DUDLEY PUBLIC LIBRARIES

The loan of this book may be renewed if not required by other readers, by contacting the library from which it was borrowed.

KU-369-500

Carla Cassidy is an award-winning, *New York Times* bestselling author who has written over 170 books, including 150 for Mills & Boon. She has won the Centennial Award from Romance Writers of America. Most recently she won the 2019 Write Touch Readers Award for her Mills & Boon Heroes title *Desperate Strangers*. Carla believes the only thing better than curling up with a good book is sitting down at the computer with a good story to write.

Discover more at millsandboon.co.uk

SHALLOW GRAVE

CASSIE MILES

GUARDING A FORBIDDEN LOVE

CARLA CASSIDY

MILLS & BOON

First Published in Great Britain 2023
by Mills & Boon, an imprint of HarperCollins*Publishers* Ltd
1 London Bridge Street, London, SE1 9GF

www.harpercollins.co.uk

HarperCollins*Publishers*
Macken House, 39/40 Mayor Street Upper,
Dublin 1, D01 C9W8, Ireland

Shallow Grave © 2023 Kay Bergstrom
Guarding a Forbidden Love © 2023 Carla Bracale

ISBN: 978-0-263-30711-5

SHALLOW GRAVE

CASSIE MILES

To my New York family: Signe, Aaron and Finn.
Can't wait to see you all. And, as always, to Rick.

Chapter One

"Are we lost?"

"Not hardly." Jackknife Jones stuck his head out the window of his ramshackle truck and spat tobacco juice onto the two-lane gravel road. "Don't you worry your purty little head. I'll get you where you're going."

Daisy Brighton turned her head—which really wasn't all that purty or little—away from the grizzled old man behind the steering wheel and stared impatiently through the filthy windshield. Over an hour and a half ago when they'd left her aunt Violet Rhodes's house in Leadville, sunset had painted the skies above the Saguache Range in shades of magenta streaked by golden clouds and framed by blue spires of ponderosa pine and spruce. A snowy-white cloak draped over Mount Elbert, even though it was mid-June.

She'd expected to reach the cemetery before nightfall. *No such luck.* Obviously, Jackknife had no idea where he was going. Jostling on unpaved roads, the truck meandered and doubled back and circled around. Dusk had settled. Daisy was furious.

The headlight beam splashed across a boulder where someone had scrawled a heart and initials: RAH + KB. She scowled. "Mr. Jones, I'm sure we already passed that graffiti."

"Like I told you, call me Jackknife." He cackled. "Don't let my name scare you."

It took more than a jackknife to frighten Daisy. For the past seven years, she'd taught high school biology in Denver, and a classroom full of teenagers was enough to strike terror into just about anybody, especially when she handed out scalpels for frog dissections.

Jackknife swerved the truck into an almost invisible right turn, and they continued to weave through San Isabel National Park and private property that was fenced off with barbed wire. They hadn't passed a town for miles.

She looked down at her cell phone. No bars. The GPS had quit working. No maps available. "You said the cemetery is near Butcher's Gulch, correct?"

"It's called a boot hill, sweet thang. Criminals and poor folks got buried there. Being left in a boot hill usually meant a violent death. These souls got kilt so fast they died with their boots on."

His description seemed apt for what she'd discovered from research into her ancestors—a motley collection of scoundrels, cheats, gunslingers and bandits. Her project over the summer break was to track down the final resting place for Sherwood Brighton, an outlaw who died in 1896. Her aunt believed her great-great-great-grandfather's grave would lead to the hiding place of his ill-gotten gains and had recruited Daisy to search. Already, she'd visited eight cemeteries.

"Just to be clear," she said. "You told Aunt Vi that you saw a grave marker in this boot hill cemetery with the name Brighton on it."

"You betcha." He tucked a fresh chaw of tobacco into his cheek. *Disgusting habit.* "Lemme ask you something about your auntie. Is she seeing anybody?"

"You mean dating?"

"I sure as heck do. Vi is a fine-looking woman."

Daisy wouldn't argue with that. Her aunt was tall and maintained her slim figure with daily exercise at the Leadville Yoga Center. The sun-streaked blond of her chin-length bob was dyed to match the color of Daisy's ponytail, and they both had green eyes. Vi was definitely stylish. Also, she was sixty-eight years old. Not that her age meant she couldn't have a boyfriend or two. But Daisy couldn't help feeling a twinge of irritation when she realized that Jackknife wanted her to play matchmaker. When was the last time a man had shown interest in Daisy? Here she sat on a Saturday night—date night—in a junky truck with a creep who'd offered to show her a cemetery.

"Violet doesn't have a steady guy," she muttered.

"Mebbe you could put in a good word for me."

Not going to happen. Her lips pinched together, holding back the obvious truth. No way would classy Vi go out with Jackknife unless he made some changes, starting with giving up tobacco. Also, he needed to shave the patchy whiskers. And it wouldn't hurt if he changed clothes and took a long, hot bath in industrial-strength disinfectant.

Still, she didn't want to alienate her ride home. Grudgingly, she said, "Maybe."

"Your auntie owns her house, right? She oughta have a man around to take care of her."

"Doesn't need a bodyguard. She's got a double-barreled shotgun."

"Does she have any other property? What about money in the bank?"

She gaped. Was this backwoods gigolo going after Vi for her money? Before she could tell him to back off, Daisy heard the discordant echo of electronic music. *In the middle of the forest?* The headlights shone on a sign for Butcher's Gulch Campground. "Finally! We're here."

"Nope, not yet," he said. "The ghost town is a coupla miles more, and then—"

"Stop. Right now." In a teacher voice that didn't allow

for discussion, she gave the orders. "You're going to drive into the campground, where I can ask for directions."

Grumbling, he parked beside the Butcher's Gulch sign. "You shouldn't get out of the truck. Ain't safe."

"I can handle some kids playing their music too loud." As if to emphasize her point, the volume lowered. "See. Not dangerous."

"The boot hill's haunted," he said. "And there's rumors of a man beast in a ski mask who attacks purty young girls like you."

Not wanting to argue until she got safely back to Leadville, she said nothing but got out of the truck, put on a denim jacket over her red cotton shirt and followed the gravel road that looped through a small campground. The two slots nearest the entrance provided parking for several vehicles, ranging from trucks and SUVs to a racy little sports car. She counted four tents and more than a dozen college-age people gathered around two fire pits. Some of them continued to dance to the tamped-down music while others guzzled beer from red plastic cups.

Asking the partygoers for directions seemed like a waste of time. This crew would be lucky to find their way to the outhouse in the middle of the night. She almost pivoted and returned to Jackknife's truck when she noticed a gunmetal-gray SUV with a National Park Service shield on the door. The tall man who reached for the door handle on the driver's side didn't wear the typical flat-brimmed hat, but he had a bison badge pinned to his dark green vest. A park ranger. He was exactly what she needed.

She approached him. "Excuse me."

The reflected blaze from the campfire flared in his deepset eyes and outlined the sharp edge of his jawbone, which contrasted with full, well-shaped lips. When he looked at her, he didn't smile, which was a bit disconcerting. "Can I help you?"

She met his unsmiling gaze with a toothy grin. "I'm looking for the Butcher's Gulch boot hill."

"Are you staying in this campground?"

"No."

"Coming to the party?" He gestured to the young people who barely looked old enough to drink but were carefully behaving within the limits of the law.

She widened her grin, probably causing him to wonder why she was so delighted to be searching for a cemetery. "You see, my ancestor is Sherwood Brighton, and I'm trying to find his grave. I'm Daisy Brighton."

He touched the brim of his weathered brown cowboy hat as he introduced himself. "I'm A. P. Carter. I go by Carter."

"Please call me Daisy." She nodded toward his badge. "You're a ranger."

"National Park Service, investigative services branch." Finally, he smiled. "And you're the heir to the legendary Brighton's Bullion."

"I am." She nodded, not surprised he'd heard the story of hidden treasure.

A pink-haired woman in skimpy cutoffs and combat boots sashayed toward them. She batted her super-long eyelashes at Carter. "What legend? Please tell me, Mr. Ranger."

He lived up to Daisy's expectations of an honorable park ranger when he put distance between himself and Pinkie. Though too young for the ranger and too drunk, she was clearly smitten. And who could blame her? Carter was a good-looking guy with a great smile when he chose to use it. He gave Daisy a nod. "Go ahead, Ms. Brighton, tell the story."

"My ancestor, Sherwood Brighton, was an outlaw. In 1887, he pulled off a robbery on the Denver–Rio Grande Railroad." Pinkie had already lost interest and scooted closer to Carter, which annoyed Daisy. Though the NPS ranger might not actually be her Saturday-night date, he could have been. At least, she was age appropriate at twenty-nine. He couldn't be more than midthirties.

To get Pinkie's attention, she used a teacher trick, waving a shiny object at the student. "Do you know how much a kilobar of gold bullion is worth?"

"A what?" Pinkie asked.

"Kilobar. It's a brick, about two pounds of solid gold."

"How big?" Pinkie held out the hand that wasn't wrapped around a red plastic cup. "Could I hold it?"

"It's about the same size as a paperback book. One kilobar is worth about $56,000 at today's rates. Sherwood Brighton stole fifty of them. He got away, and the bullion was never found." The math, she suspected, would be beyond Pinkie. "Fifty kilobars at fifty-six thou each. That's $2.8 million."

"No way." Pinkie downed her beer with one glug, straightened her shoulders and motioned to the others. "Hey, we've got to look for the kilobars."

Carter leaned close and said, "Should I give her the bad news or will you?"

"Let me." Daisy waited until the dancers and drinkers gathered around. "Brighton's Bullion has been missing since 1887. Hundreds have searched. No one has found it." Which was why she had no problem telling the story.

"I wish you luck on the search." Carter stepped forward and addressed the party-goers. "In the meantime, you people need to keep the music low, watch your fires and don't drive drunk. If I get another complaint about disorderly conduct and have to come here again, tickets will be issued and some of you will be taken into custody."

When they started to complain, he slashed his hand and cut off their voices. "That's final."

"Excuse me," Daisy said. "Directions to the boot hill?"

He took her arm, escorted her to the passenger side of

his vehicle and opened the door. "Might be easier if I take you there."

She was about to regretfully refuse when she glanced toward the entry sign. The truck was gone. Jackknife had dumped her without transportation in the middle of San Isabel National Park. Though justifiably ticked off, she wouldn't complain. The old tobacco chewer's indifference resulted in her riding with Ranger A. P. Carter, which had to be pure serendipity. Cheerfully, she climbed into his SUV.

"Where did you park your vehicle?" he asked.

"At my aunt's house where I'm staying in Leadville."

"You're a long way from home." His smile dissolved, and he regarded her with the same kind of authoritative hostility that had silenced the pesky campers. "How did you get here?"

"I caught a ride with a friend of my aunt. We got lost, and when I saw the sign for the campground, I wanted to stop and ask for directions. He must have taken off."

"Not much of a friend. Come with me."

Carter's SUV had been kept in tip-top condition, ensuring a smooth ride, a quiet engine and precisely controlled temperature, but she couldn't relax. Daisy didn't like his disapproving attitude. She wasn't a flake and had never been a troublemaker. The opposite, in fact—she was the sort of woman who solved problems and was prepared for crises. Even now, when she might have been helpless and stranded, she'd thought to bring her cell phone and had a wallet with twenty bucks and a credit card in her pocket. It might be too far to get back to Leadville tonight, but she could manage.

When he looked toward her, she studied his face in the glow from the dashboard. His eyes were bright blue, and his hair was black. His smile had disappeared. "You're not a happy camper."

"Don't worry, Ms. Brighton. I'll make sure you get home in one piece."

"Call me Daisy."

"Okay… Daisy. Now, what's the procedure when we get to the cemetery?"

"I find markers and read names. Some are carved in stone. Others are faded scribbles on weathered wood. Many of the old cemeteries have undergone restoration, which means the graves are neatly outlined with stones and the inscriptions displayed clearly." The tombstones often left poignant epitaphs, such as "lynched and deserved it" or "trampled in stampede, died too young" or "stabbed by heartless wife."

"What led you here?" he asked. "What is it about this particular boot hill?"

"The guy who abandoned me said he saw a marker with Brighton written on it. Don't know if I can believe him, but it's worth a look."

Carter tapped the brake and brought the SUV to a near stop before bumping off the road and over the shoulder onto a track through high grasses and sagebrush. After about fifty yards, he parked and announced, "Welcome to Butcher's Gulch."

Before she left the SUV, he handed her an extra flashlight from the glove compartment. Outside, she noticed more of a chill in the air and fastened two buttons on her denim jacket. Her imagination cranked into high gear as she approached the ruins of the ghost town. The beam of her flashlight slid up and down a stone fireplace attached to a crumbling stone wall. A window without glass stood above the rickety planks of a porch. The ruins of what might have been a main street formed a line on one side. There was another fireplace. And a broken-down wagon with a busted wheel. A tire swing hung from a low tree branch.

Her gaze lifted, and she looked up at a million diamond-bright stars and a quarter moon. Whatever life energy populated Butcher's Gulch had scattered on the summer breeze and vanished in the pine-scented mountain air. She didn't believe in ghosts but felt the presence of memories. Long ago, these tumbledown houses had been filled with laughter and the sounds of children singing. Families had embraced. Lovers had kissed. But there had also been tears and tragedies. A shiver constricted the muscles in her neck. Had there been fear? Were there screams that slashed through the night?

WALKING SLOWLY AND enjoying the cool summer night, Carter came up beside Daisy. When he touched her shoulder, she reacted with a shiver. Her face tilted up toward his, and her gaze flickered as though afraid to settle too long and become trapped.

"Something wrong?" he asked.

"I had an illogical premonition of danger."

"Not so odd. We're on our way to a boot hill."

"But I don't believe in superstition. I'm a scientist—a biology teacher."

"Science can't explain everything."

Being a ranger, alone in the national parks for many hours per week, he'd learned to prepare for the exceptions rather than trust in the rules. Mother Nature was an unpredictable old broad. Just when he thought he had things figured out, his expectations would be turned upside down. When he set out tonight, he'd never thought he'd meet a woman with the cheerful name of Daisy Brighton who was looking for a gold bullion in a graveyard. Never thought he'd be attracted to her wide, confident smile and her irritation when she tucked messy strands of her curly blond hair behind her ear. He liked that she was an organized woman and got a kick out of how annoyed she seemed when things got out of hand. She'd be fun to tease.

With his flashlight, he pointed downhill toward a tumbledown stone wall surrounding a clearing at the edge of the forest. "That's the boot hill over there."

"How do you know?"

"I've been here before. That's what park rangers do. We range. And we explore. The campground is only a mile from here through those trees." Again, he used the beam of his flashlight as a pointer. "Listen."

She went silent and appeared to concentrate. "I hear it. Do you have to go back and shut down the party?"

"Not yet. I told them they could play their music until ten thirty."

Taking care of drunk and disorderly campers wasn't his usual job as an investigator, but Carter had added an extra layer of vigilance, personally checking out every complaint. A couple of people reported a Peeping Tom, some guy in a ski mask. It was his job to protect those who came to enjoy nature—the innocent hikers, sightseers and campers. He glanced at Daisy and added treasure hunters to his list.

She swooped her flashlight in a circle. "I think I see a marker over there to the left. I'll hike down and take a closer look."

"I'll start at the opposite side," he said. "We can meet in the middle."

Ambient light from the moon and stars helped him find his way to the remnants of a low stone wall. Four ponderosa pines loomed over the graves at the northern edge. Shrubs and high grasses had taken over much of the cemetery. He found a cluster of weathered wooden crosses with the names rewritten in black lettering. These four graves were occupied by the same outlaw gang.

He called out to her, "Are you okay?"

"I'm a lot better off than this guy whose marker says he was killed by a moose."

He moved closer to the trees and heard the rippling from

a creek. He crinkled his nose. The night breeze carried a rotten stench. He might be having a premonition of his own. When he peered into the forest, he saw a reflection from the watching eyes of a nocturnal predator, probably a coyote or a wolf. Why would a night hunter lurk so close to humans? He unsnapped the safety strap on his belt holster, making it easier to draw his Beretta if it became necessary.

Looking down, he saw that someone had gone to the trouble of outlining a grave site with stones. Carter took care to walk around the edges rather than stepping on a final resting place. He was probably more superstitious than Daisy.

Before walking to the middle of the boot hill, he returned to the north edge to make sure he'd seen everything. Beside a clump of chokecherries, he found an open grave. Shallow, it couldn't have been more than five inches deep. The woman who lay supine on the overturned soil had been dead long enough to attract predators. Her flesh was torn. Half her face was gone. The blood on her clothing had dried to ugly brown stains. In the moonlight, her skin took on a gray-blue tint, deeper in places from bruising. The stench of putrefied flesh clogged his nostrils. He saw a wound at her neck that was partially covered by a flowing silk scarf.

Two weeks ago, he'd seen another body laid out and similarly displayed at a graveyard in Glenwood Springs. Her name was Hannah Guerrero. She'd also worn a scarf.

"Carter, come here." Daisy's voice trembled. "Hurry. I found a woman. She's dead."

A third victim.

According to the FBI, three murders meant they were looking for a serial killer.

Chapter Two

In the boot hill, at the edge of the forest, Daisy crouched beside the body of a woman lying on the ground with her legs stretched out. Her flashlight lay beside her with the beam shining through the tall grass toward stone and wooden markers. Aware that the young woman was very likely dead and should be left untouched for the CSI investigators, Daisy was compelled to feel for a pulse. Her flesh felt cold. A delicate butterfly tattoo floated above her wrist. No pulse.

The onset of rigor mortis had tightened her muscles and caused her jaw to clench. Her eyelids squeezed shut. Her long, straight brown hair fanned out around her face. A pretty face, not peaceful in death but tense and somehow frightened.

The person who had arranged the body—the murderer—had taken care with her, making sure the buttons on her blouse were fastened and her khaki slacks weren't bunched or wrinkled. Bright red blood glistened on the wound that slashed across her throat. A long, flower-patterned silk scarf tied around her neck obscured most of the laceration. The freshness of the blood made Daisy wonder if the killer was still nearby.

She peeked over her shoulder and peered into the deep, dark forest. Anyone could be hiding there. *Cougars, coyotes and bears, oh my.* Again, she called out, "I need you, Carter."

"I'm on my way."

She placed the woman's hand across her flat stomach, where it had been before. "I'm so sorry," Daisy whispered. She didn't believe the dead woman could hear her words but wanted to show respect. "I hope your life was well lived."

Though adrenaline pumped through her, Daisy didn't experience feelings of shock or fear. This wasn't her first dead body. When she was in high school taking an advanced placement biology class, she'd been lucky enough to share a cadaver with other students. Since then, she'd seen other corpses in college-level classes or at the body farm where she studied forensic anatomy.

She stood and picked up her flashlight. Newly killed, this victim was unique in her experience. Daisy wiped the nervous sweat from her forehead. Facing this dead woman disturbed her more than studying a medically prepared body laid out on an examination table. Surely, there was something she could learn. Slowly and deliberately, she directed the beam from the top of the woman's head to the scarf and death wound, then down her body to her feet, which were bare. Leaning down, she inspected the soles. Not dirty at all.

As Carter approached, she noticed that he walked in a zigzag pattern to avoid stepping on graves. *Superstitious?* When he came close, his flashlight beam shone on her, then the body, then back to her. "I'll be damned. Another one."

"What do you mean?"

"On the other side of the cemetery, I stumbled across a shallow grave. Another dead woman."

"A serial killer?"

"Could be." Though she couldn't see his eyes under his cowboy hat, she felt his gaze assessing her as he said, "You seem calm. Doesn't this upset you?"

"Of course it does. Murder is a terrible thing. But…"

"What?"

"I teach biology, and I usually get cadavers for my students. Those bodies are medically prepped for us to study, but they're still dead people."

"Uh-huh."

"And I've also taken classes and worked at the body farm outside Denver, where the dead are buried in different conditions and left for students to study. The smell there is—well, it's something else."

"Uh-huh."

"Anyway, I don't believe this woman was killed at this location. Look here—you can see that her bare feet are clean. She didn't walk through the forest or the grass."

He leaned down to see. In the reflected glow of the flashlight, she noticed that his skin had paled under his tan. His lips pinched tightly together in the tense expression of a person who was holding on to self-control with both hands to keep from losing it.

"Good observation," he said in a coarse voice. "You're right about the feet."

His squeamish reaction surprised her. She'd figured that—in his work as a ranger—he was either a hunter or familiar with their procedures, like field dressing and skinning an elk, which was way more gruesome than this. Also, since he worked as an investigator, he'd certainly seen dead bodies before. "Sorry, Carter. I didn't mean to gross you out."

"I'm fine." He pointed his flashlight up the hill. "Walk with me. I need to go to my car and radio headquarters for backup support."

"Doesn't your cell phone work?"

"Reception is spotty around here." He took a couple of backward steps and waited for her to do the same before hiking toward the ghost town.

For a moment, they walked without speaking. The crunching sound of their footsteps on dry pine needles mingled with other noises—the distant echo of music from the campground, the breeze whispering through the pine boughs and the incessant skittering of nocturnal creatures. And killers. Was he close? Had he been watching them?

Carter hadn't asked for her opinion but hadn't told her to pipe down. She volunteered another comment. "If I had to make an educated guess, I'd say time of death was no more than three hours ago, probably more like two."

"Why is that?"

"The blood at her throat is fresh, rigor mortis is just starting to set in and there's minimal evidence of flies, maggots or animal predators."

"I've got to tell you, Daisy, you're not what I expected." He stopped beside the broken-down chimney at the edge of Butcher's Gulch, took off his hat and raked his fingers through his thick black hair. "I thought you were a city woman visiting her auntie and poking around at Western history. After a couple of weeks, I figured you'd be bored and run back to Denver."

She had to admit that he wasn't altogether wrong. "I'm not deeply invested in the search for Brighton's Bullion. But my aunt Vi is my last living relative, and I care about her enough to make the effort."

"There's something more to your visit than spending time with family," he said. "You were drawn to the mountains. You're not panicky about finding a body because you consider death to be natural. You aren't nervous about coyotes or bears."

She wasn't sure if he was complimenting her or making fun of her. "What are you trying to tell me, Carter?"

"I'm saying you fit in. You're comfortable here."

"Maybe or maybe not. I've always lived in the city." Every morning she awoke with the sun and happily greeted the majestic outline of the front range of the Rockies from her bedroom window, but she had no desire to come here like a pioneer and settle into a log cabin. "Did you grow up in the mountains?"

"I was a cop in Denver before I became a ranger." He replaced the hat on his head. "I love my job, and I'm usually good at it. I kind of hate that I got queasy. And that you pointed it out. You're a little bit pushy."

"Guilty." As if she needed his approval.

"I'm not judging."

"No?"

"I like you, Daisy."

His statement was simple, direct and totally charming. It took a confident man to leave himself so vulnerable. What if she shot him down? Or the opposite, she might take his comment as an invitation to sex. Confused, she said, "Thank you?"

"I appreciate your intelligence, and I'd be a damn fool if I didn't take advantage of your expertise. What else can you tell me about the dead woman?"

Relieved, she returned to a topic she knew something about. "When I first arrived, I took her hand to feel for a pulse. I noticed her fingernail polish was chipped, and one nail was torn. Makes me think that she fought for her life."

"Anything else?"

"There was a strange smell. Not the typical aromas I associate with the dead."

"I noticed it, too," he said. "Bear repellent. I don't put much stock in dousing your campsite with weird combinations of ammonia, garlic, sulfur and other stuff, but there are people who swear it will keep the animals and the insects away."

She made the logical assumption. "The killer must have used repellent because he didn't want predators to damage her body. That fits with the way he arranged her and fixed her hair."

"And tied a scarf around her throat. The other body also

had a scarf. I wonder why." He frowned. "Maybe it'd be useful to consult a profiler."

A profiler? Talking with that type of expert could be extremely interesting. In spite of her respect for the dead woman, Daisy felt a glimmer of selfish excitement. She could be part of a murder investigation. *Cool!*

Headlights flashed behind Carter's SUV as Jackknife's beat-up truck pulled up and parked. The old man jumped out, spat tobacco juice, waved his scrawny arm and hollered, "Howdy, sweet thang. I'm back. Bet you're glad to see me."

Carter aimed his flashlight into the grizzled face. "Stop right there."

When the beam hit Jackknife, he squinted. "You got a problem, sonny boy?"

"NPS Ranger Carter," he identified himself. "Show me your registration and license."

"It's okay," Daisy assured him. "This is Mr. Jones. He drove me here."

"And left you without a ride. Not a real nice guy." His flashlight didn't waver. "I need your identification."

The old man spat again. "If'n I don't feel like showing it, what's gonna happen?"

With lightning speed, Carter flipped his flashlight to his left hand. With his right, he drew his Beretta. "Hands on top of your head, Jones. I don't have time to play games."

If Jackknife considered fighting back, that notion disappeared when Carter took a determined step toward him. The ranger wasn't goofing around, and Jackknife knew it. He put both hands on top of his John Deere cap with the leaping stag logo. "I'll do whatever you say, Ranger. I'll cooperate."

In a few efficient moves, Carter cuffed Jackknife with his hands in front, took his car keys and helped him climb into the driver's seat of his truck. "Stay here until I have time to take your statement."

"Statement about what? What the heck is going on here?"

"Murder investigation," Carter said.

"Somebody got killed?" His voice creaked into a higher octave. "I don't know nothing about it. Tell him, Daisy."

She opened her mouth to speak, but before she could get a word out, Jackknife continued, "And what about her, huh? If'n I can't drive, how's she gonna get home?"

"I'll arrange for her ride," Carter said.

"I couldn't ask you to do that now," she said, not wanting to be a bother in the middle of an investigation. "It's a long way back to Leadville."

"What are you talking about?" He shot her a puzzled glance. "It's only about forty minutes—less because there's no traffic or snow."

"Only forty minutes, huh?" She glared at Jackknife. "We were in your truck for more than twice that long."

"Mebbe I got lost."

More likely, he was playing a joke on her. *Not funny.* "I suggest you get comfortable in that rattletrap truck, because Ranger Carter has a lot of work to do before he talks to you."

She turned her back on him and strode toward the NPS vehicle.

Carter came up beside her. "How well do you know that guy?"

"Not well at all."

"Do you have any reason to suspect him?"

She couldn't believe her aunt would let her get into the truck with Jackknife if she thought he was up to no good. But Aunt Vi wouldn't count this grungy, tobacco-spitting old man as a friend. "He's kind of a jerk but probably harmless."

"That's how the neighbors of serial killers always describe them. They always say that the monster was harmless, a nice guy who kept to himself and wouldn't hurt a fly."

She reconsidered. If her time-of-death analysis was accurate, Jackknife could have murdered that woman and returned to Leadville before he picked her up. They were on the road for over an hour and a half before they got close to Butcher's Gulch. Why would Jackknife purposely delay? Why would he drive around in circles? A possible answer hit her—he might have been waiting for darkness to fall.

He might have planned a murder scenario for her. Shivers scampered across her back like a herd of spiders. "Jackknife Jones could be the killer."

"Jackknife, huh? I don't even want to guess how he got that nickname." Carter opened the driver's side door of his car. "I'll be with you in a minute. I need to put through a call to headquarters."

She had a similar thought. Her aunt deserved a call so she wouldn't worry, but Daisy's cell phone still didn't have reception. Earlier when they were driving to Butcher's Gulch in Carter's SUV, she'd noticed a bunch of screens and communication devices attached to the center console, including a heavy-looking phone on a charger—a satellite phone, too bulky to carry in your pocket but essential in areas without good access to cell phone towers.

Standing just outside the open driver's side door, she watched as he took that phone rather than using his police radio that would alert anyone listening on that open line. Apparently, he wanted privacy when he talked to headquarters.

"Excuse me," she said. "Can I use your sat phone to call my aunt?"

"When I'm done." Taking the phone with him, he left

the car, locked the door and started back toward the boot hill. "Come with me. Stay close."

Further warning was unnecessary. She'd seen the murdered woman and knew there was a killer at large. If not Jackknife, then who? There didn't seem to be anyone living in this area. When she scanned the forested hills and rocky cliffs, she didn't see house lights. Could they have come from the campground?

She half listened while Carter rattled off instructions to NPS headquarters. He wanted assistance from the local sheriff's office, the state highway patrol and agents from the FBI. He repeated "FBI" twice and added, "Tell them we're looking for a serial killer. They need to arrange for the autopsies."

Plural—as in more than one. She shuddered and fidgeted. Though she stayed close to Carter, Daisy wandered through the graves, shining her flashlight beam on the markers. This side of the cemetery featured several fieldstone markers with names roughly chiseled and occasional embellishments, usually angels or hearts and flowers. Daisy tripped over a chunk of granite that was almost completely obscured by the high grasses. Kneeling, she lowered her flashlight beam and read the inscription: "Annie Brighton. Wife, Friend and Lover."

There was no date of birth or death. No indication of what killed her. But Daisy knew she'd found the final resting place of Sherwood Brighton's wife.

Chapter Three

Ranger A. P. Carter ended his call to Joaquin Stanley, his supervisor at the National Park Service headquarters in Salida, and hiked through the graves to where Daisy knelt beside a tombstone. She shook her flashlight at a rugged stone, causing the beam to flicker. "Read it."

"'Annie Brighton. Wife, Friend and Lover.'" He wasn't thinking about treasure hunting. Not now. The double— no, triple—murder investigation would be hell to coordinate among the several law enforcement jurisdictions and would take his full attention. "Is this good news or bad?"

"It's unexpected. I was looking for Sherwood, not his wife, and I don't know much about her. Also, this marker is sort of vindication for Jackknife. He wasn't lying about seeing the name in the Butcher's Gulch boot hill."

"Don't be so quick to forgive. There's no explanation for why he pretended to be lost."

"I'm not defending him. Jackknife is a total jerk but probably not be a serial killer." She shrugged. "May I use your sat phone to call my aunt? She'll be pleased about finding Annie."

"First, there's something I want your opinion on." He hooked the sat phone onto his belt. "The county sheriff has been alerted, and his deputies will arrive soon. When they do, I won't be able to talk with you."

"Why? Am I going to disappear?"

"You're a civilian, Daisy. Some of these guys will try to shove you out of the way. They won't understand or accept your expertise, but I do." Holding her slender hand, he led her down the hill, hoping he wasn't making a mistake by recruiting a high school biology teacher as a consultant. "I want you to take a look at this shallow grave."

"Where is she?"

"Down this slope."

He'd debated with himself before trusting her. Though he appreciated her straightforward analysis of the other victim, he couldn't get around the fact that she wasn't a cop or a ranger or a medical examiner. He had hesitated because sharing the details of a murder smacked of unprofessional behavior. But what the hell should he do? This case was different. He'd never investigated a serial murder and had never faced the possibility of more victims being attacked if he didn't solve it quickly. Carter needed all the help he could get.

Walking slowly behind him, she pinched her nose. "This one has been dead long enough for the flesh to putrefy."

"How long is that?"

"At least three days."

Knowing the medical details before the deputies showed up gave Carter an edge. While they were gagging and puking in the forest, he could plan the strategy for his investigation. The timing of the murders—especially when combined with what he'd seen of Hannah Guerrero in Glenwood Springs—was an important factor. He rubbed at his nose, trying to erase the stench. "You know, Daisy, if you don't want to go any farther, it's okay."

"I don't mind the smell. When I was working at the body farm, I got used to it." She kept moving forward. "I'd like to ask a favor from you."

"Go ahead."

"I've never seen an actual autopsy. Can you arrange for me to watch?"

For the life of him, he couldn't figure out why he was attracted to this woman. "I can arrange for you to sit in."

Her thank-you and enthusiastic smile would have been appropriate for someone who'd been given freebie tickets on the fifty-yard line for a Denver Broncos playoff game. "Where will it take place?"

"That's up to the FBI," he said. "I'm guessing Pueblo."

At the edge of the shallow grave, he forced himself to, once again, look down at the dead woman whose clothing was ripped and bloodstained. What was left of her face appeared to be bloated, and her discolored flesh had turned a dead gray color.

Daisy crouched and slid the beam of her flashlight up and down the body. "It's hard to believe this is the handiwork of the same killer. The other woman was handled delicately, while this one looks like she was abused. The only item of clothing that appears to be clean is the long scarf around her neck. Do you see the bruises on her arms and ligature marks on her wrists? She might have been tied down. If you call in a profiler, they could draw a lot of inferences from this."

"I'll make sure we have photos of both bodies." He hadn't been so diligent with the Glenwood corpse. Not his jurisdiction. Not his case. But Daisy was correct. A profiler would add a different perspective, especially when studying similarities among the victims. They were all young and fit, average height and weight. Their coloring was different. Hannah Guerrero had black hair and olive skin. The woman Daisy found had long brown hair. This one was platinum blonde. The killer didn't seem to have a preferred type. "What else?"

Using a stick she found on the ground, Daisy lifted the hand and showed him the limp wrist. "She's already gone through rigor, and the stiffness has worn off. Like I said, time of death was probably over two or three days ago."

"Can you narrow it down?"

"Not with precision," she said. "Body temp won't be a good indicator because she's been outdoors, and temperature at this time of year fluctuates by several degrees from day to night. And I don't have a liver thermometer."

He wished real-life forensics could be as clear and infallible as portrayed on television. Hannah had been killed in Glenwood ten days ago. If this woman had been dead for three days, that meant a seven-day difference before he killed a second time. The body that Daisy found was recently murdered, which meant the interim had grown shorter.

Without hesitation, Daisy leaned close and aimed the flashlight beam at the dead woman's horribly mangled face. "Maggots. Do you see the eggs?"

Carter looked into the wound. Small, pale eggs mingled with crawly insects. "I see them." He gagged. This was as close as he'd come to vomiting at a murder scene. He would have preferred being stoic, but his nausea occurred as an automatic reflex.

"There isn't too much damage by predators. Torn clothes. Teeth and claw marks here and there. I suspect there was something shielding her body." She sat back on her heels and looked up at him. "Or she might have been murdered somewhere else. He might have allowed the blood to drain before bringing her to this shallow grave."

"Can you tell how much she bled onto the dirt below her?"

"Not without moving the body," she said, "and I don't think your medical examiner would appreciate that much interference. Also, I can't turn her to check on lividity— the way the blood settled after death."

So many questions, and he needed to find answers to

all of them. If there had been something covering her and shielding her from local predators, he needed to search. If she'd been held somewhere else, he might find that the killer lived in the area. Or he could have loaded the dead woman in his car and brought her here.

He started a mental checklist: Check for tire tracks. Search for something that covered the body. Look for a shovel or spade. Search the forest in this area. So much to do and so little time before he handed over jurisdiction of the investigation.

AFTER DAISY MADE her phone call to Aunt Vi and returned the sat phone to Carter, she heard the wail of a police siren bouncing off the canyon walls. Together, she and Carter hiked up the gently sloping hill to the ghost town and greeted the deputies who emerged from an SUV with the county sheriff's logo on the door. Though she stood ready and willing to help, the two officers—Graham and Escobar—barely acknowledged her presence. Carter had predicted that she'd be ignored as a mere civilian, and he'd been correct.

Not being a person who demanded a lot of attention, she was glad to step back and quietly observe what was happening. Deputy Graham—a clean-shaven, athletic-looking man in a dark green uniform and a baseball cap with the county logo—brightened when Carter told them they might be dealing with a serial killer. He immediately covered his unacceptable grin with a scowl, but she'd seen his excitement, and she understood. Serial killers were strange and terrifying creatures. Legendary, like boogiemen or vampires, they haunted nightmares and struck fear in the hearts of average citizens. Tracking one down meant a major challenge for a young deputy in a mainly rural county.

Carter asked, "Do you have lights for the crime scene?"

"Sure do," Graham replied as he hooked his thumbs in

his belt on either side of a shiny rodeo championship buckle for bronc riding.

"How about some of those throwaway booties so we don't mess up footprints?"

"I got those and latex gloves, too."

"Let's gather the gear and set up at the location of the first body."

"There's more than one." Graham stated the obvious description of a serial killer. "Are they all in the graveyard?"

"Two are here. Ten days ago, there was a third." Carter turned to the other deputy, a middle-aged guy wearing the uniform shirt with weathered jeans and boots. "I'd appreciate if you stay here and meet the others who have been contacted."

Cool and casual, Deputy Escobar nodded. "We'll have another vehicle from our office. And I expect you contacted the NPS, so there will be a couple of rangers. Who else?"

"State patrol, coroner, ambulance and FBI. Could be more than that. My supervisor made the calls." Carter matched the calm, controlled attitude of the older lawman. "I don't want a herd of investigators trooping through the graveyard messing up evidence. If you need more information about what we're dealing with, you can talk with Ms. Brighton."

She straightened her shoulders, glad to be helpful, and gave a small wave to the deputy. Escobar signaled for her to come closer. "Want some coffee, Brighton?"

"Call me Daisy. And yes on the coffee."

He led her to the passenger side of the SUV, pulled out a long silver thermos and poured hot liquid into a disposable cup. "I hope you like it black. My wife sends me out the door with plenty of sandwiches and strong coffee when I'm on night shift."

"Black is perfect." She sipped. Even though the coffee

wasn't delicious, she knew the caffeine would lift her spirits. "Thanks, Deputy. Do you have any questions?"

He leaned against the front bumper of his vehicle and watched as Carter and the younger deputy gathered equipment from the back. "What were you doing in the graveyard?"

"Research," she said as though it was the most normal thing in the world to be poking around in a graveyard after dark. "Carter was kind enough to help me, and I found the first body."

"That must have scared you."

"Not at all."

She rattled through an explanation about being a biology teacher who regularly handled cadavers and segued into forensic descriptions of the two murdered women. Occasionally, Escobar asked questions, and she answered as best she could.

She had a question of her own. "Have you worked with Carter before?"

"A couple of times. He's a good man." He tasted his coffee and slanted a wise glance in her direction. "You like him."

"I didn't say that."

"Didn't need to. Your eyes did the talking." He grinned. "And why not? You two go together like peanut butter and jelly. You're both smart and good-looking. You're both concerned about other folks."

"How do you figure?"

"He's a ranger. You're a teacher. Caretakers."

"There's nothing going on between me and Carter."

She truly wished relationships could be as simple as matching a few personality traits, but she'd never found attraction to be easy, and she hadn't really had enough time to analyze the possibilities. Of course, she found Carter to be physically appealing. He was tall and lean and looked like the romantic archetype of a cowboy in his hat, boots and jeans. The curly black hair, expressive eyes and great smile were additional pluses. If she'd been younger, she might have jumped into a brief fling with the ranger, but she was twenty-nine and ready for something more than a quickie—as Aunt Vi would say, "a roll in the hay." Daisy wanted to settle down, get serious and start a family.

Nothing long-term would work between her and Carter. He was a mountain man. And she was a city woman.

She was saved from further embarrassing conversation with Escobar by the arrival of three vehicles: one from the park service, another from the county sheriff and a patrol car with the Colorado state logo on the door and red and blue flashers whirring on the roof. The officers, rangers and deputies gathered around while Escobar told them to stay put until Carter came back up the hill and explained the situation. "He doesn't want y'all tromping around and messing up the evidence." Escobar craned his neck, scanning the group. "I don't suppose there's a coroner here."

"We heard this was a serial killer," one of the state police officers said.

The two rangers complained that this was really their crime scene, and they needed to be with Carter. There was more grumbling all around.

"Settle down," Escobar said. "Ms. Brighton, would you mind heading down to the site and telling Carter to come up here?"

She was delighted to walk away from the impatient crew of rangers and officers. Though she'd already made a couple of trips through the graveyard, she still needed her flashlight until she got close to where Carter and Graham had positioned two portable, battery-operated units that spotlighted the scene like a movie set. Though she saw more details, the body looked as unreal as the plastic cadavers she sometimes used for her classes.

Graham stood as far away from the dead woman as possible without disappearing into the shadows while Carter got in close and personal to inspect the fatal wound at her throat. His queasiness seemed to have diminished. He waved her over. "Daisy, take a look at this."

When she leaned down beside him, she caught a whiff of the mentholated gel that was supposed to mask the stink of bear repellent and death. Graham must have brought it. "What did you want to show me?"

With latex gloves covering both hands, he gently separated the scarf from the blood. "There are already insect eggs."

"Blowflies," she said. "They're drawn by the smell of carrion and show up immediately."

He ordered the deputy to make sure he took close-up photos. To her, he said, "There's a crowd gathering at the top of the hill."

"That's why I'm interrupting you. Escobar could use some help dealing with them."

"Has the FBI arrived?"

"Not yet," she said. "Why do you ask?"

"With their state-of-the-art databases and forensic equipment, they typically assume jurisdiction on serial murders. I need to talk to the feds before I hand over control."

"It doesn't seem fair for you to just step aside."

"What's fair is finding the killer before he strikes again," he said as he stood. "You're not wearing your booties."

"My bad." She rose tilted her head to gaze into his vivid blue eyes. This was the first time she'd gotten a good look at him in clear light, and she wasn't disappointed. The spotlights for the crime scene reflected off his high cheekbones and the smile that hid his true nature as a sharp, decisive man. Was that also a trait they shared? She suspected it was. She and Carter were both people who got things done.

Whoops and laughter resonated from the thick pine forest beyond boot hill. She saw Pinkie step away from the trees followed by several others from the party at the campground. They were about a hundred yards away.

Carter whirled and started toward them. "Daisy, come with me. Graham, go up to the top of the hill and tell the crew that one person from each vehicle can come down here."

"They need to wear gloves and booties," Graham said.

"Make sure they do. That's your responsibility."

Daisy followed as he marched toward the raucous partygoers, who must have followed the path from the campground. The woman with pink hair appeared to be their leader. She gave an enthusiastic but sloppy-drunk wave. "Hey there, Mr. Ranger. What's with all the cop cars?"

"There's an investigation underway." Carter continued to stride toward them. Even in his baby blue paper booties, he exuded authority.

"Cool!" Pinkie said. "What kind of investigation?"

As they approached the group of five people, Daisy recognized some of them from the party—three men, Pinkie and one other woman with red hair in two ponytails. One of the guys seemed totally wasted, but the other two were alert. The tallest, a husky guy with a buzz cut, looked a bit older than the others, maybe in his early thirties. He explained, "We heard the sirens and wanted to find out what was going on."

"That's her." Pinkie jabbed her index finger in Daisy's direction. "She's the lady who's a treasure hunter."

"Brighton's Bullion," said the tall guy. "Had any luck?"

"Not really." No point in telling him about Sherwood's wife's grave.

The other relatively sober guy squinted through horn-rimmed glasses and tried to step around Carter. "There's lights set up over there. It looks like a body on the ground."

With his arms spread wide, Carter herded them back toward the trail. "I need you to stay out of the way."

"Is he right?" Pinkie asked. "Was somebody murdered?"

"Yes." Carter dropped his arms. "And you're witnesses. I need information from—"

"Wait a minute." Her eyelids twitched, and she looked like she was going to cry. "Is she about my height? Does she have brown hair?"

"Yes."

"And a tattoo?" Pinkie said. "A butterfly tattoo on her left wrist."

Daisy couldn't help nodding when Pinkie looked toward her.

"Oh my God." Pinkie sobbed. "It's Rene."

Chapter Four

Carter hated the disorganized way this investigation was unfolding. Even if he didn't have the jurisdiction to hunt a serial killer, he'd hoped to hand over a coherent package of evidence to the FBI agents instead of a jumbled mess. From literally stumbling over the bodies to having a half-drunk, pink-haired woman blurt out the identity of the victim, every bit of information had come in random, unexpected bursts. Nothing—with the exception of Daisy's forensic observations—had been the result of logic or intelligent discovery. He needed to step up and take charge, even if he ultimately handed off the investigation to the FBI.

Leaving Daisy to keep an eye on the five partygoers who had stumbled out of the forest, he went to the boot hill to wrangle the crew of law enforcement personnel. His assignment for the state patrolman was to take fingerprints from the victim and run her photo through facial recognition software to get a solid identification. The deputies were given forensic tasks, and he sent the rangers back to the campground to take statements before the partygoers dispersed. Daisy would stay with him to record his interviews with Pinkie and her friends. *Unprofessional? Yeah, probably.* He shouldn't use a civilian for investigative business, but he needed to talk to these people before they had time to put their heads together and make sure their stories matched. One of them might slip up and say something useful. One of them could be the killer.

Their spokeswoman was Pinkie. The death of her friend had sobered her up, and she gave cogent answers to his questions. The woman with the butterfly tattoo was Rene Williams, twenty-three years old and a part-time student at the University of Colorado campus in Denver, as were most of the attendees at the party. Rene had gone missing the night before last, but nobody worried about her absence. She'd come on this camping trip to escape her depression after breaking up with her boyfriend. "I thought she wanted to be alone," Pinkie said. "That was why she left."

"Do you have a phone number and address for the boyfriend?" Carter asked.

"I don't. He and Rene lived together, but he moved out a week ago. I never knew his phone number. Do you think he…" She sucked down a breath of mountain air and forced herself to continue. "Did he kill her?"

"Too early to speculate. How long have you been camping?"

"The original group, including Rene, has been here for four days. We're all going back to Denver tomorrow."

The conditions for these interviews couldn't have been much worse. All five of these people were functioning at varying levels of intoxication. They could overhear each other. And he only had a small recorder and spiral notebook to keep track of what they said. *Definitely not ideal.*

He considered backing off, waiting for the FBI agents to swoop in and take over. The evidence he uncovered would be checked and rechecked anyway. He felt a light squeeze on his arm and gazed down at Daisy. The spark of intelligence in her light green eyes encouraged him more than a pep talk. She didn't need to say out loud that she believed in him. Her attitude radiated confidence. He suspected that she was a hell of a good teacher.

"The guy with the buzz cut," she said, "might be one of the last people to see Rene alive. His name is Slade Franklin."

He grinned, glad that he had this smart, lovely civilian for backup. "You're paying attention."

"I remember what you said about finding the killer before he attacked anyone else. It's up to you, Carter, to protect the people in this forest."

A big job, and he might not be up to the challenge. But she was right. He had to try. Turning toward the others, he waved the big guy over. "Slade Franklin, join us."

After Daisy read back her notes and repeated his name and address in Pueblo, Slade took a seat on a sawed-off tree stump that stood taller than the sagebrush. Carter remained standing for this interrogation. "Tell me about the last time you saw Rene."

"She wasn't hanging around with the others. She looked lonely, and I felt bad for her. So I went over and talked to her."

"You didn't know her before you came to the party."

"No, sir."

"What did you talk about?"

"Her dumbass ex-boyfriend. I never met the guy, but I can tell you right now that he didn't deserve Rene. There was something about her that made me think I'd met her before."

"But you hadn't."

"No."

Carter asked, "Did you think she might go out with you?"

"I guess so. She didn't have any problem going skinny-dipping."

"Both naked?"

"Naw, she wore her underpants and bra. We went to my camper truck to change afterward. She was real pretty." He gave a sheepish grin. "I knew it was a bad idea to date a woman who was getting over a breakup, but I didn't care."

"Did you try to kiss her?" Carter considered the possibility of Slade making an unwanted advance on Rene. "Maybe you rubbed her back while she was changing clothes."

"She didn't want me to get close, and I had to back off. My mama taught me to be polite." In spite of his size and his buzz cut, Slade seemed to be a sensitive guy. "I know what it feels like to get dumped. It's miserable."

"Then what happened with Rene?"

"We left the campground and went to a nearby lake. It's called Teacup on account of its small and almost perfectly round. She gave me some good advice about my relationship with my ex. And then her boyfriend showed up."

Carter checked his notes. "Josh Santana?"

"Yeah, it was Josh. He grabbed her and started kissing her, and she seemed to like it, even though she told me he was a jerk."

"That must have made you mad."

"It sure did."

Carter's sat phone buzzed. Caller ID showed a name he didn't recognize. "Excuse me, I need to get this."

The call came from the Pueblo-based FBI agents assigned to the investigation. They were on the road but lost, which wasn't a big surprise. The locals could easily find the ghost town, but Butcher's Gulch wasn't on regular maps. He told the agents to track the campground on their GPS, and the rangers who were there could give them directions.

When he returned, he found Daisy asking questions. "Are you a student, Slade?"

"No, ma'am. I'm thirty-one, and I work as a carpenter."

"How did you hear about the party?"

"I didn't," he said. "I came up here in my truck camper to get away from the heat in Pueblo. It's only June, but it's hotter than August. The mountains are always ten degrees cooler."

"By yourself?" she asked with just enough edge to suggest there might be something strange about a solo trip.

"Nothing wrong with that." Taken aback, he scowled at her. "You came here alone, didn't you? Somebody might think it was strange for you to be hanging around in a graveyard."

"I couldn't leave."

"Why not?"

"Because, Mr. Franklin, I found the body."

Until she allowed him to turn the focus back on her, she'd been doing a good job, even though she wasn't a trained investigator. Carter stepped in to derail this line of questioning. "Sorry for the interruption."

"No problem."

"Let's go back to what happened at the lake, Slade." Carter used the other man's first name to emphasize that the ranger was the person in authority. "After Josh arrived, did you go back to the campsite?"

"I didn't feel like socializing. I went to my camper and hit the sack." He exhaled a heavy sigh. "Maybe I sat outside for a while and watched for Rene. But I never saw her, never again."

Flashing lights and a siren from the direction of the many vehicles in the ghost town announced the arrival of an ambulance. Though these victims had no need for paramedics, the ambulance might be needed to transport the bodies to a place designated by the FBI for autopsies. They still had to wait for the coroner and/or medical examiner.

Carter kept juggling as fast as he could, but his interviews with the other three people were rushed. Over objections from Pinkie and Slade who wanted to stay close to the action, he sent them back to the campground and told them to report to the rangers on-site.

He motioned to Daisy. Together, they returned to Butcher's Gulch, where the paramedics stood beside Deputy Escobar's vehicle. They were staring at him, challenging him with their gazes. Again, he felt the pressure of being in charge, figuring out who should do what.

Daisy said, "I'd like to help."

She didn't belong here. A high school biology teacher and part-time treasure hunter had no business taking part in a murder investigation, but he wanted her to stay, wanted to hear her opinion after the dust settled. He seized on the only excuse he could think of. "You can't leave until the FBI takes your statement. After that, I'll arrange for a ride to Leadville."

"I'd rather wait until you can take me."

He was exceedingly glad to hear it. "It could be late."

"Don't care." She shrugged. "I have a vested interest, after all. You promised I could watch an autopsy."

"Fine with me." More than fine, actually. Though practically a stranger, she seemed like the only friendly face in this crowd. He handed her his car keys. "If you want to get away from the chaos, feel free to hide out in my car."

When another SUV joined the others, the ghost town began to resemble a backwoods parking lot. Unlike the other vehicles, this black Chevy Tahoe had no special logo. It dodged around the ambulance, the state police car, the deputy's SUV, the two from the National Park Service and Jackknife's beat-up truck. When they parked, two men emerged. Both wore black vests with *FBI* stenciled on the back. Without waiting to consult with anybody else, they stormed down the hill toward the body. The feds were here to take control and catch the killer.

DAISY AVOIDED THE FBI and the paramedics, making a bee-line for Deputy Escobar, who still leaned against the fender of his SUV. Apparently, his task was to direct all these people to the various sites, and he didn't seem to mind playing the role of traffic cop. She guessed his age was close to fifty, old enough to have developed a thick skin and a steady calm.

From the corner of her eye, she watched Carter shake hands with the special agents. One of them seemed to know him, but they weren't friendly. In the hierarchy of local law enforcement, the feds had to be the top of the food chain. Carter had readily admitted that they had the best experts and equipment.

Standing beside Escobar, she had a sweeping view of the boot hill and noticed that the second body site was also illuminated by the portable spotlights. She glanced at the man beside her. "I bet you've seen this before."

"Whenever there's a major crime, everybody comes sniffing around. Hail, hail, the gang's all here."

"Have you ever investigated a serial killer before?"

"Never have." He folded his arms across his chest. "And I've never heard of a killer who left his victims in a graveyard. You know there was another one, didn't you?"

She nodded. "Two women."

"Three bodies," he said. "There was another in Glenwood Springs. Three of them. That's why the murderer counts as a serial killer."

"I think Carter might have mentioned it. But he didn't give me details."

"Do you want to hear?"

She bobbed her head. "But first, I remember that you mentioned sandwiches."

"There's a cooler in the back seat. Help yourself."

Escobar was, by far, her favorite among all the investigators…except for Carter, of course. She stuck her head into the back, found the heavy-duty thermal cooler, unzipped the top and peeked inside. Escobar's wife had packed six meat-and-cheese sandwiches with sliced tomatoes and lettuce in plastic bags to the side.

She called out to him. "Do you want anything?"

"I'm sticking to coffee. Help yourself to bottled water."

As she added the tomatoes and lettuce to her basic sandwich, Daisy realized that she hadn't eaten since lunch. She hadn't planned to spend so much time being lost with Jackknife, finding bodies and recording information from suspects. Nor had she expected to run into someone like Ranger A. P. Carter, who made her want to stay even later and spend time with him.

She returned to stand beside Escobar. "Thanks so much. I'm hungry."

"Even after looking at dead bodies?"

"Yup."

"You're a strange one," he said. "I wish my kids had a teacher like you. Somebody who makes learning fun."

"I love my job." She chomped into the sandwich. Hadn't Carter said something exactly like that about liking what he did for a living? They had so much in common. Too bad he lived in the mountains and she in town. Daisy wasn't a fan of long-distance relationships.

"The first victim," Escobar said, "was found about ten days ago in the Linwood Cemetery in Glenwood Springs. I saw it in police reports. She was lying in the dirt outside the wrought iron fence around the marker for Doc Holliday."

"Have you been to the grave?"

"Took the kids. My wife said it was educational. The legend on the marker says, 'Died in Bed.' A disappointment to Doc, because he wanted to die in action."

The ongoing commotion in the Butcher's Gulch boot hill and the many different law enforcement entities made her wonder about jurisdiction in that first murder. "Why was Carter involved? I thought crimes committed in cemeteries were investigated by the city."

"Glenwood Springs PD," he said with a nod. "The Park Service was called to consult because of the unusual lay-out of Linwood Cemetery. To reach the memorial for Doc Holliday, you have to hike almost a mile through a forest."

"Like Buffalo Bill Cody," she said. "Do you know about him? He's buried on top of Lookout Mountain outside Denver."

"Doc Holliday wasn't much like Cody. Buffalo Bill was a showman. Doc was a gunslinger, famous for the part he played in the shootout at the OK Corral and flat broke when he died. His part of the cemetery was a potter's field for poor folks."

"Sad." She sighed. "Doc Holliday didn't get really famous until the movies."

Escobar chuckled under his breath. "Remember that line from *Tombstone*? About being someone's huckleberry. In the movie, Doc says that to Wyatt."

Meaning Doc would follow his friend anywhere like Tom Sawyer and Huckleberry Finn. She wondered if that sentiment might apply to her and Carter. Hopefully not. She wanted to be more than a pal. She wanted to press herself into his embrace and feel his lips against hers. Pushing those thoughts aside, she said, "We've gotten off topic."

"Not much else to say about the victim in Glenwood. Her name was Hannah Guerrero, and she was a dental assistant."

"Wasn't Doc Holliday a dentist?"

"Irony."

She noticed that yet another vehicle had parked at the end of the line of cars winding through Butcher's Gulch. An older man carrying an old-fashioned doctor's bag ambled toward them. Escobar introduced her to the county coroner, a retired general practitioner with a thick white mustache. The coroner nodded to the deputy and asked what was going on.

Graciously, the deputy deferred to her. "Ms. Brighton discovered the first body. She's a biology teacher and can give you details on the medical stuff."

"I can sum it up in one word—dead." She appreciated the gesture from Escobar but didn't want to mislead this former doctor. "Is there anything specific you want to know?"

"I doubt I'll have enough accurate information for the death certificate. The ME will have to fill in the blanks." He shrugged. "Can you tell me how these women died?"

"Homicide," she said. "There were bloody wounds at the throat, but I can't say for sure that cause of death was exsanguination."

His bushy eyebrows lifted, and she saw respect dawning. "What about time of death?"

She ran through her observations on body temp, onset of rigor, bloating, skin discoloration and the presence of blowfly eggs and maggots. "But I agree with you. The actual TOD is better left to the medical examiner."

One of the paramedics joined their group. "You need to sign off on the bodies so we can figure out whether or not we need to transport them."

"Well, that's going to depend on who's in charge—the county sheriff's deputies, the Colorado state patrol, FBI or NPS."

With the investigation spinning in so many different directions, she couldn't imagine how Carter was going to proceed. After she thanked Escobar for the sandwich, Daisy made her way through the array of vehicles to Carter's SUV. Jackknife's truck was parked directly behind him, and the old man yelled at her as she came close. She blocked out his words. He was not her problem.

Glad that Carter had the foresight to give her access to his car, she opened the door using his key fob, slipped into the rear and stretched out across three seats. Though the night wasn't cold, she was glad to find a plaid wool blanket and a pillow. If Carter had attempted to sleep back here, he would have been totally uncomfortable. Though she was slightly taller than average, she fit nicely.

Before she fell asleep, her imagination conjured up an image of herself lying beside Carter with his arms encircling her. She was ready for sweet dreams.

Chapter Five

Daisy jolted awake when the car parked. The engine continued to hum, and she heard triumphant instrumental music from the CD player. *A soundtrack? For what?* Her eyelids blinked open, and she remembered climbing into the back seat of Carter's SUV. Sitting up, she held the plaid wool blanket in front of her to block the chill. Outside the windows, she saw a wall of trees.

She shook off the vestiges of sleep, stretched her spine and rotated her shoulders. Daisy had always been a morning person, quickly alert. "Where are we?"

"Not too far from Butcher's Gulch," Carter said as he twisted around in his seat to look at her. "It's after five thirty, the edge of dawn."

"So early."

"Or late," he said, "depending on your point of view."

Last night when she curled up in here, it had been before midnight. She'd slept for over five hours—must have been more tired than she realized. She inhaled a deep breath and listened to the classical music as Carter hummed along to the music from *Star Wars* by John Williams. "May the force be with you."

"I like to think it is."

Up till now, he'd kept the geekier side of his personality hidden, like his smile. But Carter was almost as nerdy as any of her high school students. "Do you think of yourself as Obi-Wan? Or Luke Skywalker?"

"Neither."

"Of course not." She groaned. "Han Solo."

"You've got to love him." He turned off the music and opened his door. "Come with me."

She didn't have time to ask where they were going. Before she had her feet planted on the ground, he was already halfway down a gradual slope. The early-morning breeze brushed against her cheeks—fresh, bracing and pine scented. With the sunrise blushing a delicate pink in the sky, flashlights weren't necessary, but she picked her way carefully until she emerged from the forest.

Standing on the rocky shore of a small lake, she watched the pastel dawn reflect on the sparkling waters and shimmer in the spiky treetops. Without saying a word, Carter stood close beside her and took her hand. Though they'd only met last night and nothing had happened between them, they shared an intimacy.

"Teacup Lake." He pointed across the crystalline waters to the north. "That's where Josh found Rene and Slade."

Her hand felt safe and warm in his unexpectedly familiar grasp. "Did you have a chance to talk to the witnesses again?"

"I did a quick interview of your buddy, Jackknife Jones. He admitted that he purposely got lost when he was driving. Somebody paid him to not take you to Butcher's Gulch until after dark."

"That's ominous. Did he say who?"

"Didn't know the guy, and I'm not sure he was telling the truth. Jackknife might have wanted to get you alone after dark."

She shuddered. "What about the others?"

"According to the one you call Pinkie, Rene used to bathe in the lake."

"Naked?"

"That's usually the way you take a bath," he said. "I talked to others at the campsite. One of the guys claimed he knew you. His name is Eric Wolff."

Irritation shot through her, and she tensed, inadvertently squeezing Carter's hand. "The Wolff family—Eric and his father, Gerald—are direct descendants of Morris Wolff, who was part of Sherwood Brighton's outlaw gang. Eric has exaggerated the role of his ancestor to partner and claims to have information that will lead to the bullion, which he thinks is half his."

"None of the others at the party recognized him as part of their regular gang."

"Like Slade Franklin," she pointed out.

"And there were a couple of other young men who were drawn to the music, free beer and women in cutoff jeans." He paused to look down at her. The first rays of the sun glowed on his cheekbones and sculpted chin. "Do you think Eric was looking for you?"

"Yes." Her gaze lowered to his lips, and she imagined what their kiss would be like—their first kiss. She looked away from him before she did something she might regret. "It can't be a coincidence that he was there."

"What else do you know about this guy?" Carter asked.

"Like my aunt, he believes the key to finding the treasure is locating Sherwood Brighton's grave." She blamed Eric and his father for her quest to locate grave sites. "His reasoning comes from letters written to Morris Wolff. I think there were a couple from Annie Brighton, Sherwood's wife. Anyway, Aunt Vi believes he's onto something."

"Did he ever mention Glenwood or Doc Holliday?"

"I don't think so." She frowned. "You're thinking of the first victim."

"Hannah Guerrero," he said.

"Was she posed in the same position as Rene and the other woman?"

"There were similarities." He turned his head to stare across the rippling waves. "Flat on her back, fully dressed with hands folded on her stomach. A long silk scarf was tied around her throat. Apparently, she'd been killed where she lay. Her blood spread across the dirt and got in her long black hair."

"Black hair?"

"She didn't resemble either of the other victims," he said. "The killer doesn't have a type."

"Was Hannah from Glenwood?"

"It was a nearby town, like Carbondale or Basalt. Her friends described her as sociable, easygoing and gullible—the kind of person who believed every crazy story, which makes me think she would have loved your treasure hunt. I wish I could have done more to find her killer."

"What did the police ask you to do?"

"To see if I could learn anything from the trail that led up to the memorial. A well-traveled path with too many footprints. Long story short—I didn't find much. No signs of a struggle. There was an imprint in the dirt of Hannah's shoes and a pair of size-thirteen sneakers."

"A big man?"

"Not necessarily," he said. "The important thing is that each of his footprints were outside hers and facing the same direction."

"How does that work?"

When she tried to move into the position the footprints indicated, he spun her around until she stood in front of him with her shoulders against his chest. "Like this," he said.

"Why?"

In answer, he slung an arm around her middle to hold her in place. With the opposite hand, he drew an imaginary blade across her throat. His action took only a few seconds. "That's one way it could have happened."

"He would have gotten blood all over his clothes."

"Unless he released her immediately." Suiting the action to the word, he dropped his arms and stepped back. "He severed the carotid. She might have staggered a few paces before she lost consciousness and fell to the ground. The blood spatters indicate that sort of scenario."

"Gruesome." Talking about the murder disturbed her a lot more than analyzing the bodily remains. She'd also been thrown off balance by their sudden physical contact. Even when he was illustrating a murder scene, Carter's nearness felt good to her.

He continued, "I also found that the killer wiped his shoes on the pine needles before he hiked down. It looked like he and Hannah walked up there together."

"Which meant he was someone she trusted."

"Or wasn't afraid to be alone with after dark."

The gap between trusting someone and not being afraid of them spread as wide as a chasm. In all the years she'd been dating, Daisy was notoriously slow to trust. Only once had she allowed a relationship to develop into living together, an arrangement that lasted only eight months. On the other hand, she was seldom afraid of being alone with a person she'd just met. Hadn't she hopped into Jackknife's truck without giving him a second thought?

She asked, "Is it possible that the killer was her boyfriend?"

"I don't remember all the details. It wasn't my case," he said. "All I've got are the basics. On the night of her murder, Hannah and her friends were at a tavern in Glenwood. She left at ten o'clock to meet a guy who was an Old West fanatic and curious about Doc Holliday's ghost."

"Sounds like Eric Wolff," she said. "I'm also pretty sure

that he was the person who paid Jackknife to make sure I got to the boot hill after dark."

"One of her friends said Hannah had the feeling that she was being stalked."

"Again," Daisy said, "that's something Eric would do."

"This friend got worried when she couldn't reach Hannah on her cell phone. She went searching and found the body."

Daisy wondered if Carter would interview this friend. If he was in charge of the investigation, he'd surely start there, contacting the Glenwood PD. "Who will you be working with on that investigation?"

"The FBI has jurisdiction on serial killers." He continued to gaze across the waters as the forest came to life with the twittering of sparrows and buntings. A speckled owl swooped across the lake, ending his nocturnal hunt and disappearing into the forest. "The feds can use their cyberexperts to search for similar murders in different states and locations. And they'll do background checks on all the suspects."

"Including Jackknife?"

"He's a suspect. I'm not taking him off my list, but he isn't in the number one slot. These murders were probably the work of a younger, stronger man."

"Why do you think so?" she asked.

"I'm guessing he was boyfriend material, good-looking enough to entice Hannah into leaving her friends at the bar. And Rene Williams, the barefoot woman you found, was probably killed elsewhere and carried to her final resting place in the boot hill. She was a small woman, but it still takes muscles to carry a dead weight."

"You're good at this." She met his steady gaze. "Are you okay with not being in charge?"

"I don't miss tangling with all those different branches of law enforcement. If I'm not the boss, I have more freedom and fewer rules." He glided the back of his hand down her cheek and tilted her chin up toward him. "And I don't have to worry about confiding in a smart, pretty civilian like you."

He thinks I'm pretty. "I wouldn't want you to get in trouble."

"You're no trouble at all."

He dipped his head and kissed her lightly. The gentle pressure started a ripple of sensation that grew more intense when she arched her back and fitted her body against him. Her lungs squeezed, and she could barely catch her breath.

As their kiss continued and deepened, she melted. Her legs turned to jelly. For a moment, she thought she'd swoon like a naive ingenue in a melodrama, but Daisy wasn't a weak-kneed damsel. Strength counted as one of her best assets. Determinedly, she stepped away from his embrace and stared at him, wide-eyed and aroused with her heart wildly palpitating. *Say something.* Her lower lip trembled. "The autopsy," she blurted. "Can I still watch the autopsy?"

"I'll do my best to arrange it."

"When?"

"Probably later today. In the afternoon."

She clung to the solid thought of seeing the autopsy as though it was a life raft in a sea of confusion. He'd have to take her to the medical examiner, which meant they'd be together, and she'd have another chance to be calm, cool and collected. "What do we do next?"

"I take you home to your aunt Vi."

She caught her breath as she climbed the hill behind him. *Inhale...exhale...inhale.* Her aunt was going to adore Carter. Since Daisy's retired parents had moved to Australia, Vi had donned the mantle of parenthood and never missed a chance to nag about how Daisy should settle down and get married. Vi would see the handsome ranger as an excellent candidate for Mr. Right.

WHILE THEY DROVE, Carter filled her in on the direction of the investigation. "This afternoon, we need to hook up with the FBI in Pueblo so you can give your statement. I've worked with one of the agents before. His name is Pat Wiley, and he's a straight shooter."

"There were two of them last night."

"The other is Mickey Hicks."

"Sounds like a cartoon character."

"That's a fairly accurate description, but he's not a mouse. He looks like Popeye."

Carter felt his eyelids drooping. He hadn't slept much last night and needed a burst of caffeine to jump-start his brain. He wasn't thinking right, which might explain why he'd kissed Daisy. Not a rational decision—he'd acted on impulse without considering the consequences. A mistake? Or the smartest move he'd ever made?

He pulled off and parked at a diner he knew had decent coffee. The food wasn't great, but he needed calories for energy. Daisy, an early bird, chowed down and chatted while downing her own coffee. Watching her gave him more vigor than the caffeine. Fairly quickly, they got back on the road.

At a few minutes after nine o'clock, they arrived at Aunt Vi's two-story, gingerbread Victorian house in the historic district of Leadville. The color scheme of gray, black and lilac qualified this place as a "painted lady" without being too showy—a description that might also apply to the woman who posed on the wide veranda and watched him park in the driveway. Like Daisy, Aunt Violet had streaked blond hair. Unlike Daisy, who usually wore her hair in a tumbledown ponytail, Vi's hair was cut to chin length, straight with bangs. Though Daisy had told him that her aunt was sixty-eight, she could have passed for ten or even twenty years younger.

When Daisy came around the SUV and stood beside

him, he said, "Your aunt looks like she belongs in that painted-lady house."

"She's perfected a style that I call classic Western. A tailored shirt tucked into a midcalf, faux-leather skirt and snakeskin cowboy boots. The jewelry is, of course, silver and turquoise." She gave her aunt a good-natured grin and waved. "On some people the outfit would be cliché, but Vi pulls it off."

When Daisy introduced him, Violet gave him a handshake and a perfect smile with precisely applied dark red lipstick. "Should I be worried, Ranger Carter, about my niece not coming home last night?"

"I apologize, ma'am. We got caught up in a serial killer investigation."

Her eyebrows lifted, but she maintained her composure. "Won't you come inside? I should mention that I have another guest. You've met him before, Daisy. Eric Wolff."

Carter scanned the curb in front of the house. His gaze stuck on a dark blue van with the logo for Wolff House Painting and a pyramid of gallon paint cans on the side. Beside him, Daisy growled. "He's not our friend. Eric showed up last night near the murder scene, which makes me think he might have been following me. As a matter of fact, I'm going to ask him right now."

She charged through the front door, leaving him and her aunt on the front porch. If Carter had been in charge of the investigation, he would have reined Daisy in before she physically assaulted a suspect, but he had neither the authority nor the inclination to stop her. Her anger might push Eric into saying something incriminating.

He held the door for Vi. "After you, ma'am."

"I hope you won't mind if I ask a personal question," she said. "Are you married?"

"Not married. Not engaged."

Her red-lipstick smile widened like a Cheshire cat. "Would you like coffee? And a homemade cinnamon scone?"

"Yes, please."

While Vi strode down the central hallway toward what he assumed was the kitchen, he followed the sound of Daisy's voice into a sitting room that was furnished with an eclectic combination of ornate antiques and furniture of many styles and eras. He didn't know much about interior decorating, but he liked this room. It showed personality.

Daisy had positioned herself in front of Eric Wolff, who slouched in a burgundy velvet wing-back chair beside a chrome end table. Her voice hit a stern, authoritative note, reminding him that she was a high school teacher who regularly dealt with cranky adolescents. The age didn't apply to Wolff, who was in his thirties, but the attitude was a fit.

"I'll ask you again," Daisy said, "did you follow me to that campground?"

"You aren't the center of the world, Daisy."

"I think you've been stalking me." She glanced over at Carter. "That's illegal, isn't it?"

"You could file a restraining order compelling Mr. Wolff to stay away from you."

Eric curled his arms tightly against his body. "I didn't do anything wrong."

His shoulder-length blond hair fell around his boyish face in limp, tangled strands. Though he wasn't fat, his cheeks were pudgy, and he had a button nose. From the interview at the campground, Carter knew Eric's age, address in Pueblo and occupation—if he could call being an unemployed housepainter a real job.

"Nice van," Carter said. "Do you take jobs in places other than Pueblo?"

"Sure." His shoulders hunched.

"Ever worked in Glenwood Springs?"

"Yeah. Why?"

"Around the tenth of June, were you in Glenwood?"

His gaze shifted nervously. "I'd have to check my schedule."

Vi entered the room carrying a tray with coffee mugs for Daisy and Carter along with sugar and cream. She placed the tray on a large marble-topped coffee table, and the fresh-roasted aroma wafted pleasantly through the room. Vi straightened. "Daisy, please come to the kitchen with me. I need help carrying the scones."

Carter sat on the long sofa nearest Eric's chair, took off his cowboy hat and picked up his coffee mug. He didn't use cream or sugar, especially not on good, strong coffee like this with subtle undertones of nuts and berries. A far cry from the diner.

He licked his lips and glanced over at Eric. Several possible questions rattled around in Carter's head, but he wasn't sure where to start. The silent treatment had proved effective for him in past interviews. Eric seemed immature and nervous—the sort of man who needed to start talking to fill an uncomfortable silence. He'd say too much rather than too little.

Daisy didn't like him, which was reason enough for Carter to suspect this thirtysomething guy who lived with his father in Pueblo. What was the deal with Eric Wolff? Was he a stalker, too afraid to approach Daisy directly? Or was he a killer?

"Do I need to get a lawyer?" Eric asked.

"Have you done something illegal?"

"Hell, no," he said. "Daisy is the one you ought to be investigating. She has all kinds of secrets. She and Vi are cheating me and my dad out of millions."

Daisy stalked into the room, carrying another tray with napkins, silverware, clotted cream and two flavors of jam. "You're a liar."

Aunt Vi followed with the scones on a separate plate. "Settle down. Both of you."

Carter wanted to pounce on the cinnamon scones and not listen to their bickering. His cell phone bleeped, indicating a text message coming through, and he grabbed the excuse. "Excuse me, I need to take this." Caller ID showed it was from the FBI.

He went to the front door, opened the screen and stepped onto the porch before tapping on the text. Agent Wiley had identified the blonde he'd found at the boot hill using fingerprints. Her name was Andrea Lindstrom. Why did that sound so familiar? Who was she? The gang partying at the campground hadn't mentioned her.

Carter studied the accompanying photo from her driver's license, and the puzzle pieces clicked into place. He knew her.

He looked away from the image on the screen. Last night, he'd stared down at her ravaged remains in the shallow grave. Half her face had been torn away. The silk scarf at her throat had been encrusted with blood. In his mind, he erased that horrific image. Instead, he remembered a day when he'd talked to this sweet, gentle woman about the tragic death of her dear friend Hannah Guerrero.

Andrea had been reported missing on the fourteenth.

Was that timing correct? Hannah was killed on June 10, and Andrea disappeared on June 14. But Daisy had placed time of death for Andrea at two or three days ago, which would have been June 17. Where had she been between the time when she went missing and when she died?

Chapter Six

Still wondering about the link between two of the victims, Carter put away his phone, opened the screen door and stepped back into the house. Standing outside the sitting room, he paused to listen before entering. He didn't hear Daisy yelling or Eric whimpering, which was a good sign, because he didn't want to spend the day on a childish spitting match. Aunt Vi was lecturing them both on the standards of courteous behavior that separated civilized beings from the beasts.

After an apology for slipping out, Carter returned to his seat and broke off a piece of scone, which he slathered with clotted cream and strawberry jam. Daisy sat at the opposite end of the sofa, as far away from Eric as she could get. Her cheeks were flushed with an angry red, her jaw thrust out at a stubborn angle and the line of her soft, sensuous lips had flattened. If Eric was angry, he didn't show it. His shoulders had caved in on his baggy midsection. His mouth trembled, and his watery blue eyes flickered on the verge of tears.

"Thank you, Miss Violet," Eric said, sounding like a child. "I never ever meant to insult you. Or Daisy."

An indecipherable rumble came from Daisy.

Vi gave her a harsh glance. "Did you have something to say, dear? Speak up."

Carter filled his mouth with scone to keep from laughing at Daisy's obvious struggle to control her outrage.

"I'm sorry for raising my voice," Daisy said. "I have a simple question for our guest."

"Go ahead and ask," Aunt Vi said, playing mediator.

"Eric, did you follow me to the campground?"

"No," he said quickly. "You didn't see me following, did you?"

Carter sipped coffee to wash down the scone. He believed Eric. Not because he was innocent, but there were other ways to keep track of another person's whereabouts. Also, he didn't think Eric was capable of following without being noticed. He wasn't a hunter.

"A follow-up," Daisy said. "Did you pay Jackknife to stall until after dark before bringing me to the boot hill?"

He looked down and shrugged. "Not really."

Carter didn't believe him.

"Another question," he said. "Where were you this morning before you came to Leadville?"

"Sleeping. Why?"

"Did you sleep in your van instead of driving all the way home to Pueblo?"

Eric gave a nod. "Nothing wrong with that."

"Think back to dawn." Carter lowered his voice to a soothing, nonthreatening level. "One of the prettiest times of the day, when the skies turn pink and the soft light reflects on the surface of the water. Don't you think so?"

"Yes," he said hesitantly.

"Birds chirping. Waves rippling," Carter said. "So beautiful."

"Yeah."

"Tell me, Eric. Were you at Teacup Lake this morning?"

"Maybe I was." As soon as the words slipped out, he clapped his hand over his mouth as if he could stuff his confession back inside. "Okay, I saw you there. Saw what you were doing."

"You're keeping an eye on Daisy," Carter said. "How are you doing it? A tracking device in her pocket? A locator hooked up to her phone?"

"Who was doing what to whom?" Vi asked.

"You're worse than a stalker." Daisy's lip curled in a snarl. "You've been spying on me."

"Listen, Daisy, all I want is for us to work together. I really need to find the treasure. Me and my dad have a bunch of debt. If we don't get some kind of payoff, we'll lose the house. I'll never have the kind of future I deserve."

"What do you think you deserve?" Carter asked.

"A home with a sweet wife and two kids, girl and boy. And a golden retriever like I had before my mother left us. She took the dog with her. What kind of woman does that?"

He sounded far more upset about losing his pet puppy than having his mother desert the family. In some ways, he seemed normal—pathetic, but normal. In others, he behaved like a creepy stalker.

"Why would I help you?" Daisy asked.

"I have information about the Brighton Bullion that would help your search, and I'll bet there are plenty of things you can tell me."

"Prove it," Daisy said. "Show me one of those letters to Morris Wolff that you're always bragging about. You said you had several from Sherwood Brighton's wife."

He dug into an inner pocket of his lightweight canvas jacket. "When we find the treasure, we split it right down the middle. Fifty-fifty."

"You get twenty percent," she countered.

"Forty."

"Twenty-five," she said. "Final offer."

He stood and held a folded sheet of paper just out of her grasp. For the first time, Carter realized that Eric might look soft and dumpy, but, under that layer of fat, he was actually above average height and in decent physical condition.

With a cold laugh, he handed her the paper. "It's a copy. When you're done reading it, call me and give me an equally important clue."

With his pug nose in the air, he stomped across the patterned Oriental rug and exited from the house. Daisy bolted to her feet and chased after him. "Wait up," she said. "I want to know how you're tracking me. Did you bug my phone?"

Carter followed her. He couldn't compel Eric to hand over his tracking devices, a fact that he considered a gigantic lapse in the legal system, but he wanted the jerk to realize that he was creating a problem for himself. Standing at the screen door, Carter said, "I'd advise you to cooperate."

"Fine." Eric's lower lip stuck out. "There's a tracker in the change compartment of your wallet."

"How did you put it there?"

"Let's just say that you should watch your purse more carefully. Anyway, you can take it out and pitch it. I won't be able to follow you on my GPS."

Daisy gave him a reluctant nod. "You better not be lying."

"And you better call me. We've got a deal."

When Carter turned back toward the sitting room, Aunt Vi stood in his way. Her small fists were planted on her hips below her Navajo concha belt. In a stern voice, she asked, "What was Eric saying about what he saw at the lake?"

"Eric was spying," he said, hoping to distract her. "It doesn't seem right that those tracking devices you can order online are legal. There ought to be a law against following a person without their permission. If he was a Peeping Tom, I could arrest him."

"I once had a peeper," she said in a whisper. "It was right after I divorced my second husband, and I wasn't accustomed to taking care of myself."

Mission accomplished: he'd diverted her from talking about the kiss. "What did you do?"

"Well, I bought a gun." A sly smile teased the corners of her lips. "The first of many. Thanks to the peeper, I discovered how much I enjoy shooting things."

Carter would definitely keep that in mind. His phone buzzed with another text message from Special Agent Pat Wiley. Both of the boot hill victims had been dosed with knockout drugs. Rene Williams also had a blood alcohol level of 0.13, indicating that she'd continued drinking after she left the party at the campground.

When Daisy came back toward the porch, where he and Vi were standing, she had her wallet in hand and had pulled out the small tracking device, which she threw down on the sidewalk and stomped on. "That's what I think of Eric Wolff."

"Are you sure you destroyed it?" Vi asked. "Should I get my gun?"

Carter couldn't tell if she was joking and decided not to hang around and find out. As he left the veranda, he spoke to Daisy. "I need to make a few phone calls, but I'll be back in an hour or so and we'll drive down to the FBI office in Pueblo so you can give your statement."

"I'll be ready and waiting."

As he strode toward his SUV, he heard Aunt Vi return to the prior topic. "This is the last time I'm going to ask, Daisy. What happened at the lake?"

At the curb, Carter ducked into his car and took off. He wasn't sure where he was headed but knew he needed some space. Any other location was preferable to a relationship discussion with the well-armed Aunt Violet.

MUCH AS DAISY wanted to avoid the topic of her kiss with Carter at the edge of Teacup Lake, she knew Aunt Vi wouldn't give up until she got an answer. "If I tell you, will you drop the subject?"

"Probably not. I need to stay informed about the doings of my niece. Leadville isn't like the big city. People here watch out for each other. And they gossip. Lord, how they gossip!"

Daisy wasn't sure how her behavior reflected on her aunt. After all, she was supposed to be a wicked woman from the big city, and they expected her to have loose morals. Her actions weren't Vi's fault. "Carter and I were kissing."

"I approve." Vi gave a brisk nod. "He seems like a nice young man with a respectable job as a forest ranger. Your summer visit might have gotten much more exciting."

"Just a kiss. It doesn't mean anything."

"But it could." Vi gave her a friendly little pat on the bottom like a coach sending a new player into the game. "Run along, dear. He's going to be picking you up again in a little while, and you should get ready. Take a shower, wash your hair and put on some makeup."

Muttering under her breath, Daisy climbed the staircase, crossed the landing and went into her bedroom on the second floor. She'd intended to get cleaned up and change clothes. Not to look more seductive but because she expected this day to be long and possibly complicated. After the FBI interview, she hoped to be attending the autopsy, which wasn't an occasion for getting all dolled up, but she wanted to look clean and sanitary.

Uninvited, Aunt Vi stepped into her room. "Maybe you should borrow something attractive. I have a closet full of outfits I've barely worn."

"Believe me, Vi, if I was planning to make a move on Carter—or any other man, for that matter—you'd be the first person I'd consult." Her aunt was something of an expert, having gone through four husbands and innumerable

boyfriends. "But there's no way I can have a serious relationship with a guy who lives in the mountains. My work
is in the city, and I love my job."

"Don't be so quick to say no."

Daisy changed the topic. "I found something in Butcher's Gulch. There was a gravestone for Annie Brighton,
Sherwood's wife."

"A clue," Vi said with evident delight. "Jackknife said
he saw a marker for Brighton, but I wasn't sure whether
I could believe him or not. He should have mentioned it
was Annie."

"He wanted to impress you. Wants you to date him and
fall in love because you're rich and can take care of him."

"But I'm not a wealthy woman," she protested. "And if
I were, I most certainly wouldn't be interested in the likes
of Jackknife Jones. I have better taste."

"I don't have a lot of information about Annie. Can you
give me the highlights?"

"She and Sherwood had three children, and she basically raised them by herself. His career as an outlaw kept
him away from home for days at a time." Vi referred to his
supposed "career" as though he'd been a busy stockbroker.
"He provided for his family, and nobody ever asked where
her money came from."

"Maybe because they were scared," Daisy said under
her breath.

"You have no call to bad-mouth your ancestor. From all
accounts, he was a gentleman."

Except when he was robbing banks. Her proper aunt
was quick to turn a blind eye when it came to the treasure. "Go on."

"Annie worked as a seamstress and was acclaimed for
making fancy wedding dresses. She lived in Cripple Creek
and Pueblo for most of her life."

"But was buried in Butcher's Gulch."

"Tell me more about the headstone," Vi said eagerly. "What did it say?"

"'Annie Brighton. Wife, Friend and Lover.'"

"Aw, that's so sweet. Sherwood still thought of her as his lover." She frowned. "But it doesn't make sense. I seem to remember that he died before she did."

"Maybe one of the kids was responsible for her marker."

Daisy was curious. Why was Annie buried in a boot hill cemetery, which was the final resting place for outlaws and the indigent? She seemed to be a decent woman who made wedding gowns. Why Butcher's Gulch? Who erected her tombstone? Instead of diving into the shower and washing her hair, Daisy sat on the edge of her bed and unfolded the piece of paper Eric had given her. There might be relevant clues in this copy of a letter—dated June 6, 1889—from Annie to Morris Wolff.

Vi sat beside her, reading over her shoulder. "That's two years after the theft of Brighton's Bullion. When I think about it, I'm certain that Sherwood died in 1896, nine years after the big robbery. What was the date on Annie's tombstone?"

"There wasn't one. No date of birth or death."

"Not completely uncommon," Vi said. "Some ladies are rather particular about revealing their age, even after they're dead."

Silently, Daisy read the first few lines, which were carefully written with perfect penmanship. Then she looked up, wide-eyed and surprised. "This is hot stuff. I guess Annie B. didn't like to waste time on foreplay."

"Those descriptions are based on references from the Bible," Vi said. "Her breasts are ripe fruit, firm and juicy. Made for his delight. Could be Song of Solomon."

Annie continued with an imaginative description of Morris Wolff's private parts, which were—supposedly— as hard as oak and hung to his knees. This letter was an

1800's version of the current trend to send naked, obscene photos via text message. Annie couldn't wait until they were "joined together from top to toe" and she could "taste every sweet bite of his quivering flesh."

"Yuck," Daisy said. "I guess we know why her gravestone mentioned that she was a lover, not necessarily with her husband."

Vi pointed to the end of the letter. "This is the only place she even mentions him."

Daisy read aloud. "'Sherwood will never know where I've put the bullion. It's mine now.'"

"Those are the words of an angry woman." Violet shuddered. "We might have been researching the wrong person. Annie seems to be in charge."

"And has possession of the gold."

Daisy had to admit that Eric Wolff had shown them a telling clue for their treasure hunt. She wondered what else he might be hiding.

Chapter Seven

With the windows down, Carter drove through Leadville, one of his favorite little towns, which was part of the territory he regularly patrolled. As he left the outskirts, the late-morning sky stretched wide and blue above him. He needed this space to clear his head. While driving to a rocky hillside he'd visited before, Carter allowed the mountains to nurture his mind and his spirit.

At an elevation over ten thousand feet, Leadville—the highest incorporated town in North America—boomed into existence during the 1889 silver rush, but the real treasure was the beauty of the surroundings. Nine fourteeners, including Mount Elbert and the aptly named Mount Massive, dominated the landscape. Carter thought these peaks, still snowcapped in the latter half of June, might have provided inspiration for the explorer who saw this mountain range at dawn when the sun had painted the snow a bright red. *Sangre de Cristo* meant "blood of Christ."

Leaving the main road, he guided his NPS vehicle to a clearing at the top of a rise with a heavy-duty picnic table and benches that had seen better days. He swung open the car door, stepped into the sunshine and inhaled the scent of resin, dust and pine cones. Though he had a desk and computer at the NPS headquarters in Salida, he considered places like this—with soul-stirring views of high peaks and abundant forests—to be his office. He'd never trade this job for a cubicle.

Wishing he'd brought a thermos of Aunt Vi's excellent coffee, he stepped onto the bench, sat on the tabletop, took off his cowboy hat and welcomed the breeze that ruffled his hair. He looked to the mountains for answers. One side of his brain popped with questions about the serial killer investigation, while the other was preoccupied with Daisy. From the moment they met, he'd liked her. He admired her smart analysis of the victims' remains. The bubbling sound of her laughter made him smile. He'd never forget the way her lips tasted when they kissed.

He stared across the foothills to the rugged mountains beyond. What the hell was he going to do? The answer came fast—first, he had to stop the serial killer.

And he needed expert advice. Using the sat phone with a strong signal, he called Joaquin Stanley. His supervisor, a former hippie, brought a unique set of skills to his work. He had degrees in forestry, environmental biology and psychology. Before joining the Park Service, he'd been a farmer, a firefighter and a therapist/counselor who specialized in the treatment of perpetrators. His analysis of the serial killer's motives would provide a solid profile.

When Joaquin answered, Carter gave him a quick rundown of the progress on the investigation, including the important fact that the FBI in Pueblo had taken over jurisdiction. "The special agent in charge is SAC Pat Wiley. I've worked with him before."

"Sounds like you've got everything covered. Why are you calling me?"

"I could use your help in profiling the killer," Carter said.

"Stop by this afternoon."

"Can't. I've got an appointment at the FBI office in Pueblo. Then I'm going to watch the autopsy."

"You?" Joaquin questioned. "You've never liked the gory part of the job."

"Yeah, well, people change."

"I'm sensing something from you. What's going on?"

"Nothing." Carter knew his supervisor well. He imagined the burly man stroking his neatly trimmed, salt-and-pepper beard, a remnant of the ZZ Top look he wore in his hippie days. "I don't know what you're talking about."

"There's definite change. You're not acting like a lonesome cowboy anymore."

"Never was a cowboy." Living in the wilderness suited him, but he hadn't grown up on a ranch and didn't ride the range. Bouncing around on a horse gave him a stiff back and an achy ass.

"You know what I mean," Joaquin said. "It's your attitude, your independent nature. You're like Gary Cooper or Clint Eastwood—a kickass loner taming the Wild West."

That description fit a lot of rangers and mountain men. "If I'm a cowboy, what are you?"

"Lumberjack," he said proudly. "My ex-wife used to like watching me chop wood. No kidding. She said it made her horny."

Though he'd come to Joaquin for his expert opinion, Carter enjoyed their wide-ranging conversations. "As long as we're talking about women…"

"Aha!" Carter heard Joaquin slam the flat of his large hand against his desktop. "I know what's different about you. You're in love. Well, good luck to you, Ranger. It's about time."

"I'm not saying you're right, but suppose I met a strong, stubborn woman who loves her life in the city and will never move to the mountains. How do I change her mind?"

"Never start a relationship thinking you can change the

other person. Either you accept her as she is or you quit your job and move into town."

"You're saying it's up to me. I'm the one who has to change."

"Not necessarily. You and your lady friend can hook up for a couple of days and then go your separate ways."

A quick affair wasn't what Carter wanted. With Daisy, something more was possible—something amazing. He'd tried marriage before, and it had lasted less than two years. He wasn't good at being half of a couple. His ex-wife called him a loner. But Daisy was independent and strong and unlike any other woman he'd met. A relationship with her would be an adventure.

His gaze lifted to the vast panorama of the Sangre de Cristos. This was his home. He never wanted to live any-where else. If she didn't change her mind…

"Profiling." He switched gears. This phone call was, after all, about the serial killer. "Here's what I can tell you about the three victims. They were all young and pretty. All were found in graveyards but might not have been killed there. Long silk scarves were tied around the fatal wounds to their throats. Two of them—Hannah and Andrea—knew each other."

"What's different about the three victims?" Joaquin asked.

"Different physical types. Hannah had black hair, dark eyes and a muscular frame. Andrea was a willowy blonde, pale skinned, not an outdoors type. And Rene Williams, the most recent victim, had long brown hair and she was petite."

"What else?"

"Different occupations. Hannah was a dental assistant. Andrea worked for an insurance company. They both lived in the Glenwood Springs area in apartments. Didn't have roommates. Rene was a college student from Denver who had just broken up with a live-in boyfriend."

"How about the times of death? When were they killed?"

"I can't be precise until after the autopsies, but Daisy made a couple of good guesses about when the women in Butcher's Gulch were killed."

"Daisy," Joaquin said. "Is she a coroner? A medical examiner?"

"A high school biology teacher from Denver." He kept his voice level to avoid betraying his feelings for her. "She teaches anatomy and studied forensic medicine at a body farm."

"And she gave you an expert opinion?"

"That's right. Records show that Hannah was murdered on June 10. Andrea was probably killed on June 17 but went missing on the fourteenth. Rene died last night, on June 20."

"First victim on the tenth, second on the seventeenth, third on the twentieth." Joaquin exhaled with a whoosh. "I can see why you need a profile ASAP. The shorter periods between kills could be an indication that he's planning another murder very soon."

"We need to act fast."

Carter heard the scrape of a chair being pushed back from a desk. He knew Joaquin was on his feet, pacing across the black-and-sienna-patterned Navajo area rug in his office. Part of his process was moving. He said physical activity jogged his brain. "When you found the bodies, what was your first impression?"

"Hannah and Rene were arranged to look like they were asleep, but Andrea's body had been mauled by predators." He thought of Daisy's suggestion that the killer had tried to shield the body. "He might have tried to protect Andrea with some kind of covering."

"Tell me about these scarves."

Carter imagined his supervisor standing at the window

of his office, looking out at the Collegiate Peaks—Mount Princeton, Mount Harvard and so on. "The scarves are similar and were put on after death. I'm thinking the killer brought them with him."

"Did you find a murder weapon?"

"No." Carter shook his head. "The autopsy will tell us about the two in Butcher's Gulch. Hannah's throat was slashed by a heavy-duty hunting knife."

"Doesn't exactly narrow it down," Joaquin complained. "Sexual assault?"

"Not on Hannah. We have to wait for the autopsy to know about the other two. My gut tells me no." He described the way Rene's hair was styled and her blouse buttoned up to the collar. "So, what should I look for? I'm hoping you can be more specific than the usual parameters for a serial killer—white male between twenty-eight and forty-five. Abusive childhood. Egocentric with lack of remorse."

"An organized killer," Joaquin said. "He planned ahead, bringing a weapon and a special scarf. It's possible that his planning extends to the selection of his victims. He might get a thrill from learning her habits, might watch her or follow her."

"A stalker."

Carter thought of Eric Wolff and the tracking device he'd planted on Daisy. Though it seemed coincidental that Eric's interest in treasure hunting meshed with serial murders, he might be clever enough to hide one by focusing on the other. It ought to be easy enough to check Eric's whereabouts on the night Hannah was killed.

Joaquin added, "If he grabbed Andrea and held her for three days before killing her, he might have been playing house with her. Following some kind of fantasy."

Or hurting her. He remembered ligature marks on the

wrists. If the killer took captives, he needed a private place to hold them. "He didn't do that for Hannah. Or for Rene."

"He might have bonded with them. You know, singing a song together or dancing. He found ways to stay close to his victims that wouldn't make sense to anyone else."

Like Jackknife Jones driving Daisy in circles. "What else?"

"His motivations are complex," Joaquin said. "I'd be surprised to learn he's driven by a sexual fantasy. Instead, look for a psychologically unhealthy connection to his mother, sister or another close family member. A trigger incident with one of those women might jolt him into the need to commit murder. It's like he's rescuing them by killing them."

"What kind of incident?"

"Triggers might involve a death, a divorce, an argument or a separation. Mom might have divorced Dad and started a new family. The son would see murder as a way to keep Mom close."

"By killing other women?"

"There's a good deal of rage braided into his sadness and/or grief."

A twisted way of thinking. "What makes you study these perpetrators? What's the appeal in forensic psychology?"

"Maybe you should ask your new girlfriend, the biology teacher, why she studies corpses." Joaquin chuckled. "Call me after you have some results from the autopsy. I'll be interested in hearing about this investigation. And in meeting Daisy."

"Not that you've figured out who she is, what should I do about her?"

"Try chopping wood."

WHEN DAISY SLIPPED into the passenger seat of the NPS vehicle, she realized that her khaki skirt—a loose-fitting A-line—displayed a lot of leg, probably her best feature in the summer when she had a natural tan. She glanced over at Carter behind the steering wheel, tempted to explain that she'd chosen a skirt for her FBI interview so she'd look respectable, but then she'd also have to justify the black V-neck T-shirt that clung to her breasts under her lightweight brown jacket. Though she wasn't trying to look seductive, her outfit told a different story. Was she subconsciously putting out signals? Why else would she have blow-dried her curly blond hair into a smooth style that swooped gracefully across her forehead?

This was *not* a date. They'd drive to Pueblo, where she'd have an interview with the FBI and observe an autopsy. She had two other graveyards she wanted to check out as long as they were in the area. *Nothing romantic about any of those plans.*

Leaning back in her seat, she gazed through the windshield at a verdant June day with fluffy white clouds skipping across an azure sky. Fresh grasses dotted with crimson and blue wildflowers blanketed the valley below jagged red cliffs. The Arkansas River, flush with runoff from melted snow, cascaded beside the highway. On a day like this, when the late-morning breeze smelled like summer and sun, she easily understood why Carter loved living in the mountains instead of being a cop on the hot, dry, city streets of Denver.

She exhaled a quiet sigh. If they hadn't been hunting a serial killer, the day would have been perfect. "What did your profiler say about the crimes?"

"He has a theory based on the way the killer grooms and cares for the victims. It's almost as if he has an attachment to them."

"Then why would he kill them?"

"I talked to my supervisor about that. I'll tell you later." His eyebrows lowered in a scowl. "There was another issue with Andrea. According to SAC Wiley, she was reported missing on the fourteenth, but you placed time of death on the seventeenth or eighteenth. Where was she during those missing days?"

Daisy shuddered to think of the platinum blonde being held captive by the serial killer, especially since Andrea had known what had happened to her friend Hannah. Her body had been too mangled by predators to pinpoint signs of abuse, but there were ligature marks on her wrists and arms. "From her wounds, I can't tell if he hurt her…" She hesitated to use the word *torture*. "I didn't see scars or bruises indicating that he injured Rene. From what you told me about Hannah, her death came swiftly."

"Joaquin—my NPS Supervisor who used to be a psychologist—suggested that these weren't random killings. He stalks, pursues and captures women who have some kind of connection to him. Possibly he imagines affection—something he might feel for a family member, maybe even his mother." Carter groped for words to explain. "He might be using his victims as surrogates for women he felt close to. He might talk to them or sing to them."

Not surprisingly, the motivation for this serial killer also mystified her. Why would he do these terrible, degrading things? How could he think playing with his captives meant he cared for them? "I'm not great at putting myself into somebody else's head."

"Not when their thinking is so warped."

"But your supervisor knows forensic psychology. He studies perpetrators. What does that say about him?"

"I might ask the same of you. Why do you study dead people?" He gazed into her eyes, making a quick but deep connection. "For that matter, I must be as weird as you and Joaquin, because I like talking to both of you."

She continued to stare after he looked back at the road. In spite of herself, she wondered if he'd noticed how mascara brought out the green in her eyes. "Do you think I'm weird?"

"Not weird. I think you're extraordinary."

Definitely a first. No one had ever said that to her before. Uncomfortable, she wanted to get back to the business of investigating. "How can we use this profile?"

"When we're considering suspects, we should look for triggers—incidents involving his mother or a woman he was close to. What can you tell me about Eric Wolff?"

"He's not a killer," she protested. "He's a jealous, small-minded treasure hunter."

"He fits some parameters for the killer. He's the right age, has a job with flexible hours and can easily transport bodies in his van. He admitted to stalking you."

Every word he spoke rang true. She'd been disturbed when Eric confessed that he'd watched when Carter kissed her. Definitely a creep. But a serial killer?

"He lives in Pueblo with his father," she said. "His mother isn't in the picture. I think she left them when Eric was a teenager."

"Could be a trigger."

"But it happened a long time ago. Eric's in his thirties. Surely he's had time to get over being abandoned so many years ago."

"Some people never do. Early abandonment can scar a person for life."

"True." Her own upbringing as the only child of older parents had been relatively stable and free from tragedy. Not for the first time, she was thankful for being average. "What we should be asking is why now? What would activate Eric's early trauma?"

"We'll have to research his mother. She might be getting married to someone other than his father. Or she might have died."

"There's an easy way to verify if he was the killer

or not," she said. "Check his alibi. Was he in Glenwood Springs when Hannah was killed? Or was that unverified?"

His mouth twisted in a wry grin. "I know why you're an anatomy whiz, but how do you know about alibis?"

"I read suspense novels," she said.

"Hannah was hanging out at a tavern with friends, including Andrea, and told them she was going to meet a guy who wanted to see the memorial to Doc Holliday. Could Eric pull that off?"

Slowly, she nodded. An awareness of danger spread through her. Her skin prickled. The first time she met Eric, he made a point of talking to her about cemeteries and the boot hill graveyards. He had convinced Aunt Vi to start looking for Sherwood Brighton's grave. Was Eric the killer?

A seed of fear had been planted in the back of her mind. During the two-and-a-half-hour drive, they discussed other suspects—including Slade Franklin, who also lived in Pueblo and was someone they'd visit while there. But she couldn't dismiss the thought of Eric Wolff stalking her through the forest.

When they got to the outskirts of Pueblo, she saw a dark blue van on the other side of the street, too far for her to make out the features of the driver. He drove out of sight before she could read the logo and see the image of paint cans. Was it him? Walking on the sidewalk, she saw a man who shuffled like Eric. This was his hometown. He could be anywhere. Waiting. Watching. Planning his attack.

Chapter Eight

The headquarters for the Pueblo branch of the FBI spread across the eighth and ninth floors of an office building around the corner from the Pueblo County Detention Center and the county sheriff's office. Daisy should have felt safe within these orderly corridors where cubicles and clusters of desks for field agents occupied open spaces and partitioned private offices lined the inner walls. Though these lawmen and women had locked their weapons away while in the office, they were equipped with the skill and training to protect her. Certainly they looked professional—most of the agents wore slacks and tucked-in shirts with blazers. Several had neckties.

A red-haired agent she recognized from the boot hill approached them and slapped Carter on the back in an aggressively friendly gesture. The agent was average height, but he appeared to be bigger due to the biceps bulging inside his shirtsleeves, giving the impression that if he flexed the seams would split. His striped necktie draped over his pecs and pointed toward his muscular thighs. When he shook Daisy's hand, she braced for a mighty grip and wasn't disappointed. She gritted her teeth to keep from flinching.

"Not sure we met at Butcher's Gulch," he said. "I'm Special Agent Mickey Hicks."

The guy with the cartoon character name. "I'm Daisy Brighton. Please call me Daisy."

"Sorry you got mixed up in this, Daisy, but don't you worry. We'll nab this guy."

She'd come here as a witness to give a statement, but Hicks's pale blue eyes seemed to accuse her. A sensation of undeserved guilt prickled across her skin like goose bumps. She hadn't done anything wrong but couldn't help but worry that some long-forgotten infraction would rise up and point an accusing finger in her direction.

Carter reintroduced her to SAC Pat Wiley, who was the opposite of Hicks. While Hicks was hard-edged and intense, Wiley reminded her of a pair of well-worn loafers—not pretty but exceedingly comfortable. He was average-looking with thinning brown hair, an easy grin and a bolo tie fastened with a circular silver slide etched with a howling coyote. *A wily coyote? Another cartoon?* His handshake reassured her, and so did his compliment—"Your analysis of the time of death seems to be right on target. We appreciate your assistance."

"I'm glad. But how did that help?"

"In the early part of the investigation, we gather as much information as possible on the actual crime. Your observations of insect larvae and the development of maggots caused you to place the time of death for these women at least two days apart. A significant detail."

A woman in a white lab coat, obviously a forensic investigator, picked her way through the desks and handed a folder to Hicks. Her tone was crisp. "DNA results confirm the identity of Rene Williams. By the way, you're welcome for the rush analysis."

Before Wiley could comment, she pivoted and left. Wiley ushered her and Carter into a small interrogation room with a table, four chairs and a two-way mirror on one wall. The space looked exactly as she expected from watching TV cop shows. Wiley gestured for her and Carter to sit on one side of the table while he took a chair opposite them, opened a fat envelope and took out a folder with forms, papers and photographs inside.

For a few moments, Carter and Wiley lobbed ideas back and forth, much the way she and Carter had on the drive. As far as she was concerned, this was unnecessary talk. The autopsy would provide information about whether the victim been restrained, raped or tortured. Carter opened a new direction to their speculation, asking about where Andrea might have been held. Did the killer live in the Glenwood Springs area where he'd met Andrea and Hannah? Or was Butcher's Gulch closer to his home base? Or was it totally unrelated to the victims? He might live in Pueblo.

Daisy lacked the ability to judge distances in the mountains, which was why Jackknife had managed to drive her in circles. When the GPS on her phone went on the fritz, she was well and truly lost. The vast distances between towns and other areas heightened her respect for Carter's job. He didn't have as many violent crimes to investigate as a city cop, but his jurisdiction covered a wide and varied topography. Looking to Wiley, he said, "No matter where he lives, we'll need warrants to get your forensic investigators inside his truck or van."

"As soon as you give me cause, I'm on it." Wiley turned his head and pinned Daisy with a surprisingly sharp gaze. She figured he was deciding whether or not he should talk about the crime in her presence. "You might be more comfortable in the waiting room, Ms. Brighton."

"It's Daisy," she said. "And I don't mind hearing about your investigation."

"Having her observe is unorthodox," Carter said, "but she could be useful. The medical examiner has already agreed to let her attend the autopsies this afternoon."

"I'm impressed." Wiley arched an eyebrow. "Dr. Julia Stillwater doesn't break the rules for just anybody."

"Plus, Daisy is connected with two of the suspects— Jackknife Jones and Eric Wolff."

"Very well." Wiley adjusted his bolo tie and consulted a report from his folder. "I have information from the Glenwood Springs PD. They initiated their investigation into Andrea Lindstrom's disappearance after receiving a call from the insurance office where she worked. Her apartment showed no signs of being broken into. None of her friends or family had heard from her. The Glenwood cops were thorough. They didn't find any leads."

Daisy absorbed his words. Was Andrea grabbed off the street? Did the killer invite her to have a cup of coffee with him? Unlikely! No way would she engage in casual conversation with a stranger after what had happened to her friend Hannah. "I wonder if she drove home after work on the day before she went missing. Where was her car?"

"In a grocery store parking lot."

A clear picture formed in her mind. "I'll bet her shopping bags were half loaded into the trunk."

"Good hunch," Wiley said. "How did you know that?"

"I'm a single woman who tries to be cautious. When I get out of my car, I hold the vial of pepper spray on my key chain, cocked and ready to fire. I don't even think about the pepper spray anymore. It's habit." Though not aware of being nervous, her voice cracked. She cleared her throat. "I'm most vulnerable when I'm in the middle of unloading stuff and my arms are full."

Under the table, Carter took her hand and gently squeezed. She hoped he didn't feel her trembling.

"Good reasoning," Wiley said. "That's pretty much what the Glenwood cops concluded."

"I liked working with those detectives," Carter said. "What else did they find?"

"Hannah Guerrero had a connection with Pueblo. Her

great-uncle died in October of last year, and she attended the funeral at Rolling Hills Cemetery."

Daisy's ears pricked up. That cemetery was on her list of places where Sherwood Brighton could be buried. "Where is that located?"

"South Pueblo. I can give you directions." He flipped a page in his folder. "That evening, she went jogging along the Riverwalk."

The few bits of information she recalled about Hannah included her occupation as a dental assistant and her high level of physical fitness. An evening jog made sense, and the Riverwalk was a charming location where the wide Arkansas River curled through the center of town. Elegantly landscaped, the sprawling acreage housed a selection of shops and restaurants. The renovations represented an integral part of Pueblo's transformation from the so-called Steel City to an artsy community with galleries, concerts and a ballet company.

"On that very same night," Wiley said, "the body of a young woman was found among the trees at the north edge of the Riverwalk. Not a well-lighted area, but she was visible from the sidewalk where Hannah and other joggers would have been running. The victim had been arranged with her back against a thick tree trunk. At first, an observer might think she was taking a break from her stroll and resting while she peacefully watched the river roll by."

"How cold was it?" Daisy asked.

"In early evening, around fifty or fifty-five. The victim wore a light jacket and jeans."

He took an eight-by-ten photo from the folder and slid it across the table to Carter, who shared the picture with her. Daisy agreed with Wiley's statement about the victim appearing to be resting. His next photo showed heavy bruising around her throat. *Strangled.*

The method of killing differed from the three women

in the current investigation, but the way the body had been arranged echoed the Butcher's Gulch murderer's careful display of his victims. She wasn't an expert on criminal behavior, but the appearance of another dead woman who was connected with Hannah had to be more than coincidence. "Did Hannah find the body?"

"She didn't report it but was definitely in the area."

Though she and Carter had discovered the most recent victims, the roots of these serial killings stretched back farther into the past. Could there have been others? How many? She imagined an endless queue of young women clutching their throats with their eyes closed in death and their mouths gaping open in silent screams.

Goose bumps broke out on her arms. She might already have met this killer, might have heard his voice and inhaled the smell of bloodlust clinging to him. Would she know him when he came close? Or would he blend in, indistinguishable until he attacked?

Her chills solidified in a frozen lump in her chest, making it hard to breathe. She groped for Carter's hand, needing his strength and reassurance, but he was leaning across the table toward Wiley, his gaze intense. His voice took on an avid tone. "Is it unusual for a serial killer to change his method of murder?"

"It happens." Wiley shrugged. "He's still defining himself."

"What about the scarf?" Carter asked. "The woman on the Riverwalk wasn't wearing a scarf."

A photograph of a silver necklace with a heart pendant joined the other two pictures on the table. "None of her friends or family recognized the necklace she was wearing. He crushed her throat with so much force that the chain embedded in her skin. A reenactment of the crime based on forensic evidence indicated that he stood behind her, perhaps fastening the heart necklace at her nape before he choked her."

"Strangulation is nowhere near as messy as a slicing an artery and seems less efficient," Carter said. "Why change?"

"We can agree that he's an organized killer who plans every detail and doesn't leave much to chance. Strangling might seem tidy, but a victim who's being choked is more likely to fight."

"Not if he grabs them from behind," Carter said.

"She might kick, might throw herself on the ground or break away and cry for help."

Daisy felt the blood drain from her face. Studying the deceased didn't bother her but hearing about the struggle before death set her imagination racing down a dark, dangerous pathway. She seldom went to horror movies. And when the scary music started playing, she covered her eyes and gritted her teeth so she wouldn't scream. "Are there others? How long has he been killing?"

"I'm waiting to get more information," Wiley said. "The Riverwalk victim came from the Southern Ute Reservation near Durango. The investigation was taken over by tribal police."

Carter nodded. "I've never had a problem dealing with the tribes."

"That's because you're a ranger, a protector of the forests. They don't see you as the enemy. You'd be surprised by how many people resent the FBI and don't want to cooperate."

Daisy understood that reluctance. Moments ago, when she entered the offices of the all-powerful FBI, she'd been nervous, expecting to be arrested for a forgotten crime, something so minor that she didn't remember. The tribal police had reason to distrust the feds, stemming from a history of broken treaties and land grabs. She could understand why they'd prefer to work with an investigative ranger like Carter who shared their respect for the land.

"In any case," Wiley said, "we're expanding our computer search to include young women who were missing or killed in the past ten years."

An endless line of victims... Unable to cope with the idea of so much fear—terror from the murdered women who knew they were about to die and from her own deep-seated nightmares—Daisy went silent while Carter and Wiley continued to discuss the investigation.

In her imagination, the murderer evolved into a monster with blood dripping from his fangs and his fingernails sharpened into talons. *Ridiculous.* According to science, the natural world contained many horrifying creatures, including the apex predators at the top of the food chain. Great white sharks, Burmese pythons and grizzlies were virtual killing machines. Horrifying and lethal but predictable, they didn't frighten her as much as an innocent-looking individual who lured his prey into danger. She wanted this serial killer caught. At the same time, she realized there wasn't much she could do to find and arrest a murderer. Daisy hadn't trained as an investigator.

As soon as they were done at the FBI office, she and Carter would observe the autopsy. A much better use of her skills.

Chapter Nine

As they approached the autopsy suite, Carter trained his watchful gaze on Daisy. In her short skirt with her practical hiking boots, her tanned legs provided a sexy distraction from his concerns about her state of mind. She'd told him repeatedly that she was fine. Her posture and athletic gait showed the confidence he'd come to expect from her. But when she reached up and brushed a shiny wing of blond hair off her forehead, she avoided looking at him. She'd been jumpy since they left Leadville. During their time with SAC Wiley in the interrogation room, her nervousness had increased. The roses in her cheeks faded to ash. Her hands trembled.

He didn't understand. He'd watched this woman calmly examine maggots on a corpse and lean close to check the wounds. But talking about the investigation had her rattled. When they got down to the official business of Wiley taking her witness statement for the record, she'd regained some of her poise, especially when she discussed the injuries on the victims.

What's she hiding? Every time he asked if she was okay, she said the same thing: "Fine." He didn't think she was lying. Why would she? But there was definitely something she wasn't telling him.

He paused outside the autopsy area and asked, "Are you sure you want to do this?"

"I've been looking forward to watching Dr. Julia Still-water work." When she gazed up at him, her green eyes widened. Her smile seemed genuine. "She's a legend. According to one of my former profs, there's nobody better than Dr. Stillwater. She's done tremendous work on facial reconstruction."

Though he believed her enthusiasm, he still saw tension. "Maybe we should grab a cup of coffee before we go inside."

"I'd rather watch."

Actually, he wouldn't mind another coffee. Last night, he hadn't slept, and it was almost lunchtime. "Are you hungry?"

"I'm fine."

Fine. He was beginning to hate that word. Because she wasn't fine. She was frightened, on edge. "Something's bothering you, and I want to know what it is."

"Nothing, really."

He had no choice but to follow her into a carpeted waiting area with its functional chairs and tables. The boring furniture was where the resemblance to other institutional settings ended. An abstract painting of the high desert landscape covered the walls in turquoise, gold, sienna and purple—colors associated with the Southwest. Leafy plants, like dieffenbachia, dragon tree and that one with the spidery leaves, ranged around the room in terra cotta pots, also painted with colorful geometric designs. A sign that said Autopsy marked the wall beside a windowed door. On the opposite side was the forensic laboratory. Haunting melodies from a wooden flute shimmered in the background.

"Mellow." Daisy's tension took a giant step toward calm. "This decor has got to be from the earth mother influence of Julia Stillwater."

He'd only met the doctor in person once before and had never attended an autopsy, but he respected her knowledge and had immediately liked this strong Ute tribal elder who supervised a clinic on the reservation in addition to her work as a medical examiner.

In the anteroom outside the large area where the actual autopsies would be performed, an intern in scrubs wearing a Harley-Davidson surgical cap and a black N95 mask took their names and directed them to the area where they could change into hats, booties, gloves, masks and disposable suits to cover their clothes.

While she got dressed in the sanitary gear, Daisy asked, "Have they started the autopsy?"

"They're still doing the external exam." The intern shrugged. "What's the deal with these victims? There's a whole bunch of observers."

Carter expected as much. There would be agents from the FBI, state police and the coroner for Pueblo County, at the very least. "It's a possible serial killer."

The intern's dark brown eyes were his only visible feature. He squeezed them closed and then open, an expression that could have meant surprise, excitement or just about anything else. "Whoa."

"Has the autopsy uncovered any forensic data, like a tox screen?"

"There was one done, but I don't have the details." He bobbed his head. "The only thing Doc Julia said was that the suggested time of death was within reasonable parameters."

Daisy nudged his arm. "Did you hear that? I'm within reasonable parameters."

They entered the autopsy room, where two stainless steel tables with gutters on either side were set up in the midst of other equipment, including measuring devices, scalpels, forceps, shears, saws and other tools he didn't recognize. Dr. Julia Stillwater turned the naked body of Rene Williams onto her side to display the dark purpling of lividity

on her back and torso. One intern held the body in place
while another took photos.

Behind her plastic face shield, the doctor wore a recording microphone headset. She motioned to the intern with
the camera and pointed to the grayish flesh of Rene's arm.
"Butterfly tattoo above the ligature marks on her left wrist.
Where there's one, often there are more."

With the intern snapping photos, they recorded five other
tats, including a horoscope sign for Scorpio and an arrangement of stars that looked like the Big Dipper. Carter
looked away from the dead woman. Instead, he focused on
the doctor as she moved in a methodical manner from the
top of Rene's head to her feet, from her fingertips to her
shoulders. Once again, they turned her onto her stomach.
With precision, the doctor and her interns recorded all the
visible scratches, bruises and wounds.

"Make sure you get a photo of that double puncture,"
she said, indicating an area on the victim's side. "Those
marks either came from a stun gun or she was attacked
by a vampire."

The investigators, including Carter, focused on this new
revelation. He was fairly sure that Hannah hadn't been hit
by a stun gun, which meant the killer had made another
change in his procedure. Had he also zapped Andrea?

On Rene's upper back above the shoulder blade, Dr. Stillwater found the final tattoo. The name *Josh* surrounded by
a heart. Josh Santana was the boyfriend. Another suspect.

Glancing around the room, Carter counted seven other
observers. None were as keenly interested as Daisy, who
kept inching closer to the examination table for a better
look. When the intern who had been taking photos stepped
back, the doctor picked up her scalpel. The overhead surgical lights flashed against the silver blade. The time had
come for the Y-shaped incision that would lay the organs
bare. Not Carter's idea of a good time.

Behind her plastic face shield, Julia Stillwater grinned at Daisy. "Are you Ms. Brighton?"

"It's an honor to meet you, Doctor."

"You're a biology teacher."

"That's right."

"Good job estimating time of death. We should talk."

"I'd like that."

Carter couldn't see Daisy's mouth behind her mask, but he knew she was smiling from ear to ear. The doctor ranked high in her estimation, and the mere thought of a chat about forensic medicine had wiped away her fears and nervousness. She'd recalibrated her mood. Now, she was really and truly, actually *fine*.

On the other hand, he wasn't altogether thrilled to be here. To be sure, he wanted and needed the forensic evidence that would be revealed when Dr. Stillwater cracked open the rib cage and cut through Rene Williams's breastbone. The doc would discover all kinds of useful details when she removed the major organs and analyzed them. Ditto for the brain.

But he really wasn't interested in the procedure. He didn't care how she reached her conclusions, didn't need to see or smell the actual stomach contents. It was enough for him to read the autopsy report and learn what Rene had eaten for her last meal.

While he searched his mind for a plausible excuse to leave the autopsy, Dr. Stillwater saved him the trouble. She returned her scalpel to the sanitary tray and stepped back from the table. "I think I'll take a break now. Half an hour or so. For those of you who are observing, don't touch the body. Feel free to visit the cafeteria for coffee or tea. Remember to suit up again when you return. Daisy, please come with me."

When she turned and strode from the room, her interns carefully covered the naked body and the surgical tools. Daisy hurried out the door and down the hallway after her idol, and Carter followed.

DAISY'S EXPECTATIONS FOR the office of an earth mother who was also a scientist were happily met when they entered a large room with two tall windows. Long wooden planter boxes filled with basil, peas and peppers stretched beneath each window and were bathed in sunlight. Tendrils of ivy dripped over the edges and touched the floor. In the corner, a big-leafed bird-of-paradise plant reached all the way to the ceiling. A set of bookshelves held intricately painted bowls and vases from the Ute Mountain pottery collection as well as woven baskets. Family photos and artwork done by grandchildren decorated the walls. A casual clutter of papers, folders and books kept the place from looking like a museum.

A small desk—stacked with incoming work—lurked in the corner, while a long, polished walnut table surrounded by comfortable chairs dominated the center of the room. Dr. Stillwater peeled off her protective gear, revealing turquoise scrubs and two long black braids that had been tucked inside her cap. She went to another table and filled the reservoir in a coffee maker with distilled water. "You'll both have coffee," she said. "Feel free to take off the gowns, gloves and masks."

As Carter stripped off the outer layer of sanitary clothing, he thanked her for her hospitality. "We've met before," he said.

"I remember you, Ranger. It's Aloysius Periwinkle Carter, isn't it?"

Aloysius Periwinkle? Daisy squelched the urge to poke fun. She'd been teased about her name that seemed to rhyme with everything, including crazy, lazy and—worst of all—easy.

"A. P. Carter IV." A sheepish grin curled his lips. "You have a good memory."

"I keep track of people who interest me." She ground the beans from a canister and set the coffee to brew. The aroma mingled with the pleasant, herbaceous scent of the room. "You've worked with tribal police more than once."

"I have respect for the men and women who keep order on the rez. I hope to talk with them about a murder that took place last October."

Daisy remembered the victim found at the Riverwalk. "Is that killing related to these two autopsies?"

"I believe so," he said. "The victim was strangled."

"Eileen Findlay," Dr. Julia said. "I did the autopsy. Give my assistant her name, and she'll pull the files." She turned her dark-eyed gaze on Daisy. "Tell me how a biology teacher from Denver ends up in a graveyard outside a ghost town."

"Ever heard of Brighton's Bullion?"

"The golden treasure."

Not wanting to waste much time on the family myth, Daisy rushed through her explanation of why she'd been searching for the grave of the outlaw Sherwood Brighton. "We found the gravestone for his wife, Annie, at Butcher's Gulch. I don't know why this respectable woman was buried in an outlaws' cemetery, but she was."

"A mystery," Dr. Julia said. "I heard that you encourage your high school students to work with cadavers."

"I don't get to provide that experience as often as I'd like. Sometimes, there aren't bodies available. Sometimes, parents refuse permission." She was always surprised when the adults wouldn't allow their children to participate. "When studying anatomy, it's best to see a real-life example of how organs fit together—and work together—in the body. I also have botany classes where I make the students start a garden. I mean, how can they understand plants when they think all produce comes prepackaged from a grocery store?"

"You're a good teacher." Dr. Julia took both of her hands and held them, making a connection. "If you ever consider leaving Denver, there's a place for you here."

Stunned into silence, Daisy absorbed this special moment in time. The warmth of Dr. Julia's touch. The scent of earth from plants and coffee. The colors and patterns of the Ute designs. She glanced at Carter, realizing that he fit precisely into this picture, these feelings.

She cleared her throat. "Thank you."

"I mean it." Dr. Julia gave her hands a squeeze and returned to her coffee maker. She filled three ceramic mugs that bore stylized sunrise designs. "We have a strong community of scientists and artists. We can use someone with your skills. And your passion."

Daisy would love to work with this plainspoken woman who was also brilliant. "I read your paper on the advantages of the Rokitansky method in organ removal during autopsy, and I agree with your conclusion about how it's important to take your time."

"Even when you have a room full of officers who are anxious to hear results." She aimed a sidelong glance at Carter. "Those are your people, Ranger."

"I try not to be impatient," he said, "but you can always bluff me because I don't understand anatomy. If you told me it took a week to study the spleen, I wouldn't contradict. I don't even know where to find the spleen."

The doctor's laughter sounded as rich as her coffee tasted. Daisy's spirits lightened. "Maybe you can help me understand something. Scientific explanations make sense to me, and I can happily study forensics all day. But when it comes to speculation and deduction, I'm totally confused."

"Give me an example."

"When Carter talks about the investigation and starts

posing theories. I imagine the serial killer as a predator—which, to tell the truth, he is. And I scare myself."

"You need solid facts to be grounded. I'm much the same. My brain works deductively. For example, I saw twin puncture marks on Rene's side below the rib cage. My deduction—she had been incapacitated by a stun gun. That's a rational conclusion. Factual."

Daisy completely understood. She looked to Carter for his opinion. "What do you think about the puncture marks?"

"I'm wondering why he used it. When did he zap her—when he first captured her or right before he killed her? Did he use the gun on his other victims? There was no mention of puncture wounds in Hannah's autopsy report." He focused on Dr. Julia. "I'll be interested to hear about the victim from the reservation. Maybe Hannah was an outlier and he didn't stun her because he knew they were completely alone."

"So much speculation." Daisy sipped her coffee. "And no way of knowing the truth. I'm already imagining this monster terrorizing the women he killed. How can we ever know why?"

"Psychology and profiling." Carter looked to Dr. Julia. "I spoke to Joaquin Stanley."

"How is the old hippie?"

"Same as always."

On the drive down here, Carter had outlined his supervisor's profile of the murderer. They should look for an organized killer who was not sexually motivated. A stalker, he was fond of his victims and might develop an attachment to them. Probably, he was triggered by a traumatic event involving a woman he cared about, i.e., mother, sister, grandmother, friend.

After he ran down the same list with Dr. Julia, she gazed across the rim of her coffee mug at Daisy. "In my culture, there is a belief that the recently dead become ghostwalkers and stay close to the body for a period of time. The killer might believe he is resurrecting a relationship that died."

She shuddered. Adding ghosts to her imagination didn't help. She dragged them back to facts. "One of our suspects admitted to stalking me. Should I worry? Am I in danger?"

"Stalking might be a part of the serial killer's procedure," Dr. Julia said, "but there are others who stalk for other reasons. Either way, it's a threatening behavior. That's a fact."

"Got it. I should take steps to protect myself from this guy."

"We might learn more from studying victimology. Again, based on fact. Killers are more likely to attack when the victim is unprotected or in a dangerous place."

Daisy thought of Hannah being drawn to the memorial, where she'd be alone. Andrea had been grabbed in a grocery store parking lot, where she was not alone but surrounded by people who were distracted by their own business. "What else?"

"Trust no one. Avoid risky behavior. And—this is really important—align yourself with a suitable guardian."

"Like Carter." She was still frightened but doubted she'd be injured when he was with her. "No more visiting cemeteries by myself, especially after dark."

Dr. Julia asked, "Do you have any specific reason to believe you might be targeted as the next victim?"

She shook her head. "Just my overactive imagination."

"There is something," Carter said. "We're examining links between these women. Hannah was at the Riverwalk when the Ute woman was killed. Andrea was a friend of Hannah's. Rene was close to the place where Andrea was dumped after she was murdered."

"I'm not part of those connections," Daisy said. "Maybe you should keep an eye on Pinkie and the other women at the party who were friends of Rene."

"Good idea," he said. "I'll mention it to the FBI."

Dr. Julia stood and drained her coffee mug. "Time for me to go back to work. Daisy, would you like to assist with the rest of the autopsy?"

"Absolutely."

She bounced to her feet as though her legs were on springs. Eager didn't begin to describe her enthusiasm. Without thinking she gave Carter a hug and a friendly kiss on the cheek. *Whoa, girl, that's not smart.* No matter how hard she tried to keep their relationship nonphysical, her natural impulses kept pushing her toward him.

Settling his cowboy hat on his head, he gazed at her from under the brim. His blue eyes shimmered. His lips curved in one of his sexy smiles while he informed her that he needed to check in at the FBI office and would return for her in an hour or so. "I might try to meet with Slade Franklin while we're in town."

She remembered the clean-cut, tall man from the party. Talking to him at Butcher's Gulch hadn't frightened her before. But now? When everybody was a suspect? It might be good for her to confront him again. "If you don't mind, I'd like to come along when you interview Slade."

He cocked his head to one side. "Why?"

"To face my fears."

"Shouldn't be a problem for you to come along." He gave her arm a squeeze. "I'll be back. Don't go anywhere else without me."

She watched the office door close behind him. For her, talking to a suspect—even someone who seemed as innocent as Slade—marked a step in the right direction. She'd treat this interview like a science experiment, separating facts from imagination. And she'd follow Dr. Julia's advice: find the verifiable truth and do everything possible to avoid risk.

Chapter Ten

After spending an hour and a half at FBI headquarters, Carter returned to pick up Daisy, who was waiting for him outside the autopsy suite. Bubbling over, she delighted in telling him every detail about the autopsy on their walk to his SUV, starting with how she and Dr. Julia had removed the organs from the body cavity, weighed them and prepared slides for further examination. According to their preliminary findings, Rene Williams had been a healthy young woman who should have lived a long life. As Daisy spoke those words, her voice quavered slightly, which might have been the first time he'd seen her show emotion about a dead person.

"It's difficult to imagine," she said, underlining this deviation from her usual detachment, "the loss of a young life. She'll never marry, never have children, never have a chance to fulfill her dreams. I wonder what she was studying in college."

He rested his hand on her shoulder, offering comfort. The cruelty, the injustice and the sorrow of every murder case he'd investigated—from his years as a cop in Denver to his career as a ranger—touched him. He'd given up trying to keep himself uninvolved and impersonal. When he thought of Rene, Andrea and Hannah, he experienced the loss and the pain. "The FBI contacted her parents. They live on a ranch in Wyoming."

"I can't imagine what this is like for them."

"Neither can I."

She paused outside the passenger door of his SUV and gazed up at him. "I haven't let you get a word in edgewise. What else is happening with the feds?"

"Forensics has a couple of clear footprints for size-thirteen shoes. The same size was found near Hannah's crime scene."

"Is that an unusual size?"

"Not really. I wear a twelve, and I'm six foot three."

"Anything else?" she asked.

"When you saw Andrea's body, you said it must have been covered or hidden so the predators wouldn't completely tear her apart. And you were correct. Forensics found scraps and fibers." He paused before revealing more. This fact might send her spiraling down the wrong path. But what was he going to do—lie to her? "The scraps come from white canvas, the kind of material that painters—or carpenters—use."

"A drop cloth?"

He knew what she was thinking. "Don't make too much of this. It's likely that Eric Wolff has drop cloths as part of his regular equipment. And Slade probably uses them when he applies finish on wood products."

"Drop cloths are inexpensive and common. I've bought them myself when I painted my kitchen." Her forehead crinkled in a frown. "Those scraps might point toward Eric, but the cloth doesn't count as a valid clue unless we find it and it's stained with blood."

"And that's just about everything I learned from the feds. Wiley was happy when I gave him a copy of Dr. Julia's autopsy report for Eileen Findlay, the woman who was found at the Riverwalk. She grew up on the Southern Ute Reservation but lived in Pueblo, where she was a student at CSU. He's working on possible connections between her and Hannah."

"Other than Hannah stumbling over her body?"

"Yep." He pushed his hat off his forehead and tilted his face toward the sun. The warmth of early summer eased the chill from the autopsy suite. Outdoors, they were surrounded by life. Robins and wrens chirped from the trees. People rushed along the sidewalks. Afternoon sunlight glittered against his windshield. Though he and Daisy had already accomplished a lot today, it was only half past four. There was more to be done. "Before we go to the graveyards you want to explore, I'd like to pay a visit to Slade Franklin."

"The guy with the buzz cut who we met at Butcher's Gulch. The carpenter who might use drop cloths. Is he a suspect?"

"It's worth talking to him. He was one of the last people to see Rene alive, and he drives a camper truck that could be used to transport victims."

"Does he have a criminal record?"

"He's squeaky clean." Which made Agent Wiley think Slade was an unlikely suspect. Interviewing him ranked as low priority. "I called his cell phone, and he agreed to meet at his house in fifteen minutes. Lucky timing. He's not working today until he has an appointment to give a bid on a project at half past five."

"What kind of project?"

"Some kind of renovation." He opened the passenger-side door for her. "The way I figure, we have enough time to talk with him and drive to one of your cemeteries before nightfall."

He got behind the steering wheel and plugged the address into his GPS. Even though he was one hundred percent mountain man, he appreciated the convenience of cell phones and other technology. He glanced over at Daisy, who was nibbling on her lower lip. Holding back words?

She piped up. "Do you mind if I tell you more about the autopsy?"

His jaw clenched. He'd really heard enough, but this was important to her...and she was important to him. "I'm listening."

She tried to keep her explanation technical but he understood the whole disturbing picture. "While studying the brain, Dr. Julia discovered evidence of a concussion, probably caused by blunt-force trauma."

"Was she unconscious before he killed her?"

"I can't say with full accuracy, but probably."

"And so," he said, drawing his own conclusion, "the killer rendered her unconscious, either by blunt-force trauma or by zapping her with a stun gun. He really wanted to keep Rene from feeling pain."

She nodded. "Is that significant?"

"Could be." He thought of Joaquin's profile that presumed the serial killer had a fondness for his victims and tried to take care of them. If he was living out a twisted fantasy about a former loved one, he wouldn't want to hurt her...not even when he slashed her throat.

"When we're talking to Slade," she asked, "is there any sort of protocol? You know, like I could be the good cop and you could be the bad."

"Just be yourself." The idea of Daisy impersonating any sort of officer amused him. Though she radiated a certain amount of authority as a teacher, she lacked aggression. "You're too well mannered to be a hardened cop."

In less than fifteen minutes, he parked at the curb outside a Craftsman-style house in an older neighborhood. Yellow with white trim, a second floor, a neatly mowed lawn and a clump of juniper bushes beside the detached garage, the house didn't look like the home of a thirtysomething single man. Too tidy. The chairs on the front porch were old lady rockers with flower-patterned cushions instead of sturdy Adirondacks where a guy could sprawl and have a beer. Slade's truck with the camper on the back was parked in the driveway.

That vehicle was one of the main reasons Carter wanted another interview. An important piece of the serial killer's MO involved driving from place to place, transporting his victims. If Carter discovered sufficient reason to suspect Slade, he'd get a warrant for the FBI forensic team to process the truck camper, looking for blood, fibers and DNA.

As he and Daisy strolled up the sidewalk to the front door, the screen door swung open and Slade stepped out. "Nice to see you, sir. And you, too, ma'am."

Though he was thirty-one, two years older than Daisy, Slade came across as younger. Long-limbed and skinny, he looked like he hadn't filled out. Though he had the beginnings of wrinkles at the corners of his eyes and his mouth, his features seemed unformed. His clothes—a short-sleeved cotton shirt tucked into beige chinos—looked totally inoffensive.

After Daisy shook his hand, she asked, "What kind of carpentry do you do?"

"I like renovations, fixing up run-down houses." He ran his hand across his brown buzz cut. "I really like tearing out old stuff. Demolition can be pretty dang cool."

Not a guy who used profanity, especially not in front of a lady. Carter suspected he'd been well trained. A stern mother? "We have a couple of follow-up questions. May we come inside?"

"Just one thing." Slade lowered his voice. "I'd appreciate it if you didn't mention that me and Rene spent time alone together."

"Why not?"

"My girlfriend is in the kitchen, and she gets jealous."

A girlfriend? Mentally, Carter moved him several rungs lower on the suspect list. Typically, serial killers weren't able to maintain relationships. "What's her name?"

"Brandi Thoreau."

"How long have you dated?"

"Off and on for a couple of years."

"Wait a minute," Daisy said. "I thought you broke up with her."

"I did." He winced. "Rene is the person who encouraged me to get back together with Brandi. She understood what love was all about, and I owe her for that. I'm sad that she died."

Carter wanted to correct this sugary remembrance to include the word *murder*, which was the most important detail about Rene's death. But the hangdog expression on Slade's face gave him pause. Carter empathized with the guy. Did Slade empathize? If so, that emotion represented another sign that he wasn't a serial killer.

In the living room, Carter settled into a patterned gray chair that matched the sofa and love seat. Not the furniture a young man would choose. Nor would he select the paint-by-numbers versions of landscape paintings. In the attached dining room, an upright piano stood by the inner wall and a breakfront displayed a collection of blue-and-white-patterned plates and bowls that could have belonged to Carter's prim and proper grandmother—one of the few adults in his family that he actually liked.

An unexpected fragrance tickled the inside of his nose. "What's that smell?"

Slade shrugged. "Some weed that grows wild in the backyard. Not marijuana, though."

"English lavender," Daisy said. "I have some growing in my yard in Denver. The fragrance reminds me of rosemary. It's native to Colorado. When you dry the stems, crumble them up and add a couple of essential oils, you have a great potpourri. Did you make this yourself?"

"Brandi did it," he said. "Come to think of it, Mama loves the smell. She puts the lavender into tiny, silky bags and tucks it into her dresser drawers."

"Sachets." Daisy perched at the edge of the love seat. If she was frightened, she wasn't showing any signs of nervousness. "You have a lovely home. Very cozy."

The swinging door to the kitchen opened, and a busty brunette in a sparkly, sleeveless tank top and skinny jeans charged through. She was a short woman in high heels. "Really?" she demanded. "Do you really think this old crap is lovely?"

Always polite, Daisy stood, faced the young lady and introduced herself. "You must be Brandi."

"That's right." Brandi shook her hand. "What do you really think about this ancient furniture? Those creepy old dishes?"

"Not my favorite style," Daisy said, "but a lot of people like the classics."

"Classic crap." Brandi rolled her big brown eyes and adjusted her long, bouncy ponytail. Her hair was an unusual reddish-brown like mahogany. "Slade's mama liked this cheesy junk. And he hasn't seen fit to get rid of it."

"Does his mother live here?"

"This was her house. He moved back home to take care of her after she had a stroke."

Slade stepped up beside her. Standing over six feet, he nearly matched Carter's height, and he towered over Brandi. "Mama loved her dishes and chairs."

"But Mama has been dead for two years." She planted her little fists on her hips and glared up at him. "Honey, it's time to let go."

Daisy shot Carter a glance, and he nodded. This circumstance—the recent death of a beloved mother—might trigger a serial killer.

"Okay, sweetheart." Slade smoothed her hair off her forehead. "Next week, we'll go shopping, and you can help me pick out dishes."

Carter introduced a different topic. "Let's talk about your work. You're an independent contractor, right?"

"There are builders and remodelers I work with a lot, but I'm my own boss." He sounded proud about the arrangement. "I like being able to plan my own schedule."

A telling comment if he was the serial killer. "Did you ever have a regular employer?"

"Before I moved back to Pueblo, I worked full-time for a builder in Denver, and he taught me a lot. He also advised me to do an apprenticeship and join the union so I could earn top dollar. All I ever wanted to do was work with wood."

"Did your father teach you the basics?" Carter asked.

Slade scoffed. His voice took on an uncharacteristic bitterness. "He left when I was five years old. I haven't seen my old man ever since."

Carter was curious about the woman who raised him as a single mother but doubted he'd get an accurate picture from Slade, who cared so much about Mama that he couldn't get rid of her furniture. Or from Brandi, who probably hadn't liked the woman and resented the hold she still had on Slade. Might be useful to talk to a neighbor.

"My honey-boo is a really good carpenter." Brandi stroked the smooth parquet top of the coffee table in front of the sofa. "He did this, and it's gorgeous. I think he ought to open a store to sell custom furniture."

"Well, sweetheart, it sounds like you've got all kinds of plans for how I ought to spend my money."

"It's not like you're broke. Mama left you big bucks." Brandi glanced toward Daisy. "The old lady was rich.

Not super-rich, but she had enough that she never needed to work."

"Don't make it sound like she was lazy." Once again, Slade's voice was bitter.

"Oh, I forgot. Mama was perfect."

Before the conversation turned into a spat, Daisy stepped in. "Brandi, my throat's dry. May I have a glass of water?"

"Sure thing." She pivoted on her extra-high heels. "Come with me to the kitchen."

Slade watched them go, and Carter watched Slade as his expression changed from a scowl to a grin. Totally appropriate if he was eyeballing his girlfriend. But he said, "Daisy is really something. Real ladylike. You'd better hang on to her."

"I intend to." *So back off.*

He exhaled a sigh. "I sure wish Brandi had spent more time with Mama. Some of her classy attitude might have rubbed off."

"Tell me about your mama. What was her name?"

"Elizabeth Hotchkiss Franklin. She never went by Lizzy or Beth. Always her full name. Elizabeth." He strolled over to a built-in bookshelf below the staircase and picked up a photograph, framed in simple gold. "She was a beauty, slender and graceful. And always well-dressed."

He held the eight-by-ten photo so Carter could see. The picture had been taken outside a wrought iron gate fitted with a weathered brass plaque for Rolling Hills Cemetery and showed a younger version of Slade in a dark suit and black necktie. His long arm wrapped around the shoulders of a dark-haired woman who almost matched his height.

"Doesn't she look great!" Slade said. "She made that dress herself."

Clean and stylish, they looked like they'd come from the

funeral of an important person. Elizabeth wore an elegant, fitted black dress with long sleeves.

Tied around her throat was a silky scarf decorated with green and blue swirls.

IN THE KITCHEN, Daisy recognized more homey touches that had likely been passed down from Mama. The salt and pepper shakers on the drop-leaf wood table were a chicken and a rooster. Some of the tiles on the backsplash behind the sink showed a Dutch boy and girl kissing. The light wood cabinetry, however, was modern and beautifully made, probably more of Slade's work.

Brandi lifted a bottle from an array of liquors on a cabinet beside the fridge. She unscrewed the top. "Would you like a taste of something more interesting than water?"

"What is it?"

"White rum. Tastes like raisins."

Though she had no desire to get blitzed, Daisy figured one drink wouldn't make a difference, and the alcohol might loosen Brandi's tongue. "Yes, please. On the rocks."

"Slade tells me you're a schoolteacher." She scooped ice from the fridge into two short, clear glasses and splashed in a healthy dose of clear rum. "I used to think I wanted to do that."

"What changed your mind?"

"School bored the pants off me." Brandi handed a glass to Daisy. "And I figured I could make more money as an online influencer. I do vlogs—that's a blog but mostly video—and podcasts about makeup and clothes and shopping."

Her occupation explained the sparkly top—an outfit too fancy for loafing around the house. "You must know a lot about computers."

"Abso-flipping-lutely." She clinked her glass against Daisy's, took a healthy sip and tossed her head, sending ripples through her mahogany-brown ponytail. "So, Miss

Schoolteacher, are you going to tell me why you and your boyfriend—who is majorly cute, by the way—are here talking to Slade?"

"Just putting together more details for the investigation."

"Nope, I'm not buying that." Brandi took another slug. "Is Slade a suspect? Should I hire a lawyer for him?"

"Do you think he needs one?"

"Hmm." Again, she rolled her eyes, which must be her go-to expression. "Do I think my sweetie pie boyfriend is a serial killer? No way in hell. Why are you here?"

Daisy took a ladylike sip of rum. Not her favorite drink, but she didn't mind the astringent burn as the liquid coursed down her gullet and splashed into her empty stomach. She hadn't eaten since they arrived in Pueblo, except for an energy bar Dr. Julia had given her. "If Slade was seriously under suspicion, do you think the FBI would send me and Ranger Carter to talk with him?"

"Never thought of that." She drained her glass and gave herself a refill. "You two aren't high-ranking interrogators. Not to be insulting, but the feds would know better than to have a schoolmarm chasing Ted Bundy. Am I right?"

"You are."

"But maybe you're undercover FBI. That would be so cool."

"But not true," Daisy said emphatically. "Things are usually exactly as they seem. For example, your boyfriend doesn't fit the profile. Serial killers don't usually have girlfriends."

"But he's weird about Mama," she admitted. "That's a serial killer thing, right?"

"Could be."

"I'm so totally glad the old lady was so much taller than me."

Daisy finished off her rum. "Why?"

"Slade keeps trying to get me to dress up in her clothes.

which are huge on me. And he wants me to fix my hair like hers. You know, that big '80s style. You can bet I told him no."

Before Daisy could say no, Brandi refilled her glass. More rum actually sounded like a good idea, but she set the glass down on the countertop. "I shouldn't have more. I haven't eaten."

"Come on. Drink up." Brandi smirked. "What can you tell me about the dead girl Slade was talking to? Do you think they did more than talk? Was she prettier than me?"

"Rene Williams was short, brunette and healthy. I don't think she and Slade did anything more than talk. She'd just broken up with her live-in boyfriend." Daisy wondered if the feds had interrogated Josh Santana. "Is Slade the kind of guy who plays around?"

"He seems shy, but I'm not so sure."

Daisy sipped her rum. "Does he often take off on trips by himself?"

"No more than any other guy. He goes hunting and fishing." Her gaze sharpened as she confronted Daisy, then she slipped back into her vlogging personality and rolled her eyes. "You can't possibly think he's killing off women in his spare time."

When Daisy shook her head, she could feel her brain rattling inside her skull—an effect of the liquor. "This serial killer likes to stalk his prey."

"Damn, that's creepy. And it's not Slade. My honey-boo is a lot of things, but subtle isn't one of them."

Daisy wondered if she'd said too much. She lacked the finesse to direct this conversation with Brandi. "Are you playing me?"

"That's how I earn a living. I influence plain girls, make them think that if they use a certain brand of mascara, their eyes will shine. If they use my lipstick, their thin lips will look full and lush like mine."

"You lie to them."

"And I get paid for it." She preened. "Listen to me, sugar buns. You're wasting your time talking to my boo."

Daisy felt the same way. She liked Slade. But didn't the people who met Ted Bundy say the same thing about him? *Such a nice young man.*

Chapter Eleven

Still staring at the photo, Carter listened to Slade's monolog about Mama, who was obviously the love of his life. She came from Philly, where her family owned several clothing stores. They'd made sure Elizabeth was well provided for, financing her lifestyle with a trust fund.

Her son thought she'd been happy and had fallen in love with the West. After his dad deserted them, Elizabeth refused to go back east. She got involved with several charities in Pueblo, supported the ballet and the art museum.

"She was a wonderful person." Slade's eyes gleamed with unshed tears.

"Never remarried?"

"She said I was the only man she needed in her life. Sweet, huh?"

"Yeah. Sweet." But Carter couldn't help cringing. It sounded like Mama had developed a fairly unhealthy relationship with her young son.

"She promised she'd never leave me and made me say the same words back to her."

A very unhealthy relationship. "Does Brandi remind you of her?"

"Heck, yes. They're both opinionated ladies. And they don't mind telling me what to do."

He often spoke of his mother in the present tense. Carter had a feeling that no other woman would ever measure up to

Mama. Time to change the topic. "I have a couple of questions about your work schedule, starting with location. Do you always work in Pueblo?"

"No, sir, I go all over the state. Mostly in southwestern Colorado."

"Have you ever worked in Glenwood Springs?" Carter held his breath. If Slade has been in Glenwood on June 10, when Hannah was killed, he'd jump to the top of the suspect list. "Maybe earlier this month?"

"Not in June. Last time I was there, it had just snowed. I think it was April."

"Do you keep a record of your jobs?"

"You bet I do. Come with me to my office, and we can check it out."

In the dining room, Slade paused to play opening from "Moonlight Sonata" on the upright piano—a haunting melody that stuck with Carter as he followed the man into a hallway that bisected the house. At the end closest to the street was a bedroom. Carter took a backward step to glimpse the nondescript furniture with double beds and blah curtains. Probably a guest room. Next to that was a bathroom, which had obviously been renovated, probably enlarged. The cabinetry and fixtures were beautiful and new, reinforcing Brandi's opinion that Slade had talent.

The home office featured a custom-made oak desk and bookshelves. Across one wall were three-drawer wood file cabinets. Though a computer sat on the desktop, Slade lowered himself into the swivel chair behind the desk, reached into the center drawer and pulled out a ledger. "What did you need to know?" he asked.

"You're very organized."

"Anything worth doing is worth doing well. That's what Mama always says."

His mother might have died two years ago, but Slade hadn't buried her. "I'm surprised you don't use the computer."

"I most certainly do," he said. "It's great for running invoices and keeping track of payments. And I've also got mailing lists. But I like to use the ledger for scheduling. I can scribble in changes or switch things up with sticky notes. The first contractor I worked for used a system like this, and I adopted it for myself."

Carter suspected Slade was a good businessman—likable, skilled and efficient. "Tell me the last time you were in Glenwood Springs. And can I see your schedule for earlier this month?"

"Sure thing."

Carter came around the desk to look over his shoulder. Entries in the ledger were neatly numbered and noted in dark blue pen. From April 21 to April 25, he had installed bookshelves and cabinets in an office and playroom in Glenwood. There were other out-of-town jobs to Durango, near the Southern Ute Reservation, and at a hunting lodge in Buena Vista. Nothing special had been noted for June 10, when he was in Pueblo for an extended period of time working for a contractor on a development of five new homes.

"When you do the out-of-town jobs," Carter asked, "do you stay in your camper truck?"

"Sometimes, and sometimes I get a motel room. Depends on how tired I am and how cold it is. I've got my camper fixed up real nice with a propane stove and lantern but no extra heat."

"Must be comfortable. You took it to Butcher's Gulch for a mini-vacation."

"I have a platform on one side for a mattress. Underneath are cabinets for my tools."

"What about water?"

"I try to camp near a lake or creek." He closed his ledger. "I've been thinking about buying a trailer or an RV."

"What's stopping you?"

"Brandi would hate that. She doesn't like sleeping outdoors, and don't get me started on how long it takes for her to put on makeup—"

Carter didn't have to wait long for the inevitable comparison. Slade filled in the blank. "—just like Mama."

From outside the office, a burst of feminine laughter erupted. Brandi and Daisy stumbled through the door. Daisy's cheeks flushed a bright red, and he was pretty sure that they hadn't been drinking water in the kitchen. Turning to Brandi, she held her forefinger across her lips in a gesture meant to convey secrecy.

But Brandi wouldn't be stopped. She held up her slender wrist and pointed to an oversize watch. "You've got to go, Slade, if you don't want to be late for your, um, appointment."

He glanced at Carter. "She's right. Are we done here?"

Before he linked arms with Daisy, Carter pulled a business card from his pocket. "I appreciate your time. Give me a call before you leave town." *Or decide to kill again.*

Slade's eyes narrowed. His smile darkened as he said, "You'll be first to know."

Carter recognized the undertone. Slade's comment was a threat.

BACK IN THE SUV, with Carter behind the wheel, Daisy inhaled and exhaled slowly and fought the dizzy sensation caused by whirling rush-hour traffic on their way toward FBI headquarters. *Shouldn't have guzzled that second glass of rum.* Especially not on an empty stomach. Brandi had been conning her, bragging about Slade and how talented and clever he was. Daisy feared she might have blurted something out. "Slade takes off on a lot of hunting and fishing trips where he's out of touch. And he tried to get Brandi to play dress-up in Mama's clothes."

"His issues with Mama are seriously abnormal." He glanced over at her. "Are you okay?"

"I kind of had a glass, or maybe two, of clear rum. Brandi was trying to get me loaded."

"Why?"

"I'm not sure. Maybe so I wouldn't give her boyfriend any trouble." *Inhale and exhale.* "Did you learn anything new from talking to him."

"You might say so."

She squinted her eyes and concentrated hard on his description of the photograph Slade had shown him. When Carter talked about the scarf, a shiver went down her spine. She sobered up quickly, thinking of the first scarf she'd seen on Rene, then the second on Andrea Lindstrom.

In her slightly inebriated condition, Daisy easily imagined monsters—scary ghouls dancing to the repetitive melody of "Moonlight Sonata" plucked out note by note on Slade's upright piano. Her pulse thrummed, but she managed to keep her emotions in check. The important thing to keep in mind—the only thing, really—was the investigation. The brutal murders of these young women had to stop, and it fell to Carter and the FBI and Dr. Julia and all the other law enforcement personnel to follow every lead and apprehend the serial killer. The photograph led Carter to believe he'd found sufficient reason to suspect Slade, but she wasn't so sure.

"You can't be certain of anything," she said.

"How drunk are you? The photo is a solid clue."

"Is it?" she questioned. "Just because his mama wore a scarf doesn't prove that Slade is a psycho murderer."

"Psycho," he said. "That's accurate. Slade reminds me of Tony Perkins in *Psycho*. He looks so innocent until he attacks. Do you remember that movie?"

She avoided horror movies and didn't want to dig into

her fears. *Inhale slowly, exhale.* She changed the subject. "What was the name of the cemetery in the photo?"

"Rolling Hills."

"It's a big one, over three hundred acres, just south of Pueblo." She kind of hated that she knew so much about graveyards. "I haven't searched there, because they have a registry with names and the locations of most of the marked graves. Didn't you mention that Hannah came to Pueblo for a funeral? Maybe she bumped into Slade at Rolling Hills. He strikes me as the sort of son who visits Mama's grave often."

"Now you're thinking." He shot her an approving glance. "I'll have Agent Wiley check on where Mama is buried. I'm sure Hannah's great-uncle is at Rolling Hills."

"I wonder whose funeral Slade and Mama were attending."

"He said it was a local church lady. I wrote the name down."

"Are you going to talk to her family?"

"Wouldn't hurt to find out what other people think of Slade and Mama Franklin." He shrugged. "I have a feeling they'll tell me he's a pleasant, hardworking young man who took good care of his mother."

"I'd probably say the same." She liked Slade and his girlfriend. Once she'd gotten past Brandi's brash exterior, she enjoyed talking to the busty brunette who was incredibly proud of her guy in spite of his poor taste in home furnishings. "If he's the murderer, why would he drop such a huge clue? Why show you a photo with a scarf in it?"

"I don't think he realized the implication," Carter said. "His breathing stayed calm and level. His expression didn't change."

"Maybe he's innocent."

"Or maybe he's a split personality, like Dr. Jekyll and

Mr. Hyde. One side is a nice, friendly carpenter while the other is a serial killer."

"I know that syndrome exists." She'd studied the neurological anomalies present with dissociative identity disorder, which sometimes resulted from concussion or another brain trauma. As soon as she focused on anatomy, her thinking became less blurry. "The pathology is similar to amnesia. There are examples of individuals with multiple personalities, but it's unusual."

He parked at the curb outside the office building with the FBI headquarters on the eighth floor. "I might mention the Jekyll/Hyde thing if that's what it takes to get a warrant for Slade's camper. When the FBI forensics team processes his truck, they'll find any evidence that exists. Blood or a hair or fiber, something to prove he used his vehicle to transport the victims."

Her suspicions circled back to Eric Wolff and the blue van he used for his house-painting supplies. "Can we also get a warrant for Eric? He admitted to planting a tracking device on me."

"We can try to get a warrant, even though it's a long shot. He can claim you're friends and you gave him permission. Your word against his. Maybe we should pay him a visit while we're in Pueblo."

"Isn't the FBI going to interrogate him?" She enjoyed imagining creepy Eric in handcuffs being led into a little room with a big mirror, even though she didn't think he was a killer. "Shouldn't the feds take him into custody?"

"I get it. You don't like the guy. But that doesn't turn him into a suspect."

"What about this—he showed up at Butcher's Gulch, admitted to stalking me and might have been in Glenwood Springs when Hannah was killed."

"We'll talk to him again. I promise."

Daisy exited Carter's car and stood very still on the sidewalk, allowing her woozy feelings to abate. She gazed toward the mountains west of town. The sun wouldn't dip behind the Sangre de Cristos for a couple more hours, but the light had thinned. Day was almost gone. "We aren't going to have enough time to explore my graveyards today, are we?"

"If we hurry, we can get to one of them before dark." He escorted her through the glass doors into the ground-floor lobby, where they were screened and issued visitor badges from the security guard at the front desk. Carter continued, "I don't know how I'm going to drop you off in Leadville, which is two and a half hours away, and return to pick you up in the morning."

"Well, I have to be here tomorrow. That's nonnegotiable." She took an adamant position. "Dr. Julia is going to let me participate in Andrea's autopsy. The exposure to the elements and mauling by animals makes her case even more interesting than Rene's. Doing the autopsies is a tangible way I can be useful."

"Then we've got a problem," he said as he clipped on the visitor's pass. "Too many things to do and not enough time to take care of business."

He was right, and she didn't want to get in the way of the investigation, especially since he seemed to be making progress. "You could take me to my aunt's house and stay over. Then we could leave together early in the morning."

He crossed the air-conditioned lobby and stopped in front of the elevators. "Or you could spend the night with me."

After a momentary burst of panic, she absorbed his suggestion. They both understood the sheer impossibility of a relationship. Nothing serious could develop between them. They were too different. If she spent the night at his house, they had to maintain a distance. *I can do that.*

Daisy wasn't a love-starved maniac like the teenagers she taught in high school. Surely she could keep her hands off the tall, sexy, blue-eyed ranger. "You live in Salida, right?"

"Between Salida, Cañon City and Florence, near the Royal Gorge. My cabin is about an hour away from here."

None of the locations he mentioned rang a bell for her. She tried to visualize a map in her head but didn't know enough to make sense of the twists and turns of the highways and side roads. The towering fourteeners formed an indecipherable, snow-covered mass. Streams, rivers and creeks traversed the landscape. He might as well have told her he lived on the moon. "I'm guessing your cabin is far away from civilization."

"You know me well." They boarded the elevator.

What if he didn't have water or electricity? Of course he did. She was being ridiculous. "Do you have a guest room?"

"Two guest rooms, two bathrooms, a fully stocked kitchen and a state-of-the-art security system to keep intruders at bay. And I have another car you could drive."

She really liked the idea of security and protection. If she agreed to stay there, she needed to make a stop before they left Pueblo to purchase a couple of T-shirts, underwear and a toothbrush. "I'll think about it."

The elevator door swooshed open, and they entered headquarters through an unmarked door. At 5:25, they'd passed quitting time, but the FBI office hummed with activity. The agents who weren't on the phone were tapping away on computer keys. Special Agent in Charge Wiley and red-haired Agent Hicks strode toward them in tandem.

Wiley shook her hand. "Dr. Julia wants me to hire you."

"So do I," Carter whispered.

"I appreciate the compliment, but I already have a job in Denver." Carter wanted her to stay. On some level, Daisy knew what he wanted, and she most definitely didn't intend to discuss the topic right here, right now, in front of Wiley and the other feds. She gestured to the busy room. "What's going on? Do you have a new lead?"

"As soon as news of a serial killer hits the internet and

television, we get dozens of leads, most of which are bogus. Nonetheless, we need follow up on each and every call."

"Even that jerk with a sheep ranch and a telescope," Hicks said. "He always reports a UFO landing and aliens killing and/or probing young women."

"Sorry to bring you more work," Carter said. "I'd like to get warrants to search the vehicles belonging to a couple of legitimate suspects."

Wiley perched on the edge of a vacant desk. "Convince me."

While Carter recounted their conversation with Slade and his girlfriend, she checked out the room. A huge whiteboard listed the victims' names along with their photographs, dates of their murders and locations. Beside it was a map of southwestern Colorado with murder sites highlighted in red marker. Forensic technicians in lab coats drifted among the desks. Most of the agents drank from mugs, and she could only hope they were having soothing herbal tea. Some used land lines, others held cell phones to their ears and a few had headsets. Several scanned their computer screens.

Though she knew the FBI had better forensic resources than state or local branches of law enforcement, the pace and volume of activity impressed her. As SAC, Wiley had his hands full coordinating the operation. Even the muscle-bound Hicks showed himself to be capable of more than flexing as he hammered Carter with intelligent, pointed questions.

Looking around, she recognized the obvious: this investigation centered on real victims and serious consequences. Her petty romantic concerns about staying at Carter's cabin seemed trivial by comparison. To spend the night with Carter or not to spend the night. Was that the question? *Grow up, Daisy.*

She could solve her own dilemma by getting a motel room here in Pueblo and using a rideshare service. Assisting Dr. Julia represented a *real* contribution to the investigation, and Daisy ought to stick to her area of expertise.

At a break in his conversation with Wiley, she pulled Carter aside. In a low voice, she said, "I'm going to stay in town at a motel, but I need to make a stop first and pick up a few things."

"I thought we were going to a graveyard." He actually looked disappointed about not visiting another cemetery. *Seriously?* "Let me at least give you a ride."

"I'll call a rideshare."

"Okay, if that's what you want, but if you change your mind or need help, don't hesitate to call me."

"Why would I need help?"

"No reason. Just offering."

In Denver, she lived alone and took care of herself. Not a problem. After a quick consultation with Agent Hicks, she had the name of a decent motel, where she booked a room. Using a cell phone app, she arranged for a rideshare to pick her up outside the FBI building in nine minutes.

She scanned the room for Carter and saw him staring in her direction. Taller than most of the people around him, he seemed to be above the chaos and furious activity. Calmly, he raked his fingers through his black hair, raised his hand to wave and offered a smile. Such a handsome man, but he looked worried.

For a moment, she remembered Dr. Julia's advice about victimology, especially the part about not taking risks and making sure that someone—like Carter—had her back. Daisy almost reversed her plan before she realized there was no reason to consider herself a target. Sure, Eric was stalking her, but he was after Brighton's Bullion, and she'd made a deal with him to share info. Slade had his hands full with Brandi.

Daisy had nothing to fear.

Or did she?

Chapter Twelve

Outside the FBI building, the rideshare Daisy had contacted
arrived precisely on schedule. She gave the driver, Marlene, the address of the motel and settled back. Marlene—a
motherly woman with short, frizzy hair and cat-eye sun-
glasses—drove a spotless Hyundai that smelled of lavender
air freshener, reminding her of Slade's mama. When she
looked out the window, Daisy spotted a dark blue van on
the opposite side of the street and was glad when it pulled
away before she had a chance to study the logo. *Not Eric
again!* She refused to let him frighten her. The creep lived
in Pueblo and might be here by coincidence. *Yeah, right.*

At the pink stucco Sundowner Motel, she asked Marlene
to wait for her to check in and if she could then drop her
off at a place where she could buy all the everyday stuff
she'd left behind when she and Carter drove away from
Leadville. After a quick peek into room number eighteen
on the second floor—plain, simple and clean, with a small
circular table by the window and two full-size beds—she
jumped back into the Hyundai. After arranging to return
in a half hour, Marlene dropped her off at a superstore
where she could purchase everything from deodorant to
diamonds. Daisy marched her shopping cart through the
automated doors.

Buying toothpaste and T-shirts gave her a pleasant feeling of normalcy. As long as there were superstores, she

could put down roots anywhere. She picked up the basics: aspirin, travel-size shampoo, moisturizer and toothbrush. The familiar array of products and the layout of the store lulled her into a sense of security—possibly a false sense. She reminded herself that Andrea Lindstrom had been grabbed in a grocery store parking lot. Shaking her head, she erased the last bit of alcohol-induced relaxation. *Stay alert.*

She headed toward the women's department, where she could pick up a change of clothes. When her cart rounded the end of the aisle, she came face-to-face with a white-haired man, tall and heavyset, hauling an oxygen tank in his cart. He glared at her.

After an aisle dance where they both went left, then right, he muttered, "I know you."

A threat. She backed away, whipping her cart in a U-turn and going to the end of the aisle. The comfortable atmosphere of the store darkened. What had made her think she was safe in here? These customers and clerks could all be serial killers…or worse. *Really?* What was worse? Before she turned into the next aisle, she thought she spotted Eric.

The old man bumped the back of her legs with his cart. Still glaring, his ruddy complexion and broken capillaries primarily on his bulbous nose hinted at alcoholism. He pointed at her and shook his head.

She zipped away from him. Her imagination soared out of control. Why, oh why hadn't she agreed to spend the night at Carter's cabin? Even if she wasn't targeted as a victim, she knew too much about the investigation—enough that the killer might consider her a threat.

But she needed to be able to take care of herself. Dashing through racks of clothes, she grabbed a couple of T-shirts, a pair of cargo pants and a six-pack of socks. Glancing over her shoulder, she saw the old man again.

Before she realized what she was doing, Daisy found

herself racing toward the sporting goods section of the store. She approached a clerk behind the counter. "I want to buy a handgun."

"Sorry, miss. We don't handle firearms anymore."

Frantically, she scanned their selection of bows and arrows and all manner of hunting knives. Who was she kidding? Unlike her aunt, a skilled markswoman, Daisy didn't know how to use any kind of lethal weapon. And she had flunked the freebie self-defense class at her gym. Still, she needed a way to protect herself—needed help, someone to back her up. She needed Carter.

Not the most independent thought she'd ever had. But a logical, rational solution. After a quick dash through the grocery section, she hit the checkout line, where she checked her rideshare app. Marlene was out in front, waiting. *Thank God!* Before leaving the store, Daisy armed herself with her pepper spray attached to her key chain.

Outside, she boarded Marlene's bronze Hyundai with her two large shopping bags and her purse. Immediately, she felt mothered and safe. As she shuffled her supplies into a zippered paisley duffel bag she'd bought for easy handling, she said, "Back to the Sundowner."

"Are you okay? You seem unsettled."

"This scary old man was following me."

"Do you want to call the police?"

Did she? Was she overreacting to an imaginary threat? *Calm down.* The interior of the car felt too confined. Inhaling and exhaling deeply, she said, "I'll be okay. Do you mind if I lower the window?"

"No problem."

Daisy buzzed the window all the way down and leaned out. At seven o'clock, the evening rush had slowed, and the orange and purple of sunset streaked the skies. She gazed toward the distant, peaceful mountains. Maybe Carter had the right idea, after all. Living close to nature was far preferable to inhaling exhaust fumes.

The Hyundai braked at a stoplight, and a dark blue van rolled to a stop in the lane beside her. Not just any van—the Wolff House Painting logo on the side featured the familiar pyramid of paint cans—but it wasn't Eric behind the steering wheel. The white-haired man rested his bulky forearm on the edge of the open window. He peered down at her with a cold, ugly sneer distorting his ruddy features.

"Hello, Daisy."

WHEN CARTER'S CELL phone rang, he had to dig through stacks of paperwork to find it. Nothing in the FBI background information he'd compiled on Slade Franklin and his girlfriend justified a search warrant for his home and camper. The couple seemed to lead a simple, law-abiding life, but he also appeared to be one of the last to see Rene alive. If the forensics team could search his truck, they might turn up evidence.

Caller ID on his phone showed Daisy's number, and he answered quickly. "Hey, lady, how's it going?"

"Bad. It's going bad, real bad. You said to call if I needed help, and I do."

Her words spilled out in a rush, faster than a churning whitewater current. "Slow down and tell me where you are."

"No, where are you?"

"Same place you left me. FBI headquarters."

"Good, good, good. I thought you might have left for home. But you haven't. Good. I'll be there in a few minutes. Come downstairs to meet me—please, please. I'm in a bronze Hyundai."

"On my way." He rose from the vacant desk where he'd been sitting and waved to Agent Wiley. To Daisy, he said, "Stay on the line and tell me what happened."

"You won't believe it. I was stalked at a superstore by a

huge, white-haired man. I didn't recognize him, but later he was driving Eric's van."

"Stalked, huh?" Carter caught up to Wiley and whispered, "Daisy found something. She's on her way here."

"Got it," Wiley said.

Carter spoke into his phone. "Eric Wolff's van?"

"I got so confused and scared. I tried to buy a gun."

Not wanting to lose his connection with her, he didn't take the elevator. Instead, he plunged into the stairwell and ran down eight levels. "You got a gun?"

"The store didn't sell guns, and I changed my mind anyway." In spite of the weird conversation, she seemed to be calming down. "Okay, we're pulling up in front of the building. I don't see you."

"Almost there." He charged from the stairwell and paused at the security guard's desk. "I'll be right back."

"Hold on, buddy. It's after seven. I need to buzz you in and out."

"Do it."

Carter went to the glass door and waited until a tiny light on a chrome panel turned from red to green. He thundered onto the wide sidewalk outside the office building. The traffic had thinned, and he easily spotted the Hyundai. When he rushed to open her door, she shoved a paisley duffel into his hands.

Turning to the driver, she said, "Thank you, Marlene. You'll get a big tip from me."

"Almost being in a chase with that van was kind of exciting." She craned her head out the window. "Is this really the FBI office?"

"Eighth floor," she said.

Carter set down the duffel, took her arms and turned her toward him. His gaze locked onto her face. "What the hell happened?"

When she looked up at him, he saw the fear in her eyes.

Her grip on self-control had dwindled, but she insisted, "I'm fine."

"Don't start this with me, not again." He didn't want to be brushed off with a "fine" when she was upset. "Tell me the truth. I won't think less of you for being scared."

"I'll think less of myself." She placed her palms on his chest, keeping a distance between them while maintaining contact at the same time. "When I hear these horror stories about murderers and feel threatened by things I can't understand or explain, I panic."

He took both her hands and guided them up around his neck. "Start at the beginning and tell me everything."

"I can't." She trembled against him. "We've got to get off the street. I don't want him to see us."

He should have realized that standing in the open on a sidewalk wasn't going to make her feel safe. Usually, he was great at handling people who were frightened, whether a troop of scouts who thought they saw a bear or a hunter who'd shot himself in the foot. Carter always knew what to do, what to say, how to make it all better. But when it came to Daisy, his natural instincts malfunctioned. Clumsily, he took her paisley duffel in one hand and wrapped his other arm around her waist. And here was another problem. He needed a third hand to signal the security guard to unlock the door.

Together, they jogged toward the entrance. If need be, he'd bust through the glass door to get her to safety. Fortunately, that drama was uncalled for. Agent Wiley must have anticipated trouble. He stood waiting to usher them into the building.

As soon as she came inside, Daisy scooted away from the windows and pulled him toward the elevators, where solid walls would hide them from those passing by on the street. Finally, she dived into his embrace and held on so tightly that he felt her heartbeat hammering against his chest.

Carter looked over her head toward Wiley and said, "She was being stalked by a white-haired giant and tried to buy a gun."

Daisy laughed—a sound more wonderful to him than music. But when she tilted back in his arms and looked up, he saw tears streaking down her cheeks. Her smile quivered on her lips. "That's not the whole story."

"Do you want to sit down?" Wiley asked.

"I want to go upstairs," she said, "and file a report so you can arrest that creep."

"Sure thing," Wiley said hesitantly as he adjusted his bolo tie. "And which creep is that?"

"Eric Wolff's father."

Carter nodded. *Not surprised.* Of all the potential suspects he'd researched, Gerald Wolff had the longest criminal record, ranging from dozens of speeding tickets to an assault and battery charge that resulted in a six-month jail sentence. For most of his life, the sixty-three-year-old man had worked a good-paying job at the steel mill. He'd been divorced for fifteen years. While he was married, his exwife had filed four restraining orders against him.

Now, it seemed, old Gerald had been stalking Daisy. Just like his son, Eric. The rotten apple didn't fall far from the tree.

Chapter Thirteen

On the eighth floor in an FBI conference room, Daisy took
the chair at the head of an eight-foot-long table and dug into
her paisley duffel for the burritos, guac and chips she'd
snagged at the superstore. Carter sat on her right, facing
the windows where a brilliant sunset devoured the mountains. On her left was SAC Wiley and Agent Hicks, who
activated a recording device so they wouldn't lose a single
word of her narrative.

Even before she spoke, she began to feel foolish about
her panic. An old man had accosted her. So what? The
whole thing was totally unimportant—unless Gerald Wolff
turned out to be the serial killer. "I might be overreacting."

"Mr. Wolff doesn't fit the standard serial killer profile,"
Agent Hicks said. "Typically, they're white males between
twenty-eight and forty-five. Gerald is sixty-three."

"I guess that means Jackknife Jones is also eliminated."

"Not so fast." Wiley flipped through his file folder and
found a photo of Jones that actually didn't look too bad.
With his scraggly hair pulled back in a neat man bun and
his chin shaved, he appeared younger. "He's on the older
side. But only fifty-two."

"I would have guessed twenty years older," Daisy said.
"I guess he's lived a hard life."

"You're giving him the benefit of the doubt," Wiley said.

"He's made his own life choices, some of which have landed him in jail. Usually on charges of petty theft."

"I really don't like having him sniff around my aunt Vi."

"Don't blame you," Wiley said.

Daisy poked at her burritos with a plastic fork. Food had seemed like a good idea, but she couldn't imagine putting anything into her churning stomach. After one small bite, her stomach groaned. Nope, nothing to eat or drink, not right now.

SAC Wiley encouraged her to get started with her narrative. "From the beginning, right after you checked in at the motel."

"After I peeked into my room, I asked my rideshare driver, Marlene, to take me shopping. She dropped me off at one of those stores that have groceries and everything else. Except for guns—I couldn't buy a handgun."

Wiley raised an eyebrow. "You're jumping ahead, Daisy. Let's go in sequence. What did you purchase first?"

She described her foray through cosmetics and her aisle dance with Gerald Wolff. "At the time, I didn't know who he was. I've never actually met the man, but he visited my aunt Vi in Leadville. Gerald and Eric think they have a claim on Brighton's Bullion because their ancestor Morris Wolff was part of Sherwood Brighton's outlaw gang."

"But you don't agree," Wiley said.

"Saying that he has as much right to the fortune as Aunt Vi is ridiculous. Sherwood was the leader of the pack and Morris was an underling. Plus he might have been having an affair with Sherwood's wife."

"Maybe Sherwood wanted to cut him out," Wiley said. "For revenge."

"Doubtful. Sherwood left records of how he planned and executed the robberies. Morris Wolff was hardly mentioned. He definitely wasn't a partner. Even if he was, even if the treasure actually exists, we've made a deal with Eric to give him a share."

Agent Hicks folded his arms and flexed his biceps. "It exists. There are lots of people who believe in the bullion."

"Which doesn't make it real," she said. "In any case, the treasure isn't connected to the serial killer. Or is it?"

The three men exchanged a look before Carter spoke up. "We can't ignore the coincidence, Daisy. If we take Eric seriously as a suspect, there might be a link."

"Let's leave that topic for later," Wiley said. "Please continue."

She ran through the rest of her narrative, taking the story to the point when Gerald peered down at her from the van and said hello. Her lips pinched together. She'd never forget the sound of his rough-edged voice—a growl that sounded like he had a mouthful of broken glass. "He threatened me."

Carter reached over and placed his large hand on top of hers. "Keep going, Daisy. You're doing great. What did he say?"

"He told me not to think I was so smart. If me and my aunt—he called her a bitch—didn't find his treasure soon, we'd be sorry."

Wiley prompted, "Did he say how you'd be sorry?"

"He didn't have a chance," she said. "I stuck my arm out of the car window and blasted my pepper spray at him."

Her action had been unplanned. Pure instinct. Scared, she'd struck out blindly. Didn't know if she hit him before she frantically buzzed the window up and yelled at Marlene to drive fast. Get away from the blue van. Go to the FBI building.

Remembering, her pulse beat as fast as a snare drum. In spite of the office air-conditioning, sweat moistened her forehead and back. She turned her hand palm up and laced her fingers with Carter's, needing his steady, calm strength to anchor herself. "And then," she concluded, "I called Carter and came here."

Hicks asked, "Anything else you can recall about the old man? Did he have a weapon? In the store, did he touch you?"

"He bumped me with his shopping cart." She glanced back and forth between Carter and the two FBI agents. What was going on here? Didn't they believe her? "He should be in jail."

SAC Wiley said, "His actions don't rise to the level of assault. We can't arrest a man for shopping. Or for saying hello."

Slowly, she stood. Her hands balled into fists at her side, ready to fight. "He called my aunt Violet a bitch and told me we'd be sorry if we didn't find his gold."

"I wish there was something we could do," Wiley said.

For most of her life, she'd been polite and controlled. She longed to throw caution to the wind, to scream her head off and color outside the lines. Why should she allow Gerald Wolff to menace her? Whirling, she pointed to the door of the conference room. "Out there, you've got a gang of agents following up on improbable leads from every weirdo in the state of Colorado. Why not the Wolff men—father and son?"

"We need evidence," Hicks said.

"They both stalked me. Their blue van appeared at the crime scene in Butcher's Gulch. And maybe they were in Glenwood."

"We don't know for sure if the timing matched Hannah's murder," Hicks said. "And she described the man she was meeting to visit Doc Holliday's grave as being younger."

"It could have been Eric. Father and son could be working together," Daisy said. "That's possible, isn't it? A serial killer team?"

Carter got up and stood beside her. "I agree with Daisy.

We can't let Wolff threaten her and walk away. I'll go to his house and interrogate him."

Her heart swelled with pride and gratitude as she took a step toward him. Carter believed in her. He stood up for her.

"Whoa there, Ranger." Hicks slammed his fist on the table. "The FBI has jurisdiction on this investigation."

"Thanks for the reminder." Carter confronted him. "I don't answer to you guys. I work for NPS."

"Shoes," Daisy said emphatically. "You've got footprints from the murder scenes, and Gerald Wolfe is a big man—probably size thirteen."

"That could be evidence," SAC Wiley said. "Maybe enough for a search warrant."

"Yes." She did a fist pump.

"Big feet aren't a crime, but we'll interrogate. Carter, you shouldn't approach him, because he already knows you're allied with Daisy. Hicks and I will talk to him."

"When?" Carter asked.

"Right after dinner." Wiley's forehead pinched in a scowl. "My wife made me promise to watch my diet. If I don't eat healthy food on a regular basis, I get cranky."

"The crankier, the better," Daisy said. "I want you to scare that old man."

"It's time for the two of you to go home until tomorrow," he said. "Hicks and I will use an open channel on a transmitter so you can both listen in on our interrogation."

Satisfied with the compromise, Daisy headed toward the door. Over her shoulder, she said, "Help yourselves to the burritos and guac. I'm not hungry."

Marching away from the FBI headquarters, she felt equal measures of bravery and silliness. Was she acting on the facts? Or had she gotten swept away by her own panic? Either way, she was happy about two things. Number one: Gerald Wolff wasn't going to get away with scaring her. Number two: Carter was on her side.

AT ROOM NUMBER eighteen on the second floor of the Sund-owner Motel, Carter paused to scan the asphalt parking lot and traffic on the street below. Not sensing a threat, he entered behind Daisy. Inside, he noted the two full-size beds. If he needed to spend the night at the motel, no problem. Of course, he'd rather take Daisy home to his cabin, where she could feel safe and he could relax and maybe, just maybe, take their relationship to a more intimate level. Their kiss this morning deserved a follow-up, and he was ready, especially when she kicked off her hiking boots and stretched out on the bed closest the door. Her well-toned, golden-tan legs almost reached the end of the mattress. She flexed her foot and wiggled her toes. Typically, he didn't have a foot fetish, but she was enough to make him change his mind.

Before he started drooling, he shifted his focus to the takeout dinner from the Happy Dragon—three large bags with veggie fried rice, chow mein, ginger beef, egg rolls, sweet and sour pork, kung pao chicken, cheese wontons, and fortune cookies. Had he overordered? Oh, yeah, he was starving. He'd also picked up a six-pack of bottled water. Before he settled down to eat, he set up the transmitter on the dresser by the television so they could hear the team of Wiley and Hicks interrogate Gerald Wolff.

Daisy rolled onto her stomach and exhaled a sound that was halfway between a groan and a giggle. "I've never had a day like this," she said. "Best of times and worst of times."

"Yeah? What was the best?" In his mind, he replayed their kiss by Teacup Lake.

"The autopsy, of course."

He should have guessed. "And the worst?"

"Being scared by the big bad Wolff."

He appreciated her sense of humor but knew she used jokes to deflect her real feelings. This woman didn't like being vulnerable. "I'm sorry that happened to you."

"Not your fault."

"I know. But if I'd been with you, Wolff never would have come close."

"True. You're definitely an alpha male."

"Can we be serious for a minute?" He stood and went to the transmitter, tuning the sensitive radio to the channel Wiley would use. "I'd feel better if I could—with your permission—keep an eye on you."

"Like a bodyguard?"

Exactly like a bodyguard. "I want to be sure you're safe."

For a long moment, she considered. No doubt weighing the positive of having protection against the negative of being watched over by a babysitter. She solemnly nodded. "Okay."

While he called Wiley and made sure they were properly connected, she spread food cartons on the small table by the window. Chopsticks in hand, they dug in. According to Brandi's influencer vlog, Happy Dragon ranked in the top five Chinese takeout places in Pueblo. Admittedly not a huge selection, but he was so hungry that he could have eaten a huge platter of Rocky Mountain oysters. At first, Daisy picked at her food, but her enthusiasm grew as she tasted the spicier dishes.

He enjoyed watching her balance large chunks of ginger beef on the tip of her chopsticks, then dab at her mouth with dainty touches. He grinned. "In your expert opinion, what's the best Asian food in Denver?"

She rattled off three different places without thinking twice. "And I love dim sum on Sunday morning, especially sticky rice and pot stickers. What about you? Cops are supposed to know the best places to eat."

"I agree with your picks." His worry that they didn't have a single thing in common vanished. Apparently, they were both foodies. "I took a class in how to make sushi."

"You've got to show me." She gestured with her chopsticks. "But how do you get good, fresh fish in the mountains?"

"Not fresh," he admitted. "We've got no ocean. But we do have refrigeration."

The transmitter on the dresser buzzed to life, and Carter went to turn up the volume.

He heard Wiley's deep, authoritative voice. "FBI. Open the door, Mr. Wolff."

Words to strike terror in the heart of a guilty person.

Chapter Fourteen

Daisy dropped her chopsticks and stared at the transmitter, amazed at the clarity of the audio. Introductions between Gerald Wolff and the FBI agents sounded like they were standing across the room instead of being miles away. Carter returned to his seat at the small table, reached over and gave her hand a gentle squeeze.

She squeezed back. "I'm glad we're not there."

"I wish we were."

A perfect illustration of the differences between them. She preferred to observe the situation from a safe distance—clinically noting facts and discrepancies—while Carter was a man of action.

From her prior encounter with Gerald, she had deduced probable alcoholism. In this conversation, he was huffing and coughing like a man with advanced emphysema. His tone was hostile. "What the hell do you feds want?"

"We're investigating the murders of two women," Wiley said. "Is your son at home?"

"Eric ain't here. And we got nothing to do with murder."

"Your dark blue van was sighted near the crime scene. Eric admitted being there. Were you with him?"

"Hell, no." He gasped and grumbled. "I hardly ever use the van. Supposedly, Eric is running things. Running his business into the ground, if you ask me."

"You worked at the steel mill," Wiley said, "but you're retired."

"The bastards made me retire early because of my disability. Can't stand on my feet all day so I don't get my full pension. I'm only sixty-three, you know."

Agent Hicks spoke up. "Do you own another vehicle?"

"None of your damn business."

"You met Ms. Brighton today," Wiley said.

"So that's why you're paying me a visit. Well, good. The little bitch attacked me. You can lock her up. Take a look at my arm. She blasted me with pepper spray."

Under her breath, Daisy said, "And I'm glad I did. I hope it hurts."

Wiley ignored Gerald's complaint. "You were stalking Ms. Brighton."

"You can't prove it. We just happened to be in the same store at the same time." She heard him grunt, probably while shifting his bulk in a chair. "Little Miss Daisy and her auntie are trying to take my bullion, my inheritance."

Wiley continued. "Eric admitted that he put a tracker on Ms. Brighton."

"A game between the two of them. Nothing but a prank. No harm done."

"I've advised her to register for a restraining order. I believe your ex-wife filed several such orders against you."

"Don't care what she did. I'm glad the ugly old sow is out of my life."

"You had domestic violence arrests, but your wife dropped the charges. Do you have a problem with women, Mr. Wolff?"

Daisy could only guess at the depth of his awfulness. His behavior—the cruelty and the rage—fit her expectations of a serial killer who lashed out at women, cut their throats and watched them bleed to death. But the behavior of this particular killer also included tenderness. He cared for his victims and tied pretty silk scarves around their throats.

Wiley switched the topic to Eric, probing to discover how he'd felt after his mother left. Did he blame his father for chasing her away? Not according to Gerald, who stated that he'd done a great job of raising his teenaged son by himself, didn't put up with whining and used a firm hand to show the kid what was expected of him.

"I taught that long-haired punk everything he knows." Gerald lapsed into a bout of coughing. "Showed him how to paint houses and how to bargain with his suppliers. And I taught him how to handle the ladies. You know what I mean?"

Wiley asked, "Did you also teach Eric how to stalk a woman?"

"When you want something," Gerald said, "you have to go after it. You've got to study your prey, see where she goes and what she likes. Then you make your move. And you take what you want from her."

"What if she doesn't want to give it up?"

"They always do," Gerald said.

Daisy groaned. *Disgusting!*

In SAC Wiley's voice, she heard barely suppressed rage. "Is Eric stalking Daisy because he wants to make her his woman?"

"Could be. She's not bad-looking."

"Does he have other girlfriends?"

"What are you getting at?" Wolff growled.

"Does the name Rene Williams mean anything to you? How about Hannah Guerrero?"

"I don't know them."

"Was it your son or was it you, Gerald? Are you the Wolff who got too close to these ladies? Eileen Findlay. Andrea Lindstrom."

She heard the ring of steel in Wiley's voice as he listed

the victims. With his thinning hair and his bolo tie, Wiley might not look like a hardened federal officer, but—according to Carter—he had one of the highest arrest records in the Rocky Mountain West.

Over the transmitter, she heard a door open. A new voice joined the others. Eric Wolff had come home. "Good evening, gentlemen. What's going on here?"

"Back off!" the older Wolff roared at his son. "I can take care of myself."

"Don't you get it, Dad? They're trying to pin the serial murders on you."

"Or you, sonny boy."

"Shut up," Eric snarled.

"Don't you dare backtalk me."

She heard confused muttering and the sounds of a scuffle. Chair legs scraped on the floor. Feet stomped. There was a loud slap. The crash of something breaking. Nervous, she looked to Carter. "What's going on?"

"Some kind of fight." He paced to the dresser where the transmitter stood. Bracing his arms on either side, he looked like he wanted to dive through the radio and join in the brawl. "Wish I knew who was involved."

"Why?"

"I'd like to see Hicks use Gerald's big, fat face for a punching bag. I don't like that guy."

Another crash. She heard Wiley take control. "If you hit him again, you're under arrest."

"He's my son," Gerald said. "If Eric needs discipline, that's my job."

"It's all right," Eric said. "I'm okay."

"You're bleeding," Wiley said. "Do you need medical treatment?"

"It's just a bloody nose. I had it coming." He cleared his throat. "Are we done?"

"What size shoe do you wear?" Agent Hicks asked.

"I'm a twelve. My dad is a thirteen."

"We'll need to take a look in your closet."

Gerald refused loudly while he coughed and huffed. Eric claimed it wasn't any good to talk to him when he was like this. After five minutes' argument, the FBI agents left. Before Wiley ended the transmission, he told Carter that he'd see him tomorrow. His last words: "We'll have a warrant to search their truck, their house and anywhere else you like."

"We win," Carter said as he turned off the transmitter.

In a dull voice, she said, "Yippee."

Daisy pushed away from the small table by the closed motel drapes. Being involved in the investigation had taken her appetite away. She cracked open her fortune cookie and read the scrap of paper inside to herself. *You will find true happiness with a tall, dark, handsome partner.*

She gazed across the table. There sat Carter—Mr. Tall, Dark and Handsome himself. Having him close did a lot to relieve her fears. She pointed at his fortune cookie. "Let's hear your future."

"Sure." He cracked it open and read out loud. "'A beautiful woman will spend the night at my cabin.'"

She grabbed for the fortune, but he pulled it away. "It doesn't say that."

He shrugged. "My real fortune says something about taking a trip over high mountains, which is kind of my job. Accurate but no surprise."

She rolled the idea of spending the night with him around in her mind, then pushed it away. Life was already too complicated. "What did you think about the interrogation?"

"SAC Wiley is a sharp guy, and Gerald is a misogynist who probably abused young Eric."

She sipped water from one of the plastic bottles. "Do those traits fit the profile for a serial killer?"

"I'm afraid so." Carter dug more deeply into the container of veggie fried rice. "Hating women is a biggie. Also, he admitted being a stalker, which suits our killer. Both Hannah and Andrea felt like they were being watched. Abusers sometimes graduate to murder. My boss, Joaquin, would say that Gerald is a narcissist who thinks he's smarter than everybody, especially the feds."

Once again, her imagination cranked into high gear as she thought of the victims seeing the big, ugly face of Gerald Wolff before they died. Instead of a celestial chorus, they'd hear his labored breathing. Something about that picture didn't fit.

She left the table and sat on the bed. "I'm leaning more toward Eric as the killer. He was abused in childhood and lost his mother in his teens. We need to find out more about her. She left him fifteen years ago. Why is he compelled to start killing now?"

He bit into a cream cheese–stuffed wonton. "Abuse is not an excuse."

"What?"

"Just saying." He studied the wonton as though the answers were hidden in the deep-fried folds. "Criminal behavior can't always be blamed on the rotten parents."

She sensed there was something more to his statement but didn't want to go deeper right now. Taking out her cell phone, she said, "It's after nine. I'd better call Vi to let her know I won't be returning to Leadville tonight."

Actually, Daisy was more worried about her aunt than the other way around. Her aunt had been in contact with two of the suspects: Jackknife and Gerald Wolff. She might make an enticing target.

After Daisy explained that she was staying at a motel in Pueblo to save driving time, she asked, "Aunt Vi, has Jackknife been in contact with you?"

"As a matter of fact, he's sitting in the front parlor as we speak."

Warning bells clanged inside her head. "Tell him to go home. Right now."

"I'm never rude to my guests. Besides, I want to reward him for making an effort before he came calling. His hair is combed, he shaved and he must have purchased a clean shirt."

Daisy remembered the photo in the FBI file that showed Jackknife in a more positive light. Still not completely presentable but better than usual. "Don't encourage him. He's a suspect in the serial killings."

"My dear girl, are you worried about me? There's really no need. I'm carrying my tiny Glock 42 in the pocket of my skirt."

Her blonde, green-eyed, sixty-eight-year-old aunt wasn't a woman who would crumble under threats. "Are you always armed?"

"Frequently. I have a concealed carry permit, after all." She cleared her throat. "Actually, I'm more concerned about you doing autopsies and interrogating criminals. Is that nice forest ranger with you?"

"Yes." She glanced across the room to the table where Carter was tidying up the cartons of Chinese food. *My tall, dark, handsome partner.* "He's not spending the night, though."

"Why not?"

"I haven't known the man for even two days. It's too soon."

"Of course, I agree," aunt Vi said. "But spending the night doesn't necessarily mean you're in the same bed. He could watch over you...like a bodyguard."

Frankly, she didn't trust herself to be alone with Carter and not make a move on him. When she caught him staring at her bare legs, her response was to inch her skirt up even higher. *Time to change into those baggy cargo pants.* Picking up her paisley duffel, Daisy scooted into the bathroom and closed the door. She turned up the water in the sink full blast so Carter couldn't hear her end of the conversation. Still, she whispered, "He invited me to his cabin outside Salida, about an hour away from here."

"Do it," Vi said. "Otherwise, you'll spend the whole night hiding under the covers and listening for the lead-footed approach of Gerald Wolff or Jackknife or any of the other suspects you've been confronting. I remember what you were like as a child."

Daisy wasn't sure what she was talking about. "Can you give me some details?"

"Your parents, especially my sister, are ridiculously overprotective. I was always the wild one, and she was a frightened little mouse. In any case, she wouldn't allow you to watch or listen to anything scary. *Grimm's Fairy Tales* were too violent for her darling Daisy. When you finally had the chance to see a scary movie at a sleepover, you were traumatized. Weeping all night. Screaming at every shadow. Once, when I was babysitting, I found you hiding in your bedroom closet with a butcher knife from the kitchen."

That bit of family background explained a lot. "I really don't remember."

"But you still get scared, don't you?" Aunt Vi's voice had an *I told you so* tone. "I saw that fear when you were talking to Eric. Right this minute, you should march up to Ranger Carter and tell him you're taking him up on his invitation. Do you want me to talk to him? You know, to let him know that you're not agreeing to a night of hanky-panky."

Oh. My. God. "Absolutely not."

"What about his boss? Somebody at the Salida headquarters, maybe."

"No phone calls, Aunt Vi. And you need to get rid of Jackknife. Whatever else you do, no more contact with Gerald or Eric Wolff."

Daisy emerged from the bathroom and shuffled toward Carter in her slightly too large cargo pants that dragged on the maroon-and-gray-patterned carpet. When she reached the table, she set down her cell phone and gazed up into Carter's blue eyes. Before she became mesmerized by the reflection of light in the facets of his irises or the way his black hair fell across his forehead or his incredibly sexy mouth, she spoke up. "I want to stay at your cabin tonight."

"I can make that happen."

Immediately, her imagination settled down. She felt safe.

Chapter Fifteen

Before Carter turned onto the red gravel driveway that led to the detached garage outside his cabin, he killed the headlights on his SUV. Parked behind a stand of leafy green aspen that hid his vehicle from the road, he drew his Beretta from the holster he'd stashed in the locked center console and adjusted the overhead light so it wouldn't flash on when he opened the door.

Daisy roused herself from sleep. In a groggy voice, she asked, "What's going on?"

"Probably nothing." She'd sunk into a heavy nap as soon as they left the lights of Pueblo, and he hadn't wakened her when he noticed headlights following them. "Stay here, and keep the doors locked."

Earlier, when he drove by the NPS headquarters in Salida, he had considered stopping and recruiting Joaquin for backup, but the office was dark. Though it was only a few minutes past ten o'clock, his boss—an early riser—might have already gone to bed at his house on the outskirts of town. Carter didn't want to disturb him for a threat that might not even be real. The headlights in his rearview mirror had disappeared right after he passed the Salida City Limits sign.

He'd contacted SAC Wiley. In a quiet phone conversation, Carter learned that the FBI had placed Gerald Wolff under surveillance—an extreme measure, but suspected serial killers got extreme attention. The dark blue house-painting van hadn't moved, which meant the vehicle stalking his SUV wasn't Wolff. Unless Gerald or Eric had sneaked out and used a different vehicle.

Carter wondered if he was turning paranoid. Never before had unfounded fear been an issue, but Daisy's imagination had infected him like a virus. He felt her panic and saw danger in every shadow. The vehicle following them hadn't come close enough for him to identify the make or model. Then, he didn't see the headlights anymore. Not until he drove on the twisting route leading to his cabin. The stalker was back.

Outside the garage, Carter slipped through the driver's-side door into the night, holding his Beretta at the ready. The waning moon and a cloudless sky full of stars shed enough light to see the edge of the wide driveway, where the adobe-colored gravel spread into thick shrubs and sage. The triple-size wood-frame garage with a shake shingle roof that matched the cabin loomed in front of his SUV. An ancient Jeep with a snowplow attachment on the front was parked under the eaves. On the near side, a rustic path with a sturdy banister led to the covered porch that stretched across the front of his log cabin. None of the interior lights were on, but the stars and moon reflected on the triple-pane glass on the lower floor windows and the twin dormers.

Pacing carefully at the edge of the driveway, Carter made very little noise. A rush of fresh wind slapped him in the face. The smell of forest and arid dust chased away the drowsiness that came from sitting too long in the car. Alert, he was ready to kick butt if necessary and almost hoped one of the suspects had been stupid enough follow them here.

If he'd been alone, he might have darted through the surrounding forest until he located the stalker. He would have turned the tables on this creep. But not tonight, not while

Daisy was nearby. His job, his main purpose until they apprehended the serial killer, revolved around her safety. After all, she wouldn't be in this predicament if he hadn't escorted her to Rene Williams's body in the Butcher's Gulch graveyard. Her involvement wasn't all his fault, but Carter deserved a measure of the blame.

Looking over his shoulder toward the car, he tried to see her shadowy silhouette in the front seat, but the night was too dark and the windows too opaque. Without visual verification of her whereabouts, he could only hope she'd followed his instructions and stayed put.

He crouched behind the row of four mailboxes at the edge of his property and watched the road. For a full ten minutes, he held himself motionless. From years of hunting, he knew how to blend into the forest and wait patiently.

Finally, Carter stood and walked to the center of the two-lane graded gravel road that passed his cabin and curled up the hill toward other properties. He saw no evidence of the other vehicle. Safe to assume he'd given up? Or was he biding his time until later tonight?

He jogged back to the SUV, clicked the locks and opened the passenger-side door. Immediately, he was hit by the smell of deep-fried wontons and spicy ginger seasoning. Daisy held one of the Chinese food containers and a pair of chopsticks.

She grinned. "Are we okay?"

"As far as I can tell." The shift in her mood from near panic to cheerful munching surprised him. Paranoid or not, the lady was unpredictable. "I'll feel safer when we get inside the cabin so I can set the alarms."

"Aye, aye." She saluted with the flick of a chopstick.

Juggling her paisley duffel, the remains of their Chinese dinner and his Beretta, he hiked up the inclined path to the covered porch, tapped a code into the security keypad, listened for the click and swung open the front door. Three years ago, when he had firmly established his assignment as an investigator for the NPS, he'd bought this two-story log cabin with dark green trim and a gray roof. He liked the views and didn't mind the need for repairs. His first improvements included upgraded locks, reinforced windows and an electronic security system designed to protect his home when long assignments kept him from returning. Next, he added the huge garage that also served as a storage area for his ATV and sports equipment. This year, his main project for the summer would be expanding his cedar deck and adding a barbecue.

After he reset the alarm, he watched Daisy stroll around his living room with the rustic stone fireplace and heavy furniture. Her too-long cargo pants lacked the charm of her short skirt, but he liked the way they outlined her firm little bottom. She passed through the dining area, which was dominated by a table he meant to refinish one of these days, and ended her tour in the large kitchen, also partially renovated, with a long, black granite–topped island opposite the dated avocado-green appliances. Her smile seemed forced. "Great place. So much potential."

"It's not perfect," he readily conceded. "My cabin is a work in progress."

"Too bad Slade Franklin is a suspect. You could use a skilled carpenter who specializes in renovation work."

"I can't believe you'd consider hiring a possible serial killer as a handyman." He unloaded the Chinese food into his fridge. "I get a kick out of working on the house. Some ranger buddies will come over and we'll make a day of it."

"Did you ever think you could maybe use a woman's touch?"

"Are you volunteering for the job?"

"No way."

Her answer came too quickly, and she emphasized by waving her hands and taking a couple of backward steps.

Apparently, Daisy wanted him to know, for sure, that she wasn't pressing for a deeper relationship, which made him contrary. Now, he wanted her to...want him. "Are you certain that you don't want to step in and be my interior decorator?"

"One hundred percent," she said. "I'm a condo dweller whose fix-up projects are limited to replacing the plants on my balcony when they die."

He offered her a choice of beverage, and she opted for herbal tea. "Are you hungry?" he asked. "I can zap something in the microwave."

"Not necessary."

After he filled the teakettle and set it on the stove top to boil, he pointed to a tall stool on the opposite side of the island. After she sat, he said, "Before you go to bed, there are a couple of questions we need to answer, starting with this one. Do you believe you're in danger?"

"I don't know," she said. "At times, I'm nervous, almost panicky, but I don't have factual evidence to validate those feelings."

In a sentence, she'd summarized the opposite sides of her personality. Should she follow her instincts? Or allow her knowledge to define her behavior? Both approaches had merit, and he didn't know which to believe.

She continued, "I mean, it doesn't make sense for the killer to come after me. I have no connection to any of the women who were murdered. I live in Denver and don't know their friends or families. We all worked in different arenas. What's his motive?"

"Killers aren't known for being rational." He set the tea to brew in a butterfly-and-flower-patterned teapot left behind by a former girlfriend. "None of the other women were connected, except for Andrea and Hannah in Glenwood Springs. They were friends."

"Fancy teapot," she said dryly.

"I know how to steep." He loaded a tray with the pot, cups, sugar, spoons and creamer. "Let's take this conversation into my office. I want to make notes."

"Charts and graphs." She eagerly rubbed her hands together. "I love that stuff."

Not surprised. He suspected her science classroom was packed with interactive displays, including the periodic table, the Fibonacci sequence, see-through models of human anatomy, plastic skeletons and skulls.

He led her down a hallway, passed the bathroom, and entered the home office with square footage nearly equal to the living room. He placed the tea tray on a coffee table in front of a sturdy brown leather sofa. Opposite the sofa stood a large whiteboard—four feet by six—on a heavy-duty frame that backed up to his desk.

With a dark blue marker, Carter wrote the names of the victims, starting with Eileen Findlay, who was killed on the Riverwalk in Pueblo, then Hannah and Andrea. Finally, Rene. "What else would you add?"

With a green marker, she filled in the blanks with each woman's age, occupation, home address and the places where their bodies were found. In front of their names, she wrote the date they were murdered. Stepping back, she regarded the whiteboard and gave a satisfied nod. "I like being organized. On the opposite side of the board we can jot down the suspects."

"Not all of them."

"There aren't that many."

"We don't have access to the complete list," he said. "There are a number of suspicious characters who the FBI keeps under routine surveillance. These are men with criminal records. Some are stalkers. Others have been arrested for harassment or other violence. Bad guys."

He circled the coffee table and poured himself a cup of green chamomile tea, to which he added two teaspoons of raw sugar. After taking a sip, he lowered himself onto the left end of the sofa, his favorite spot, and turned on a brass table lamp. "Our investigation," he said, "is limited to the Wolff men, father and son, Slade Franklin, and Jackknife Jones."

On the other half of the whiteboard, she listed the names. "Not Rene's boyfriend?"

"The FBI in Denver is keeping an eye on him."

While he watched, she filled in pertinent information about their suspects, including age, address and occupation. He was happy to leave the charting to her and wanted to believe being organized would make a difference.

"I'm glad we're doing this," she said.

"I'm going to ask you again," he said. "Are you in danger? Yes or no."

"Yes."

He saw the fear in her green eyes and heard the tremor in her voice. She believed the answer she'd given, even if she couldn't explain why.

And so did he.

DAISY WANTED THESE serial killings to make sense. Staring at the whiteboard, she picked up a pink marker and said, "This is for alibis or lack thereof."

Sipping his tea from a dainty china cup decorated with butterflies, he looked like a cross between a rugged cowboy and a fancy-pants gentleman. "Explain."

She drew a line connecting Eric to both victims found in Butcher's Gulch. "We know he was in the area and could have committed both of these murders."

"Don't forget," Carter said, "Andrea was abducted on the fourteenth in Glenwood Springs, killed on the seventeenth and her body wasn't found until the twentieth. Did Eric hold her captive for three days?"

She groaned. "I don't suppose he has an alibi for the time period."

"He's self-employed. Timing is based on *his* records, which means he could have gone to Glenwood and lied to us about being there."

She scribbled an *E* for Eric and a pink question mark beside Andrea and Hannah. The line to Eileen Findlay slashed directly across the whiteboard. "Because he lives in Pueblo, it's possible that he doesn't have much of an alibi for the woman found in the Riverwalk."

A similar pattern emerged for self-employed Slade Franklin, who had shown the record of his schedule to Carter without any sort of verification.

Stepping back, she studied the chart and shook her head. "We know almost nothing about the whereabouts of Gerald Wolff. Ditto for Jackknife. He could have been in all those places or in none of them."

Carter joined her at the board. In purple, he wrote a note between the victims and the suspects and drew a circle around a single word. "Warrants," he said. "Wiley promised he'd have the necessary paperwork tomorrow. With any luck, that should produce evidence."

She prepared a cup of tea for herself with one spoonful of sugar and a dab of creamer. "After the ace FBI crime-scene team searches Slade's camper truck and the Wolffs' van, we could have proof that one or more of the victims had contact with our suspects. Otherwise, we have a lack of forensics. No witnesses. No cameras in the area. No DNA or prints."

She sat at the opposite end of the leather sofa and tasted her chamomile tea. The warmth, flavor and fruity apple scent relaxed her. After such a long day, she'd expected to be tired, but the nap on the drive here must have refreshed her. She felt wide-awake—disturbingly so. Her busy brain had begun to spin sexy fantasies about her and Carter, and she had to remind herself to shut down her desires before they got started. Aunt Vi had given her good advice. Spending the night together didn't mean they had to be in the same bed.

In her peripheral vision, she watched him pace in front of the whiteboard. With a yellow marker, he wrote another single-word notation and read it aloud. "Motive."

"That's a good one." Her gaze lingered on his wide shoulders and narrow hips. He was too handsome, too perfect. Talking about these other creeps tarnished her thinking. "We know what makes Gerald tick. He hates women."

"And Jackknife?"

"I'd have to say greed. Didn't he agree to drive me in circles for a payoff?"

"That's what he told me the first time we talked at Butcher's Gulch. He said he got the cash from a kid—an unconnected third party—and didn't know who was behind it."

"How much?"

"He wouldn't say. I had the idea that it wasn't much."

She frowned. "And it doesn't explain how he might make money from the other victims?"

"Jackknife isn't a great suspect, and his motive is weak." He shrugged. "Let's move on. We've got mother issues for Slade and Eric."

"Slade has an unhealthy attachment to Mama. And Eric erupted with rage when he talked about how his mom left with the golden retriever." She gazed at him and smiled. "It's ironic—I know quite a bit about our suspects but almost nothing about you."

"Right back at you."

She wanted to fill in those blanks, wanted to have a clear picture about who he was, what he loved and what made him laugh. His favorite movie? Favorite song? "Tell me all about yourself."

Chapter Sixteen

From her position at the end of the long sofa, Daisy concentrated on her chamomile and tried to ignore the magnetic pull that impelled her toward Carter, who sat on the opposite end with his legs crossed in a figure four. She kicked off her hiking boots and stretched out her legs across the sofa cushions. Her pose created a barrier between them, but not a very effective one. When he caught hold of her bare foot and lightly massaged the sole, she felt the tingling effect throughout her body. *Pull your foot back.* But, oh my God, his touch felt good.

She forced herself to focus. What were they talking about? Oh yeah, getting to know him. "Let's start with your unusual name," she said. "Aloysius Periwinkle Carter IV. Why?"

"The name is sick, and not in a good way. Could be that my family is a gang of sadists."

"Who was the first Aloysius and where did he come from?"

"According to our romanticized family history, he was Scotch-Irish and immigrated to Virginia with others from his clan. He was a poet—a worthless job that went well with the fancy Periwinkle part of his name."

"The periwinkle is a flowering vine, common to Europe and North America. Sometimes called the myrtle."

She knew her botany. "Mildly poisonous with some medicinal properties."

"A good description of my family," he said.

"One of the common varieties has beautiful blue flowers."

He opened his eyes wide, showing off the color of the iris, which could, in fact, be called periwinkle blue. "Another family trait that's been passed down."

With his index finger, he drew a line down her foot from her middle toe to her heel and back again. A tremor climbed her leg to her hip, stimulating the sciatic nerve, which was the longest and largest in the entire body. She tensed and released, tensed and released and forced her voice to remain calm. "How did the original Aloysius get from Virginia to Colorado?"

"In addition to being called a poet, he was an adventurer. As a young man, he packed up his kilt and headed west during the Pike's Peak gold rush, hoping to make his fortune."

A familiar story. Many of the early pioneers hoped to strike it rich—the same type of naive people who believed in Brighton's Bullion—and many were disappointed. "What did he end up doing instead?"

"A. P. Carter didn't fail. He found a mother lode near Cripple Creek and partnered up with an engineer who knew how to build a functional mine. That partner was his first bit of luck. The second was his wife, an accountant. She wisely invested their profits and made them all rich. Carter started a newspaper in Colorado Springs and opened a pub."

His gentle narrative washed over her and lulled her into a pleasant mood while his clever fingers teased her foot and kept her trembling with awareness. "They had four children, and the oldest male was named for his father. The tradition passed down to my dad. And to me."

"I hope you don't plan to carry Aloysius forward with your firstborn." She'd never saddle her son with such a jawbreaker name. *Her son?* As if she had any reason to think of having children with Carter? *What's wrong with me?*

"Are you all right, Daisy?"

She exhaled a long sigh, almost a groan. "So you inherited the name and the eye color. What else was passed down?"

"A whole lot of money. Investment in Colorado property, especially near Aspen before the ski lodge and real estate boom, paid off nicely. The Carter clan has always done well for themselves financially." His voice took on a ragged, rough edge. "They weren't so lucky when it came to genetics."

Alarmed, she focused on his profile. "An illness?"

"You could say that." He stared down at the arch of her right foot. "Alcoholism. We have a lot of drunks in the family, including my younger brother, Theodore, and our dad."

His charming story about the wandering Scotsman who found gold in them thar hills turned dark and foreboding. She had an idea about the origin of his bitter statement when they realized Gerald Wolff mistreated his son. Carter commented about how abuse didn't excuse bad behavior.

"And you?" She might as well come right out and ask. "Are you an alcoholic?"

"I dodged that bullet." He held up his china teacup and toasted her. "Some might say I controlled my impulses by concentrating on professions that strictly define right and wrong. Studied law in college but changed my mind and went to the Denver Police Academy instead. Dad hated my decision. He never held a steady job and bounced from one supposedly great opportunity to another. Some weren't exactly legal. Worse, he dragged Theo along with him."

"Did they stay in Colorado?"

"Moved to Idaho after my mother divorced the old man." His well-shaped lips curved in a sardonic grin. "I guess I managed to turn out okay. After some serious rehab, Theo also got his act together. He's running the ranch in Idaho, raising cattle. One day at a time."

"I'm sorry," she said, "for all you had to go through."

"While we're on the topic of unhappy twists of fate, I should mention my marriage that lasted less than two years. She hated being married to a cop, and I can't say that I blamed her. After we split, I focused on becoming a ranger. Best job I ever had."

"And you never want to change?" She heard her voice rise on the last word, turning her statement into a question. A hopeful question. Was there a chance for them?

"I didn't think so. Not until recently."

Her spirits lifted. "Recently?"

After one last squeeze of her toes, he placed her feet onto the sofa, stood and went to the whiteboard where they had been trying—futilely—to bring order to their findings. "There's another way we can look at this data. We have four victims, enough to form a pattern."

She had the distinct impression that he had changed the subject as a way to avoid continuing the conversation about his personal life. Discussing the past wasn't easy, and she was willing to play along. "Okay, what kind of pattern are you talking about?

"You're the scientist. What kind of statistics should we use? Some kind of graph or a ranking?"

"We could try a four-way Venn diagram," she said. "Four circles with one section to represent an intersection with all four."

He flipped the whiteboard to the back side, which was blank. He started their diagram with the most recent victim: Rene Williams. While Carter drew a circle and filled in the pertinent data about her, Daisy padded across the hardwood floor to the board in front of his desk and did circles for the other victims.

Next, they filled in the overlapping details. Three had

been found in cemeteries. Two were students. Hannah and Andrea had both been employed full-time and lived in the Glenwood Springs area. Three had died from exsanguination due to a slashed carotid, but Eileen was strangled.

The central overlap that showed similarities for all four had only a few notations: All in their twenties. All the bodies were found outdoors.

"It's not much," he said.

"We don't even know their horoscope signs." Daisy turned to him. "What's yours?"

"Aquarius, the deep-thinking loner. Let me guess yours."

Though she didn't believe in the zodiac, she appreciated all the charts and data that had been collected based on date of birth. "Go ahead, guess."

"Scorpio," he said with a seductive smile. "The sexiest sign."

Bingo! She'd heard that thumbnail sketch before and didn't really believe she was a sexy bombshell. "Scorpios are also creative and good with numerical calculations."

"But mostly sexy," he said as he looked at the whiteboard. "We need to go deeper in our analysis. Just like you did with me."

"You and I will never understand how the mind of a serial killer works…" *Thank God for that.* "…but we can break down the logical pieces and maybe put the puzzle together."

"You lost me."

Daisy was a teacher. She could explain. "Take Hannah, for example. She met up with the killer because he conned her into taking him to Doc Holliday's grave at night. What sort of woman agrees to such a risk?" She answered her own question. "I hate to admit that it could be someone like me, someone who agrees to go for a ride with Jackknife Jones. I guess I'm gullible, too."

Realization dawned in his periwinkle-blue eyes. "And

Rene Williams hung out with Slade at Teacup Lake because she thought she was helping him solve a girlfriend problem."

"Again, gullible." She bobbed her head. "We don't know what the killer might have said to Andrea in the grocery store parking lot, because there were no witnesses."

"I read about a scam used by Ted Bundy," Carter said. "He'd approach a woman in a mall or a parking lot and tell her that he needed a woman's help, doing something like taking a child to the bathroom or choosing a color of paint. He played on their sympathies."

"That leaves Eileen, and we don't know enough about her. Tomorrow, when I sit in on the autopsy with Dr. Julia, she might be able to tell me about Eileen Findlay."

"And I can call the tribal police," he said. "We have a good working relationship."

Finally, they seemed to be making progress. The killer stalked his victims, found women who appealed to him and used their gullible/sympathetic nature to lure them into his grasp. She shuddered. These supposed facts—based on inductive reasoning—didn't calm her fears the way she'd hoped they would. She still saw the killer as a monster. A predator. A sociopath.

From the kitchen, she heard her ringtone and dashed to answer. Fortunately, her cell phone was perched at the top of her duffel. She answered, "Hello?"

"Hi, Daisy. I hope it's not too late."

The voice was familiar, but she couldn't quite place it. "Who's this?"

"It's me. Brandi Thoreau." *Slade's girlfriend?* "There's something I need to talk to you about."

WHILE CARTER CLEANED up the tea tray and cups, he eavesdropped on Daisy's phone conversation and heard the tone of her voice shift from frightened to concerned. Her idea about determining similar personality traits of the victims had given him another way to look at their serial killer. He went after empathetic women who could be lured into dangerous situations. Such a person fit Dr. Julia's lessons about victimology. What else did they have in common? All young, all found outdoors, three out of the four were in cemeteries…what else?

More importantly, how did Daisy fit into this picture?

Tonight, on the drive from Pueblo, another vehicle had followed them. *A stalker?* Stalking might be part of the killer's standard procedure. Both Andrea Lindstrom and Hannah Guerrero had mentioned that they felt like someone had been watching them. Most definitely, Daisy had been stalked by Eric Wolff, who admitted using electronic devices to keep track of her whereabouts. Why? And why was a stalker after Daisy? What had she done? Why was she like the others?

He heard her on the phone making plans to meet Brandi for lunch tomorrow outside the building where the autopsy would be done. And then she ended the call.

Still hungry, he took a package of chocolate chip cookies from the upper shelf beside the sink and made a short stack of four. "What's up with Slade's girlfriend?"

"She thinks he's cheating on her because he takes off for hours at a time and doesn't tell her where he's going. Sounds suspicious, right? And Brandi wants me to investigate."

Based on his first impression of Brandi, Carter figured she had the cleverness to run a vlog and be an influencer but not a whole lot of intelligence. "Does she know you're a high school science teacher and not a cop?"

"She seems to think that you and I are working on the same case, and I'm some kind of law enforcement, probably FBI. A compliment, really."

"And you agreed to meet her."

"After the autopsy at one o'clock." She stood and slung

her paisley duffel over her shoulder. "We need to return to Pueblo early. It's best if we get some sleep."

Though he didn't want the night to end with Daisy tucked into the queen bed in the guest room, which was far away from the extra-long king that took up half the floor space in the primary bedroom, he didn't know how to switch the topic. He couldn't come right out and ask if she wanted to have sex. Too creepy. Sweeping her into his arms for a passionate kiss didn't work for him, and he couldn't think of any suave, seductive lines to charm her off her feet. He was a forest ranger, dammit. Not smooth. Not clever. Just a guy.

Following her through the house to the staircase, he watched the subtle sway of her hips and the bouncy swing of her curly ponytail. Her energy and vitality made her a pleasure to be around, and he wanted to let her know how much he appreciated her. *Tell her.* The words stuck in his throat. Talking about a serial killer felt easier. *Safer?*

"The feds are going to serve their warrants on Wolff and Slade first thing tomorrow," he said. "We ought to have preliminary results by lunchtime."

She paused on the staircase and looked down at him. "That means Brandi could hear something about the evidence before our lunch date. Slade might be cleared of suspicion."

"Or not."

"It's weird, you know. We're investigating her boyfriend for murder, and she couldn't care less. She's worried about him being unfaithful."

"Not so strange." He moved up one stair step nearer to her. "If she actually thought he was a killer, she'd run."

"How could she not know?"

"Dr. Jekyll and Mr. Hyde," he reminded her. Sometimes, a heinous murderer lived in the same body as a gentleman. Her lips parted as though she had more to add, but she stopped speaking. Her opaque green eyes widened as she gazed at him. They stood so close together that he could smell the minty scent of her shampoo, feel the warmth from her body and see the rise and fall of her breathing. A soft pink blush colored her cheeks. Gently, he touched her arm. When she didn't bolt away from him, he tilted toward her.

Her attitude mirrored his. He could feel her attraction rising and mingling with his own, but instead of relaxing into his embrace, she stiffened. Quickly turning away from him, she dashed up the last few stairs and stood on the landing with her gaze darting from one side to the other, not knowing which way to go. His bedroom was at the front of the house to the left. Diagonal to that was the larger of two guest rooms.

He gestured toward the rear of the house. "That way. The bathroom is over here to your left."

Without a word, she disappeared into the bedroom, turned on the light and closed the door. Tonight, nothing would happen between them. He accepted that condition, but it was hard to accept the disappointment. "Good night, Daisy."

Carter went into his bedroom and quietly closed the door. Without turning on the light, he crossed the Berber carpet to his extra-long bed, sat on the edge and pulled off his boots. After a day like this one, he should have been exhausted. And yet, when he lay back on the chocolate-brown duvet, he knew sleep wouldn't come easily. Details about the investigation marched through his mind, making vague and tenuous connections. And then there was Daisy.

She was attracted to him. He knew it. When she looked at him, he saw a warm invitation in her amazing green eyes. In her ever-logical voice, he heard the promise of intimacy. And on the very few occasions when they touched, the sensual chemistry raced through him like a lit fuse.

She liked him but had decided they shouldn't start something they couldn't finish, and the two of them—both adults with fulfilling careers in different locations—weren't permanent relationship material. Could a city gal love a mountain man? Vice versa?

He heard the gush of water in the shower next to his bedroom and groaned as he imagined her, beautifully naked, stepping into the glass enclosure while steam from the hot water billowed around her. Not usually a drinker, he found himself craving a shot of tequila.

This had to stop. He pushed off the bed and stalked toward the glow of moonlight from the dormer. From the second-floor window of his cabin, which was at the top of a small ridge, he had a clear view of his garage, the mailboxes and the road that led past his cabin. Peering into the forest, he noticed movement. A dark shadow, nearly indistinguishable, crept through the trees.

The stalker had returned.

Chapter Seventeen

Carter stood motionless at the dormer window and stared, watching the dangerous shadow slip through the trees on the opposite side of the road. The mysterious dark form melted into the dark silhouette of a jagged boulder. The stalker didn't have a flashlight and wore a baseball cap to cover his hair. The surrounding trees, rocks and leafy shrubs hid his height and size. Though moonlight illuminated the forest, Carter hadn't caught a single glimpse of his face.

Since he knew every inch of these woods and had hiked from the foot of the canyon to the highest point on the cliffs above his cabin, he had an advantage. But he couldn't leave Daisy alone in the cabin, not even with the doors locked. Carter needed backup.

Staying at the window, he took out his phone and hid the screen so the light wouldn't attract attention. He called his boss, who lived nearby. "Joaquin, I've got a problem."

"What's up?" The big man's voice rumbled. "Where are you?"

"Daisy and I are at my cabin. There's a stalker outside in the forest. I need your help."

"Tell me what you wat me to do."

"Park outside my garage, come to the front door and let yourself in." He gave Joaquin the code to bypass the alarm and told him to go into the kitchen. "You take care of Daisy. I'll go after the stalker."

They didn't waste time with more talk. Carter ended the call, returned his phone to his pocket and looked toward the bathroom. The shower was off, and he heard Daisy humming. Now came the hard part. He had to tell her that her worst fears had come true—the imaginary monster she feared had materialized.

He tapped on the bathroom door. "Daisy, open up."

"Not a good time, Carter."

"I need to talk to you. Now."

When she peeked around the edge of the door, he saw that she'd wrapped herself in a fluffy blue towel. Her damp hair curled around her face. "What is it?" she asked impatiently.

He couldn't explain, couldn't be expected to make sense while standing here talking to a half-naked woman. "Get dressed. Joaquin is coming over. He's on his way."

"What's wrong?"

"The alarm system will be engaged. Don't touch it." He turned away from the door. "Hurry."

He heard the bathroom door slam as he returned to his post at the dormer window. After peering into the forest for a moment, he once again spotted the shadow, still lurking. Carter needed to be prepared for whatever came next. He put on a pair of lightweight hiking boots and a dark gray jacket from his closet. Then he armed himself with his Beretta automatic and an extra clip in the holster attached to his belt. Still not turning on the bedroom light, he fished around in the top drawer of his dresser until he touched a knit cap, which he pulled over his black hair. In his bedside table, he found a tin of black camouflage paint that he smeared across his cheekbones and around his jaw to eliminate the reflection of moonlight on his face.

He saw Daisy approaching on the landing, wearing nothing but a long T-shirt."

Don't turn on the light," he said.

"Why do you have goop on your face?"

"The stalker is here. I saw him on the other side of the road."

She gasped in surprise. Her eyes flickered with panic. "What should we do?"

"I contacted Joaquin to act as backup, and he's on his way. When he gets here, he'll come directly into the house and go to the kitchen. He'll stay here with you."

"And you? What about you?"

"Right now, I'm going outside to position myself. After Joaquin gets here, I'll go after the stalker."

She swayed and braced herself against the doorjamb. "Don't go."

Gently, he eased her into his arms and held her, hoping to shelter her from the fear that had become reality. "This might be my best chance to nab this guy."

Her freshly washed hair smelled of vanilla and orange blossom. Not a fragrance he'd ever used; she must have purchased shampoo at the store. That light, feminine scent would stay with him forever. "Joaquin will be here. You'll be okay."

She exhaled a shuddering breath, then separated from him, stepping backward onto the well-lit landing. When she lifted her chin, he saw a blush rising from her throat. Her green eyes hardened with determination. "Come back to me, Carter. You have to come back."

He didn't know the magic words to assuage her fear. And so, he talked about strategy. "I'll go downstairs first. Right now, the lights are off in the kitchen. After I go out the back door and reset the alarm, you go to the kitchen, turn on the light and wait for Joaquin."

Before he could take a step toward the staircase, she

caught hold of his sleeve. She clasped both of his arms, went up on her tiptoes and kissed him on the mouth with an outpouring of passion that had been building all night— actually, it had been building from the moment they met.

Her soft lips contrasted the pressure of her kiss. Her breasts crushed against his chest, and her hips joined with his. Unintentionally, she was making this moment more difficult. He didn't want to leave her. But he had to try to catch this stalker.

Tearing himself away from her, he rushed down the staircase and through the house. Carter didn't breathe until he'd gone out the kitchen door and reactivated the alarm system. The fresh, cool night air brushed his cheeks but did nothing to douse the fire she'd started in his heart. Their connection felt deeper than any attraction that might develop in a few days. He didn't believe in fate or kismet or any of that other romantic stuff, but he couldn't help a rising belief that they were meant to be together.

Yeah, great…but before the big, dramatic love scene got underway, he needed to catch a serial killer.

He ducked into the forest, taking a narrow path that led uphill, where he'd have a better view. Crouched behind a large, flat-topped boulder, he peered past his cabin to the opposite side of the road. The shadowy figure had barely moved. *Should have brought my rifle.* Though Carter didn't have a clear shot, he had skills as a marksman. He could make this shot.

His thinking recalibrated. *I'm not a sniper. Not a murderer.* His job was to apprehend this man and bring him to justice. To keep him from harming more women.

He heard Joaquin's Range Rover approaching and saw him pull into the driveway. Carter kept his gaze trained on the seemingly motionless shadow across the road. The stalker dodged the Rover's headlights, then stood to watch when his boss parked in front of the closed garage door.

Joaquin climbed out and strode up the inclined pathway to the door.

Though Carter couldn't see the front porch from where he hunkered down on the hillside, he heard the door close and assumed Joaquin had gone inside. How would the stalker react? Settle back and wait? Try to sneak close and peek through windows? Or would he run?

If he ran, which way would he go? Probably, he'd left his vehicle down the hill on his way to the cabin. There were several turnoffs and wide shoulders where he could have parked. Carter counted on the stalker going left, which was why he'd taken a position on the left side of his cabin. He was ready.

The muscles in his thighs tensed as he crept from behind the boulder. He wanted to get as close as possible before he made a charge. One silent step after another, he went downhill.

For no apparent reason, the stalker jolted into action... but he didn't go left. Instead, he jogged through the trees, heading up the road to higher ground.

Carter had to move fast. Still trying to be quiet, he broke into a run, dodging through trees and over rocks. About a hundred yards from his cabin, the road swerved. When the stalker reached that point, he'd be out of direct sight. In the moonlight, he saw the shadowy figure race around the curve.

Carter hit the road and turned up the speed. After struggling to find his footing on the forested hillside, the two-lane graded gravel road was a relief. Carter broke into a sprint. In seconds, he rounded the curve. To his right, a driveway led to his neighbor's cabin. Didn't look like anybody was home. He kept running uphill, careening around another twist in the road.

In the stillness of the night, he heard a car engine start up. *He's getting away.* Several yards ahead, he saw the unlit taillights of a car, driving fast and swerving. At the next zigzag in the road, the lights came on. The vehicle swiveled into the turn and disappeared.

Breathing heavily, Carter stopped in the center of the road. He stared at the turn where the taillights had been. Frustration poured over him. He hadn't seen the license place. Didn't know what kind of vehicle he was chasing. Those red lights hadn't belonged to a truck or a van—just a regular sedan like thousands of others on the road. His sighting of the stalker hadn't moved the investigation forward one bit.

He had to wonder if he'd actually seen anything. Was he so desperate to find answers that he'd invented a stalker the same way Daisy imagined monsters? He tilted his head up toward the thousands of diamond-bright stars scattered across the dark sky. They seemed to be laughing at him. In his black cap and camo makeup, did he look as ridiculous as he felt?

Jogging down the road, he went to the place he thought he'd seen the watcher. Behind a waist-high boulder, the grasses were trampled and branches on shrubs had been snapped. He took out the compact Maglite attached to his key chain and shone the beam around the area. The light showed him a flash of color. A long scarf in yellow and orange draped over a shrub.

No doubt about it. The stalker had gotten the last laugh.

As soon as Daisy heard Carter at the front door, she hopped off the kitchen stool and darted toward the sound. Joaquin followed, and she suspected he stayed close to protect her in case the person at the door wasn't Carter after all. The big man who ran the Salida headquarters for the National Park Service was about as subtle as a grizzly bear when it came to bodyguard work, but she appreciated his honest concern. Shortly after they'd met, he busied himself in the kitchen brewing herbal tea and talking about organics and the garden outside his cabin, where he cultivated indigenous Colorado plants, like wild onion, asparagus and skunk cabbage. He believed in living off the land. As a biology teacher, she totally agreed.

When Carter stepped through the door, she wrapped herself around him. If he'd been injured while trying to protect her, she would never have forgiven herself. She loosened her grip long enough for him to disarm and reset the alarm.

"In case you're wondering," Joaquin said, "you were never in real danger. If the intruder had tried to break in, Carter's alarms and my physical presence would have protected you. If all that failed, Carter would step in. He doesn't look tough, but our guy is kind of a badass."

"Takes one to know one," Carter murmured.

"I'm guessing the stalker got away," Joaquin said. "Any new evidence?"

Instead of answering Joaquin, Carter concentrated on Daisy, as though he was assessing her state of mind. "Maybe it's best if—"

"You can talk in front of me." Daisy wanted to know if her panic had any basis in reality. "How about this? You tell us what you found, then go wash the goop off your face."

"Fair enough." He glanced between her and Joaquin. "He took off before I could catch him, but I caught a glimpse of his taillights. It wasn't Slade's camper truck or the Wolff painting van. He was driving a regular compact sedan."

"A second car," Joaquin said.

"He was too far away for me to recognize the make or see a license plate." Carter shrugged. "I came back to the place where I'd seen him hiding. The grasses were trampled, branches broken, and I found this."

From the inner pocket of his jacket, he pulled out a plastic evidence bag. Inside was a silky scarf with streaks of orange, peach and yellow like a mountain sunrise.

Daisy turned her head and looked away. "I hate that he left this. Like a taunt."

"That's the reaction he wants," Joaquin said. "Part of the serial killer profile is narcissism. He's asserting his superiority by literally waving a flag in your face, daring you to catch him."

"Why?" She clenched her fists. "Why us?"

"My guess? He sees Carter as an adversary. I'm not sure why he's after you, but he is. It's almost like he's obsessed."

"Joaquin's good with profiles," Carter said. "This old hippie has spent much of his life studying people. He was a therapist before he joined the park service."

She'd already guessed the hippie part from the faded Ramones T-shirt under his uniform. Looking to him for an answer, she asked, "More specifically, why me? Why is this person coming after me?"

"Let's talk about it," he said, sounding like a therapist as he took her arm and guided her toward the kitchen. "Carter, you go wash your face. The camo makeup makes me think you should be in hand-to-hand combat with a gang of video game mercenaries."

Back in the kitchen, Joaquin freshened her tea and sat beside her at the black granite–topped island. He stirred a teaspoon of raw sugar crystals into his tea. "Before Carter comes back, I want to tell you about a phone call I got earlier tonight."

Daisy groaned. "Let me guess. My aunt Violet."

"Violet Rhodes of Leadville," he confirmed. "She's concerned about your safety and wanted a character reference on Carter."

"I'm sorry she bothered you."

"Not a bit." He smiled. "We talked awhile, shared a couple of gardening tips, and she grilled me about the weapons I carry."

"A long time ago, she had a peeper and bought a handgun for self-defense." She exhaled a sigh. "That was how her arsenal got started."

He stroked his salt-and-pepper beard. "After our conversation, I looked her up on the computer. She has a beautiful house and a very nice…garden."

Joaquin personified the sort of man Aunt Vi liked. Educated and healthy with a good job, plus he wore a uniform. Daisy ought to warn him before he became Vi's husband number five.

Carter strolled into the kitchen, wiping the last vestiges of camo makeup off his face with a towel. "What are you two talking about?"

"Daisy's aunt," Joaquin said. "She's coming to Salida tomorrow to look into the serial killer situation, and I promised to show her around in Pueblo."

Though Daisy would be delighted to have Joaquin involved in the FBI investigation, she really didn't like the idea of Aunt Vi being close. "Do you think it's dangerous for her to come?"

"I'll just have to protect her," Joaquin said. He turned to Carter. "Have you met the lady?"

"I have, indeed."

"Let me ask you, is Violet Rhodes a woman who likes a man who chops his own wood?"

"Wait and see."

Chapter Eighteen

The next morning, Daisy and Carter hit the road by seven o'clock. He'd brewed fresh coffee and filled two silver travel mugs. The excellent coffee and an energy bar she'd already gobbled up provided all the breakfast she wanted. After the excitement last night, Daisy hadn't expected to get a good night's sleep, but as soon as her head nestled into the pillow in the guest room, she sank into a deep slumber and didn't waken until Carter roused her this morning.

Holding her mug with both hands, she took a sip and quietly relived the moment when her eyelids had fluttered open and she'd seen him sitting on the edge of her bed—showered, sexy and shirtless. The sunrise had cut through a split in the blue plaid curtains to highlight his lips and his high cheekbones. The blue in his eyes was as deep and pure as…periwinkle flowers.

Her waking thought had been that she was dreaming, but then he'd kissed her forehead with a light pressure that, nonetheless, sent a buzz through her nerve endings. She'd pulled him down on top of her for a deeper kiss. Her hands had stroked his warm, well-muscled chest. More, she'd wanted more. But common sense had reared its ugly head, and she'd rolled away from him.

She raised her mug to her lips, took another sip and turned her head to study his profile as he drove. "What's going to happen after the investigation is wrapped up?"

"We take things one day at a time," he said. "The drive from Leadville to Salida is a couple of hours, not far enough to count whatever we have going on here as a long-distance relationship. We can still see each other."

"In a month, I'll be back at my regular job in Denver. My time at Aunt Vi's is temporary." She recalled their conversation last night. "Speaking of my aunt, what did Joaquin mean when he asked about chopping wood?"

"Recently, he told me that his ex-wife liked to watch when he cut logs for their fireplace." Carter grinned and wiggled his eyebrows. "Watching him get all sweaty made her horny."

"Oh, that's not good. He's thinking about Aunt Vi and sex before he even meets her. Once he gets the full flirting treatment, the poor guy doesn't stand a chance."

"He's not helpless, you know."

"But my aunt is really good at teasing and making men fall for her, even Jackknife Jones. Seduction is kind of her superpower."

His ringtone sounded, and he answered the cell phone attached to the dashboard. "Good morning, Agent Wiley. I have you on speaker. Daisy is in the car with me."

"FYI, we're in the process of serving a warrant at Slade Franklin's house. Forensic techs are crawling all over the place, and our boy Slade isn't happy."

"Didn't think he would be."

"We've already turned up evidence in his camper truck. A pair of pink cotton underpants and several long brown hairs."

Daisy's pulse beat faster as she remembered the first time she saw Rene Williams at the cemetery with her long brown hair fanned out around her head. "It's Rene."

"About the panties," Carter said. "Slade has a girlfriend."

"We've met, and she's almost as mad as her boyfriend. Not about him being a suspect, but she flew into a rage when she heard about the panties in his camper truck. She said they weren't hers. Apparently, she doesn't wear cotton. Only silk."

"Did she spend the night with Slade last night?"

"She was working as an internet influencer—whatever that is—until midnight at the opening of a new tavern, then she came to this house and stayed the rest of the night."

Daisy nodded. The timing made sense. If Slade had been stalking the cabin last night, he might have rushed home to meet Brandi, who gave him an alibi. "Anything else?" she asked. "I don't suppose you found blood."

"No such luck," Wiley said, "but we're impounding the vehicle for a closer inspection. Slade has serious objections. He uses his truck for work, and he's scheduled to be at a church renovation all week."

"Does he have another vehicle?" Carter asked.

"A 2012 Toyota Corolla. Not a lot of trunk space, but he can transport most of his tools."

She exchanged a glance with Carter. Slade might have been driving the four-door Toyota last night. The more they learned about him, the more suspicious he looked.

"Thanks for calling," Carter said to Wiley. "After I drop Daisy off at the autopsy suite with Dr. Julia, I'll be in touch."

When he disconnected the call, they were driving past the NPS headquarters in Salida. She saw only one SUV with the NPS logo in the small asphalt lot. Joaquin's car? Last night, he'd told her that Aunt Vi expected to be in Salida early this morning. She hadn't seen fit to contact Daisy with an update. *Typical!* Her aunt had scented adventure in the air and wanted to be a part of it.

"It's too bad Slade has an explanation for those hairs and panties," Carter said. "The first time we talked to him, he told us that he and Rene went skinny-dipping in Teacup

Lake. She changed clothes in his camper truck. It's possible she dropped a pair of panties."

Daisy would check the inventory of Rene's clothing from the autopsy to discover if she was wearing underwear when she was killed. Not that it made much difference. She might have left the panties a day or two before her murder.

"When we found Rene's body," she said, "she was barefoot, and her feet were clean, which meant she hadn't been walking through the forest. Maybe she'd just come from skinny-dipping with Slade. He might have slashed her throat while they were in the water, let her bleed out and carried her to shore, where he dressed her."

Images from that scenario flashed through her mind like a horror movie. She hated the way her imagination conjured up these scary pictures.

"I think you're onto something," Carter said. "Slade is a muscular guy. He wouldn't have any trouble carrying a petite woman like Rene. Did the autopsy show she'd been in the water?"

"She wasn't drowned." Daisy squeezed her eyes shut, trying to banish the mental image of tall, rangy Slade carrying the lifeless body of Rene through the trees. "He'd have to be naked, of course. So he wouldn't get blood on his clothes."

"Are you visualizing the scene?"

"I am." Her throat tightened. "It's horrifying."

"You have a talent, Daisy. I know you consider your imagination to be a curse, but it's also a gift. With the way you think, you could be a terrific detective."

But she didn't want to solve crimes. Involvement in the serial murders had showed her a peek behind the curtain separating civil behavior from nightmare insanity, and she had no desire to go deeper. She lifted the coffee mug to her lips and took another swallow. "I'll leave the detecting to others, thank you very much."

"Don't you want to catch the bad guys and see justice done?"

"Of course I do. But not by scaring myself half to death." She changed the topic. "Where should I take Brandi for lunch? You're a foodie. Give me some suggestions."

"I'm guessing the big-deal influencer will know where she wants to go. When you know where you're headed, text me. I'll join you."

"I hope she's not blaming us for the FBI raid this morning."

Daisy expected Brandi to be angry about the warrants and the search. It might be best to check with her before lunch. Until then, she intended to take a deep dive into practical anatomy, watching Dr. Julia perform the autopsy on Andrea Lindstrom.

AFTER CARTER PARKED and escorted Daisy to the door of the building where the autopsy would be performed, he texted SAC Wiley. The forensic team was in the process of serving Gerald Wolff with a warrant to search his vehicles and his home. Wiley invited Carter to join them.

When he parked in front of the Wolffs' house, he needed no introduction to recognize Gerald Wolff, who sprawled on the front porch of a two-story grayish house that was—ironically—in desperate need of a paint job. One of the front windows had been broken and patched with duct tape and cardboard. An aura of disrepair and neglect hung over the property.

In his worn cotton bathrobe, sleeveless T-shirt and striped boxer shorts, Gerald Wolff matched the unkempt house. His short white hair stuck out in spikes. The grungy plaid robe barely covered his belly. An oxygen tank sat beside him, and a cannula hooked into his bulbous nose.

Daisy had mentioned the reddened complexion common to heavy drinkers, and Carter agreed with her diagnosis.

Gerald squinted at him and demanded, "Who the hell are you?"

He pointed to the bison badge fastened to his belt. "National Park Service."

Realization dawned in Gerald's small, piggy eyes. "You're the park ranger who hangs out with Daisy. She attacked me, you know."

Carter had no problem seeing this angry, hostile old man as a murderer, but he couldn't picture Gerald lifting and carrying the victims or tying silk scarves around their throats. Sad to say, he didn't have the macabre style of this serial killer.

SAC Wiley opened the front screen door and motioned for Carter to come inside. "There's something you've got to see."

When Carter walked around the old man, he caught a whiff of the whiskey in his coffee. Inside the house, he wasn't surprised to see stacks of magazines and unopened mail. Used plates and mugs were scattered across coffee tables and on chairs. In spite of a central air-conditioning system and ceiling fans, the stench of rotting garbage mingled with the smell of turpentine from jars holding used paintbrushes.

He followed Wiley up the staircase, where the clutter persisted in a large bedroom. The covers and sheets were tangled in a wad at the foot of the bed. The bedside table held no fewer than four empty bottles of generic-brand whiskey. No doubt, Gerald's room. Across the landing, Eric's room seemed to have been transported from a different home. Tidy, dusted and vacuumed, the shelves held a neat array of books and photos, including several of Eric as a small, towheaded boy standing with a smiling woman who much have been his mom. Other photos showed his golden retriever. A flat-screen television sat beside a desk-top computer.

"An amazing contrast," Carter said. "Looks like Eric went out of his way to be as different from his father as possible."

"Not entirely." Back on the upstairs landing, he pointed Carter toward a closed door. "See for yourself."

In a small room, not much bigger than a walk-in closet, Eric had made an office with file cabinets and a narrow table that stretched all the way across one wall—a wall en-tirely covered with corkboard. Opposite, he'd hung a de-tailed map of southwestern Colorado with several locations marked by colored pushpins. Another table held a laptop and printer to create photographs from his phone. Eric had been busy. Dozens of photos of landscapes—lush hillsides, oddly shaped boulders and trees—decorated the corkboard.

After a brief study, Carter recognized the forest outside Butcher's Gulch. He saw the fence surrounding Doc Hol-liday's grave marker. These were photos of cemeteries.

Scattered among the graveyards, photos of people popped up at random. A picture of Violet Rhodes showed her at an outdoor shooting range wearing ear protection and aiming a tiny Glock 19. Several snapshots of an older woman who resembled the person Carter assumed was Eric's mother lined the right edge of the wall. There was one of Jackknife Jones, looking like a bum. Three photos of Daisy centered on the wall in a triangle. In one, she had a dreamy look in her green eyes as she leaned against the porch banister outside her aunt Vi's house. Another caught her in action, running toward the entrance of the FBI build-ing. The third picture had been taken at Teacup Lake, when Daisy had melted into Carter's embrace and they kissed.

Chapter Nineteen

Daisy observed Dr. Julia's skillful technique as she opened the skull of Andrea Lindstrom while preserving the damage done to her face and neck by animal predators. Previously, Dr. Julia had confirmed Daisy and Carter's hypothesis about Andrea being placed in the shallow grave at Butcher's Gulch and wrapped in a drop cloth, which the coyotes and other animals tore open. The really important discovery from this autopsy had been the presence of immature ten-lined June beetles in Andrea's ears and her other wounds. This species wasn't found in the higher elevation of Glenwood Springs and probably not at Butcher's Gulch. The ten-lined beetle was common in high desert areas like Pueblo.

Daisy couldn't wait to tell Carter. The beetle gave them tangible evidence that Andrea had been taken from Glenwood and brought to this area, where she might have been held for the three days between when she disappeared and when her body turned up at Butcher's Gulch. The killer might have a lair in this area. *A lair?* She shuddered at the thought and hoped the FBI searches at the Wolff house and Slade's might show where Andrea—and possibly others—had been held.

Other autopsy findings: faint ligature marks on her ankles and wrists, which indicated the use of restraints, but not in a painful way. She hadn't been handcuffed or duct-taped. There were no signs of torture. They found puncture wounds from a hypodermic needle.

The tox screen showed Andrea had been drugged as well as zapped with a stun gun. During that three-day period, sedatives could have been used to keep her quiet and under control but not unconscious.

The time for Daisy's noon appointment with Brandi was rapidly approaching. Though she hated to leave the autopsy suite, where she felt comfortable, Daisy waved goodbye to Dr. Julia and pointed to the time on a wall clock over the door.

Julia nodded. Through her plastic face shield, the doctor smiled. In a talk with Daisy, she'd shared contact information and encouraged her to visit while she was in the mountains. In addition to her responsibilities with autopsies, Julia ran a clinic on the Ute reservation and experimented with the medicinal properties of native plants.

"*Towaoc.*" Daisy whispered the Ute word for "thank you," truly grateful for the opportunity to spend time with this wise, generous woman.

On her way out, Daisy shed her personal protective equipment: mask, gloves, hair covering and suit. She strode through the pleasant waiting room into the hallway and out the door to the parking lot. Carter must have warned her a million times to avoid going anywhere by herself, but just in case, she held her key chain with her trusty pepper spray.

Brandi had arrived earlier and posed beside her cheery yellow Ford SUV that made a pretty contrast with her red, white and blue–striped T-shirt and red mini. Her long mahogany hair was parted in the middle and pulled up into two cute ponytails. She waved to Daisy, pursed her mouth in duck lips and snapped a selfie. Daisy groaned inwardly. *This is going to be a long lunch.*

"Hope you don't mind if I take photos for my vlog,"

Brandi said. "Is it okay for me to tell people you work for the FBI?"

"I'm a high school science teacher in Denver." Not comfortable with having her face splashed across the internet, she shook her head. "Don't mention the FBI."

"Yeah, right, you're a schoolteacher. Well, that's a snooze."

"Think about it, Brandi. You don't want me to tell all your followers that the FBI served a warrant on Slade, do you?"

"Guess not." She rolled her big brown eyes, clearly bored and frustrated. "What else can I say about you that's interesting? Something cool."

"Brighton's Bullion," Daisy said.

Brandi adored the story about Daisy's ancestor—the outlaw Sherwood Brighton—who left behind a treasure in gold bullion that had never been found. While they drove to Herbivore's, a trendy restaurant on the downtown Pueblo Riverwalk that offered a full vegetarian menu plus twenty-six different flavors of fruit drinks.

"I have a special parking permit," Brandi said as she zipped into a parking slot. "All this week, I'm visiting different locations on Riverwalk, promoting them and vlogging about their specialties."

"Is that where you were last night?"

"Yeah. I asked Slade to come with, but he said no. His loss."

Inside the restaurant, greenery abounded, and the air was redolent with the fragrance of mint, lavender and basil. Daisy ordered a mint iced tea, nonalcoholic.

"It's better with schnapps," Brandi said.

But Daisy didn't want a repeat of yesterday's mild intoxication. She needed to have her wits about her. Following a suggestion from the waitress, she ordered vegetarian lasagna with béchamel sauce. Brandi opted for a beet and broccoli salad with hard cider to drink.

After organizing a simple recording setup with a small camera and lavalier mics for both of them, Brandi asked Daisy to repeat her order into the camera. She did the same, then she clearly described Daisy's claim to the family treasure of gold bullion worth millions of dollars. "Tell me, Daisy Brighton, how big are all those gold bars?"

"It's about enough to fill a steamer trunk."

"Or a coffin." Brandi mugged for the camera. "Is that why you hang around at cemeteries?"

Daisy evaded the potentially dangerous part of that topic by launching into a fact-based discussion about cemeteries in the Old West and boot hill graveyards. Though Brandi kept smiling, Daisy could see the other woman's eyes glaze over. *Another snoozefest.*

When their food came, Brandi took pictures on her phone and engaged the waitress in a conversation about preparation. Finally, she turned off the recording equipment. "Nobody wants to watch us eating," she said. "Or talking with our mouths full."

After tasting the vegetarian lasagna and loving the creamy flavor, Daisy pursued her own line of questions. "You and Slade seem so different. Is he often gone on jobs?"

"He's kind of a loner. On the plus side, he's tall, has a great body and photographs well." She snatched up her phone and flipped to a handsome photo of Slade with his shirt off. On his upper left bicep, he had a heart tattoo that said, "Mama."

"See?"

"You've been dating for a couple of years, right?"

She nodded. "Since before Mama died. But we've broken up a couple of times."

"Were you taking a break from each other when he met Rene Williams?"

"Can you believe that little witch?" Brandi took a swallow of her cider. "Leaving her cheap pink panties in my honey-boo's camper? She didn't waste any time moving in on him."

Apparently, Brandi had never heard the old adage about not speaking ill of the dead. "Are you aware that she was tragically murdered?"

"Yeah, yeah." She rolled her eyes. "Boo-hoo."

Daisy moved to a wider focus. "Have you uncovered other evidence that he's been unfaithful?"

"I found a necklace. Actually, there were two of them, as if he bought one for me and one for some other girl. When I showed the jewelry to him, he said they were both for me. He was trying to decide which he liked best." She rolled her eyes. "But they were identical."

Daisy recalled the heart pendant worn by Eileen Findlay, the Ute woman whose body had been found not far from where they were eating. "What did the necklace look like?"

"A little heart. Cute but kind of chintzy. I wear it when I'm trying to relate to the people who follow my vlogs and podcasts."

Daisy asked, "Did he ever give you a scarf?"

"He tried. Mama was big on scarves, but I don't like them. I'm real careful putting together my outfits and don't want a drapey piece of material covering me up."

She remembered Brandi talking about how Slade had tried to get her to dress like his mother. "His mother kind of ran his life."

"Wasn't a bad deal. She left him a lot of money. You know, he's weird about being rich. Prefers to pay cash for everything." Brandi paused and looked around the restaurant as though scanning for other influencers who might steal her thunder. "This is why I wanted to talk to you."

"Okay."

"I think Mama left her sonny boy another property outside town."

Daisy felt a spike of adrenaline. "Like his own secret lair?"

"Or a love nest," Brandi said. "I think he goes there on his long weekends and fixes the place up. Then he takes his little girlfriends there."

"Do you know where it is?"

Pushing the beets around on her plate, Brandi shook her head, clearly unhappy about the idea of her honey-boo with another woman. "I need you to help me find it."

"Have you asked him about it?"

"He swears there's no special place. Tells me that I'm his one and only, but I've got a sense about this. Can you use your FBI contacts to find the location?"

"I can try." Though it seemed likely the FBI could turn up an address, she didn't know for sure. "Do you have any other clues about the love nest?"

"The old bat who lives next door to Slade, Mrs. Gallagher, used to be tight with Mama. Hates me, of course. But Slade does little repairs around her house, and she thinks he's wonderful. Could you talk to her?"

"I don't see why not," Daisy said.

She spotted Carter at the door of the restaurant, wearing jeans and a lightweight tan blazer to hide the clip-on holster on his belt. She waved him over. Though she'd checked before inviting him to join them, Daisy noticed that Brandi's expression darkened as she watched Carter's progress. She muttered, "I blame your ranger friend for the FBI raid."

With one hundred percent honesty, Daisy said, "Carter wants what's best for everybody." *Which means finding the serial killer.* "I'm sure he'll help find Slade's secret property." *If only to call in the forensic team.*

"Yeah? Well, okay." Brandi rose to shake hands with Carter. "Wish I could stay, Mr. Ranger, but I've got a full day."

"Nice restaurant," he said. "I've never been here before."

"Lunch is on me." She waved the waitress over and paid with a $100 bill. "Get them whatever they want."

"How can I get in touch with you?" he asked.

"Daisy has my number."

"What about Slade's cell phone?"

"He might answer but probably not. He's doing renovations for a little chapel in the forest. And he never gives me names and numbers for his clients." Before flouncing away from Herbivore's, she gave Daisy a hug and whispered, "If you find anything about you-know-what, call me."

"I will," Daisy promised. And if Slade turned out to be a killer, she'd make sure Brandi had an appointment with a reputable therapist.

When Carter took a seat beside her at the table, she couldn't tear her gaze away from him. If possible, he seemed to get better looking every time she saw him. "Sorry you didn't get to ask Brandi any questions."

"I didn't expect much. What did she tell you?"

"She wanted me to use my FBI contacts—as if I had any—to find the location of her boyfriend's love nest in a property left to him by his mama. Can we do that?"

"We can ask. If there's a record, we can probably dig it up."

"Hungry?"

Quietly, he said, "I grabbed a burger before I came here. I'm surprised all these noncarnivores can't smell the beef on me."

She took her last bite of the truly delicious lasagna. "Want to get out of here?"

"This is not a good place to discuss serial killers. Too healthy."

They stepped outside into a spectacular, clear, blue-sky day. Not yet as hot as July and August but warm. She was glad to take off her long-sleeved dark blue sweater. As they strolled along the paved path following the winding course of the Arkansas River, a light breeze slid across the water and ruffled the manicured foliage that lined the walk. Bronze statues of bison, antelope and an old-time cowboy on horseback hid among colorful displays of daisies, lavender and sage.

For a carefree moment, she reveled in the scent of fresh-mowed grass and the laughter of kids who chased each other through the park. An involuntary smile lifted the corners of her mouth. On a day like this, with Carter at her side, Daisy felt upbeat and positive. But happiness didn't last forever. The monsters in her imagination hadn't vanished—they were merely hiding.

She turned to him. "You need to know about the ten-lined June beetle."

"Something you found in the autopsy?"

She nodded and explained how the immature beetles were only found in high desert terrain in late spring or early summer, which meant Andrea had been brought to someplace like Pueblo. "Maybe to his lair. She must have been killed here and dead for several hours, which is how the beetles got into her wounds."

"Then he wrapped her in a drop cloth and took her to Butcher's Gulch."

A growing awareness reminded her that another victim had been found on the Riverwalk. Daisy didn't want to know the location—didn't want those dark thoughts to take seed and grow. "I guess we've pretty much decided that Slade is the killer."

Taking her hand, he pulled her off the walkway to a bench, where they sat, watching the kids playing and the tourists and paddle boats shaped like giant rubber duckies. He cleared his throat. "I have to tell you what the FBI found at the Wolff house."

She braced herself, knowing from his serious expression

that this wasn't good news. She lifted the brown cowboy hat from his head so she could see the truth in his periwinkle-blue eyes. "What is it?"

He told her about the office Eric had designed for himself on the second floor of the house—a private space with a corkboard wall where he posted photographs, mostly of outdoor scenery. "Cemeteries. Including the boot hill at Butcher's Gulch and Doc Holliday's grave."

"Murder sites." In spite of the warm sun beating down on her back, her blood ran cold. She laced her fingers with his and held on tight. "What else?"

"There were pictures of a woman I think is his mother, who divorced Gerald. Also, photos of Aunt Vi, Jackknife Jones and you. Three photos of you, including one of us kissing."

All the clues pointing toward Slade crumbled to dust. Here was tangible proof that Eric Wolff was, at the very least, a creepy stalker. At worst...a serial killer.

She inhaled a deep breath, hoping to pump fresh air into her lungs. "Anything else?"

"I talked to Joaquin earlier. Before I left the house, he showed up with your aunt."

Compared with being the star photo on a stalker's corkboard, Aunt Vi's appearance almost counted as good news. "Did they see Eric's office?"

"I managed to keep Vi away from there, even though she demanded full access to everything. I also hid an envelope Eric had addressed to you."

"Isn't that illegal? Tampering with evidence."

"I fully intend to hand it over to Wiley." He reached into the inner pocket of his tan blazer and pulled it out. "I thought you should see it first."

She opened the unsealed envelope and took out a photocopied letter. Like the last one Eric had given to her, this was from Annie Brighton to Morris Wolff. The language of the long-ago lover was graphic and dripping with long-ing—until she mentioned the bullion.

Daisy read aloud. "'Sherwood thinks he's the boss, but the old fool is utterly wrong. Mark my words. I'll take that gold to the grave with me.'"

She thought of the grave at Butcher's Gulch. They needed to get an exhumation order.

Chapter Twenty

After Carter put in a call to Wiley about tracking down the out-of-town property that Mama Franklin had left to Slade, he and Daisy got back into his SUV and set out to visit Mrs. Gallagher, the neighbor lady who liked Slade but not his girlfriend. These efforts were important but not his primary goal. Everything he did, every motivation, every thought centered on one job: protect Daisy.

Eric the stalker was obsessed with her and a definite threat. Papa Wolff, Gerald, might attack for no other reason than Daisy had zapped him with her pepper spray. As for Slade… Carter didn't know why the mama's boy would be interested in Daisy, but he was dangerous.

When he parked outside Slade's house, he noticed the lack of vehicles. Slade's camper truck—usually in the driveway—had been confiscated by the FBI for further processing. His garage doors were open, showing an empty space where he probably kept his Toyota. And Brandi hadn't returned with her yellow Ford. Nobody was home. *Good.*

As they approached the next-door neighbor's front door, Daisy said, "I think you should do the talking. This lady seems to be partial to men."

Mrs. Gallagher opened the door a few seconds after Carter pressed the doorbell, which made him think she'd been watching and waiting. A tiny woman with a crest of red hair and bright eyes magnified by oversize glasses, she reminded him of a woodpecker. He introduced himself and showed his badge. "Ranger Carter of the NPS. Are you Mrs. Gallagher?"

"A forest ranger, eh?" She squinted up at him. "I saw you next door. And this lady?"

Daisy stuck out her hand. "I'm a high school science teacher."

"Oh, my." Mrs. Gallagher shook hands but wasn't friendly. Her skinny arms wrapped around her middle, and she didn't ask them to come in. "What do you want?"

"We're working with the FBI," Carter said. "And we heard that you were close to the late Mrs. Franklin."

"I'll bet that Brandi girl told you." She sniffed, sticking her nose in the air. "Elizabeth would have despised her. She wanted the best for Slade, and that ain't Miss Brandi, flaunting herself all over the computer. Shameless, that's what she is."

Carter hoped to keep this meeting short, and so he didn't push her to invite them into her house. "Do you know if Elizabeth Franklin owned a property outside town?"

"What if she did?" Mrs. Gallagher stuck out her pointed chin. "There's no law against having four acres of property right near a lake that's full of trout."

"Sounds like you've been there."

"Maybe I have, but not in a long time. The last year before she passed, Elizabeth wasn't up to taking trips. I saw her almost every day, though. Brought her and Slade casseroles and roast beef for sandwiches. Slade loved my snickerdoodle cookies."

Once she got started talking, she didn't have a stop button. He interrupted, "Do you have an address? Can you tell us where the property is located?"

"Sorry, Ranger. I don't see very well, and I didn't drive. It was in a forest. Not the mountains. The name of the lake was Shelby or something like that. Elizabeth's cabin was at the end of a road that was blocked off with a gate and a sign—No Trespassing."

The perfect place for a love nest. Or a villain's lair. "Do you remember anything else?"

"Ask Slade? She left the property to him." She pushed her door open a bit wider. "Say, why don't you come inside and have some cookies and milk?"

He took a step backward, fearful that if they went through that door, they'd never escape. "Thank you, Mrs. Gallagher, you've been very helpful."

"Come back any time." She waved as they walked away.

At the street, Daisy grinned. "I was right. She prefers good-looking men. Did the location of Elizabeth Franklin's cabin sound familiar?"

"Too familiar. There are hundreds of lakes with little cabins and No Trespassing signs." He'd need to cross-reference names of lakes on a map. "Let's check in at the FBI. Maybe they have something more accurate."

The tide of evidence had begun to turn in their direction. Every move they made turned up another piece of the puzzle. When they found Slade's lair/love nest, he hoped they'd uncover evidence that he'd taken the victims to that place. Or not.

"What happened with Aunt Vi and Joaquin?" she asked.

"I'm hoping they went back to Salida, but I doubt it. Your aunt wants to investigate."

"Not surprised," Daisy said. "I'll bet she thinks that if she looked into the case, she could solve it in a snap."

"The opposite. When Vi talked to Wiley and Hicks, she spewed dozens of compliments about the brave FBI. She might even have squeezed Hicks's bicep and giggled."

"Catching more flies with honey than with vinegar," Daisy said. "I told you she was really good at flirting."

Not like her niece. Aunt Vi was beautifully groomed, manicured and polished, while Daisy didn't seem to care about her appearance. Her beauty seemed natural and almost careless. Instead of flirting, Daisy blurted. She managed to get her way but lacked subtlety and skill in manipulating others. Instead, she came right out and said what she thought. Though he liked her straightforward attitude, her rational explanation of why they shouldn't start any kind of physical relationship didn't make him happy. A little flirting might have softened the blow.

Glancing across the console, he noticed the glimmer of sunlight in her blond hair, and he wanted to comb his fingers through the strands that fell from her ponytail and curled around her neck. He appreciated her posture and her sharp attention to all that was going on around her.

"Look over there." She pointed through the passenger-side window. "I know that truck."

"Jackknife Jones." What the hell was the old codger doing in Pueblo? More importantly, why had Carter dismissed him as a suspect? "He doesn't seem to be following us."

She winced. "He could be after Aunt Vi."

Though Carter could have turned on his flashers and forced the beat-up truck to pull over, he'd rather see where Jackknife was headed. "I'm going to follow him."

Apparently, the old man wasn't familiar with traffic patterns in Pueblo, and Carter knew from prior conversations that the aged truck didn't have GPS. They trailed him in a meaningless meander through the streets until he hit the one-way street with the FBI headquarters building. Jackknife zeroed in on his destination. Joaquin's NPS vehicle was parked in front.

"You're right," Carter said. "He's not after you. It's Aunt Vi."

"How would he know where she is?"

"Let's find out."

When Carter turned on his flashers, Jackknife pulled

over to the curb in a No Parking area in front. After he parked and told Daisy to stay in the SUV, Carter got out of his car and drew his weapon, following standard procedure. "Show me your hands. Out the window."

Jackknife did as he was ordered. As soon as he saw Carter, he snarled. "You! Again?"

"Step out of the truck. Keep your hands in clear sight. Brace yourself against the bed of the truck and spread your legs."

"How come you're getting up my butt? I ain't done nothing."

"Assume the position."

Grumbling, Jackknife leaned against the car. He'd taken the trouble to clean up—probably hoping to impress Vi—and didn't look as disreputable as usual, despite the chaw of tobacco pushing out his cheek. Carter didn't actually think Jackknife was the serial killer, but the old man had been involved from the start. He patted him down, snapped on handcuffs and turned Jackknife around to face him.

"I have questions. If you answer correctly, you can go."

Jackknife nodded his head toward the building. "What about Vi? She said she was going to the FBI headquarters in Pueblo, and I wanna see her."

"Did she tell you she wanted to see you?"

"Maybe not. But I don't like her riding around with that other ranger guy."

"You drove around in circles before you dropped Daisy off near Butcher's Gulch. Why?"

"I was lost."

How dumb was this guy? He'd already admitted to taking a payoff. "Did someone pay you to make sure she didn't arrive until after dark?"

"I don't have to tell you."

"Suit yourself." Carter clamped his hand around Jackknife's upper arm, headed toward the FBI headquarters and started reciting the Miranda warning as if he intended to arrest the old man. "You have the right to remain silent. Anything you say—"

"Okay, stop right there. I'll talk," he said. "A punk kid showed up at my doorstep and gave me an envelope."

"What else?"

Inside were two $100 bills and instructions. If'n I drove Daisy around till after dark, I'd get another two bills." His mouth pulled down in a scowl. "I'm still waiting on the second half of the payoff."

"Why didn't you tell me this before? You never mentioned $100 bills."

"Because. I thought you'd take them away from me."

"Had you ever seen the kid before? Did you know the person who paid you?"

"That's a big, fat no."

His story didn't amount to proof but was very suggestive. Slade preferred to keep his money in cash, and Carter had seen Brandi pay for lunch with a $100 bill. If Jackknife had kept the payoff, they might be able to get prints. "Do you have either of the hundreds?"

"Hell, no. I already spent it." He stuck out his chest. "This here is a new jacket. I figured Vi would like it."

Carter believed Jackknife leaned toward a career of cheating, lying and petty scams. But was he a serial killer? Booking him at the local jail felt like a waste of time and effort. "Turn around and let me take the handcuffs off."

"You're cutting me loose?"

"With a warning. Until this serial killer is arrested, stay away from Daisy Brighton and her aunt Vi. If I catch you sniffing around again, you're going to jail for being a public nuisance."

He rubbed his wrists and gave Carter a sly grin. "See you around, Ranger."

"One more question. Did you really see Annie Brighton's grave at Butcher's Gulch?"

"The person who paid me gave me that hint." He shifted his tobacco from one side of his mouth to the other. "Maybe it was that Eric Wolff kid. He's always hanging around."

The pendulum swung back toward Eric. Which was it? Eric or Slade? Carter needed the answer before anyone else was killed.

Chapter Twenty-One

When Daisy strolled into the FBI offices with Carter, she immediately recognized the tension that came from having an outsider—her aunt Violet—who thought she knew better than everybody else because she'd watched every episode of a TV crime show. Though Vi's flirting had bewitched Joaquin, the other officers and agents had not succumbed.

Special Agent in Charge Pat Wiley pulled Daisy aside and said, "Your aunt is a busy little bee. She's tidied up stacks of filing, made fresh coffee, organized the condiments in the snack room and lectured me on the proper use of DNA evidence. She reminds me of my mom. I don't want to hurt her feelings, but—"

"I understand." Daisy empathized. "I might be able to convince her to come with me to explore the two major graveyards in the Pueblo area."

"Yes, please."

Should have been an easy solution, but Carter didn't want Daisy to go anywhere without him. He cornered her in the hallway by the elevator and spoke softly. "Another graveyard? I don't like this idea."

"Wiley loves it." She grinned. "I should go. I don't want to be in the way."

"In my mind, you're the center of this investigation. Everything revolves around you. And you are in dan-

ger." His blue eyes—periwinkle blue—pleaded with her.
"Don't go."

"I don't want to hang around like an unnecessary appendage."

"A what?"

"An appendix." She chose a more appropriate comparison. "An organ that seems useless but can become infected and ruin everything."

"Not useless," he said firmly. "You're a lung or a liver."

"Or a pancreas?"

"Stay with me today." He glided his hand down her arm and took her hand, setting off a chain reaction of sizzling awareness. "Tonight, come home with me to my cabin."

Though his invitation wasn't specific, she understood exactly what he was proposing. As they stood in a public hallway where any number of people, including her aunt, could walk by, Carter drew an invisible curtain around them, shielding them from interruption. Tonight could be for them. Finally, they could lie together in his bed and make love.

She wanted that closeness, wanted to kiss him until her lips were bruised, to stroke her fingertips across his chest and to inhale his clean, masculine scent. No matter how irresponsible and impossible their relationship, she needed to join with him.

"I will come home with you tonight." Still, she didn't capitulate. "For right now, I should go to the cemeteries with Aunt Vi. Joaquin will be with us. He'll keep us safe."

He brushed her cheek with a light kiss and whispered, "Until tonight."

She could hardly wait.

DAISY STOOD IN the main parking lot at Rolling Hills Cemetery south of Pueblo and waited for Joaquin to run around to the passenger side of his SUV to open the door for Vi.

Before they left FBI headquarters, Daisy had checked the cemetery's registry for the 114,988 people who were buried on the nearly three hundred acres of manicured landscaping and statuary. According to the records, Elizabeth Franklin, Slade's mama, had a plot in a central area near the reflecting pool. Though she didn't know the first name of Hannah's uncle, there were several members of the Guerrero family. The most recently interred had a spot near Mama. Could that be how Slade met the young woman from Glenwood Springs? In spite of Eric's wall of stalking photos, she leaned more and more toward Slade.

Aunt Vi exhaled an impatient breath as she marched toward Daisy. "I don't know why we're wasting our time here."

Joaquin shuffled along behind her, his reluctance obvious. Like Carter, he preferred nature to human interaction, especially when the human—the lovely and somewhat irritating Violet Rhodes—thrived on conflict. She continued, "There's no record for Sherwood Brighton. Rolling Hills had barely been established when he died in 1896."

"I was thinking of Annie Brighton," Daisy said.

"His wife? But, sweetheart, you already found her grave in Butcher's Gulch." She glanced at Joaquin. "My niece is a genius in anatomy but sometimes forgets everyday details."

"Her burial site is important." Daisy reached into her backpack and found the letter from Annie to Morris Wolff that Eric had addressed to her. "Check out that line about taking the treasure to the grave."

Aunt Vi slipped on her silver-frame half glasses to read the sexy letter. She frowned and read it again. "Once again, it seems that our great-great-great-grandmother was a bit of a floozy, despite her renown as a seamstress of wedding dresses."

"There are a number of unmarked graves here," Daisy

said. "And it occurs to me that Annie might have been buried under another name."

"Wolff?" Aunt Vi groaned. "I hope you aren't suggesting that she married that cur."

"It's worth a search as long as we're here." She looked toward Joaquin. "Am I right?"

He gazed toward the west, where the late-afternoon clouds had already begun to take on the pink and gold of sunset. "We've got one and half or two hours of good light. We should use it."

Daisy handed out maps she'd printed from the online site and pointed them toward a section at the far southeast corner where tombstones with incomplete inscriptions—only a date or a first name—mingled with others. Vi charged toward that area while Joaquin and Daisy followed, strolling along a paved pathway. She continued to study the map, noticing that the grave of Slade's mother, Elizabeth Franklin, wasn't far from where they were walking.

This cemetery had an open, pleasant atmosphere. It was as friendly as a graveyard could be with plenty of visitors and groundkeepers. She felt safe enough to make a suggestion. "I want to make a quick stop. Why don't you catch up with Vi?"

"She's something else," he said as he watched her stride ahead of them. "Is she dating anyone else?"

"Second time this week someone's asked." And Joaquin Stanley ranked so much higher than Jackknife that they were hardly the same species. "At the moment, she's single."

"May I ask a personal question?"

"Go for it."

"How many former husbands?"

"Four. Two divorces and two deaths, including the love of her life. That was six years ago. She might be ready to get back into the game."

"Sounds reasonable."

Not wanting to interfere in this budding romance, she waved him on. "Keep going. Vi is waiting."

"And leave you by yourself? Hah! Carter would kill me."

"You can time me. This won't take more than five minutes."

"Just last night, you were being stalked."

Vi waved. "You two, hurry up."

"Go," Daisy said. "I'll be fine."

Reluctantly, he moved away from her as a group of ten or twelve mourners milled around them. "I'll be watching."

After consulting the map, she hurried along a pathway toward the central area, where she quickly found a square reflecting pool with a white marble statue of a praying angel with beautiful wings and flowing robes. In a quick moment, she found the white marble marker for Elizabeth Franklin. The epitaph said it all: "Gone but Never Forgotten. I Love You, Mama."

As Daisy reached out to touch the stone, she heard a voice. "Ever since the first time I saw you, walking alone and so serious, I imagined you here, close to Mama."

Slade loomed over her, gun in his hand. It was a huge weapon with an attachment on the barrel. She'd fallen into his trap. "What do you want?"

"If you make a sound, I'll kill your aunt and her ranger friend." He grasped her upper arm and yanked her away from the throng of mourners and closer toward him. "Come with me. Move fast."

When she stumbled, he poked the barrel of his gun into her ribs. "Quiet and fast."

She had no choice but to obey. When Vi and Joaquin were no longer in danger, she could deal with Slade. Maybe talk him into letting her go. Bide her time and find a way to escape.

Clearly, he knew his way around this cemetery. He dodged onto a narrow path that led between a mausoleum and a small chapel. No one—not Joaquin or Vi or any of the other people in the cemetery—could see them. Daisy hoped they wouldn't try to follow. But she heard Aunt Vi calling her name. If she and Joaquin ran toward the central area of the cemetery, Slade would have a clear shot—and he was a killer who wouldn't hesitate.

He slowed as they approached an open area with a low fence separating the cemetery grounds from a small parking area. Taking long strides, Slade dragged her forward. She heard her aunt shouting. Joaquin's voice joined hers.

A sob caught in Daisy's throat. Too late. *I'm going to die.* Should have stayed with Carter. Tonight they could have made love. Why did she wait?

At the parking lot, a man stepped out from behind a truck. Jackknife Jones had a gun of his own. He spit a wad of tobacco onto the asphalt. "You've got to be the guy who owes me two hundred bucks."

Slade cursed under his breath. "I don't know you."

"The hell you don't. I came to Pueblo to find you. Now gimme my money."

"Wasn't me."

"Then who?" His jaw dropped. "That Eric Wolff kid? It was him, wasn't it?"

Slade released his grasp on her, aimed and fired a handgun with a long tube attached to the barrel. A silencer? Jackknife went down.

Before Daisy could react, Slade pressed a stun gun against her neck. The painful shock of fifty thousand volts paralyzed her. She went unconscious.

No point in blaming each other. Or in rehashing what had happened and what they could have done differently. Joaquin and Vi had responded to the gunfire and witnessed enough of Slade's escape to say he'd headed west. They were on their way to FBI headquarters.

Carter went into action, charging into full-scale action, organizing an FBI task force dedicated to finding and arresting a serial killer. With authorization from SAC Wiley, he launched an aggressive police search for Slade's Toyota Corolla, using the license number on file. Following his suggestion, the FBI called in helicopters to scan the roads near Rolling Hills Cemetery.

Another possible source for information was Jackknife. Not dead. Not yet. An ambulance had taken him to the nearest hospital, where an ER nurse told Carter over the phone that he couldn't speak to the patient until after surgery. She'd also conveyed a message. Jackknife wanted to tell Carter he was sorry for lying. He thought the person who gave him two hundred bucks was Slade Franklin, but he was wrong. Eric Wolff, it was Eric.

Would it have made a difference if Carter had learned that information earlier? Eric was guilty of stalking Daisy, but Slade was a killer. He'd abducted her. Where the hell had he take her?

Agent Wiley picked his way through the cubicles and stepped up beside him. "I've got an off-road map and coordinates for Elizabeth Franklin's property near Lake Charlotte. A squad using a chopper can be there fast. To catch the bastard off guard."

"Do it."

Wiley gave him a thumbs-up and made a call.

Though Carter agreed with the plan, he didn't have a good feeling about Mama's cabin behind the No Trespassing sign. The location seemed too obvious, and Slade was as slippery as a weasel. If he felt them closing in, he'd dodge…and take Daisy with him.

When Wiley ended his call, Carter asked, "How fast can we get there?"

"We?" The veteran FBI agent combed his fingers through his thinning hair. His easygoing smile flattened into a stiff, straight line. "We aren't involved in this operation, Carter. This is a crack team from Fort Carson. They'll get him."

"I want to be there."

"Sorry." Wiley shrugged off Carter's concerns. "Leave this op to the experts. They're expert in hostage extraction."

It made a difference when the hostage was Daisy. They had to think of every detail. The cabin could be booby-trapped. An overeager squad member might discharge his weapon too soon. Was Daisy drugged? Wounded? Too many things could go wrong.

Before a tornado of doubt overwhelmed him, he paced away from Wiley and exited from FBI headquarters on the eighth floor. Through the floor-to-ceiling window at the far end of the hallway, he saw the last vivid orange and purple streaks of sunset. Nightfall didn't bode well for a search.

An hour and a half ago, he and Daisy had been standing close together outside the silver elevator door at the other end of the hall, talking about spending the night together. The ding of the arriving elevator startled him. When the door opened, Joaquin charged toward him, red-faced and out of breath. "Never should have taken my eyes off her."

"And I should have known better than to send her to the cemetery where his mama was buried. Slade knows his way around that place."

"Swear to God, it was only a minute."

"Not your fault," Carter said. "Not yours. Not mine. Not Wiley's. Not Daisy's. The only one to blame is Slade Franklin."

"Wise words." Joaquin nodded. "I'm the one who is trained to be a counselor, but you're catching on. Now, what can I do to help?"

"Come with me. We're going to visit a little old lady named Gallagher."

When they left in Joaquin's SUV, Carter phoned Wiley,

told him that he was checking for other leads at Slade's house and asked him to report on the raid at the Lake Charlotte cabin. He looked over at Joaquin, who was making good time scooting through the streets of Pueblo at the tail end of rush hour. "Okay, counselor, give me the straight scoop on Slade."

"Narcissistic psychopath. Thinks he's smarter than everybody else. Has no moral filter to distinguish right from wrong."

"Why does he kill? Why these women?"

"I don't have enough information," he said. "Something to do with his mama."

Carter nodded, then changed the subject. "Where's Aunt Vi?"

"I was too distracted to watch her, so I contacted a local cop and arranged for him to drive her back to NPS headquarters in Salida. Travis can keep an eye on her until I get back."

"She could be in danger," Carter said. "I still don't trust Eric Wolff."

"Travis can handle it." Joaquin whipped into an illegal left turn and flew down a main road. "I like the lady. When this is over, I intend to take her to a steak house. You wouldn't think a dainty woman like Vi would go for a T-bone, but she loves beef. And carries a gun."

At this point, Daisy would have warned Joaquin about moving too fast with the much-married Aunt Vi. Thinking of her caused an ache in Carter's heart and an overwhelming need to bring her home safely.

Joaquin parked at the curb outside Slade's tidy yellow house with white trim, but Carter pointed him toward the neighbor's place. As before, Mrs. Gallagher answered the doorbell immediately. She smiled at Carter and peered through her extra-large glasses at Joaquin, scanning him from the top of his head to his size-thirteen boots.

"Well now," she said, "you're a big fella, aren't you?"

"Yes, ma'am."

"I'll bet you boys want some cookies."

Carter wanted information. Anything and everything she could tell him about the handsome, supposedly kindhearted son of her deceased friend Elizabeth… Slade Franklin, the serial killer next door.

Chapter Nine

Chapter Twenty-Two

A hoarse cough scraped the back of her throat. When she tried to swallow, the interior of her mouth felt dry and gummy. A headache stabbed between her eyebrows and penetrated all the way to the back of her skull, killing sensation and pinning her imaginary fears in place. How could she be afraid when confronted with all this reality, all this pain? Forcing herself to breathe, she inhaled sawdust and the sweet fragrance of lavender.

Daisy needed to waken but feared more agony. *Go back to sleep.* No. She couldn't quit. Not now. Nothing could hurt more than the full-body cramps twisting the muscles in her arms and legs into knots. Curled up on a long, wood bench, she cautiously tried to change positions. A soft cotton rope bound her wrists. Another linked her ankles. She was barefoot.

She opened her eyelids a slit and peered through the tears. In spite of many windows and a high, arched ceiling with open beams, the room held more shadows than light. Outside, night had fallen. Where was she? How long had she been asleep?

A soothing melody played on a discordant piano. "Moonlight Sonata" by Beethoven. She'd heard this music before. Recently. She poked her tongue through her lips, tried to swallow. So dry—her mouth was so dry.

She remembered. The first time she and Carter had visted Slade's house, he'd played the sonata. He must be here, plucking out the repetitive music on the keys. *He's here.* Now she was scared. She had to get away from him. Had to escape.

Struggling through the pain, she wriggled out from under the worn blanket covering her shoulders. She swung her legs down to the floor and sat upright on the first pew in a small sanctuary. The music surrounded her, choking off all other sounds.

Squinting, she sharpened her focus and saw a spinet piano beside a carved wood panel that separated the choir stalls from the altar, which was also lavishly decorated with a design of wheat and flowers. Slade's handiwork? Had he designed this place? For a homicidal psychopath, he was skilled.

And there he sat. Her captor. The man who would kill her.

Shoulders hunched, Slade continued to play the same notes over and over. He didn't seem to notice she was awake. This might be her best—maybe her only—chance to escape. Bent from the waist, she maneuvered her bound wrists so she could work on the knotted rope restraining her ankles. Unable to grip, her fingers were weak and clumsy. Her headache pounded mercilessly.

Slade abandoned the melody to hammer tunelessly on the keys. The harsh noise jolted.

"Daisy, Daisy," he sang. "Give me your answer, do."

Gritting her teeth, she tugged at the ropes. The loop around one ankle loosened. Would it be enough? Could she wiggle her bare foot and get free?

Slade rose to his full height, towering over the spinet. "Where are my manners? I should offer you a beverage. A glass of water?"

Sitting up and hoping he wouldn't look at her ankles,

she tried to respond but could only manage a few gam
bled syllables.

"What was that?" he asked. "You want a clear rum lik
the stuff Brandi gave you? Oh, I don't think so. Mam
wouldn't approve."

"Wa-wa-water."

"Much better."

With a dramatic flourish that didn't match his outfit c
jeans, flannel shirt and work boots, he pivoted and strod
through a door behind the choir stalls. Now was her chance

She inhaled a deep breath, pushed her foot free from
the rope and attempted to stand. For a terrifying moment
she balanced on the razor edge of equilibrium. *Don't fall
Don't fall.* Her mind spun out of control, shattering her vi
sion into a kaleidoscope. Into the past, the present and th
unknown future. *Can't move.* Hopeless, she sank dowr
onto the pew. Her eyes snapped shut, and she embrace
the familiar darkness. *Think. Use your head.*

She remembered the autopsy suite and Dr. Julia's calm
nurturing voice as she listed the combination of drugs Slad
had used on prior victims to control them. First, he hit them
with a stun gun to immediately disable their natural reac
tions. Then came the parade of sedatives, most of which
were designed to wear off quickly.

When she twisted to the left, she felt a possible spo
where he had administered a hypodermic—using the sam
technique he'd used on Andrea. When he appeared agair
in the sanctuary, it felt like she'd been waiting for an hour
But it had probably only been a minute or two. After con
gratulating herself on making sense of her drugged reac
tions, she tried a nonthreatening smile to let him knov
she'd cooperate.

He held the water glass to her mouth. "Small sips. Don'
want you to glug it and vomit."

Hoping desperately that he hadn't put a drug in the water

she tasted. The cool liquid moistened her lips. Instant relief lifted her spirits. She tried to speak again. "Head hurts."

He held the glass for her again. "You're going to be fine, aren't you? You're a strong one. I saw that in you at the first glimpse."

"When was that?"

"Butcher's Gulch. Don't you remember. You had just found Rene."

Of course she remembered. But if that was the first time he'd seen her, he couldn't have arranged with Jackknife to drive in circles. It didn't make sense, not unless the payoff came from Eric Wolff.

After he placed the water glass on the floor, he sat beside her and dug a vial of pain relievers from his pocket. He tapped out three. "Wash these down with water."

Reminding herself that none of his victims had been raped or shown signs of torture, she didn't fight him. But there was no way she trusted him enough to take his meds. "I'm okay."

He ran his large hand over his bristly, buzz-cut hair. "We both like graveyards, you and me. Such peaceful places, even those that aren't landscaped or as well maintained as Rolling Hills. I knew you'd go there sooner or later."

She tried to nod, but the motion proved too difficult. Her head lolled forward before she regained her balance. "Reflecting pool."

"It's pretty, isn't it? I knew Mama would enjoy having a plot close to the center of the cemetery. It took some masterful negotiating to get that space for her, but I persevered."

"You're a good son." She chose her words deliberately, expecting that he wanted to hear how much his mama cared about him. "She loved you."

"But I still haven't made her happy." He frowned. "Mama wanted me to find the perfect mate, someone who could clean my house and cook and take care of me. Are you that girl, Daisy?"

Hell, no. She didn't speak. Just nodded.

"I brought a pretty yellow scarf for you, just like the kind Mama wears. But I lost it."

When he was hiding outside Carter's cabin. "Do you have another?"

"Six or seven. Maybe I don't need to get more. Maybe you're the girl I'm looking for. Should we go into the kitchen and see how well you can cook?"

The fog in her brain had begun to dissipate. If she could convince him to take her into the kitchen, dozens of weapons—knives, boiling water, heavy fry pans—would be close at hand. Before she attempted her escape, she had to be able to run. When she flexed the quadriceps in her upper thigh, the muscles trembled. Not ready for action.

"I'll cook for you." She stammered. "W-w-what's your favorite food?"

"Mac and cheese, made from scratch with cheddar and gouda." He stretched his long legs straight out in front of him. "I was going to make some later. I've got all the ingredients, even the cheese, in the kitchen behind the rec room."

"Where are we?"

"The Nature Chapel of DSC, which stands for Divine Spirit Church." He looked around with a proprietary air. "I did most of the wood finishing in here. Now I'm renovating the kitchen. The pastor and the board had me submit a bid. As if there was any doubt? They hired me on the spot. I do good work."

That must have been his evening appointment after she and Carter visited him and Brandi. "You worked for them before?"

"Sure have. DSC is Mama's church." He scowled. "Your FBI buddies made my life difficult when they confiscated my truck. I couldn't bring all my supplies."

She didn't want him to be angry at her. "Not me."

"I know that, Daisy." He slid the back of his hand down her cheek, and she held herself very still to keep from flinching away from him. "You're a good girl. I don't like Ranger Carter."

Hearing his name spoken by this murderer disgusted her. Carter was such a good person, moral and strong and so damn handsome. Thinking of him, believing that she would see him again, gave her strength.

Slade gazed toward the altar, and his dark eyes softened. "I remember Andrea Lindstrom. A very good cook."

He'd held on to Andrea for an extra three days. Hadn't brought her here because he didn't have the job until a day ago. His lair? "Was she the sort of woman Mama would like?"

"Very much so. With her blond hair, she looked like you."

Not really. Andrea had had platinum hair, while Daisy's curls were streaked and honey blond. Still, she nodded. "I guess so."

"We were happy, me and Andrea. Then she tried to run away from me."

"Were you at your house in town?"

He gave her a suspicious look. "Why do you want to know?"

"Curious." She had to be careful. If he thought she was investigating him, he'd clam up—or, more likely, he'd decide she wasn't worth the risk and kill her. "Because Brandi is so jealous."

"Yeah, she is." He chuckled. "I took Andrea to a little cabin that Mama left to me. Very secluded. Private. Maybe you and I can go there."

She flexed her quads again and felt the strength returning to her muscles. Supposedly, Slade liked the cabin, but he hadn't taken Rene to his lair. And he'd killed Hannah on the spot at Doc Holliday's tomb. She wondered about Eileen Findlay, the Ute woman. "Did you take anybody else to Mama's cabin?"

"Too many questions," he said. "All you really need to know is how to take care of me the way Mama did."

"Can't help it." She managed to raise and lower her shoulders in a shrug. "I ask questions. I'm a scientist."

"Okay, Miss Scientist. You can ask one question. Only one."

Her investigation with Carter had answered many of the mysteries surrounding the serial murders, but they'd never understood the motivation. Knowing full well that the profile for a serial killer wouldn't fit the parameters of logic, she still wanted to hear what he had to say. "Why me?" She asked, "Why any of us, but mostly, why did you choose me?"

He stood and went to the low altar rail, which was carved and sanded to match the other wood in the sanctuary. Slowly, he paced from one end to the other with measured steps. "You probably won't understand."

Try me, you narcissistic creep. "I'll try."

"About a year after Mama died, my grief became so intense that I wanted to lie down in the grave beside her and end the torture of loneliness. I knelt by her grave, waiting for a sign, and I saw a young woman, also in pain about the death of a loved one. We wept in each other's arms."

She couldn't feel sorry for Slade. Not when she knew this tender story ended in murder. "What was her name?"

"No more questions." He resumed his pacing. "I took her to Mama's cabin near Lake Charlotte. She stayed with me, cleaned my house, cooked for me. After a few days, she wanted to go home, to return to her family. I couldn't let her leave me."

And so, he killed her. Adrenaline rushed through her

bloodstream, counteracting the influence of the drugs he'd given her. She said nothing.

He continued to pace and to talk. "I took her to Rolling Hills after dark to give her one more opportunity to say she'd stay. She didn't. I squeezed her neck until she stopped moving and laid her beside the grave of her loved one."

Pivoting, he faced Daisy. "That woman broke my heart. I waited by her body until dawn, when another woman came to the cemetery. That was when I knew."

Knew what? With the obvious questions burning in her throat, she waited.

"The woman who found the body was meant to be my mate," he said. "Mama sent her to me. That's how I've found all of you."

So random. And yet so specific. He had selected his victims based on who found the body. Eileen Findlay, killed in Riverwalk Park, was found by Hannah Guerrero, who was found by Andrea Lindstrom, who was found by Rene Williams. And now it was Daisy's turn. She had found Rene's body. This was her fate.

WITH TENSION RISING, Carter urged Joaquin to drive faster. He had to reach Daisy and know that she was all right. The narrow road leading to the Nature Chapel of the Divine Spirit Church was rutted, narrow and didn't look like it went anywhere. "Are you sure this is the right way?"

"I've been here before," Joaquin said. "I give lectures at local churches about fire safety and pass out souvenirs to the kids."

The road was so narrow that tree branches brushed against the passenger door. "This is too remote for a church."

"DSC has a huge congregation in Pueblo, but this chapel is only used for retreats and special events, like marriages and anniversaries."

"And abductions?"

Joaquin took his eyes off the road for a moment and shot him a meaningful look. "You care about her. I can see it. You've only been together a few days, but there's a connection."

Carter didn't bother denying their relationship. In addition to his education and training as a counselor, Joaquin was one of his best friends. "Damn right, I care. If he hurts her—"

"Don't go there. We'll stop him. We're lucky to have found this lead."

Luck had very little to do with it. Carter had been operating on a logical basis when he looked up Mrs. Gallagher. After she served "the boys" a plateful of snickerdoodles, she'd mentioned that her neighbor Slade—one of her favorite people—had a renovation job at the chapel and wouldn't be home until late. Moments later, Joaquin and Carter had set their destination.

During their drive into the forest, SAC Wiley kept them updated on the speakerphone about the progress of the hostage extraction squad from Fort Carson. Their approach to the little cabin near Lake Charlotte sounded like an action-adventure movie with choppers making strategic landings, surveillance from drones, heat-sensing equipment and flash-bangs.

After one particularly dramatic report, Joaquin said, "I'm feeling underequipped."

"Not me." Carter stared into the night. "I could tear this guy apart with my bare hands."

Joaquin pulled off onto a wide shoulder of the road. "We're here."

The Nature Chapel was about fifty yards from where they'd parked. Through the tree trunks of a pine forest, Carter saw lights from a square, white clapboard building with a short, fat steeple and a cross on top. An attached structure had a row of windows with no lights showing.

Carter heard a piano playing "Moonlight Sonata"—Slade's favorite melody.

From the speaker, he heard Wiley's report about the property at Lake Charlotte . "They broke into the cabin. Nice, neat parlor. Functional kitchen. On the dining table, he has an array of cutting and whittling tools. One of the closets is full of long, silky scarves. There's blood on the floor. This is the place. The serial killer's lair. But I'm sorry, Carter. He's not there."

"I know."

"How?"

"I'm listening to him play the piano."

While Joaquin gave SAC Wiley directions to the Nature Chapel, Carter dodged through the trees. As he approached the chapel, the music fell silent. Something was happening.

In the long, flat-topped building attached to the chapel, lights went on. Holding his Beretta at the ready, Carter got close and peered through one of the dirty windows. Slade chattered mindlessly as he helped Daisy walk through a casual gathering area that seemed to be a rec room. Her unfastened hair fell around her face, her gait was stumbling and she was shoeless. A soft, gray rope bound her wrists. She appeared to be unharmed.

While Slade escorted her around an open counter into a kitchen, Joaquin stepped up beside Carter. He gestured toward the end of the long building, and Carter nodded agreement. Ducking low so they wouldn't be seen through the windows, they moved to the end of the building. Carter turned the handle on a simple wood door. Unlocked.

"Inside, we split up," Carter whispered. "We go to the kitchen."

"I'll take the far door. You take the closer."

They slipped into the rec room and made their way

across a checkerboard pattern of green and red tiles—
Christmas colors. At the end closest to the door was a
three-foot-tall stage with a curtain. Several long, collaps-
ible tables were arrayed on the floor.

He heard Slade talking about how Mama made the best
mac and cheese. "You've got to boil the pasta until it's soft."

"Sure," Daisy said. "I can't cook unless you untie my
hands."

"Well, I guess that makes sense."

When he did as she asked, Carter was proud of her.
Smart move. He eased around the counter into the kitchen,
which was, apparently, where most of the renovation work
was being done. On the countertop near the sink, he saw an
electric handsaw and a nail gun. Hammers, chisels, screw-
drivers and other tools littered the other surfaces.

"Do you have any bacon?" Daisy asked. "I like to crumble some on top."

"I suppose we can try it, but that's not what Mama did."
Slade took the bacon from the double-wide refrigerator and
laid it on the counter beside her. "Anything else?"

"Frying pan," she said.

He lifted a cast iron skillet from under the counter and
placed it on the burner. Carter could tell from the way Daisy
looked at the pan that she was considering using it as a
weapon. He needed to act fast, to gain control. He stepped
around the center island and aimed his Beretta.

"Freeze," Carter shouted. "Police."

From the opposite side, Joaquin echoed the warning.

Slade ignored both of them. He bolted toward the counter, picked up the nail gun. Before he could shoot, Daisy
stepped up with the cast iron skillet and whacked him on
the side of the head. Slade went down.

Half collapsing, Daisy almost followed him to the floor.
But Carter caught her and held her close. He nuzzled her
hair, kissed her forehead.

"You found me," she said.

"And I'm never going to let you go."

After Joaquin secured the cuffs on Slade and put through a call to SAC Wiley, he turned toward them. "I'm sorry, Daisy. I did a lousy job of taking care of you."

"Not your fault."

Carter guided her away from the rec room and into the adjoining sanctuary. So many things he wanted to tell her. So many promises he longed to make.

He seated her in the first pew facing the altar and went down on one knee in front of her.

Alarm crossed her face. "No," she said.

"You haven't heard what I'm going to say."

"Better not be a marriage proposal."

He took her hand. "Daisy Brighton, I want more time with you. I don't know how long. Days, weeks, maybe a lifetime. Will you promise to spend time with me?"

"I will."

And then they kissed.

Epilogue

Three months later, in September, before the first big snow-fall, Daisy had started teaching science at the high school in Buena Vista, which was halfway between Leadville and Salida. Though she maintained her own apartment near the school, she spent a lot of time at Carter's cabin. On this particular Saturday morning, she stood in front of the clothes she'd hung in his closet, trying to make up her mind.

When he entered the bedroom, wearing only his black jersey boxers and his cowboy hat, she asked, "What's the appropriate outfit for an exhumation?"

"I don't think the dead will care." He set a steaming mug of coffee on the bedside table and slipped up behind her for a hug and a nibble on her earlobe. "You'd better decide quick. We've got to get rolling."

She took a swallow of rich coffee, turned to face him and groaned with pleasure. The taste was great. Looking at him was even better. She loved the way the morning light from the dormer outlined his muscular shoulders and the sprinkle of soft black hair that arrowed down his chest. "Do we have time for a shower?"

"We do. Wouldn't want you to turn up at Butcher's Gulch all dirty and stinky."

"I'm never stinky."

"After a day in autopsy with Dr. Julia, you're not exactly a bouquet of roses."

Taking a shower together saved water and was always a treat, even on mornings like this when they had to rush through the soaping, rinsing and naked groping. It had taken a long time for them to decide to make love, but once that switch was turned, they couldn't keep their hands off each other.

Stepping from the shower, she wrapped herself in a fluffy yellow towel, dashed into the bedroom and selected a forest green pantsuit—practical, sensible and respectful. She'd worn this outfit often during the trial of Slade Franklin. His insanity plea failed, despite evidence to the contrary, and he was found guilty of at least four murders and sentenced to life in prison. Brandi did live interviews during the trial, and her vlog became even more popular.

Daisy jumped into Carter's SUV, and they drove to Butcher's Gulch. This morning, Aunt Vi had arranged for the exhumation of the grave of Annie Brighton.

Though Daisy and Carter were early, a crowd had already gathered. Aunt Vi and Joaquin Stanley led the pack, and she was supervising three men with shovels who were digging into the soil of boot hill. Jackknife Jones—fully recovered—waved to Daisy and then spit tobacco juice on a nearby grave. She wasn't happy to see Gerald Wolff and his son, Eric, who had put together that stalker's wall that he explained to the police was only an artistic expression of his search for the bullion. He also admitted to paying Jackknife as a prank, a sick joke on Daisy.

After greeting Aunt Vi with a kiss and hugging Joaquin, she took Carter's hand and leaned toward him. In a whisper, she asked, "Isn't there something you can arrest one or both of the Wolff men for?"

"No law against being a jerk."

"When we find something," Aunt Vi said, "we promised to give them twenty-five percent."

"If we find something," Daisy said.

They watched while the hired men dug. Aunt Vi had gone to a lot of trouble to obtain proper paperwork, even though the boot hill wasn't owned or supervised by anyone. If they found anything…there was a question of ownership. The loot had been stolen, after all.

One of the shovels made a heavy clunk as it hit a solid surface. The coffin. In minutes the plain wood box was uncovered.

In spite of herself, Daisy was excited.

The lid was torn off. A sheet removed. Inside the coffin, packed from one end to another, was gold bullion—the treasure Annie Brighton had taken to the grave.

* * * * *

GUARDING A
FORBIDDEN LOVE

CARLA CASSIDY

To Darlene, the daughter of my heart. I love being your mother. You make me laugh and you make me proud. I love you…more!

Chapter One

Harper Brennan sat on her sofa and stared at the birthday cake in the center of her coffee table. The cake was a beautiful dark chocolate, frosted with a rich raspberry buttercream and baked in her very own bakery, the Sweet Tooth.

She'd planned a very small birthday party for herself this evening with two of her best friends. Unfortunately, they had both canceled at the last minute. So now Harper was having a pity party for one and she was the guest of honor.

She grabbed one of the silly pointed party hats she'd bought for the occasion and fastened it atop her head. She then stared at the single candle in the center of the cake. There was only one because there was no way the cake could hold forty-five candles.

Forty-five. She'd never dreamed at this age she would be celebrating a birthday all alone. A little over six years ago, she'd been happily married and had dreamed of opening her own bakery.

She'd managed to see her dream of the bakery come true, but her marriage had ended when her husband had left her for a twenty-five-year-old woman. Jerk. At least the happy couple had moved away so Harper didn't have to see them together every day.

She now sighed and picked up a lighter to light the single candle. In the mood she was in, she felt like bingeing on the cake and eating half of it or more. But she'd only eat a small piece because lately it seemed she only had to look at food and extra pounds jumped right to her tummy and hips. Damn middle age.

Before she could light the candle, a knock sounded at her door. Maybe one of her friends had made it after all. She jumped up off the sofa and hurried to the front door. She opened it to see Sam Bravano standing on her front porch.

"Hi, Harper. I'm here about the ad." He smiled, revealing a dimple in one cheek.

Sam Bravano. She'd seen him around town many times, but nothing had prepared her for seeing him so up close and personal.

Lordy, if she were ten years younger, she would so jump his bones. And fine bones they were. With his broad shoulders and slim hips, and his slightly shaggy dark hair and his unexpected, yet vivid green eyes, he was definitely a piece of hunky eye candy.

"Harper?" His smile faltered and she realized she'd just been standing there staring at him and maybe mentally drooling a bit. God, she hoped she hadn't really been drooling.

"Oh, yes…the ad. Uh, come on in." She opened the door wider to allow him entry. As he passed by her, she caught the scent of sunshine, a hint of a spicy cologne and intoxicating male.

"Please, have a seat." She gestured him to the chair facing the sofa.

"It's your birthday?" he asked as he sat.

"It is. Would you like a piece of cake? I'd planned a little party for myself with a couple of friends, but at the last minute they couldn't make it."

"That's a shame. It's no fun to celebrate your birthday all alone." He stood, and to her utter surprise, he grabbed one of the party hats from the coffee table and put it on his head.

Even the silly hat didn't detract from his attractiveness.

The man definitely knew how to wear a pair of worn jeans and a T-shirt. His skin was nicely tanned and overall, he just looked incredibly fit.

Harper sank back down on the sofa. "I was just about to light the candle when you knocked on the door."

"Then by all means, light the candle," he replied and that charming dimple winked at her once again. "How many other candles should there be?"

She laughed. "Enough to burn this house down." She lit the candle.

"Now, wait to blow it out," Sam said. "What's supposed to happen now is everyone sings 'Happy Birthday.' So, here goes…" to her surprise again, he stood up and began to sing the traditional song.

His lovely baritone not only filled the room, but shot a rivulet of warmth straight through her. She swallowed against unexpected tears that burned at her eyes. He was obviously being very kind to a lonely older woman.

"Now, make a good wish and blow out your candle," he said when he finished singing.

She made her wish and blew. "You can take off that silly hat now," she said as she took off the one on her head and set it aside. She picked up the cake server, cut a liberal piece, placed it on one of the decorative plates and then held it out toward him.

He swept the hat off his head and took the cake. "Wow, this looks delicious."

"I hope it is." She handed him a fork.

"Aren't you having a piece?" he asked.

"I'll, uh, have one later. You said you were here about the ad. Sam, I know your work around town and I know you've seen my storefront. It obviously needs a lot of work."

She'd gotten an amazing price on the piece of real estate on Main Street because it had needed a lot of cosmetic work and the mortgage company was eager to sell after the last owner had defaulted on their loan years before.

Since opening the business a little over two years ago she'd focused most of her work and finances on the inside. Now she had enough money saved and a small loan in place to begin the necessary work on the outside.

She'd placed an ad in the local *Millsville News* requesting a carpenter. Sam and his two brothers were all carpenters who often worked at one project or another around town. However, they weren't the only carpenters in town.

"It just needs a bit of a face-lift," Sam now replied.

Yeah, that makes two of us, she thought wryly. "I'd like to do a bit more than a face-lift in the back." As she told him her plans, he set aside his half-eaten cake and pulled out a notepad and pen from his back pocket and began to make notes. He also asked her some questions to clarify exactly what she wanted.

She was acutely aware of him. She'd had men in her living room before, but none of them had filled the space quite like he did. Even sitting, energy wafted from him. It wasn't an uncomfortable energy, rather it was soft and soothing and would instantly put a person at ease.

And yet she felt oddly on edge. Maybe it was because of the way he looked at her so intently, like what she said was the most important thing in the world. Or maybe it was because he exuded a self-confidence and strength in a quiet way. Then there was that dimple…

Oh, the young ladies in town must be positively mad about Sam.

"Business must be good for you to plan all these renovations," he said. He picked up his piece of cake once again.

"It helps to be the only bakery in town," she replied.

"There is that," he agreed with a grin. "But from what I've heard, you're good at what you do. And if this cake is any indication, you're damn good at what you do."

She felt a blush warm her cheeks. "Thanks."

"Did you always want to be a baker?"

The personal question surprised her. "From the time I was a little girl, I liked to bake and dreamed of having a place where I could sell my goodies to other people. My mom loved to bake, too, and we often worked together in the kitchen."

A quick wave of sadness fluttered through her. She'd lost her mother a little over a year before to a heart attack. It was three years after her father had passed away from the same ailment.

"Did you always want to be a carpenter?" she asked in an effort to stave off her sad thoughts.

"My dad was a carpenter all his life and I often went to jobs with him. I wanted to follow in his footsteps. Besides, I enjoy working hard and then seeing something tangible. I enjoy building something new, or rebuilding something old." He laughed. "And that was probably more than you wanted to hear."

"Not at all," she protested. "I've always been interested in what people do and why." She shrugged and felt a blush once again heat her cheeks. "I guess I've always been a people person."

"That's a good thing considering your business, right?" He smiled at her.

"Yes, I suppose it's a good thing," she agreed. She held his gaze for a long moment and then looked down at the cake. "So, what happens now?" She gazed at him once again.

"What I'd like to do is come to the bakery tomorrow morning and take some measurements and check things out. It's the only way I can give you a close estimate as to what all this is going to cost," he replied. "Will nine o'clock work for you?"

"That would be just fine," she agreed.

He stood. "I would encourage you to get several estimates, but I'm betting I can beat anyone else's price and I definitely do better work than anyone else in town." His green eyes sparkled brightly at his last words.

She got up as well and walked with him to the front door. He was a tall drink of water and towered over her shorter frame. She opened the door and then gazed up at him. "Thank you, Sam, for sharing my birthday with me."

He smiled. "It was my pleasure, Harper. I'll see you tomorrow."

Good Lordy, the man looked every bit as good going as he had coming. When he reached his pickup truck in the driveway, she closed her door and locked it.

As she carried the cake and then the dirty dishes to the kitchen, she thought about Sam's suggestion that she get estimates from other places. She didn't intend to waste her time.

She'd already spoken to several people who'd had work done by Sam and his brothers, and everyone had said they were hardworking, delivered on time and had been very fair with their prices. So, why get other estimates?

The only reason she'd placed the ad in the paper was because she had been afraid that Sam and his brothers would already be tied up with other jobs.

She sat at the kitchen table with a small slice of cake before her. It was a slow time at the bakery right now. Fourth of July had passed and the next big holiday was still a couple of months away. Thank goodness she had regular customers who came in daily for coffee and a cinnamon roll, a slice of cake or cookies.

Her birthday cake was delicious and once she'd put it into the refrigerator, she headed for her bedroom even though it was relatively early. Bedtime always came early for her because she tried to be in the bakery by five in the mornings.

Once she was in bed, she couldn't help but think about Sam. He seemed like a nice guy. She guessed he was around thirty years old. Too bad he wasn't, at the very least, ten years older, although even then he would be far out of her league.

She turned over on her back and stared up at the ceiling where moonlight danced in and created flickering shadows. She wouldn't mind having a man in her life again. She missed eating dinner with somebody. She missed intriguing conversations and laughter. She missed watching something as simple as a sunrise or a sunset with a special somebody.

She finally fell asleep and into totally inappropriate and delicious dreams of Sam Bravano.

SAM WHISTLED A cheerful tune as he left Harper's place. The cake was still a delicious taste in his mouth and the woman who had baked it intrigued him.

Harper was a cute little thing with short, curly dark hair and bright blue eyes. She had captured his attention more than once, whenever he saw her out and about in town, although he knew little about her. All he really knew was she had been divorced years ago and owned the bakery.

It had definitely been kind of pathetic to walk in on her having a birthday party all alone. She'd looked charming even with the silly party hat atop her curls. He had no idea what had possessed him to sing to her. He didn't normally do things like that but it had just felt like the right thing to do in the moment.

He pulled away from her house and headed home. As he drove down the main drag of the small town of Millsville, Kansas, a sense of enormous pride filled him. He loved this town and he had worked on several of the storefronts, transforming them from old and tired facades to colorful places that breathed of new life.

He wasn't surprised when he pulled up in his driveway to see his two younger brothers lounging in the two wicker chairs on the front porch. Tony and Michael almost looked like twins despite there being almost two years' age difference between them.

They both had the Bravano dark hair and brown eyes. Sam had no idea where he'd gotten his green eyes from. His father had joked that the mailman had bright green eyes, but there was no doubt that Sam was his father's son. He looked just like his father where Tony and Michael favored their mother. The two brothers sat up straighter in the chairs as he pulled into the driveway.

Sam had bought the two-story house a year ago. He'd gotten a good price for it because it had needed a lot of work and the former owners had just wanted out. His idea was to get it back into good shape and either remain in it or flip it, depending on what the housing market was doing when he got it all finished.

Because his two brothers still lived at home with their mother, they often popped in at his house in the evenings to drink a few beers and shoot the breeze.

Tony wasn't dating anyone in particular at the moment and Michael had an on-again-off-again with his girlfriend named Paula.

"Good evening, boys," he said as he approached them.

"Hey, Sam," Tony said and got up from his chair.

"Where have you been?" Michael asked, also rising from the chair.

"Since when do I need to check in with you?" Sam asked good-naturedly as he unlocked his front door.

"Just wondering, that's all," Michael replied as he and Tony followed Sam through the front door. Tony beelined directly into the kitchen and reappeared a moment later with three beers in hand.

He tossed one to Michael, who had reseated himself on Sam's sofa, and then one to Sam, who then eased down in his recliner. "So, what's new?" Sam asked once they were all seated with their beers cracked open.

"Paula and I broke up again last night," Michael said mournfully.

"Have you ever considered that maybe she's not the right one for you?" Sam asked.

"But I'm crazy about her," Michael lamented.

"You're a schmuck," Tony said. "That girl leads

you around like a puppy dog. When she snaps her fingers, you jump. You need to get better game, bro."

"What he needs is a better girlfriend," Sam observed.

"I love Paula. I just need to figure out what she really wants from me," Michael replied. "Once I figure it out, we'll be just fine."

As his two brothers complained and moaned about their love lives or lack thereof, Sam silently sipped his beer. Sam was ten years older than Michael and eight years older than Tony.

At thirty-three years old, Sam had been through the romance wringer. He'd dated a lot of women, but hadn't yet found that special someone. Lately, he felt a quiet desperation wafting from the women he dated. It was the desperation to get married and have babies before time passed them by.

While Sam would love to find a woman who would want to share his life with him, he'd never really wanted children and he wasn't even sure the whole marriage thing was right for him.

Of course, his mother was on him all the time about giving her grandbabies, but he figured his brothers or his older sister, Lauren, could fulfill that wish for their mother.

"So, really…where were you this evening, Sam?" Michael asked again when the conversation about their love lives had finally waned.

"I answered Harper Brennan's ad in the paper for

a carpenter. She wants to have a little work done at the Sweet Tooth," Sam replied.

"Does that mean we all have a new job?" Tony asked. "We've still got to finish up the gazebo in the town square." Several weeks ago, the members of the town council had hired them to build a gazebo that people in town could enjoy.

"There isn't that much left to do on that job. I figure you two, along with Bud and Aaron, can finish things up there," Sam replied. Bud Kurtz and Aaron Palmer were a couple of teenagers who were always up to earn extra money by working for the Bravano brothers.

"What exactly does Harper want done?" Tony asked.

"I'm not exactly sure. I'm meeting her in the morning to discuss the specifics. From what little she already told me I should be able to handle a lot of it on my own. However, I'll need you two to help me there in a few weeks or so," Sam said.

He found it odd that for some reason he was reluctant to share with his brothers too much about his time spent with Harper this evening. He also found it odd that he was also reluctant to have them working with him there, at least initially.

"Have you heard if Dallas has any more clues in Cindy's murder?" Tony asked, changing the subject.

"That was creepy as hell," Michael said darkly.

"As far as I've heard he's no closer to finding her murderer," Sam replied.

It had been a little over a month since the body of Cindy Perry, a young woman who had worked as a waitress at the local café, had been found in Lucas Maddox's cornfield.

She'd been trussed up to a pole like a human scarecrow. She'd been stabbed to death and, according to local gossip, her mouth had been sewn shut with thick black thread and her eyes had been missing.

Dallas Calloway, the chief of police, had quickly let it be known that Lucas wasn't a suspect in the murder. Unfortunately as far as Sam had heard, there didn't seem to be any viable suspects. The murder had definitely cast a pall over the whole town.

"It's got to be somebody Cindy made mad," Tony said.

"The person who did that to her was more than mad," Michael added darkly. "It was somebody who was sick to do those things to her.

Thankfully his brothers didn't stay too long after that and the next morning at quarter 'til nine, he pulled up and parked in front of the Sweet Tooth Bakery.

The bakery was in a good location on Main Street, and Harper's house was just a little over a block away. The commercial building had rotting boards and was painted a fading, tired brown. The only saving grace was the large bright pink sign that hung over the doorway. It not only had the name of the place on it, but also an illustration of a cupcake with white icing and pink sprinkles.

The sign could remain, but most all of the wood on the front either needed to be replaced or painted. The air just outside of the building smelled absolutely mouthwatering.

He'd never been inside the business before even though he enjoyed cakes and cookies and such as much as the next person. But his mother baked goodies regularly so he'd never felt the need to go into the bakery.

He opened the front door and stepped inside. In here the scents were even more delicious. Directly ahead of him was a long glass display case holding beautiful cakes, cupcakes and a variety of other sweets. A coffee machine was behind the counter, one of those fancy ones that spewed out straight coffee or cappuccino or hot chocolate.

There were several high round-topped glass tables with pink-and-white-striped chairs. The walls were white with pink trim and there were several large photos on them depicting cakes he assumed Harper had baked. Harper was nowhere to be seen but there was a bell on the counter and so he rang it.

She came through a doorway that led to the back. She was clad in a pair of jeans that hugged her slender legs and a blue blouse that did amazing things to her blue eyes. Over it all, she had on a blue-and-white apron that sported a bit of flour.

"Sam, I'm sorry, I didn't hear you come in," she said with a smile.

"It's okay. I've just been looking around. It's quite inviting in here."

"Thanks. It's a total disconnect with the outside, right?"

"Right, but we're going to fix that," he said confidently. "We'll make sure the outside is as inviting as the inside."

"That's the plan," she agreed with a wide smile that lit up her entire face.

"I just wanted to let you know I was here and that I'll be outside doing some measuring and then later I'll come back in and give you an estimate."

"That sounds perfect to me," she agreed. "I'm really looking forward to getting the process started." Her eyes sparkled brightly. God, she had pretty eyes with long dark lashes.

"Then I'll see you back in here in about twenty minutes." With a smile, he turned and walked out of the shop. He whistled as he walked back to his truck and retrieved his tape measure and a small pad and pen.

Before he could start measuring, Joe Rogers approached the shop. "Hey, Joe. How's life?" Sam greeted. Sam would guess that Joe was in his late fifties or early sixties. He was divorced and lived on a small farm at the edge of town.

"It's going," Joe replied. "Although my days don't really begin until I get a cup of coffee and one of Harper's big cinnamon rolls. Looks like she's finally ready to do something to spruce up the place."

"That's why I'm here," Sam replied. "See you later, Joe, and enjoy your cinnamon roll."

"I always do," the man said and then disappeared into the bakery.

For the next twenty minutes or so, Sam measured and made assessments about what needed to be done and what supplies he would need. He worked enough in the business that he had a rough idea about the cost of lumber and other supplies he would need to buy.

When he was all finished, he reentered the shop. Joe was seated at one of the tables and Harper stood behind her display case. Sam walked up to her. "I'd like a cup of black coffee and one of your cinnamon rolls. Joe led me to believe they must be really good. Then whenever you're ready to talk, I'm ready." He pulled out his wallet.

"Put that away," she said. "It's on the house this morning."

"Is that because you like me?" he teased.

"No... I mean yes..." Her cheeks turned a charming pink. "Why don't you have a seat at one of the tables and I'll be right with you."

"Harper, I'm taking off," Joe said. "I'll see you tomorrow morning."

"Okay, Joe," she replied. "See you tomorrow."

As Joe left, Harper carried the coffee and the cinnamon roll to where Sam sat. She set the things on the table and then took a seat across from him. "So, what have you got for me?"

"This is only an estimate on the front of the building. You'll need to walk out back with me to show me what you want specifically done out there," he explained.

As he went over the supplies and the cost, he was only interrupted once when Letta Lee, president of the gardening club, came in.

Letta was a sixty-something-year-old woman who Sam believed was one of the most judgmental snobs in town. She was also known to be a big gossip. Thankfully, she picked up a cake she'd ordered and then left without speaking to him, which didn't surprise him.

"So, when can you start work?" Harper asked when she rejoined him at the table.

"As soon as you want," he replied.

"As soon as you can," she said.

"I'll draw up a contract for you to sign this afternoon and then I can get started," he replied.

"A contract? Is that really necessary?"

He smiled at her. "It not only protects me, but it protects you as well. So yes, it's necessary." He got up from the table. "I'll be back in about an hour or so with the paperwork."

"I'll be here," she replied.

Two hours later the financial aspect of the job had been hammered out, the contract had been signed and Sam left the bakery once again to head to the lumber yard to arrange for the supplies he would need.

He was eager to get started on the job and he was even more eager to get to know Harper better. For the first time in a long time, a woman interested and attracted him.

He wasn't sure what it was about her, but he felt a spark with her and he couldn't wait to explore it…and her. He would be spending long days working outside her shop, but he'd also make sure he got plenty of opportunities to spend some time inside her shop and engage her on a more intimate basis.

Chapter Two

Harper leaned on her elbows over the display case, her chin in her hands as she watched Sam working outside. She knew it was miserably hot and humid outside and fifteen minutes ago Sam had stripped off his T-shirt. Lordy, just the sight of his bare broad shoulders and six-pack abs made Harper feel hot and humid despite the coolness inside the building.

Earlier that afternoon supplies had been dropped off just to the side of the front door. There were all kinds of lumber and exterior wall boards and everything else needed to transform the outside of the front of the building.

However, at the moment her sole attention was on Sam. He used a crowbar to take off some old wood trim, and as he did, his arm muscles bunched and danced. Oh, but the man was hot.

He suddenly stopped his work and peered into the shop. A slow grin curled his lips and he winked at her. Harper straightened up and looked down into the display case, appalled that he had caught her staring at him.

It had been a slow morning and was winding up to be an equally slow afternoon. Joe had been in earlier for his usual cup of coffee and cinnamon roll. A couple of other regulars had also come in.

Mandy Creighton, a nice lady, had come in to pick up a birthday cake she'd ordered for one of her sons' birthdays. Other than that, it was just too hot outside for people to enjoy walking around and shopping. Harper had a feeling today people were thinking more about crisp salads and cold pasta dishes than baked goodies.

It was around three when Sam entered the shop. He had pulled his T-shirt back on and announced it was break time for him. She hadn't even seen him take a lunch break.

He walked up to the counter with that smile that filled Harper with unexpected heat. Or maybe she was just on the verge of having another one of her hot flashes.

"I'm determined to try all the sweets in here, and I mean all the sweets." His green eyes pierced into hers as another slow smile curved his lips.

Good golly, was he flirting with her? Surely not. She was old enough to be his…well, not his mother, but his much older sister. "So, what would you like to try today? A slice of cake or some cookies?" She hated that she sounded like a half-breathless schoolgirl.

"I'd think I'd like to try your cookies today," he replied. "A couple of those raisin oatmeal ones. I'd also like a cup of coffee and since nobody else is in here maybe you can sit with me at one of the tables."

"I can do that," she replied.

"Now, how much do I owe you?" he asked.

"It's on the house," she replied.

"No," he said firmly. "We're not doing that. You run a business here and I pay my own way. You should never give away what you work hard to create. Now, how much do I owe you?" he repeated.

She told him and he paid and then she waved him toward the tables. He must want to discuss some of the work outside, she thought. Otherwise, why would he want her to join him? "Go ahead and sit down and I'll be right there."

As he sat, she plated a couple of the big cookies, got his coffee and then joined him at the table. "So, what's up?" she asked.

He frowned. "Nothing's up."

"Then why did you want me to sit with you?" she asked.

"Because I'd like to get to know you better."

She blinked and then stared at him. "Why?"

He laughed, the deep, pleasant sound rolling over her like a warm blanket on a cold day. "Why not? I'm going to be working for you here for a while and besides, I find you very attractive."

His words left her momentarily speechless. "Oh

well…uh…we can certainly visit when you take your breaks and there's nobody else in the shop," she finally sputtered.

"Are you dating anyone at the moment?" he asked.

"Uh, no." Once again, he'd caught her off guard.

"Good, I was thinking maybe we could visit even more if I took you out to dinner tonight," he replied.

Once again, she stared at him. Was this some kind of a joke? Maybe he'd made a bet with one of his brothers or some friends that he could get the much older baker woman to fall for him. Or maybe he was just being foolish.

She finally laughed. "You're funny."

"I wasn't trying to be funny. I am being completely serious. I'd like to take you out to dinner at the café. If tonight doesn't work for you then I'm free any other night."

"That sounds like a date and, Sam, there's no way on earth I'm going out on a date with you. The whole idea is positively absurd."

"It's not absurd at all." His eyes twinkled and he leaned forward. "This just means I need to work a lot harder to show you my charm and to entice you to go out with me."

She laughed again. "Good luck with that." She was just grateful that her voice didn't betray the slight breathlessness the whole conversation had caused inside her. The idea of going out on a date with Sam Bravano was wildly appealing, but utterly ridiculous.

"So, what have you been doing this morning? I've seen you using your crowbar and hammer," she said in an attempt to change the subject.

"I've been removing some of the rotten wood across the front. With that gone, I can then start replacing the rotten wallboard underneath. What's your favorite color?"

She sat back in her chair. "Pink. What's yours?" she asked. The man was positively incorrigible.

"Blue. What's your favorite kind of food?" He bit into one of the cookies and washed it down with a sip of coffee.

"I like all kinds of food, but Mexican is probably my favorite. What's your favorite?"

"Burgers. I love a big, juicy cheeseburger with a side of fries."

"Are you going to ask me what my sign is now? I'm a Libra and as stubborn as you seem, I would guess you as a Taurus. Why are you asking me all of this?"

He tilted his head slightly and the dimple danced in his cheek as he grinned. "I like to learn as much as I can about the woman I'm going to date."

She laughed and got up from the table. "You are some piece of work, Sam Bravano."

"Speaking of work, I'd better get back to it." He

ate the last bite of cookie and took a drink of the coffee. "Those were the best cookies I've ever tasted."

"Thanks," she replied. "I'm glad you liked them." She watched as he threw his plastic plate and napkin away and then started out the door, but before he could completely leave, he paused and turned back to her. "And just for your information, I'm a Cancer. I love deep and hard and I enjoy taking care of my partner." With that, he left.

She released a deep sigh. It had been fun to spar with him a little bit, and she had to admit his flirting with her had definitely tickled her. It had been a very long time since a man had flirted with her. Even if he'd just been toying with her, she admitted to herself that it had still been fun.

She sighed and picked up a cleaning cloth in an attempt to ignore the man, who was once again shirtless and working just outside her front windows. He was definitely more than a bit of a diversion.

For the rest of the afternoon, she cleaned the display case and all of the tabletops. She kept herself busy so she wasn't caught again just standing and watching Sam. It had been bad enough that he'd caught her staring at him one time.

She gathered up all the cleaning cloths she'd used during the day and carried them through the kitchen and into a small laundry room. She threw them into the washing machine and set it to wash. She went through tons of the cloths in a day and it was wonderfully convenient to have the washer and dryer here.

At quarter 'til four she made a fresh pot of coffee and at four one of her best friends walked into the shop. "I see work has begun," Becky Barlow said as Harper poured them each a cup of the fresh brew.

Becky sank down at one of the tables and Harper carried the coffee to the table and then joined her friend there. Harper and the blond-haired, brown-eyed woman had been friends for years. They'd gone all through school together and had become really close during high school.

Becky was happily married to her high school boyfriend. They had a son and a daughter and they had just enjoyed the birth of their first grandchild. Becky worked as a third-grade teacher at the school and had always been wonderfully supportive of Harper through all her ups and downs.

She now sat facing the window and as Sam passed by, she let out a low whistle and then grinned at Harper. "Nice view," she said.

"Really? I hadn't noticed," Harper replied with pretend airiness.

Becky laughed. "Yeah, right. Harper, I've got news for you. You're divorced, not dead."

"Okay, so maybe I have noticed a little bit," Harper said with a laugh of her own. "In fact, I'll admit the view has been a bit distracting all day."

"No doubt," Becky replied. "If I was ten years

younger and single, I swear I'd take that hunky boy to bed and make his head spin."

"Becky." Harper laughed once again. "You're feeling pretty feisty this afternoon."

"I'm just trying to make up for the crummy day I had."

"What made it crummy?" Harper asked curiously.

"Benny McGraw threw up all over the back of Lizzie Dominic and then while Alice Jackson was trying to escape the puke, she slipped and slid and fell right into it. So, math class involved one sick, crying boy and two screaming, crying girls. It took almost an hour to finally get it all sorted out and for the class to calm down again."

Harper couldn't help but laugh at the visual picture Becky had painted. "I'm just sorry I can't offer you anything more than coffee," she said sympathetically. "Sounds like you need something much stronger."

Becky laughed. "It's okay. I'm fine with the coffee. As far as I'm concerned, the day was just an example of how teachers are warriors who tackle short attention spans, crazy parents and puke. By the way, on another subject, I'm really sorry I missed your birthday party."

"It was no big deal," Harper replied even as a vision of Sam sitting in her living room filled her head. She was almost glad now that her two friends hadn't been able to show up.

"So, tell me, what's new with you?" Becky asked and then took a sip of her coffee.

"Not much. I'm really excited about getting the outside of the bakery cleaned up and once that's done, we'll start work on the backyard. I have all kinds of exciting ideas that I want to see back there."

"I think you'll see a big uptick in sales once the outside of the bakery looks just as good as the inside," Becky said.

"From your lips to God's ears," Harper replied.

"People just don't know how nice it is in here by looking at the outside." Becky took another sip of her coffee.

For the next few minutes, the two continued to visit and when the coffee was gone, Becky got up from the table.

"Time for me to get home. Larry told me he was cooking dinner for me tonight and it would be ready by five."

"Lucky you," Harper said, also rising from the table. "Go enjoy your dinner and tell Larry I said hi. I'll see you sometime next week."

Becky stopped by about once a week or so for a quick cup of coffee after work. She told Harper it was her decompression time before she headed home.

Sometimes their other friend, Allie Crawford, joined them, but her work hours didn't always allow it. However, occasionally the three of them would go out to dinner together.

Once Becky was gone, Harper cleaned the table-top once again and then poured herself a tall glass of water. If she drank any more coffee, she'd be up half the night. She already had to deal with hot flashes and occasional night sweats that often disrupted her sleep. Perimenopause, the doctor had told her. Early hell as far as Harper was concerned.

At five o'clock she turned the sign on the door from Open to Closed. She went back into the kitchen and made sure everything was clean and ready for the baking she would do the next morning. She switched the cloths from the washer to the dryer, turned it on and then grabbed her purse and walked out the front door.

Sam was in the process of putting his tools away into a large wooden carrier. "Harper, hang on a minute." She stopped in her tracks and then watched as he loaded the carrier into the back of his pickup truck. Then he hurried back to where she stood.

"Now I'm ready," he said with a wide smile.

"Ready for what?" she asked curiously.

"To walk you home," he replied. "I'm assuming you usually walk to and from work."

"Uh…well yes, I do. It seems silly to drive less than two blocks from my house to here. The only times I do drive is if it's raining hard or too cold and snowy. Although sometimes I don't mind walking through the snow. However, I usually enjoy walking instead of driving here."

She shut her mouth, aware that she was rambling. For some reason Sam made her nervous, not in a bad way, but rather in an inexplicable good way.

"So today, if you don't mind, I'd enjoy walking you home." He cast her that smile that made his dimple dance and her knees weaken.

"I guess I don't mind if you don't mind," she replied. She was so confused by him.

What on earth did Sam Bravano really want from her?

THEY TOOK OFF down the sidewalk at a leisurely pace. He walked close enough to her that he could smell the scents of sugar and cinnamon and everything sweet. But there was also an underlying fragrance of something hot and spicy. That scent he found exceedingly attractive and it called to something deep inside him.

"You look very pretty today," he said to her. It was true, the pink blouse she wore enhanced the darkness of her hair and the bright blue of her eyes. The cut of the blouse, along with the skinny black jeans she wore, also showcased her lush body to perfection.

"Thanks," she said, her cheeks dusted with a pink color to rival her blouse.

He found her blushes positively charming. It had been a long time since he'd seen a woman blush. "It looked like a friend came in to visit with you this afternoon," he said.

"Yes, Becky Barlow. She and I have been good friends since we were sophomores in high school. She's a teacher at the elementary school and we've seen each other through a lot of ups and downs over the years. Do you have a best friend?" she asked.

"My best friends are my two brothers, even though they are quite a bit younger than me," he replied. "They're my friends, but since our dad passed away two years ago, I'm also kind of like a father figure to them."

"Oh, I'm so sorry about your father. I lost mine four years ago and then my mother last year," she replied.

He heard the sadness in her and it resonated with a grief in him. His father had been his hero. Anthony Bravano had been bigger than life, a gregarious man who never knew a stranger and who had loved his family fiercely. When he'd died, a huge hole had been left behind not only in the family, but also deep inside Sam's heart.

"Do you have siblings?" he now asked her.

"No, I'm an only child," she replied.

"Sometimes I wish I was," Sam said with a laugh. "So, what do you like to do in your spare time? I know the bakery is closed on Sundays."

"The one thing I don't do on Sundays is bake. I like to do a little gardening and I enjoy reading. Things I'm sure you would find pretty boring."

"Actually, I don't find those things boring at all. I

like to do a little gardening, too, although I don't do as much reading as I should," he confessed.

"I imagine you spend a lot of your spare time at Murphy's," she said, naming a popular bar in town.

"Ha, not at all. I outgrew the bar scene a long time ago," he replied. "I haven't been to Murphy's in years."

He saw the disbelief that flashed in her eyes. "Then what do you do in your spare time?"

He was pleased that she was asking questions of him. Surely, that meant she had a little interest in him. "I bought a house last year that needed a lot of work, so that's what I do in my spare time."

"So, you work hard all day long and then go home and work some more," she said. Again, her voice held more than a touch of disbelief.

"Why am I getting the impression that you don't believe me?" he asked.

She stopped walking and turned to face him. "Sam, a man who looks like you has got to have a…uh…robust social life."

"I'd like to have a social life with you, Harper," he said.

She started walking at a quicker pace. "There you go, being totally ridiculous again."

"I'm not being ridiculous," he protested and quickly caught up with her. "Harper, why can't you believe that I'd like to take you out on a real date?"

By that time, they had reached her front porch.

She turned and faced him once again, her beautiful eyes filled with skepticism. "What did you do, Sam? Make a bet with your buddies that you could romance the old lady in the bakeshop? Are your friends waiting to see if you're successful or not? How much money will you get if you succeed?"

"God, no." He was appalled that she would even think such a thing about him. "There's no bet and you aren't the old lady baker. How can you even refer to yourself like that? I see you as a very attractive, lively woman who I'd like to spend more time with."

She unlocked her front door and then turned and looked at him. "Sam, you seem like a very nice young man. Go find somebody your own age to play with."

Before he could reply, she flew into her house and closed the door. Sam stared at the door for a long moment and then turned around and headed back up the sidewalk.

He was more determined than ever to get her to go out with him. He now knew what he was up against. She believed he couldn't possibly be attracted to her because of the age thing.

Well, she was dead wrong. For the first time in a very long time Sam looked forward to seeing and talking to a woman again. He really had no idea exactly what drew him to her, but something was definitely there.

And despite what she said, he thought she was

drawn to him, too. If he truly believed she had no interest in him then he would just show up at the bakery and do his job. But his plan right now was to show up there and do his job and try to convince her to go out with him.

HE WAS BACK to work at eight the next morning when the bakery opened. For the next hour or so, people he assumed were regular customers came and went.

It was another hot and humid day, although not quite as bad as it had been the day before. Just after one there was a lull in the customer traffic and he was ready to take a break inside the cool interior.

He went inside where Harper stood behind the display case. Today she was clad in a pair of black slacks and a bright yellow blouse. She also wore an apron that read Sweet Tooth across the front.

"Afternoon, Harper." He walked up to the counter. She definitely looked like a sweet treat he'd like to savor. There was just something about her that drew him to her. Maybe it was her bright smile or the sparkle in her big blue eyes.

"Hi, Sam."

"You look like a bright ray of sunshine today...a very pretty ray," he said.

He was unsurprised by the faint blush that filled her cheeks. "Thank you. Now, what can I get for you?"

"How about three of those cookies that I like...the

oatmeal raisin ones, and a cup of coffee," he said. He pulled some money from his wallet and then watched as she got everything ready for him. "You going to come and sit with me?" he asked once he'd paid.

"Uh…not today. I need to clean some things up back here," she replied, not quite meeting his gaze.

"Okay then," he replied easily. He carried the cookies and his coffee to a table nearest the display counter and sat. "It looked like you were fairly busy this morning." He watched as she began to clean the top of the display case, which he suspected was already clean.

"I think almost all my regulars came in. Then I've got two cakes and two dozen cupcakes going out this afternoon."

"That's good, right?"

"That's about normal for a Friday afternoon," she replied. "There are always parties on the weekends and thankfully people want cakes or cupcakes."

"So, the people in Millsville like their cake."

"Thank goodness for me," she replied with a laugh. He liked the sound of her laughter. It was a musical sound that was quite pleasant to the ears.

"Have you ever considered hiring somebody to help you out here so you aren't working from five or six in the morning until five in the evening six days a week?"

She paused with her cloth in hand. "I've considered it, but I've been saving every penny I can scrape together for the renovations. Once those are all done and paid for then I'll maybe consider hiring another person to work here part-time. Although I have to admit I'm a bit of a control freak and the idea of having somebody else in my kitchen kind of stresses me out."

"That reminds me, maybe right after work today we could go around back and you can tell me exactly what you want done out there," he said.

"That will work," she replied. "I'm eager to show you what I want. I have to warn you, it's going to be a lot."

"Then it's a date," he said with a grin.

"No, Sam, it's not a date. It's a…a…business appointment," she replied.

He laughed. "You are one stubborn woman."

"And you are one tenacious man," she returned with a small grin of her own.

"I just know what I like and when I like something I go after it," he replied. "So, this is a fair warning, Harper Brennan, I intend to do whatever I can to prove to you that I want to date you."

Her eyes sparkled brightly and she laughed. "Just remember I am one stubborn woman and right now I don't see that happening at all."

"Ah, but you haven't seen the full brunt of the Sam Bravano charm yet."

She laughed once again. "At this point in my

life, I've got to warn you, I'm pretty immune to charm, Sam."

She might say that now, but she'd cleaned the same spot on the top of the display case three times now. He ate his cookies and finished up his coffee and then headed back outside. Maybe one of the ways to Harper's heart was for him to work hard and give her the storefront she'd always dreamed of.

He knocked off at five o'clock and went into the bakery right before Harper closed for the night. She appeared to be ready for him. Gone was her apron and the minute he was inside she turned the sign on the door to indicate the business was closed and then she locked up.

"We'll go out the back door. I hope you brought your pad and pencil because there are a lot of things I want done out back," she said.

"Got them right here," he said and patted his back pocket.

"Okay then, let's go." There was a lilt to her voice that spoke of her excitement.

He followed her into a pristine kitchen with commercial-grade equipment. "So, this is where all the magic happens," he said.

"I don't know about magic, but this is where all the work is done," she replied.

"I'm sure it's hard work," he agreed quickly.

She smiled. "It is, but it's work I absolutely love.

Let's head outside," she said and led him through the laundry area.

"After you," he said and opened the back door. She walked out before him. She took about three steps out and then froze and suddenly screamed.

Then he saw it…a scarecrow standing in the backyard. However, it wasn't a scarecrow made of corn husks and hay. Rather it was a human scarecrow. He immediately recognized the young woman despite the fact that her mouth was sewn shut with thick black thread and her eyes were missing.

It was Sandy Blackstone, who worked as a teller at the bank. She was dressed in an ill-fitting pair of jeans and a red-and-black plaid shirt, a straw hat set atop her head at a cocky angle. It took only an instant for his mind to process the horrendous sight.

He grabbed the screaming Harper by the shoulders, whirled her around and drew her into his arms, not wanting her to see the horrible scene for a moment longer.

Chapter Three

Harper clung to Sam and was grateful for his big, strong arms holding her tight. She'd finally stopped screaming but now wept uncontrollably into the front of his shirt as the vision of Sandy tied to the pole with her mouth sewn shut and her eyes missing continued to fill her head over and over again. It was positively horrifying.

"You're okay," Sam's deep voice said softly… soothingly. He rubbed her back in small circles, obviously in an attempt to calm her down. "I'm so sorry you had to see that, Harper."

She nodded, her face still buried in the front of his T-shirt as her tears continued to fall. Who would do such a thing? Dear God, who was even capable in this small town of doing such unspeakable things to a pretty young woman?

"Come on, let's go back inside. I need to call Dallas." He gently guided her toward the back door and when they went back into the kitchen, she sank down on the folding chair she kept there.

She tried desperately to pull herself together as Sam made the call to the chief of police. But the vision of Sandy was burned into her brain and caused icy shivers to rush up and down her spine. Along with the horror was the grief of a young woman lost…a young woman dead far before her time. Dear God, who had done those terrible things to Sandy?

Sam hung up his phone, tucked it back into his pocket and then knelt down in front of her. "Are you okay?" he asked. He ran his thumbs down the tear tracks on her cheeks. His touch was infinitely gentle and for some reason made her want to cry all over again. But she swallowed against her tears and nodded.

"I'm okay. But, why here?" She finally managed to say. "Why was she left here, Sam? She's never even been in the bakery before. I only know her from the times she's waited on me at the bank."

"Dallas will sort it all out when he gets here," Sam replied. His beautiful green eyes seemed to reach out and caress her. "I just need to know that you're all right. You've been through one hell of a shock."

"I… I'm okay," she repeated even though it wasn't really true. She was definitely shaken up to her very core and still aghast by what she'd seen. "D-did you know her?" she asked, trying to wrap her mind around everything. "Did you know Sandy?"

"Like you, I only knew her from the bank." He rose to his feet. "We need to go up front to meet Dallas."

She rose and preceded him into the shop, where they both sat at a table near the window to wait for the lawman. "You might want to make a pot of coffee, it's probably going to be a long night," he suggested.

She jumped back up, grateful for something… anything to do, even though nothing could distract her from the horror in her backyard.

Poor Sandy. She'd always found the blonde with her bright blue eyes and wide smiles very pleasant whenever she'd helped Harper at the bank. Why? That was the question that kept racing through her head.

Why had Sandy been killed and why had she been left behind the bakery? It was just like what she'd heard about Cindy Perry being found in Lucas's cornfield. Who was committing these heinous murders of young women?

The coffee had just finished brewing when Dallas and two of his officers showed up. Dallas Calloway was a nice-looking guy with curly black hair and silver-gray eyes. Right now, he looked as grim as she'd ever seen him. Officers Joel Penn and Darryl O'Conner looked just as serious as their boss.

Harper offered the coffee to them, but all the men declined. As Sam told Dallas about them going out to the backyard to look at the building, Harper poured herself a cup of the coffee and returned to her chair. She wrapped her fingers around the warmth of the mug in an effort to heat the iciness that remained deep inside her.

"I've called Josiah so he should be here anytime," Dallas said. Josiah Mills was the town's undertaker and the county coroner. "Is there access to the backyard any other way than besides through here?"

"The yard is fenced, but there's a gate on the east side," she said. "D-do you need me to go back out there and show it to you?" She didn't want to go back there again. She didn't want to see Sandy like that again.

"No," Sam replied quickly. "There's absolutely no reason for you to go back out there. I'm sure we can find the gate without your help."

She smiled at him gratefully. She knew he was trying to protect her. What she wanted right now was to be back in his strong arms. She wanted to bury herself in his scent of sunshine and a faint spicy cologne and forget that there was a dead woman tied to a pole in her backyard.

Instead, he and the rest of the men went out the back door, leaving her alone in the bakery. Dear Lord, this made the second woman who had been killed by the man dubbed the Scarecrow Killer. One murder had been frightening enough, but now with two victims, it was possible…probable that Dallas was dealing with a serial killer. The very idea shot a new wave of horror through her. She'd never dreamed something like this could happen in her small hometown. Things like this happened in big cities, not here in Millsville…at least that was what she'd always believed before now.

Hopefully Dallas would be able to find something…anything that would lead him to an arrest. The killer definitely needed to be behind bars or in a mental institution as soon as possible. Anyone capable of doing something like what had been done to Sandy, and Cindy Perry before her, had to either be mentally ill or just plain evil.

She jumped as a knock sounded on the door. It was Josiah along with his younger assistant, Gary Walters. Josiah was in his mid to late sixties. From what she'd heard about him, when anyone asked him when he intended to retire his reply was always that he'd stop working when he was dead. He occasionally came into the bakery for a dozen cookies or a couple of cupcakes. Harper knew he was a widower and lived on the outskirts of town.

On the other hand, Gary was in his late twenties or early thirties. He was as shy as Josiah was boisterous. He was unassuming with rather drab brown hair and eyes, but he had a beautiful smile.

He'd never been in the bakery before, but Harper had interacted with him and found him very helpful and caring when both of her parents had passed and she'd been grieving.

She quickly unlocked the door and let them in. "Harper, not so good to see you under these inauspicious circumstances," Josiah said.

"Definitely not the best of circumstances," she agreed. "Hi, Gary."

"'Evening, Ms. Harper," he said.

"Dallas and…uh…she's in the backyard," she said and then gestured them on out the back door.

The minutes ticked by and slowly turned into hours. Several times Sam popped in to check on her. Finally, after what seemed like forever, Sam and Dallas came inside and asked for a cup of coffee. She jumped up to serve them and then Dallas gestured her back to her table, where all three of them sat.

"Harper, I need to ask you a few questions," Dallas said. "First of all, did you know Sandy Blackstone outside of her work at the bank?"

"No, she was just a teller who occasionally helped me when I went into the bank, but I didn't know her personally at all," she replied.

"I know you must hear some gossip in here. Have you ever heard about anyone else having a problem with Sandy?" Dallas asked.

She shook her head. "I've never even heard anyone mention her name."

"When was the last time you went out into your backyard?" he asked.

She frowned thoughtfully. "It's been at least a week or so. H-how long has she been out there?"

Sam reached for her hand and she was grateful for the slightly calloused fingers and palm that swallowed her smaller hand in welcomed warmth. "Not long, Harper," he said softly.

A small sense of relief fluttered through her. She would hate to think that poor girl had been in her backyard for days and days without anyone discovering her. It was bad enough she was back there at all.

Dallas only had a few more questions for her and then for Sam. "I have more men coming and we'll probably be in your backyard for at least several more days collecting evidence, but since we can access it through the side gate, you can operate your business in here as usual. You and Sam are now free to go. You can lock up the front and back doors. I'm assuming you'll both be available if I have any more questions."

"Absolutely," she said and Sam echoed her sentiment.

Sam released her hand and she got up from the table. Dallas disappeared out the back door once again and she emptied the last of the coffee and set the machine up for the next morning.

"I'll drive you home," Sam said.

She started to protest, but darkness had fallen outside and suddenly the idea of walking home all alone was abhorrent. Somewhere on the streets of

Millsville there was a killer on the loose. "Okay," she agreed. "I appreciate it."

"If you'll give me the key, I'll lock up the back door for you," he said.

Once again, she looked at him gratefully. She didn't want to go back there again. She didn't want another vision of Sandy trussed up like a human scarecrow in her brain and Sam must have known that.

She gave Sam the key and minutes later they walked out the front door and to his truck in the parking lot. His truck interior smelled just like him, of a touch of sunshine and the cologne she found so attractive. She leaned back against the padded seat and watched him walk around to the driver's-side door.

Thank God he'd been with her when she'd stepped out the back door. Thank goodness he'd been there to hold her and comfort her. She would have come completely undone if he hadn't been there for her and she'd had to face that horrible sight all alone.

"I feel like I'm stuck in a very bad dream…like I'm in a horrible nightmare and I can't wake up," she said as he started the truck engine. "I know it's crazy, but I somehow feel guilty…like I've done something terribly wrong. Otherwise, why was she left in my yard?"

"Harper, this had nothing to do with you personally and you did absolutely nothing wrong. This is just like when Cindy Perry was left in Lucas Maddox's cornfield. That had absolutely nothing to do with Lucas. This is some sort of a crazy random thing and you need to stop any thoughts of guilt you might be entertaining."

"That poor woman. She must have suffered so much pain." Tears once again filled her eyes as she thought about Sandy's horrendous ordeal at the hands of her murderer.

"If it's any consolation at all, Josiah said she was already dead from several stab wounds to her abdomen when her mouth was sewn shut and her eyes were removed. Damn, don't tell anyone her eyes were removed. Dallas is hoping to keep that information from the public."

"Don't worry. I don't intend to ever talk about this again to anyone," she replied. "I don't even want to think about it. Still, that poor woman."

By that time, they had reached her house. He parked in the driveway and together they got out of the truck. He threw his arm around her shoulder as they walked to her front door. Once again, she welcomed his body heat warming her.

"Are you going to be all right here all alone?" he asked when they reached her porch.

She unlocked her door and then turned to face him. She released a deep, weary sigh. "Yes, I'll be fine." She'd been fine all alone when her husband had walked out on her and she'd been fine when she had lost her parents. She would be okay alone because she had to be.

"If you aren't fine, you have my phone number. Call me, Harper, if you need anything...anything at all," he emphasized. His gaze was so warm, so caring and she wanted to lean forward and feel his arms encircle her once again. But she didn't.

"Thank you, Sam...for everything. I don't know what I would have done without you there with me tonight."

"I'm glad you weren't alone to walk out there and find her like that, and I was glad I could be there for you," he replied.

For just a moment she thought he was going to kiss her. He leaned slightly forward and she saw a flash of something dark and strangely delicious in his eyes.

"Good night, Sam," she said before anything crazy could happen. It had already been a crazy and absolutely awful night. Of course, there was no way she thought a kiss from Sam would be awful. But it also wouldn't be right.

He straightened. "Good night, Harper."

"Thanks for bringing me home," she replied.

"It was no problem."

She stepped into her house and closed and locked the door behind her. She leaned against the door for several long minutes.

She wondered what her dreams would be tonight.

Would she dream of horrifying human scarecrows or would she dream about being held in Sam's arms with his mouth plying hers with heat?

She desperately hoped it was Sam that filled her dreams and not terrifying nightmares of murder.

BY THE NEXT morning word about the latest murder was out. The headline on the front page of the *Millsville News* read "Scarecrow Killer Strikes Again." To Sam's dismay the story not only named the previous victim and the new one, but also named the bakery as the scene of the crime, which probably meant a lot of people would stop in to ask Harper questions today.

Aside from her initial screams and tears, she had been so strong last night. Despite her fear and her horror, she'd pulled herself together in a remarkably short amount of time. He admired the core of strength she obviously possessed.

Now driving to the bakery, he couldn't help but think about how she had fit so neatly in his arms. It was as if she'd been specifically made for his embrace.

He'd almost kissed her the night before. He'd desperately wanted to pull her back into his arms and take her lips with his. There was no question he was developing a very serious crush on his boss.

He glanced over to the cooler that set in the passenger seat. If she wouldn't go out to dinner with him at the café, then he would bring dinner to her at the bakery.

Today, he was bringing her one of his mother's specialties and he hoped she would take a few minutes and eat it with him after the bakery closed for the day. He hoped it would help take her mind off what had happened the day before, even if just for a few minutes.

He was taking a big chance. She'd already rejected the idea of him taking her out for a date. She might tell him to take the meal and get out. But it was worth taking the chance that she might actually appreciate his effort.

Of course, he wanted to take her out on a real date where they could sit and be waited on and have plenty of time to really get to know each other better, but she seemed to think he was just joking about wanting to take her out. And he wasn't sure how to make her realize he was serious about it…serious about her.

This morning it was certainly much easier thinking about Harper than the horror he had seen the night before. The vision of Sandy was going to be lodged in his mind for a very long time. He could only imagine how Harper was coping today.

Dallas must be pulling his hair out over this latest murder. One had been appalling enough, but two deaths with the women tethered to poles like scarecrows indicated an active killer who probably wasn't done yet.

Who had committed these heinous murders? Certainly, that would be a question on everyone's mind today and for the foreseeable time to come until Dallas had somebody under arrest. He just couldn't imagine anyone in the small town being capable of something like that. But somebody was living with dark secrets and a thirst for murder. He hated that this was happening in his town. He hated that it was happening at all.

He pulled up in front of the bakery and frowned as he saw four other cars already parked in front. So, it had already begun...the lookie-loos would want to see the backyard and others were probably quizzing Harper for any information they could glean from her.

There were also three police cars pulled up along the side of the building, letting Sam know there were officers out there still processing the scene.

Thankfully the backyard was fully fenced with not only a tall privacy fence but also with tall conifer trees that helped add to the seclusion. But it wouldn't help that it was a Saturday when most people were off work and would be able to come to the "scene of the crime."

Although the bakery wasn't really the scene of the crime. Sandy had been killed someplace else and only staged to be found at the bakery. The newspaper that morning had definitely gotten that fact wrong.

He parked and got out of his truck. Usually, he got right to work outside, but today he beelined inside. There were five people seated at tables and talking to Harper, who wore a slight furrow of uneasiness...of anxiety across her forehead. When he walked in, she smiled at him in what appeared to be immense relief.

"Good morning, Sam," she said.

"'Morning, Harper. I thought I'd start my day off with a cup of coffee and one of your big cinnamon rolls," he said.

"We were just asking Harper about what happened here last night," Joe said.

"You were here last night, Sam. What did you see?" Letta Lee asked. The older woman had never deigned to talk to Sam before. She'd always turned up her nose when Sam was around.

She sat with one of her garden club buddies, another older woman named Mabel Tredway. Mabel had always acted like speaking to the carpenter might dent her standing as one of the "society" women in the small town. Fancy that, they both were willing to talk to him this morning.

"Actually, Harper and I have been firmly instructed not to talk about anything that happened here last night," he replied.

"I've been trying to tell them that," Harper said with a touch of frustration in her tone.

"Oh, surely you can give us a little tidbit of information that wasn't in the paper this morning," Mabel wheedled with a smile. "I heard the birds had pecked out her eyes." She gave a visible shudder. "At least tell us if that is true?"

"Sorry, Mabel. I can't answer that. The last thing Harper and I want to do is tangle with Dallas," he replied firmly. "He told us not to talk about any of it and both Harper and I intend to respect his wishes."

By that time Harper had his coffee and cinnamon roll ready. He paid and then sat at a table. Letta and Mabel left soon after, but several more people drifted in to take their places.

Again, the questions started and Sam repeated what he had told Letta and Mabel. He made the decision then to sit inside for the remainder of the day. Easing Harper's stress today seemed far more important than hammering in a couple of boards.

As the day wore on, Sam changed from coffee and a roll to iced tea and cookies. People continued to drift in and out. The good news was Harper was probably selling more in this single day than she ever had.

The bad news was the customers were all seeking information about the murder that had occurred. He didn't blame them for their curiosity, much of which he believed was driven by fear.

Nothing like this had ever happened in Millsville before. Before Cindy Perry had been killed, Sam

couldn't even remember the last time the town had
seen a murder.

People would be wondering who they could
trust…who might secretly be the killer. Neighbors
would be looking askance at each other and family
members would be thinking about that odd one in
the household.

Sam continued to intercede for Harper by repeat-
ing the same thing over and over again to people all
day long. He and Harper were not allowed to talk
about the crime. Dallas had told them not to discuss
anything.

At a few minutes before five, Sam went out to
his truck and grabbed the cooler and carried it inside the bakery. He returned to his table and set the
cooler at his feet.

Hopefully she would agree to share the meal with
him, and hopefully it would erase the lines of stress
that had stretched across her forehead throughout
the day.

Finally, the last person inside aside from Sam left,
and Harper hurried toward the front door where she
turned the sign to Closed and then locked up. She
turned off the interior lights although there was still
plenty of sunshine pouring in through the windows.

She sank down in the chair across from Sam and
released a deep sigh. "Jeez. What a long day. Thank
you, Sam, for once again being here for me. I'm sure
the last thing you wanted to do was spend your entire

day in here fielding questions, but I really appreciate how you ran interference for me."

"At least you sold a lot of cookies today," he said, hoping to see a sparkle return to her eyes.

He achieved his goal. Her eyes not only sparkled, but a small laugh escaped her as well. "There is that," she agreed. "In fact, I sold out of every single one of the cookies I baked this morning. That's never, ever happened before."

"So, it was a good day for cookies but a stressful day for you."

She smiled at him. "Made a bit less stressful thanks to you."

He reached down and picked up the large cooler and placed it in the center of the table. "What's all this?" she asked curiously.

"Since you won't go out to dinner with me, I thought I'd bring a little dinner to you, and I hope you like Italian." Before she could protest, he opened the cooler and brought out the containers that had been packed inside.

"You're in for a real treat. I've got some of my mom's homemade lasagna and meatballs. There's also garlic bread and a bottle of red wine. If you just sit tight, I'll take all these things back to the kitchen and warm them up." He knew she had a microwave in the kitchen.

"Sam…" There was a weak protest in his name. "Why did you go to all this trouble?"

"Because I think you're worth it," he replied easily. He got up from the table and walked behind the display case where he knew she kept plastic cups. He grabbed two and then went back to the table, where he cracked open the bottle of wine and poured two cups.

He set the cooler back on the floor and grabbed the food item containers. "I'll be right back with the meal."

She merely nodded. He was encouraged by her allowing him to do this for her. Once in the kitchen he used the microwave to heat the lasagna and meatballs and threw the garlic bread under the broiler. A few minutes later he plated the food and then carried the two plates back to where she remained seated, sipping her wine.

When he placed her plate before her, she looked up at him with eyes that appeared slightly misty with tears. "Sam, I can't believe you went to all this trouble."

He grinned at her. "If Mohammad won't come to the mountain, then the mountain will come to Mohammad. Now, enjoy."

"Oh, my gosh, this is absolutely amazing," she said after taking her first bite.

"Mom cooks something like this at least once a week and she always sends me home with enough leftovers to feed a small army."

"Do you cook?" She looked at him curiously.

"I do. When I moved out of my parents' home, I quickly realized the only way I was going to get to eat was if I learned how to cook."

"Are you any good at it?" she asked.

He laughed. "I don't know how good I am, but I haven't poisoned myself yet." He was rewarded with her laughter. "What about you? Do you cook anything other than sweet treats?"

"Yes, I cook normal dinners," she replied.

"Are you any good at it?" he asked teasingly.

"I haven't poisoned myself yet," she replied, making him laugh in return.

"What's your specialty?"

"Oh, I don't know. I make a pretty mean parmesan cheese–encrusted pork chop," she replied.

"Hmm, that sounds really good."

For the next few minutes, they ate and talked about different kinds of food. From there, the conversation went to favorite movies and television shows. Like him, she enjoyed watching crime dramas and comedies.

The subjects were safe and easy to talk about and yet gave Sam a little glimpse into who she was as a person…as a woman.

This was exactly what he had wanted, some uninterrupted quality time with her. The more he learned about her, the more attracted he was to her. He was pleased to learn that they seemed to have a lot in common despite their very different jobs.

She liked old country tunes, as did he. She enjoyed long evening walks and crime shows that challenged her. She loved living in Millsville and insisted she would never want to live anywhere else. It was exactly the way he felt about their hometown.

Much to his dismay soon the food had all been eaten and the wine was almost gone. "I'll take care of the dishes," she said.

"Nonsense, I'll help." He got up from the table with her and carried his plate to the back where she had a dishwasher. She rinsed and loaded the plates and then they went back into the front where he packed his now-empty containers back into the cooler.

"It always seems like I'm thanking you for something, Sam," she said once everything was cleaned up.

"If you really want to thank me then you'll agree to go out with me," he replied.

She stared at him for a long moment. "Okay."

He looked at her in stunned surprise. "For real?"

"For real."

"So, you're saying you'll go out with me on a date."

She grinned at him. "That's exactly what I'm saying."

"When?" he asked. "How about tomorrow night around six? We'll go to the café for dinner."

"That sounds good to me," she agreed.

"Then it's a date, right?" He wanted to make sure he was hearing her right.

She laughed. "Yes, Sam, it's a date." Together they walked to the bakery's front door.

"Would you like me to drive or walk you home now?"

"No, I'm fine. I've got a few more things to do here before I leave so I'll just see you in the morning." She unlocked the front door. "Good night, Sam, and thank you again for the wonderful meal among other things."

Sam whistled a happy tune as he walked to his truck. He was grateful that the one thing they hadn't talked about was the body in her backyard. He'd hoped to take her mind off the grisly sight and he believed at least for a little while he had done just that.

What made him even happier was that finally, Harper was seeing him as somebody to date. He wasn't sure why she had changed her mind about him, he was just glad it had happened. For the first time in years Sam was excited about a woman. She not only drew him in physically but emotionally as well.

The last time he'd felt that way about a woman he had fallen in love hard and fast. He'd been twenty-four years old and had believed he'd found the perfect woman who he wanted to spend the rest of his life with.

Sharon was funny and smart and pretty and he'd

loved her desperately. Unfortunately, she hadn't felt the same way about him. After six months of dating, she'd broken up with him. He'd been absolutely devastated.

He was finally willing to put his heart on the line once again. He hoped Harper wasn't just humoring him. His cheerful whistle halted as another thought entered his mind.

Maybe Harper was just toying with him so she could boast to her friends that she was dating a much younger guy. Maybe he was nothing more than a trophy boyfriend for her. Perhaps it would be best that Sam hang on to his heart before seeing where this all was going.

Chapter Four

What have you done? Girl, you must have lost your ever-loving mind. What in the world were you thinking? The next evening at five forty-five, Harper stared at her reflection in her bathroom mirror. What on earth had made her agree to go out on a date with the much younger, very hunky Sam Bravano?

Even as the question shot through her head, she knew the answer. She'd agreed to go out with him because he had been so gentle and caring with her on the night Sandy Blackstone had been found. She'd agreed because he had sung her "Happy Birthday" and brought her dinner.

Ultimately, she'd capitulated because he made her laugh and because he'd been so tenacious about wanting to take her out on a date. Besides that, she'd agreed because she genuinely liked him.

"It's just one night," she told the reflection in the mirror. It wasn't like she was going to sleep with him, although the idea was certainly appealing.

She'd go out with him this one time and then not again. The whole idea of him wanting any kind of a real romantic relationship with a slightly chubby, menopausal woman who was years older than him was ridiculous.

She turned away from the mirror and left the bathroom.

Her makeup had been applied and she was clad in a lavender sundress that hid her tummy and hips and instead skimmed the length of her body. White earrings and sandals completed her outfit.

She went into the living room and sank down on the sofa to await Sam's arrival. She'd spent the day waffling between phoning him to call the whole thing off or biting the bullet and going. She'd finally decided to bite the bullet. One and done, she told herself firmly. He probably wouldn't want another date with her anyway.

She'd also spent the day doing a little housework and reading a novel by her favorite author. It had been a restful day after a crazy and disturbing week.

The town was all still buzzing about the Scarecrow Killer and his newest victim. The idea of a potential serial killer at work in the small town was frightening, indeed.

Dallas had called for a town meeting in the community hall the next night and she intended to be there. She was sure that most of the people in town, along with all the farmers on the outskirts of town, would also attend.

Still, even with all these things swirling around in her head, it was thoughts of Sam that took precedence. Out of all the women in town, why did he want to spend time with her?

She'd been tossed away by her husband because she hadn't been young enough, hadn't been fun enough. She'd been left behind because she wasn't pretty enough, wasn't witty enough to keep the man who had vowed to love her forever. So, why on earth would she be enough for Sam?

She was getting way ahead of herself. By the end of this evening, she was fairly sure Sam wouldn't be interested in another date with her. She supposed this one date wouldn't hurt anything. All she really wanted from Sam was his expertise as a carpenter. This night was just the result of him catching her at a weak moment.

At precisely six o'clock a knock fell on her door. Her heart did a crazy dance in her chest. She got up, grabbed her purse and then answered. It was Sam...a very hot, handsome Sam. She'd never seen him dressed in anything but jeans and a T-shirt. Tonight, he wore black slacks with a short-sleeved forest green dress shirt that showcased his beautiful green eyes.

"Hi, Harper. You look positively stunning," he said as his gaze swept the length of her.

She felt the blush that warmed her cheeks. "Thanks. I'm all ready to go." Even though she didn't believe him when he said things like that to her, there was no question that it was still nice to hear.

"Are you hungry?" he asked once they were in his truck. He smelled as delicious as he looked with the spicy cologne that she always found so wonderfully attractive.

"I am." A nervous tension fluttered inside her as she thought of going out in public with Sam. The café was always packed on Sunday evenings. There would be a lot of people there who would see the two of them together out on a social basis. What on earth would they think? "What about you?"

"I'm definitely ready for a big juicy burger. Unfortunately, I don't think the café does Mexican food very often."

She was surprised he'd remembered that she'd mentioned in passing that Mexican was her favorite type of food. "They don't, but I always find something good on the menu."

"It's a nice night," he said. "Although still a little warm."

"At least it's cooled off some from this afternoon," she replied.

The closer they got to the café, the more nervous she was becoming. She should have never agreed to this. What were people going to think when they saw the two of them out together?

"Relax, Harper," Sam said as if reading her mood. "It's just a meal out, not a lifetime commitment."

She laughed. "I realize that."

"Have you ever been to the Farmer's Club?" he asked as they passed the place.

The Farmer's Club was a small bar on Main Street mostly frequented by the older farmers and couples in the area. "No, I've never been in there, although I've heard about it from some of the people who come into the bakery."

"It's a nice place that caters to an older crowd versus Murphy's, which is much bigger and noisier and caters to more of the singles in town. Maybe next time we go out we can have a drink and relax at the Farmer's Club."

She didn't feel like this was the appropriate moment to tell him there wouldn't be a next time. "At least you'll be able to get one of your big juicy cheeseburgers for dinner," she said in an attempt to change the subject.

"Yeah, and I'm definitely hungry tonight. On another note, I heard that the long-term weather forecast is for a couple of days of rain this week. And just so you know, this man doesn't work in the rain," he replied.

"I wouldn't expect you to," she replied. "I guess your work is at the mercy of the weather at times."

"Definitely," he agreed. "Rain can keep me off a job for days, so I'm not particularly fond of rainy days."

"Sundays… I don't mind a rainy Sunday occasionally."

He shot a quick glance at her and smiled. "And what do you like to do on rainy Sundays?"

"Nothing exciting. I enjoy curling up on my sofa under a nice warm blanket and watching movies all day."

"So, you aren't one of those crazy women who like to get naked and dance in the rain?"

"Good grief, no," she replied with a laugh.

By that time, they had arrived at the café. Just as she had feared, cars were parked not only in front of the place but also all the way down the block.

"Looks like we'll have a little walk," he said as he pulled into a parking space across the street and down the block from the eating establishment. He cut the engine and smiled at her. "Sit tight."

He got out of the truck and then walked around to open her door and help her down. She murmured a thank you and then they started walking side by side toward the café.

It seemed only natural when he reached out and took her hand in his. The warm, slightly calloused hand felt familiar and good and she remembered how he had held her hand the night that Sandy's body had been found. But she didn't want to think about that right now.

"It looks like there's a big crowd here tonight," she said.

"Yeah. Hopefully we'll be able to grab a booth or a table without waiting too long," he replied.

He dropped her hand as they reached the café door and he ushered her inside. A cacophony of sound greeted them, the clinking of silverware and dishes and people talking and laughing together.

Along with the sounds were the heavenly scents. They were the fragrances of cooking meats and onions, of simmering stews and veggies. Finally, there was a hint of yeasty rolls and fresh-baked pies.

The decor in the café was an homage to the local farmers. One wall held big golden hay bales with bright red roosters. Another wall depicted a yellow cornfield with the three tall silos that were part of the town's skyscape, and yet another was farmland in patterns of browns and greens and golds.

Harper had always found the café to be a pleasant, calming place to eat. But tonight, as Sam spied an empty booth in the back and as they made their way toward it, she was aware of gazes following them and conversations suddenly turning to whispers. She also caught a quick glance of her friend Allie Crawford and her husband, Ed, seated at one of the tables they passed.

She had no idea who else might be in the café

that she knew for she tried to keep her gaze straight ahead, not making eye contact with anyone. She didn't want to see the expressions on their faces, although she definitely felt the stares.

She was grateful to slide into the booth where at least she couldn't see everyone who had been staring at them. She immediately grabbed one of the menus that stood between the salt and pepper shakers and held it up in front of her face.

"Harper." Sam's deep voice made her lower the menu and look at him over the top edge. "Relax. I promise you, it's going to be just fine."

She released a small, nervous laugh and lowered the menu all the way. "I felt like everyone in the whole café was gawking at us and whispering about us. I'm sure they're wondering what you are doing here with such an old lady."

He frowned at her. "Harper, you have got to stop thinking of yourself that way. You are not an old lady. You are a beautiful and vibrant woman and to be perfectly honest, I don't care what other people think. I'm here with the woman I want to be here with. Now, smile and at least try to look like you're enjoying my company." He grinned, causing his dimple to dance in his cheek.

She laughed again. "Okay, I'm relaxing as you speak."

"Good, now let's take a minute and decide what we want to eat."

She returned her gaze to the menu, but her thoughts remained on Sam. There was no question he made her feel good. He made her feel pretty and girly. She couldn't remember the last time a man had told her she was beautiful. Did she believe his words? Not really, but she definitely enjoyed hearing them. In any case, after tonight they would go back to being only employer and employee.

Regina Waltz, a pleasant young blonde, appeared at the side of their booth to take their orders. "Hey, Sam… Harper, what can I get for you two this evening?"

"I'd like the turkey bacon club with fries on the side," she said.

"And I'll have the big bacon cheeseburger with a side of fries," Sam said. They both ordered iced tea and Regina left to put their orders in.

He put their menus back in place and then settled back in the booth and smiled at her. "So, how was your day off today?"

"Nice and quiet. I did a little housework and then read for a while. It's too hot to do much of anything outside, although I certainly don't have to tell that to you. What about you? How was your day?"

"Fairly productive. I finished ripping out the ugliest lime green and yellow linoleum you'd ever want to see out of my kitchen."

"What are you putting down instead?"

"I haven't quite decided yet. It's either going to

be some nice, big neutral ceramic tiles or some sort of a wood product. Maybe you could come over to my place one evening and give me a woman's perspective on it."

His gaze on her was so warm, so inviting. Yet, she was also aware of the couple at the table nearest to them shooting her disapproving glares. "We'll see," she finally replied.

For the next few minutes, they small-talked about the weather and then the town meeting the next night. By that time their dinners had arrived.

Even though she tried to completely relax, there was still a core of anxiety inside her. How much gossip was now flying around with her and Sam as the main subjects? She was far too old for Sam and most of the people in town probably thought she was an extremely foolish woman.

It didn't help that Sam was so danged hot…that he could probably date any young beautiful woman the town had to offer. And everyone knew that. If people weren't outraged by the idea of their May-December date, then they were probably pitying Harper for being stupid enough to believe there could ever be something between her and Sam.

And what were they saying about Sam? They probably couldn't imagine what was in his head to want to be with Harper. And as she gazed into Sam's beautiful green eyes, she knew the foolishness had to stop tonight. Even if he didn't want it to stop, she would put an end to it.

Because she liked him…she liked him far more than she should.

SAM HAD BEEN aware of the curious gazes that had followed them as they had walked to their booth. He could also feel Harper's discomfort and he truly hated that for her.

She definitely didn't see herself as Sam saw her. He found her beautiful and with a wonderful sense of humor. She was strong and a successful business-woman. He didn't feel any age difference when he was with her, when he was talking and laughing with her. For him, she was the complete package and he couldn't believe she hadn't been snapped up by a man long before now.

"Do you date a lot?" he now asked, eager to learn as much as he could about her.

She paused with a French fry halfway between her plate and her mouth. "Oh yes, I have a date every couple of decades or so," she replied dryly.

He looked at her in genuine surprise. "I'm shocked that your social calendar isn't full with dates every weekend. What's wrong with all the men in this town?"

She laughed. "I've asked myself that several times in the past few years."

Oh, he loved the musical sound of her laughter,

and the way her mirth not only filled the air but also caused her eyes to sparkle so brightly.

"You were married for a long time, right?"

"Almost nineteen years," she replied.

"What happened to cause a divorce?" He immediately winced. "Or maybe I'm getting way too personal. If so, I'm sorry and please just ignore the question."

"No, it's okay. What happened to cause my divorce? Her name was Ginger and she was a twenty-five-year-old with big breasts and a desire to marry my husband. According to my husband, she was everything I wasn't…fun and lively and gorgeous among other things. I'm not sure how long he was cheating on me with her, but ultimately, he told me his happiness was with her and so he was leaving me." She released a small sigh. "That afternoon he packed up his bags and left and that was pretty much that."

Even though the words were said matter-of-factly, he saw the flash of pain that momentarily filled her eyes. So, she'd been replaced by a much younger model, and after nineteen years of marriage that had to have been a big blow to her very soul.

"I'm so sorry that happened to you," he said. "He was obviously a jerk who only had half a brain. He apparently didn't know how to appreciate the finer things in life."

She laughed. "I like the way you think, Sam."

"Well, it's true. Do you ever miss him?"

"My husband? No, not at all. He obviously wasn't the stand-up man I thought he was. But there are definitely times I miss having somebody to talk to…to share with." She shrugged her shoulders. "Still, if I'm meant to be alone, then I'm just fine with that. I don't mind my own company and I'm comfortable in my own skin. I have my work and for the most part that fulfills me."

That was one of the many things that drew him to her: the fact that she knew who she was and she was fine with it. He liked her sense of self-confidence. He found it sexy as well.

They were quiet and concentrated on eating for the next few minutes. "What about you?" she finally asked, breaking the silence that had been between them.

"What about me?" he asked.

"Do you have a sob story about a love in your past?"

"Certainly nothing like what you experienced with your marriage. I was twenty-four years old when I fell in love for the first and only time. She was everything I thought I wanted for the rest of my life and for six months I thought it all went wonderfully well. But before long I realized there was trouble in paradise."

He paused to take a drink and then continued.

"I guess I was so crazy about her, I hadn't seen or really paid attention to all the red flags."

"Like what?" Harper asked. He was glad to see that she was no longer looking around at the other diners but rather completely absorbed in their conversation.

"She mentioned several times to me that she didn't really like small-town living. She also hinted around that she wanted me to find a different job, something more impressive than a mere carpenter. But I pretty much ignored those things and then was completely blindsided when she broke up with me and ended up moving to Kansas City to be with a man who was a lawyer she had met on the internet."

"I'm so sorry that happened to you," she replied. "Broken hearts always hurt, whether you've been married for years or are together for a shorter amount of time."

"At least my heartbreak was a long time ago," he replied. "Did you miss some red flags with your husband?"

She laughed again. "Oh my gosh, I missed a whole parade of red flags. In the last year of our marriage, he was suddenly working late most evenings when he had never had to work late before. There were many times he didn't answer his phone when I'd call. He had one dumb excuse after another, for not answering the phone or not being where he'd told me he would be, yet I always believed him. Despite all those things, I never suspected for one minute that he was having an affair until the day he left me."

She picked up a French fry and dragged it through a pool of ketchup on her plate. When she looked up at him her eyes were clear and bright with no shadows or pain to cloud them. "You like to think the people you trust have the same integrity and morals as you, but I guess it doesn't always happen that way."

"That's why it's so important that two people have open communication and conversations about such things. Personally, I've always believed in ending a relationship before starting a new one and I consider myself a monogamous man who would never cheat if I was married."

She smiled at him. It was a real, open smile that lit up her entire face and created a pool of heat that swirled around deep in his stomach. "It's time to lighten up this discussion. Why don't you tell me more about your family?"

For the next half an hour or so he regaled her with stories from his childhood, making her laugh over and over again. He loved making her laugh and he had plenty of funny stories about life with the Bravano family.

"I always wanted a sibling, and your stories about life with your brothers make me feel like I definitely lost out."

"Were you lonely as an only child?" he asked.

"Not always, but there were certainly times when

I was. My mom and dad tried their best to make sure I wouldn't feel that way but their efforts didn't always succeed. According to my mother, they hadn't intended for me to be an only child and they tried to give me a sibling, but it just never happened."

By that time their meals were done, but he wasn't ready to call it a night. He wasn't ready to take her home and tell her good-night yet. "I'm thinking maybe a piece of apple pie and a cup of coffee would be good right about now," he said. "What would you like for dessert?"

"I would usually say nothing, but if you really force me to have dessert, then apple pie and coffee sounds good," she replied. He was glad she didn't indicate that she was immediately ready to go home.

He grinned. "You have total permission to blame me for you ordering and enjoying dessert." He motioned to Regina and ordered their pie and coffee.

Minutes later they were enjoying their apple pie and talking about other favorite desserts. "Of course, my favorite is cake," she said.

"I wouldn't expect you to say anything else," he replied with a grin. "And I would assume your favorite cake is the kind you baked for your birthday."

"You would guess right," she replied.

"I have to admit, I'm now a total fan of your cookies."

She smiled. "I've noticed."

She then began to entertain him with bakery horror stories, from accidentally using the wrong ingredients to giving the wrong cake to the wrong people.

"I once baked a cake that was to be served after an older man's funeral and at the same time I had a birthday cake for a six-year-old girl going out," she began.

"Oh no, don't tell me," he said with a laugh.

"I'm telling you. I'm not sure who was more horrified, the people after the funeral who got the pink-and-yellow-flowered birthday cake or the little girl when her mother opened the cake box to discover a black cake that read 'We'll miss you, Grandpa.' But I definitely heard from both unhappy parties."

She was a lively storyteller. Her eyes sparkled and all her features lit up. Was that the way she would look when making love with him? The thought jumped into his brain unexpectedly. But once it was there it refused to dislodge easily.

He was definitely physically attracted to her and would take her to bed in a fast minute, but he knew he couldn't rush things with her. He didn't want just a quick hookup. He wanted something more meaningful than that. He needed to woo her a little longer. Besides, he had a feeling she was well worth the wait.

Finally, it was time to go. Their dessert plates were empty and their coffee was gone. He waved to Regina to get his check and after paying they got up to leave.

Immediately he felt the tension fill Harper once

again and he knew it was because they had to walk through the café to get back to the front door.

She walked stiffly beside him, her gaze directed straight at the door. He hated that she was so self-conscious about being seen with him when he was so proud to be seen with her.

The tension appeared to leave her the moment they stepped back outside. Once again, he reached for her hand. He loved the way hers felt enclosed in his. Her hand was small and dainty and her skin was so soft and warm.

"I am so full," she announced once they were back in his truck and headed to her house.

"That makes two of us," he replied.

"I probably should have said no to dessert."

"Ah, but never regret the dessert you eat. Instead regret the dessert you don't eat," he said.

She grinned at him. "Did some wise old man tell you that?"

He laughed. "I don't remember, but it might have been my mother."

"Ah, a wise woman," she replied.

Night had fallen and she looked enchanting in the soft illumination from the dashboard. Once again, a wave of intense physical attraction toward her punched him in the gut.

"So, it's back to work tomorrow," he said, breaking the silence that had momentarily grown between them.

"Yes, it's back to cakes and cupcakes and everything sweet for me," she replied. "At least I feel well rested to start a new week."

"That's good. I'm ready to get back to work, too." By that time, he had reached her house. He pulled into her driveway, shut off the engine and then hurried around to the passenger door to help her out.

When they reached her front porch, she unlocked her door and then turned back to face him. "Thank you, Sam. I really had a lovely evening tonight."

"I really enjoyed it, too." He took a step closer to her, so close he could feel her body heat wafting toward him and smell the seductive scent of her. "Harper, can I kiss you good-night?"

Her eyes flared wide, but to his encouragement, she didn't step back from him. "I… Uh…okay, I guess."

Before she could change her mind, he gathered her into his arms and took her mouth with his. Oh, she tasted so hot and sweet, with just a hint of the apple and cinnamon from the pie she'd just eaten. When she opened her mouth to him, he quickly deepened the kiss, swirling his tongue with hers.

Oh, the woman definitely knew how to kiss. Her lips were pillowy soft and he felt himself quickly getting aroused. The kiss lasted only a few moments and then, with a small gasp, she halted it and stepped back from him. "Thank you again, Sam. Good night."

"Good night, Harper."

She went into her house and he turned and headed to his truck.

It had been a really great night. Hopefully the ice had been broken with the date tonight. And hopefully she would want to go out with him again.

Everything he learned about her only drew him closer to her. He wanted to discover so much more about her. He wanted to know what she thought about a hundred…a thousand things. He wished to learn all her likes and dislikes and all of her hopes and dreams.

He only hoped she felt the same way about him. He knew the age thing bothered her, but he was hoping with more time she would see her way past that. The difference in their ages certainly didn't bother him at all.

He didn't know where things were going with her. All he could hope for at this point was that she wanted to go out with him again.

HE LEANED FORWARD in his chair, the *Millsville News* in front of him. He was back in the news, headline status. The Scarecrow Killer had returned with a vengeance and he knew the whole town was afraid. There was even a town meeting planned that would be solely about him.

The very thought made excitement roar through him and his entire body positively tingled with intense pleasure. Nobody in this town had ever really seen him before, but they were definitely seeing him now. He knew the young women of Millsville were going to bed every night with fear in their hearts. Some of them were probably having nightmares. All because of him.

He loved it. He loved all of it. He loved sedating them and dragging them into his car. He loved the warmth of their blood when he stabbed them and their pleas and cries before that, while they bargained for their lives.

He liked slowly stripping them naked and then re-dressing them in their special scarecrow attire. Once they had been dead for a couple of hours, he then sewed their lips together.

He saved the best thing for last. The eyes. The windows to the soul. The very last thing he did was take out their eyes…blue eyes like his mother's, God rest her soul.

He now looked over to the wooden shelving where two jars sat side by side. One held Cindy's eyeballs and the other held Sandy's. Unfortunately, they hadn't kept their bright blue color but instead had turned a milky faint bluish white.

Even though that had initially disappointed him, he now realized maybe it was better that way, for if he sat and stared at the blue eyes that so reminded him of his mother, he would not only be filled with a rich rage, but also with the trembling fear she'd always evoked in him.

That bitch. She had terrorized him until five years ago when she'd "accidentally" fallen down the basement stairs and broken her neck. To the outside world she'd been admired as a strong woman who was a single parent. But to him…she'd been the very devil.

There was no fear inside him today, only a sweet, heady jubilation. He pushed the papers aside, leaned back in his chair and instead looked around him. This was actually the basement of the small ranch house his mother had left to him upon her tragic death, but he thought of this space as his killing lair. After all, his first murder had been that of his mother, who had died at the bottom of the stairs.

The shelving not only held the two jars of eyeballs, but also the items he would need for future kills. There were straw hats and flannel shirts, jeans in a variety of sizes, along with his killing knife and the instruments necessary to sew together lips and remove eyeballs.

There was also a stack of thick, sturdy poles, perfect for binding a woman to in order to make her an impeccable scarecrow. And he had plenty of poles… plenty of all the supplies he needed to keep him in the headlines. Plenty to keep the young women of Millsville terrified for a very long time to come.

Looking at it all now, the hunger inside him rose up…the intense hunger to make another scarecrow.

But he'd practice self-control. He'd wait. He'd attend the town meeting tomorrow night and he'd act like another concerned citizen. It would be such fun to feel the terror of the entire town as they all came together to talk about him.

After that, he'd go hunting again and when he found the perfect woman, he'd turn her into a perfect scarecrow. Maybe this one would finally stop the screaming in his head.

Chapter Five

The next evening, the community center was packed with people. Dallas was supposed to begin talking at seven. At six forty-five Harper entered the large room where chairs were set up before the stage, upon which stood a podium.

A gathering like this was always a big deal. The café had set up coffee and brought doughnuts for everyone and Harper had packaged up dozens of cookies and cupcakes to give away for the event.

The last time she remembered there being a big town meeting like this was four years ago when spring storms had torn through the area, leaving some of the farmers with damage to their homes and outbuildings.

At that time the meeting had been about supporting those neighbors in their time of need. Garage and bake sales were set up with all the proceeds going to the people who needed extra help in just getting the basics. Volunteer task forces were also set up to provide physical aid in rebuilding and repairing.

The room now buzzed with dozens of conversations as neighbors greeted neighbors. The talk wasn't just about the recent murder, but also about weather and crops and kids and other current events. Many in the farming community didn't come into town very often, so this was a good opportunity for them to catch up with other people.

It appeared that everyone in the whole town had shown up. Still, despite the crowd, as she made her way to one of the empty chairs, Sam appeared at her side.

She had spent the entire day once again distracted by him as he'd worked outside of her shop. Just after noon he'd come inside for his cookie lunch break and since it was just the two of them inside at that moment, she had sat with him.

As always, the conversation had been a combination of him lightheartedly flirting with her and her laughing in response. Before Sam, she hadn't laughed very much. Before him, she hadn't felt pretty and worth flirting with.

"Hey, stranger," he now said to her with the brilliant smile that always warmed her deep inside.

"Hi, Sam," she replied. He had offered to bring her tonight but she had declined his offer. Still, every time she saw him, every time he flirted with her and she remembered what fun it had been to be out with him, her resolve to never go out with him again weakened more than a little bit.

"Mind if I sit with you?" he asked.

"Not at all," she replied.

They found two empty chairs toward the back of the room and once again she felt some of the disapproving looks that followed them. Jeez, surely these people had something other than who the baker was sitting with to worry about in their lives. They were here about a couple of horrid murders, for crying out loud.

"You're going to have to get used to it," Sam leaned over and whispered to her. "Because I don't intend to let a bunch of small-minded people deter me from seeing you."

So, he noticed the glares, too. It warmed her that apparently she was the woman he wanted to be with…at least for now. Should she not see him anymore because other people disapproved? Should she deprive herself of his company even though she enjoyed him a lot? This whole situation with Sam confused her.

Even now, with the crowd surrounding them, the scent of him enticed her. His nearness excited her. The kiss they had shared after their date had been more than wonderful. So, should she stop dating him because some people might want to criticize her for it?

Before she could answer any of her own questions, a hush fell over the crowd as Dallas took his place at the podium. He looked quite handsome in his uniform, but he also appeared tired and grim.

"As you all have probably heard by now, Sandy Blackstone lost her life several days ago. She was killed by the same man who we believe murdered Cindy Perry," he began.

He then went on to speak about how the victims were found, dispelling any rumors and gossip that had swirled around. However, the one thing he didn't mention was that Sandy's eyes had been removed. Harper had heard through the grapevine that Cindy's eyes had been missing as well, but Dallas didn't mention anything about her eyes, either.

"There is still a lot about these crimes that we don't know. Obviously, we don't know who the killer is. We also don't know where these women were killed before they were staged to be found first in a cornfield and then behind the bakery," Dallas continued.

"We don't know why this person is killing or why the bodies are being left where they are. So, I'm calling on you all to keep your eyes and ears open and come to me with any information you might have. So far, both of the victims have had blond hair and blue eyes, but we're not sure this will be a pattern that continues. Therefore, I'm telling all women to travel in twos or a group whenever you're out and about. Be aware of your surroundings and who you let into your personal space."

His words were sobering and shot a chill up Harper's spine. Basically, he was telling them that any woman could be the next victim. Any women in Millsville could become the next horrific scarecrow.

At the end of his speech, Dallas took no questions. He left the stage and immediately disappeared. Sam turned toward her. "I think I'm going to go grab a couple of cookies and a cup of coffee. Would you like for me to get you something?"

"No, thanks. I'm good."

"Will you sit and wait for me to get back?" he asked.

"Okay," she agreed.

He had only been gone a minute or two when Harper's friends Becky and Allie appeared in his place. "Hey, girls, what's happening?" she said in greeting.

"I think what's important is that you tell us what's happening with you," Allie replied with one of her dark eyebrows raised.

"What do you mean?" Harper asked in confusion. "There's nothing really going on with me."

"Apparently there is. Allie told me you and Sam went out to dinner together," Becky said as she sat in the chair Sam had vacated. "Please tell me it was a strictly business dinner."

"Actually, it was a date…a strictly for pleasure dinner date," Harper replied.

"My God, Harper, what on earth are you thinking? Have you completely lost your mind?" Allie asked. "You know he's probably just toying with you. He can't be seriously attracted to you."

"Gee, thanks," Harper replied dryly.

"You know what I mean," Allie replied. "Harper, you know I think you're a real catch, but not for a man who is so much younger than you."

"What does he really want from you?" Becky asked.

"Nothing. Nothing but my company," Harper replied defensively.

"Honestly, Harper. I just thought you had more sense than this. Surely you can't believe this would work out," Becky said with a disapproving shake of her head.

"Who says I want anything to work out with him?" Harper finally got a little bit hot under the collar. "Maybe I'm just having a bit of fun with Sam. What's wrong with that?" She looked at each of her friends with a touch of defiance.

"There's just been some talk. People don't like it. They don't think it's right," Becky said.

"So, I should stop having fun with Sam because some people in this town don't think it's right? Maybe they're all just jealous."

"Oh, Harper," Becky said with dismay.

"I don't think that's the case," Allie protested.

"Well, no matter what the case is, I'm not going to let anyone make my decision about whether I see Sam on a social basis or not. I'll decide that for myself." Harper sat up straighter in her chair. "But thank you both for thinking about my happiness."

"Harper, the very last thing we want to do is make you mad or upset. We just want to protect you. You just have to wonder what a hot-looking young man like Sam is doing with you." Allie took Harper's hand. "Still friends?"

"Of course," Harper replied. But she was definitely irritated with the two of them. Who did they think they were to tell her what to do with her life? Who to see or not see in her spare time? It wasn't as if the two of them were jumping to spend any real time with her. Heck, they'd both even missed her little birthday party.

And why were they so certain that Sam couldn't really be attracted to her? That he couldn't truly enjoy her company without wanting anything from her? That really hurt her feelings and reminded her of the negative way she had felt about herself when her husband had left her.

They finally left Harper's side and Tom Adamson stopped by her chair. Tom was one of her morning regulars and greeted her with a friendly smile. "How are you doing this evening, Harper?"

"I'm doing fine. How are you doing?" she asked.

"Okay. Troubling meeting, right?"

She nodded. "It was definitely troubling," she agreed.

"Well, I'm heading out now. I'll see you at the bakery tomorrow," he said.

"See you, Tom."

The older man murmured a good-night and then wove his way to the end of the aisle.

Sam returned with his coffee and cookies. He sank back down next to her and smiled. "Thanks for waiting for me. I hate to eat cookies all alone."

She laughed and for the next couple of moments he munched on a cookie and drank his coffee. "At least the crowd is starting to thin out a bit. By the time you finish your coffee and cookies we should have no problem getting out of here," she said.

"Yeah, that's why I figured I'd wait until the initial mad dash for the exit was over before trying to leave," he replied.

"Is your family here?" she asked curiously.

"My mother didn't come but my two brothers were here earlier however they've already left," he replied. "I saw you visiting with a couple of your friends."

She frowned. "We weren't really visiting. They were basically telling me I was a fool and needed to stop seeing you." She looked down at her lap. "They couldn't believe that you would really be interested in me and they're sure I'm going to get hurt. They implied that I look like a foolish old lady with you and that people disapprove of us together."

"Harper, look at me." She looked up and into his beautiful eyes. "If I were you, I'd get really tired and more than a little bit angry at people implying that you somehow aren't enough to hold my attention. If it's a matter of them thinking I'm somehow using you, then what am I using you for? For your money? I don't need your money, I have plenty of my own. Do they think I'm using you for a quick hookup? To be perfectly honest I could get a hookup every single night of the week, but that's not what I'm looking for."

"Then what are you looking for with me?" she asked.

"Aside from the fact that I think you're beautiful both inside and out, I find you intelligent and I enjoy having conversations with you. You have a wonderful sense of humor and I like laughing with you. I like that you're a strong woman who is confident in your own skin."

He paused a moment and then continued, "Harper, I'm just into you and some things don't need to or can't be explained. It's a matter of chemistry. Now, are you going to allow other people to dictate who you should or shouldn't date?"

He reached out and took her hand in his. "Harper, right now we're a novelty item to gossip about. People would rather gossip about us than think about the two murders that have occurred, murders that have everyone frightened. But tomorrow or the day after everyone will find something else to gossip about. I promise you this will pass and eventually nobody will care what we're doing together. Now, I'd like to ask you out again. Are you in?"

She held his gaze while a million emotions and thoughts flew around in her head. She had been so sure she wasn't going to go out with him again. One and done, that was what she'd believed where dating him was concerned.

However, ultimately it came down to one important thing: What did she really want for herself? And in this moment, she decided she wanted Sam.

"I'm in," she answered.

He smiled and squeezed her hand. "That's my girl. How about tomorrow night I take you to the Farmer's Club for drinks and some good conversation?"

"That sounds nice," she replied. To heck with everyone else and what they thought. She was willing to see where this thing with Sam went. It wasn't as if her heart was involved. She was just enjoying his company. Right now, she was just having fun with him.

As he finished up his last cookie, she looked around the room and realized there was almost no one else left inside. The coffee machine had been packed away, the doughnuts and cookies had disappeared and three men were folding up the chairs and carrying them to the storage closet next to the stage.

"We need to get out of here, otherwise we're going to be folded up and shoved in the closet," she observed.

"That would not be a good thing," he said with a laugh and together they rose. "I'm going to follow you home," he said as they exited the building.

"Why? That really isn't necessary."

"I think it's necessary and it's because it's after dark and you're all alone and your safety matters to me," he replied.

"Oh…okay, thanks." It had been a very long time since anyone had cared if she got home safely from someplace or not. After all the warnings they had just gotten from Dallas, she wasn't going to turn down his offer.

He saw her to her car and then hurried across the parking lot to get into his truck. She waited until his truck was right behind her to pull out of the parking lot.

She had another date with Sam and she was probably going to catch more hell from her friends. But she didn't care. She'd been alone for a very long time now and it felt good to have somebody to share things with,…somebody to talk to and laugh with. She was doing this for herself and not to please anyone else and, aside from her work, it had been a long time since she'd done something to make herself happy.

When she reached her house, she parked in the driveway and got out of her car. She waved to Sam and then hurried toward her front door, thankful that she'd left her porch light on.

She saw it immediately and her heart began to thunder loudly in her ears as the back of her throat closed up in stunned shock.

"It" appeared to be an old woman fashion doll hanging on a wreath holder she had on her front door. A nail file was pushed through the doll's head and a note was folded and tucked beneath one of her arms.

Who had done this? Who had left this horrible thing on her front door? She stumbled several steps backward. She spun around toward where Sam's truck was still parked at the curb. He opened his door. "Harper, is everything okay?" he yelled to her.

"N-no, it's not." That was all she could manage to say as her throat continued to squeeze closed with shock.

And that was all she needed to say for Sam to jump out of the truck and came running to her side. He immediately saw the doll and ripped it off the wreath holder. "Let's go inside," he said tersely.

With trembling fingers, she unlocked the door, opened it and then flew into her living room. Sam followed her in and shut and locked the door behind him.

She walked with shaky legs to the sofa and sank down. He joined her there, plucking the note from under the doll's arm and then placing the doll on the coffee table in front of them.

A deep frown cut across his forehead as he opened the note. "What does it say?" she asked, consciously trying to keep her gaze away from the horrible, mutilated doll.

"'Have you lost your brain?'" he read. "'Date somebody your own age.'" He tossed the note on the coffee table. "This really pisses me off." He got up from the sofa and pulled his cell phone from his back pocket. "I need to call Dallas. Maybe he can catch the bastard who left this for you."

She nodded and fought against an icy chill that threatened to crawl up her back. Who had done this? Who had left this atrocity on her door? Who cared so much about who she was dating? Obviously, it had to have been somebody who saw them together tonight at the town meeting and had left the community center before them. That was almost the entire town.

She was vaguely aware of Sam making the call to Dallas and then he returned to sit next to her. He took her hands in his and she welcomed the familiar warmth of his touch against her icy fingers.

"Honey, don't be afraid," he said softly. "This was done by a coward…a jerk who wants to try to bully you. I hope you don't let this get to you."

"I just can't imagine who would do such a horrible thing. Who would care enough about my dating habits to go to all this trouble?" She searched his handsome features as if she might find the answers there.

"Hopefully, Dallas will be able to tell us who did this," he replied.

"Us." It was nice to know she wasn't all alone in this, that Sam was taking this on as his issue, too. "Has anyone else asked you out recently? Maybe somebody who would see me as their competition?" he asked and released his grasp on her hands.

"No," she replied. "Nobody has asked me out for at least a year or so."

A little over a year ago she had gone out on one date with Billy Jackson. He was a nice older man who worked at the post office. They had gone out to dinner together at the café but had quickly realized they had very little in common and there had been absolutely no sparks between them. They hadn't gone on a second date and he had just recently married a nice woman who worked at the grocery store. Since then, nobody else had asked her out. Nobody had shown any kind of a romantic interest in her. Not until Sam.

She and Sam sat in silence for several long minutes. She was still trying to wrap her mind around the horrid doll that had been left for her. Who on earth would even think to do such a thing? Who would think to drive a nail file into a doll's head? It was positively sick.

"Harper." Sam said her name softly. She turned to

look at him again. "It's going to be all right. I swear it's just a stupid scare tactic."

"Well, it worked because right now I'm scared," she replied.

"Try not to be," he replied. "I really believe whoever did this isn't a real threat to you."

She desperately wanted to believe him, but she couldn't help the shivers of fear that continued to race up and down her back.

Again, they fell into silence and minutes later a knock sounded at her door. It was Dallas, and she was hoping the lawman would be able to tell her whether she should really be afraid or not.

As Dallas questioned Harper, Sam once again took one of her hands in his to show his support. Her hand felt so small and trembled slightly as she told Dallas she had no idea who would be this angry that she was seeing Sam.

Dammit, he hated that she was so frightened. He hated the dark shadows that had taken over the beautiful sparkle of her blue eyes… the fear that tightened her lush lips into a thin slash. And he hated that this had happened because he was seeing her.

"Two of my girlfriends talked to me tonight after the meeting about not liking the fact that I'd gone out with Sam on a date," she now said.

"Their names?" Dallas asked.

"Becky Barlow and Allie Crawford, but neither

of them would stoop so low as to do something like this," Harper said. "They're nice women and they would never, ever even think about doing something as crazy, as awful as that." She gestured to the doll in front of her.

"What about you, Sam?"

Sam straightened up and looked at Dallas in surprise. "What about me?"

"Are there any women out there who might have a problem with you seeing Harper?"

"Not that I'm aware of," Sam replied.

"Any women who have made it clear they'd like to go out with you?" Dallas asked.

Sam was aware of Harper gazing at him curiously. "Uh, Celeste Winthrop has let me know on more than one occasion she'd like me to ask her out, but I've tried to make it clear to her it isn't going to happen." He tightened his hand around Harper's. It felt a bit awkward to discuss this in front of Harper. "But honestly I can't imagine Celeste doing something like this."

"You'd be surprised what some people will do," Dallas replied dryly. "We know somebody here in town is hiding an evil secret as far as the murders are concerned. Why wouldn't Celeste harbor a secret hatred of Harper if she was desperate enough for a date with you?" He released a deep sigh and stood. "I'll just run out to my car and get an evidence bag.

I'll dust the doll for fingerprints and maybe we'll get lucky."

As he walked out the front door, Harper pulled her hand away from Sam's. "Are you okay?" he asked her worriedly.

"I will be," she replied. "I just have a few questions for Dallas." She leaned back against the sofa cushion with a frown working lines across her forehead. "I hate that we even had to bother him with this. He already has so much on his plate with the two murders that have occurred."

"True, but he also needs to know the other things that are going on in his town. I wouldn't have felt right not calling him about this," he replied.

At that moment Dallas came back through the door. "I'm assuming you don't want to keep this nasty piece of work," he said as he pulled on a pair of gloves.

"I definitely want it gone out of my house as quickly as possible," she replied fervently.

Once he had his gloves on, Dallas took the doll and placed it in the bag he'd brought in. He also put the note in the bag. "I hate to tell you this, but right now no real crime has been committed here. If things like this were to continue then I might be able to make a case for stalking or trespassing at the very least. What I hope is I can hunt down the person who did this and have a stern talk with him or her and make sure this kind of nonsense stops."

"I just want to know if I should be afraid or not," Harper said, her voice trembling slightly. Once again, a rich anger ripped through Sam. Damn whoever did this. Damn whoever had frightened her like this.

Dallas frowned thoughtfully and raked a hand through his hair. "It is a thinly veiled threat, but I don't think you need to be overly concerned with it. Honestly, people who do things like this are rarely a real physical threat. Of course, there are always exceptions to the rule, but they are rare. All I can really tell you is what I said earlier tonight at the town meeting…watch your surroundings and stay aware. Don't let anyone get into your personal space unless you want them there."

"Thank you, Dallas, for coming out here for this. I know you have far more important things to deal with right now," she said.

Dallas smiled at her. "I'm glad you called me. It's important that I know everything that's going on in this town," he said, mirroring what Sam had told her moments before.

Sam got up and walked the lawman to the door. "Thanks, Dallas. We appreciate it."

"No problem. I'll be in touch and let you know what I find out," he replied.

The minute Dallas left Sam returned to his seat on the sofa next to Harper. "Harper, I hope you don't give this creep the power to make you stop seeing me," he said.

She stared at him for several long moments and then a slow smile curved her lips. "You know what they say about bullies. They say the best way to deal with one is to stand up to them, so I don't intend to change anything I'm doing right now."

"That's my girl," Sam replied with a smile of his own. From the moment he'd seen the doll and the note, he'd been afraid that Harper was going to tell him she was done with him.

"Are you sure you wouldn't rather date Celeste Winthrop? She's a beautiful woman and she's much more your own age," Harper said.

"Why would I want to date a woman who seems superficial and rather vacant when I can date a woman who is warm and real and can actually have a meaningful conversation with me?"

"And why would I date an old man when I can date a handsome young hunk like you?" she replied.

He was grateful to see the light back in her eyes, taking the place of the dark shadows of fear that had been there minutes before.

"I *am* totally a hunk," he replied.

She laughed. "And a humble hunk at that."

"So, we're still on for tomorrow night to go to the Farmer's Club?" he asked.

She hesitated a moment and then nodded. "Yes, we're still on."

"Then we'll firm up the time tomorrow during my lunch break."

"Sounds good to me," she replied.

He got up from the sofa. "It's getting late and I know you have an early morning so I'm going to get out of here." She got up as well and walked with him to the door.

He opened it and then turned back to her. "Are you okay to be alone tonight?"

"You'll have to work harder than that to get into my bed, Sam Bravano," she said wryly.

"No... That's... It's... That's not what I meant," he sputtered.

She laughed. "Sam, I'm just giving you a hard time, but in any case, I'll be fine. I've got good locks on my doors and windows."

"Harper, if you get scared or just feel the need to talk, no matter what the time, you know I'm only a phone call away," he said. "And I can be here in less than five minutes if you need me."

"Thank you, Sam. I really appreciate it."

He raised an eyebrow and winked at her. "Do you need a kiss to get you through the night?"

She shoved him toward the door with another laugh. "You are incorrigible. Good night, Sam."

"'Night, Harper." He stepped out on the front porch as she closed the door behind her. He waited until he heard the satisfying sound of her door lock clicking and then a dead bolt being turned.

As he walked to his truck, he used the faint light of a nearby streetlamp and the moon overhead to make sure nobody was lurking around her house.

Driving home, he tightened his hands around the steering wheel as a sharp anger stabbed into him once again. Who had left that damned mutilated doll for her to find? Who cared that much about who Harper was dating? Unfortunately, he had no idea. She had no idea, either, and he seriously doubted that Dallas would be able to find the culprit.

There was also an anger and a small amount of guilt that he was the cause of that doll being left for her. What was he supposed to do? Stop seeing her because some creep had a problem with it? Dammit, he wasn't ready to stop seeing her, especially not because of a doll and a note.

In the time he'd been working for her, he hadn't noticed anyone showing any kind of a romantic interest in her. Sure, she had several male regulars who came into the bakery, but as she'd told Dallas, none of them had ever asked her out or indicated to her that they had romance on the mind where she was concerned.

Was it possible it was some woman in town who was angry at Sam? Celeste? The woman had definitely been chasing him for the last couple of months or so. Was it possible she had done this? Maybe when he got home, he'd find something disgusting had been left on his door, too.

He needed to call Dallas and tell him there were several other women in town who had been pretty forward in wanting Sam to ask them out. He hadn't wanted to rattle off a list of names with Harper sitting right there next to him. It would have not only been embarrassing, but it had felt like it would be disrespectful to Harper.

Despite the growing lateness of the hour, his two brothers were seated on his front porch when he pulled in and parked. "Don't you two have a home?" he asked after greeting them. He unlocked his door and the two followed him inside.

"Yeah, we have a home, but we like yours better," Michael said as he flopped down on the sofa.

"You know Ma goes to bed really early and we weren't ready to call it a night yet," Tony said as he took up the other half of the sofa.

"Why don't you move out and into your own places?" Sam eased down in his recliner, his thoughts still on Harper and what had happened. Nothing had been left on his front door which led him to believe it was somebody Harper knew who was upset about the two of them dating each other.

"You know we don't want to leave Ma all alone," Michael said.

"She would probably be happy to be all alone, and you mean you don't want to leave a place where your meals are cooked and your clothes are washed and where the two of you are babied," Sam replied.

"Well, there is that," Tony said with a laugh.

"I haven't heard from Lauren in a while. How's she doing?" Sam asked.

A touch of guilt shot through him as he thought of his older sister. Lauren was two years older than Sam and the two siblings had always been close. They usually touched base by phone at least once a week or so, but at least two weeks had gone by since the last time he'd talked to her.

"She's fine. Her and Russ have been busy putting together her shop," Tony said.

Lauren had married Russ Lincoln three years ago. Russ was a nice guy who worked as a firefighter and was helping Lauren's dream of opening a trinket and dress shop on Main Street come true.

"How's the shop coming along?" Sam asked.

"According to what Lauren told me, the interior has all been painted and the shelving is mostly in," Tony said. "You should go by and check it out. I think it's going to be really nice."

"I'll do that," Sam said.

"On another note, you'll be happy to know that Paula and I are back together again," Michael said.

"He's such a schmuck," Tony said with disgust.

"I'm happy about it if you're happy," Sam said.

"I'm totally happy," Michael said with a wide grin. "She's definitely what I want."

"Schmuck," Tony replied.

"So, what did you think about the meeting tonight?" Michael asked, obviously ignoring Tony.

"As far as I'm concerned there were no real surprises," Sam said.

"I feel bad for Dallas," Tony said. "He's got to be pulling his hair out over this. One murder was bad enough, but two is horrible. Sandy was a real nice woman."

"Yeah, she was, and it sounds like Dallas has no clues to help him solve the murders," Michael added.

"He's a smart man. Eventually he'll figure it out and get the murderer behind bars," Sam said.

"I found one thing very surprising about tonight," Michael said. "What are you doing with Harper Brennan?"

"I'm dating her."

Tony straightened up and stared at Sam. "For real?"

Sam nodded. "For real."

"Why?" Michael asked.

"Ah duh, because I like her," Sam said. "I like her a lot and I'm enjoying spending time with her."

"Yeah, but you could date any hot young chick in town. Why Harper? Isn't she a lot older than you?" Michael asked.

"I don't want any of the hot young chicks in town. I've already dated my share of them. Harper excites me. The age thing doesn't bother me at all. I just really like being with her," Sam said. "She's smart and funny and I'm eager to get to know her even better."

"Don't you worry that maybe she's dating you as some sort of a trophy? She must be happy for everyone to see she can score with a hot younger man," Tony replied.

That thought had crossed Sam's mind, but he knew better now. "Harper isn't that kind of a woman and right now I intend to keep seeing her whether you guys like it or not," Sam said.

"I don't have a problem with it, I just think it's kind of weird," Tony replied.

"And I give it two weeks and you'll be ready to move on to a younger, hotter woman," Michael said.

The conversation suddenly irritated him and he was glad when they didn't stay long after that. He didn't need to hear their negative opinions about dating Harper. Couldn't anyone be happy that he and Harper were happy together? And who had left that doll on her front door?

Right now, Sam had two worries in his head. The first was Harper's safety, even though he tended to agree with Dallas that the creep who'd left the doll was probably harmless.

His other concern was that Harper would bend to the pressures around her and stop seeing him.

For the first time in his life, he'd found a woman he wanted to fight for and he wasn't just walking out of Harper's life without a battle.

Chapter Six

Harper checked her reflection in the mirror and mentally pronounced herself ready for another date with Sam. She'd tossed and turned all night long, thinking about the doll and her friends and Sam.

There was absolutely no way she believed Allie or Becky had anything to do with the doll. They'd certainly speak their minds, and had during the meeting, but Harper believed there was no way they'd stoop to such a level as to leave that horrendous doll for her to find. They just weren't that kind of people.

The easy thing for her to do would be to stop seeing Sam in any kind of a social way. Then her friends would be happy and whoever had left the doll for her would be happy. Everyone would be happy except her.

That day when Sam had taken his lunchtime inside the bakery with her, he'd reminded her of just how much she enjoyed his company. He caused a girly breathlessness deep inside her at the same time he made her laugh.

His presence in her life had eased the deep core of loneliness that had been with her since the day her husband had walked out on her. And somehow, she didn't believe anyone else would have done that as well as Sam had.

All the pushback she had gotten about dating him had made her wake up that morning with a new determination that she was going to see Sam whenever, however she damn well pleased. To heck with everyone else.

She wasn't a complete fool. She didn't believe they had any kind of a real future together, but for the first time in her life, she was doing something to please herself. He made her happy, and she hadn't really been happy in her personal life in a very long time. She would continue to see Sam as long as he wanted to see her.

She now left her bathroom and went into the living room to wait for Sam's arrival. It was going to be a very low-key night, drinks and conversation at the Farmer's Club. After last night she was definitely looking for a low-key, drama-free evening.

It had been another hot day and so she wore another sundress this evening, this time in a bright pink. She'd worn it several times before and had always gotten compliments, so she knew it looked good on her. And she wanted to look as good as she could for Sam.

She jumped up as a knock sounded on the door. That would be him and her heart did a crazy little dance as she went to answer. She opened the door and a new warmth swept through her at the sight of him. Nobody wore a pair of jeans as well as Sam, and the emerald green polo shirt he wore brought out the beautiful color of his long-lashed eyes. He looked totally hot.

That charming dimple winked in his cheek as he grinned at her. "Wow, you look absolutely gorgeous," he said as his gaze swept the length of her. It wasn't just his words, but the light in his eyes that heated the pool of warmth that was already in her stomach. His eyes told her that his words were true. He really thought she looked gorgeous.

"Thank you, and you clean up real nice, too," she replied.

She stepped out into the warm evening air and after locking her door, together they headed for his truck. Gray clouds overhead portended the possibility of a rainstorm. She knew the farmers in the area were probably hoping for rain after the past couple weeks of unrelentingly hot days.

"The bakery is looking better and better every day," she said once they were in his truck.

He smiled. "Yeah, it won't be long now before

it's ready for a fresh coat of paint. Have you thought about what color you'd like?"

"Something bright and fun. I'm thinking maybe a cheerful yellow," she replied.

He laughed. "I was sure you were going to tell me you wanted it painted a hot pink."

She also laughed. "Trust me, I considered it, but in the end, I decided I don't want a big pink building."

"Yellow would be nice, and some of the trim could be pink."

"That sounds perfect," she replied, glad that they were on the same page. "The building would look like one of my lemon cupcakes."

"You still need to show me what you want in the back of the building," he reminded her.

Instantly, a vision of Sandy Blackstone on a pole with her eyes gone and her mouth sewn shut with thick black thread sprang into her head. The idea of going out into the backyard again still filled her with a deep anxiety.

"Sooner or later, you've got to go back out there," Sam said softly, as if reading her thoughts. He reached out and lightly touched her hand. "We'll make something really beautiful out there." He returned his hand to the steering wheel.

Once again, her heart warmed with his words. He always seemed to know exactly what to say to make her feel better. He always seemed to know what was important to her. Sam was definitely getting under her skin and the last thing she wanted was for him to get into her heart. That would definitely make her a foolish old woman.

He pulled up and parked in front of the Farmer's Club. The bar was located in a small building just off Main Street. The front of the bar was quite unassuming, with blinds in the windows and one small neon beer sign.

He helped her out of the truck and then they entered the bar. Instantly her nose was assailed by the scents of frying onions, hamburgers and beer.

There was a long, polished bar on one side of the room and booths and tables on the other. Along the back was a dartboard and a shuffleboard area where two older couples were currently playing.

She was surprised that Sam was greeted not only by several of the old men seated at the bar, but also by the bartender, Ranger Simmons. He also greeted her, as he was one of her morning regulars.

She knew that Ranger had lost his wife years ago. He had a farm on the outskirts of town that he had ultimately given to his son. He'd been the owner of this place for over twenty years and now lived alone in the rooms upstairs.

Sam led her to an empty booth and once they settled in, Ranger walked over to them to take their orders. "Hey, Harper, you look really nice tonight. That pink is really your color."

"Thanks, Ranger," she replied with a smile.

"She looks good in any color," Sam said.

"That's true, and the bakery is looking better already," Ranger said.

"That's thanks to Sam," she replied with a warm look across the table.

"You'd better do right by her, Sam," Ranger said.

Sam laughed. "I know if I don't, I'll have to answer to all the regular customers she has."

"You got that right," Ranger replied with a laugh of his own. "Now, what would the lady like this evening?" he asked.

Harper wasn't really much of a drinker, but occasionally she enjoyed a beer or a gin and tonic, so she ordered the latter. "With a double twist of lime," she added.

Ranger smiled at her. "Ah, a perfect drink for a hot summer night. What about you, Sam? The usual?"

"That works for me," Sam replied.

"Any food for the two of you?" Ranger asked.

Sam looked at Harper. "Please, order anything you like. Ranger is a master of all kinds of bar food."

"Thanks, but I'm good for now," she replied. She had eaten a sandwich before Sam had picked her up. She especially felt good right now given the fact that nobody in the bar had looked at them askance. In fact, several of the other couples had nodded and smiled at them pleasantly. It was definitely a nice change from their night in the café.

Within minutes they both had their drinks and she discovered Sam's regular was a whisky and soda. The music playing overhead was soft, an old George Jones country tune, and the other conversations in the room were nothing more than soft murmurs.

"Do you come here often?" she asked.

"Not too often, but occasionally. It's a good place to come alone and unwind with a drink. Of course, it's much nicer to have you here to unwind with," he said with that smile that always melted something deep inside her.

"I'm glad to be here with you," she replied.

"Sometimes I enjoy coming here and sitting with some of the old-timers. I like talking to them about a variety of topics," he said.

For the next few minutes, they talked about the work on the bakery and some things she would like to see in the backyard behind it.

"I want a nice covered patio where on nice days families can come and sit and enjoy the ambiance along with the food," she said. "I'll run different kinds of family specials that will hopefully bring in more people."

"That's one of the things I admire about you, you're a smart businesswoman," he said.

She laughed. "I'll tell you a little secret. I mostly fly by the seat of my pants."

"Then you have darn good instincts," he replied.

"My brothers and I have our own business, the Bravano Brothers Renovation and Construction Company."

She looked at him in surprise. "I didn't realize you all were an actual company. I just thought you and your brothers casually worked with each other."

"I know that's how it appears, but we are an actual LLC company. I keep the books. Everything that we make goes into the business bank account and then we pay ourselves out of that."

"I've seen your brothers working on the gazebo in the park." She took a sip of her drink. "It looks like that's going to be beautiful for everyone to enjoy."

He nodded. "It is going to be nice. They should be finished with that job just in time to help me at the bakery."

"You seem to have plenty to do around town."

"We stay really busy during the summers. The buildings in this town need a lot of work and there seems to be a general mood among the building owners that now is the time to renew things."

"And then what will you do when everything is done here in Millsville?" she asked curiously.

"I figure by that time I'll be ready to retire. Then I'll be your houseboy and clean and cook for you and eat delicious cakes every night," he said with that charming twinkle in his eyes.

She laughed. "It's nice to know you have your future all planned out for yourself."

He took a drink and then gazed into her eyes once again. "What do you see for your future?"

"To be honest, I don't think about my future too much. I tend to live in the here and now," she replied and then took a sip of her drink.

"But if you were to really think about it right now, what do you foresee for yourself?" He leaned forward slightly and his gaze seemed to be probing deep inside her.

"Oh, I don't know. I'd like to work the bakery for a long time and then maybe when it's at the very height of being profitable, I'd sell it and live on the proceeds."

"And then what? Do you see yourself traveling or writing a book, or just swinging in a hammock?" he asked.

"Definitely not swinging in a hammock or writing a book, but a little traveling would be nice. I've never been out of Millsville," she said.

"Ever?" he asked in surprise. "Didn't you and your ex-husband ever travel on a vacation?"

"My ex-husband's idea of a vacation was to drive out to Johnson's pond and go fishing," she replied. Ed Johnson lived on a farm on the outskirts of town and had the biggest, best fishing pond in the area. He was a cantankerous old widower who charged people for fishing privileges.

"Then we have to plan to take a trip together," he

said, the twinkle back in his eyes. "Where would you like to go for your first trip out of Millsville?"

"Oh, I'd love to fly to New York City and visit Times Square, or maybe jet off to Las Vegas and try my hand at the tables." She laughed. "If we're really fantasizing here, why not a quick trip to the Bahamas or another beautiful island. Have you traveled a lot?"

"Not a whole lot, but I've done some. I've been to New York City and to San Francisco. I've also been to the Grand Canyon and to Niagara Falls. However, I've never been out of the country. There's so much to see and explore right here in the United States."

"I definitely agree with that. I've just never felt like I could close up shop and take any real time off," she replied.

"But you should. At least once a year you should close down for a week or so and get out of town. It would be good for you and the people of Millsville will survive without their cake and cookies for a week. I've never been to Las Vegas. Maybe sometime in the future we could plan a trip together there."

She smiled. "We'll see," she replied. However, the idea of traveling somewhere, anywhere with Sam was incredibly appealing. Part of the reason she'd never traveled anywhere was because her husband had never wanted to and then after he left her, she didn't go anywhere because she was a woman all alone.

Now her head filled with visions of her and Sam walking hand in hand down the Vegas strip. They would gamble a little bit during the day and then they could eat dinner together in a castle or some other fun restaurant. Then they would head back to a hotel room where they would...

She stopped the thoughts before they could take her to a place where she'd blush and fill with a heat to rival one of her hot flashes.

He ordered another round of drinks for them and the topic of conversation went back to family. "If you don't mind my asking, why didn't you and your husband ever have any children?" he asked.

"My husband never wanted children and to be honest, I wasn't one of those maternal women who wanted to get married and have babies. I spent a lot of my marriage working hard to save money to open up the bakery. That's my child." She paused and took another drink, then gazed at him once again. "Do you want to have children?"

He smiled. "No, I've never been one of those paternal men who wanted to get married and have babies. Having children just isn't in my wheelhouse."

"Are you sure you won't change your mind about that in the future?" she pressed. This was definitely an issue that concerned her if she and Sam were to continue having a relationship. She couldn't give him a child if that was what he wanted. Of course, she still didn't believe there was any kind of a future with him, especially that kind of a long-term future.

"I'm positive, although I'm looking forward to being an uncle to my siblings' children." There was a note of finality in his voice. "And now I want to ask you a very important question."

"Wait, if it's a very important question then I'd better have another sip of this." She picked up her glass and took a big gulp, then looked at him with a touch of anxiety.

He laughed. "It's not that important, Harper. I just wanted to know if this Sunday you'd come over to my mom's house and have dinner with my family. I'd really love for you to meet everyone."

"Oh, I don't know," she replied and took another sip of her drink. The idea of meeting his family was more than a little bit daunting.

"Come on, Harper. I promise you none of us bite and Mom is making her eggplant parmesan, which is absolutely delicious. You can officially meet my mom, my brothers and my sister and they can meet you."

"Sister?" She looked at him in surprise. "I didn't know you had a sister. You've never talked about her before."

He nodded. "Yeah, Lauren. She's two years older than me and happily married. Now, don't change the subject. Will you come to dinner on Sunday? I'll pick you up and take you back home." He reached across the table and took her hand in his. "It's important to me, Harper. I'd really like for you to come."

Oh, his green eyes pulled her in and as always, the touch of his hand around hers both thrilled her and made her feel oddly safe. "Okay," she relented. "I suppose I'll come."

His dimple winked as he gave her a huge smile. "That's my girl." He squeezed her hand and then released it.

She released a deep sigh. "I wish I could introduce you to my parents. My father would have liked you."

"And your mother wouldn't have liked me?" One of his dark eyebrows shot up.

"Oh, no…she would have liked you, too. But my father and you would have had a lot in common. Even though he worked as a janitor at the high school, he liked to do a little woodworking on the weekends."

"I'm sorry I can't meet them," he said softly. Once again, he reached out, took her hand in his and gently squeezed.

"Yeah, me too," she replied and cast him a bittersweet smile.

It was just after ten when they left the Farmer's Club. By the time they left, Harper had a little buzz on and she wasn't sure if it was from the two drinks she had consumed or from having Sam's undivided attention for so long.

He definitely had the ability to make a woman

feel like she was the most important, most beautiful woman in the room. He made her feel witty and smart. It was a heady feeling and one she had never experienced from a man before.

Her husband had been a rather cold man, short on compliments and even shorter on attention and affection. Looking back now, she wasn't even sure why she had married him. She must have loved him at one time, but after the affair it was now difficult to tap back into any loving feelings she might have once had for him.

Sam was a whole different kind of animal. He was gregarious and attentive. He was affectionate and caring and he filled a hole inside her soul that she hadn't even known was there.

"I've enjoyed this evening, Harper," he said as he walked her to her front door.

"I really enjoyed it, too. Thank you for inviting me," she replied. She unlocked her front door and then turned back to him.

"I'll pick you up on Sunday about noon, and we usually eat about one or so," he said. Lightning flashed in the distance, followed by a low rumble of thunder.

"Okay, now you better get out of here before you get wet," she said with a glance up at the thick clouds overhead.

He grinned at her. "A little rain never hurt me.

Besides, before I leave, I'm hoping to get a good-night kiss."

Her heartbeat quickened as he leaned closer to her, so close she could feel his body heat and see the tiny gold flecks in the very depths of his green eyes. "So, am I going to leave here brokenhearted or are you going to let me kiss you good-night?"

She laughed. "Oh, jeez, you're so dramatic. I certainly don't want to be the one to break your heart."

He immediately drew her into his arms and claimed her lips with his. She opened her mouth to him and their tongues moved together in a heated dance.

As the kiss continued, she reached up and wrapped her arms around his neck and he pulled her intimately close against him. She loved the feel of his strong, broad chest against her breasts and the fire that had ignited inside her grew more intense.

He finally pulled his lips from hers and blazed a trail of teasing nips and kisses down her throat. She threw her head back to allow him access. She was lost…utterly lost in the desire he stoked inside her.

It had been so long since a man had held her so tightly, so long since she'd experienced the fluttering heat that now rushed through her.

It was him who finally released her and took a step backward. His eyes glittered hot with desire and he swept a hand through his hair. "Oh, woman. You are so in my blood." His words shot another rivulet of delicious heat through her.

At that moment the skies opened up and rain began to pour down on them. "Go, get inside before you drown," he said with a laugh.

"Good night, Sam. I'll see you tomorrow," she replied and then hurried through her door.

However, she didn't see him the next morning. The rain system that had moved in the night before had stalled overhead and rain continued to fall the next day.

Just because Sam couldn't work didn't mean he was out of her thoughts. In fact, he was all she could think about as she baked her goods for the day and then opened the bakery for business.

Things seemed to be moving incredibly fast with Sam. There had been a moment at the door the night before while he was kissing her that she'd actually considered letting him come inside to make love with her.

Her intense desire for him had shocked and surprised her. That desire wasn't just built on the fact that Sam was good-looking and had an awesome body. Rather she wanted him because he was a good man who drew her in emotionally as well as physically.

She also knew now that he desired her. Last night as he'd pulled her so tight against his body, she'd realized that he was fully aroused. That had only made her desire for him grow hotter and more intense.

And this Sunday she was going to meet all his family. Yes, everything with Sam was definitely moving fast. She still had no idea where things were going with him or how long they would be going at all. Right now, she was just thoroughly enjoying the ride.

Surely there would come a time when Sam would realize she was too old, much too staid for him. Surely he would eventually tire of her company and want someone livelier...somebody younger. She knew that time would eventually come and that was why she needed to hang on to her heart where he was concerned.

She was just enjoying Sam's company and having fun, she kept telling herself, and she assumed that was what he was doing with her as well. But when the fun was over, she knew he'd move on.

Could she sleep with him and still hang on to her heart? She believed she could. Was she ready to take that next step with him? She wasn't sure.

The dreary, rainy morning kept everyone away from the bakery. Even her regulars didn't show up for their usual coffee and cinnamon rolls as rain pelted down from the gray skies.

It was early afternoon when Sam called her. "What's happening with my favorite baker?" he asked, his deep voice rolling over her in pleasant tones.

"Absolutely nothing," she replied. "Not a single soul has been inside this morning."

"Really? That's unusual," he replied.

"It's just too rainy for anyone to want to get out."

"Do you miss me?"

"I plead the Fifth," she said with a laugh.

"There you go again, playing hard to get."

She laughed again. The truth was she did miss him. Even though he worked outside, it was always nice to know he was there. It was definitely nice to watch him work. She was going to miss him in the next hour or so when he normally came inside for his break.

"What are you doing today?" she asked.

"I'm moping around."

She laughed. "You are not."

"Okay, I'm not. I just got finished painting the bathroom in the basement."

"I knew you were probably working on something. You aren't one to just sit idle for too long."

"If you've been there all alone all morning that means you've had a lot of time to think. You haven't changed your mind about Sunday, have you?" he asked.

"No, I haven't changed my mind," she replied.

"Good, I'm really looking forward to it. I know my family is going to love you."

"I hope so." A wave of anxiety swept through her as she thought about spending the day with his family.

They chatted for a little while longer and then said their goodbyes. Hopefully the weather would be better by tomorrow and Sam would be back working as usual.

At around two o'clock the rain finally stopped, but the clouds remained thick and gray overhead. It was just after two when Annie Cook came through the door. Annie was a pleasant young woman who had two children, and she frequented the bakery often.

"What a miserable, dreary day it has been," she said as she came through the door. "How are you doing, Harper?"

"I'm about to die of boredom. It's been a very slow day. In fact, you're my first customer of the day," Harper replied.

"Oh, wow, you probably have been bored in here all by yourself. It's been such a dismal day I decided to treat my kids and hubby with some cupcakes," Annie said.

"What kind would you like? I have chocolate, vanilla, and dark cherry ones today," Harper explained.

"How about two of each," Annie replied.

"How are your kids doing?" Harper asked as she began boxing up the cupcakes.

"Right now, they're at my mother's for a little while. I love my kids, but to be perfectly honest I'm more than ready for summer to be over and school to begin."

Harper laughed. "I imagine all the mothers in town are feeling that way about now."

"Especially on rainy days like today," Annie added. "My little angels suddenly turn into little monsters when they're cooped up inside for too long." Annie pulled money out of her wallet. "I definitely needed a little break from them. I should feel guilty that I dropped them off at my mother's earlier, but do you want to know a secret? I don't feel guilty at all."

Harper laughed again. "I promise your secret is safe with me."

A few minutes after Annie left, RJ Morgan strode into the bakery. RJ owned the tattoo shop next door. He was a walking advertisement for his business. His bald head and face were heavily inked, as were his thick arms. He was a big, burly man who Harper had always found rather intimidating.

"Hi, RJ," she said with a smile. He'd only been in the shop once before and that had been when she'd first bought the building and, on that day, he had been very angry. Apparently one of his buddies had intended to buy the bakery building and he'd been angry that she'd bought it before his friend could get all his finances together.

He didn't return her smile. "Harper, when is all the crap you have outside going to be cleaned up?"

She took a step backward, surprised at the question. "As soon as Sam Bravano is finished with renovating the front of the bakery," she replied.

"There's so much crap, it's a damn eyesore out there," he replied, his brow pulled down to his bushy eyebrows in a deep frown. He was half leaning over the display counter, slightly menacing in his nearness.

"It's all the materials Sam is using to do the job," she countered.

"Why can't he put them out around the back where they can't be seen?"

"Why would he do that when he's using them on the front of the building?" she replied.

"He'd better use them up damn fast. I'm sick of seeing it all."

Harper raised her chin defensively. "It's on my property and it can be there as long as it needs to be." A hot flash suddenly took hold of her, heating her face, her neck and her chest.

She knew her face was probably turning a beet red as small dots of sweat sprang out on her forehead. "Nothing is on your property or bothering your business, so you have no right to complain about anything."

Her voice might have sounded more strident than she intended, for RJ took a step backward. Or maybe he moved back because he saw her turning bright red and he was afraid she might explode.

"If any of that material gets on my property, I'll burn it," he said and then turned and exited the shop.

Harper released a deep sigh and then hurried over to the sink. She wet an unused cleaning cloth and wiped it across her face and neck in an effort to cool down.

The hot flash slowly passed and as usual left her slightly chilled. She sat on the chair behind the cash register, wrapped her arms around herself and released another deep sigh.

RJ was a total jerk. There was no way the material Sam had stacked outside her store in any way affected the business in the tattoo shop next door. He'd been mad at her ever since she'd bought the building. He must have just been waiting all this time for something to bitch to her about.

At four-thirty a light rain started up again and Harper began to get things ready to close. She put the items that froze well into the freezer and then packed up some of the other things for Elijah Simpson to pick up.

Every Wednesday he came in for any of her leftovers for the food bank he ran out of the basement of his house. She knew there were some people in town and around the area who sometimes went to bed hungry, and that absolutely broke her heart. Even though she only had sweets, she was always happy to give Elijah whatever she could.

At ten 'til five, Elijah came through her door. He

was a tall, thin Black man with salt-and-pepper hair, a wide, warm smile, and a kind and gentle spirit.

"Hey, Elijah, how's it going?" she greeted him with a smile.

"It's going okay," he replied. "How are you doing, Harper?"

"Okay, although I've decided I hate rainy days."

He laughed. "Most of us do, but the farmers in the area will be happy with all this rain. They've definitely needed it lately." He eyed her for a long moment and then grinned. "I've been hearing that besides the latest murder, you're causing a bit of a stir on the gossip scene."

Harper sighed. "Apparently so. It's amazing how many people in this town are interested in my personal life."

"It's probably not that many but rather just a loud few," he replied.

"Are you going to tell me what a foolish old woman I am?"

Elijah laughed. "First of all, you aren't an old woman. Secondly, what I'll tell you is to do what makes you happy. Life is far too short, and lately, too full of sadness, not to try to find your own little piece of happiness. And once you find that, don't let anyone take it away from you."

"Thank you, Elijah. That's exactly what I believe and I'm trying to ignore all the naysayers," she replied.

"That's exactly what you should do," he said.

"Now, I've got two big bags for you today." She bent down to retrieve the things she'd packed up for him and then placed them on the counter.

"God bless you, Harper. I always try to make sure your items go to the families with children so that occasionally they can get a little sweet treat."

"I'm just glad it helps," she said.

"Oh, it helps. Every little bit helps," he replied. "And I thank you for what you donate to me."

Minutes later Elijah was gone and Harper turned the sign in the door to Closed. She was glad to close up after the long, boring day. Hopefully tomorrow the rain would be gone and business would be better.

Thank goodness she had driven her car this morning for it was raining once again and a preternatural darkness had fallen outside.

Once she'd set up things in the kitchen for the next morning, she pulled on the lightweight yellow raincoat she'd worn that morning and then went out the front door. She locked it behind her and then ran to her car parked along the side of the building.

The police had finally finished up with their investigation and released the backyard to her. However, she still hadn't made herself venture back out there yet. She just hadn't been able to force herself to go back there.

Visions of Sandy once again filled her head. She tried not to think about what she had seen, but occasionally unbidden thoughts of the horror sprang into her mind. She now consciously pushed the horrible images out of her head.

Once inside her vehicle, she shook her head and brushed the raindrops off her shoulders and then put the key in the ignition. She turned the key.

Nothing. No roar of the motor, not even an ominous click. She tried it once again with the same results. *Oh jeez*, she thought. *What now?* She waited several minutes and then tried it again. Still nothing. Obviously, the car wasn't going to start.

Damn. The rain continued to patter down on her car windows. Of all the evenings to have car trouble, she thought with a sigh. She was certainly no mechanic, but it sounded like a dead battery and she was in no mood to sit around and wait for somebody from the garage to come and jump her.

Her house was only a block and a half away. She could run home and call somebody to take care of the car in the morning. A little rain certainly wouldn't hurt her.

She sat for a few minutes longer and thankfully the rain turned into a heavy mist. Decision made, she opened her car door and stepped out.

At least the mist wasn't cold, but rather refreshingly cool. Still, she put her head down and walked briskly. Hopefully the car issue really was just the battery and would be a quick fix in the morning.

A dog barked nearby and a squirrel raced across the sidewalk in front of her. She thought she heard a footstep behind her and she stopped and turned around as the hairs on the nape of her neck raised up.

There was nobody behind her on the sidewalk. All she saw were the dark shadows that the clouds overhead had created. She turned back around and continued her brisk walk.

She was grateful to reach her front door. She now felt soaked and chilled throughout and a touch of un-easiness had risen up inside her. She inserted her key and unlocked the door and then gasped as somebody grabbed her by her shoulder and spun her around.

For a brief moment she couldn't comprehend what was happening. A man faced her. He wore dark pants, a black shirt and a ski mask that dis-guised his identity.

"Bitch," he hissed and then shot out a fist. She saw the glitter of the knife blade in his hand at the last minute and with a gasp, she whirled to the side.

The knife slashed through her thin raincoat and pain seared through her shoulder where the knife had glanced off. Terror slammed into her, tightening the back of her throat and making it impossible for her to draw a breath, let alone scream.

What was happening? Her brain struggled to make sense of it. Who was this man? Even as those questions flew through her head, she knew they didn't matter. She was in imminent danger.

Get away. Run! an inner voice screamed in-side her head, but he had her trapped with her back against her door and with nowhere to go. He stabbed at her again…and once again she managed to deflect it from hitting anything vital on her body. Still, the knife sliced into her forearm and again a searing pain roared through her.

He continued to slash at her, cutting her over and over as she did her best to dodge and weave away from the knife. Tears of pain…of terror blurred her eyes as she continued to twist and turn to escape a deadly stab.

Fight back, the voice screeched inside her. *If you can't run…then fight*, the voice continued. Sooner or later his knife would do deadly damage to her if she didn't do something, anything to stop him. She needed to act. She needed to do something to get herself out of this dangerous situation.

She finally found her voice and began to scream as loud as she possibly could. As she continued to shriek for help, a porch light blinked on across the street. A frisson of relief swept through her as she realized her screams were being heard.

The attacker paused for a brief moment and shot a glance across the street. She took the opportunity and slammed her knee up, catching him hard between his legs. He grunted and stumbled backward a step. While he was off balance, she shoved him with all the strength she could muster. He fell off the front porch and to the ground. He roared in obvious rage.

In a frantic panic, she quickly turned to her door

where the keys still hung in the lock. She yanked them out, opened the door and ran inside. She immediately slammed the door behind her and locked it.

Leaning with her back against the door, she tried to catch her breath even as deep, frantic sobs ripped through her. Oh, God, what had just happened? Who was that person?

She remained against the door only a moment. She ran to her front window and pulled the curtain aside. She looked all around but there was nobody there. Apparently, her attacker had melted back into the mist and out of sight.

Who was he? Why had he attacked her? More importantly, was he still out there and would he try to get in to finish the job he'd started?

Chapter Seven

"Sam, I... I need you." Harper's voice trembled as it came across the phone line. It was obvious she was half sobbing and that was all he needed to hear from her.

"I'll be right over." He disconnected the call, grabbed his wallet and keys and then flew out of his house. He had no idea what was going on, but it must be something drastic for Harper to call him in tears.

I need you. Her words resonated deep inside him. He drove like a bat out of hell, his heart beating a frantic rhythm. What was going on? What had happened? Dammit, he should have asked her some more questions before he'd disconnected the call.

The rain had finally stopped, but he had to slow down several times for standing puddles in the road. The wind had picked up, sending leaves and errant trash flying through the air.

When he finally turned onto the street where Harper's house was located his heart fell to the pit of his stomach as he saw Dallas's car parked in the driveway. What on earth had happened with her that required the chief of police to respond?

Sam pulled up behind the police car and flew out of his truck. He raced for the front door and when he reached it, he didn't bother to knock. He stepped inside and when Harper saw him, she jumped up from the sofa and flew into his arms. She sobbed with her face buried in his chest as he threw a questioning look at Dallas.

"Harper's car didn't start tonight when she was ready to leave the bakery, so she decided to walk home. She got to her front door and somebody attacked her," Dallas said.

"Attacked her?" Sam echoed in stunned surprise.

"He...he tried to kill me," Harper said amid sobs. "Sam, he t-tried to st-stab me to death."

"She has several places where he managed to slice her up," Dallas said. "I've got an ambulance coming so one of the EMTs can check her out. She insisted she didn't want to go to the emergency room."

Outrage swept through Sam as he led Harper to the sofa. He pulled her down to sit next to him as she finally stopped crying. For the first time Sam saw the slashes in her raincoat sleeves and the blood that still looked wet and sticky.

"Who in the hell did this to her?" Sam asked angrily.

"I was just about to ask Harper some questions

when you came in," Dallas said. He sat in the chair facing the sofa.

As he began to interview Harper on the details of the attacker, it quickly became clear that there would be no way for Dallas or anyone else to identify who it had been.

The only information Harper could give Dallas was that the attacker was male. "It all happened so fast. I'm sorry, but I can't even tell you how tall he was or what kind of body type he had. I was too busy trying to keep him from stabbing me in the stomach or chest to pay any attention to anything else."

Sam pulled her closer against his side, his outrage and anger morphing into a fierce protective mode and abject fear for her. Somebody had tried to kill her tonight and what scared him was that there was a very strong possibility that he would try to kill her again. And the next time he might be successful.

"Did this person say anything to you?" Dallas asked.

"No...uh...yes," she replied. "He called me a bitch right before he tried to stab me for the first time."

"I'm assuming you didn't recognize the voice." Dallas said it as a statement.

She shook her head negatively, looking positively miserable. "It was just a gravelly hiss. I would never be able to recognize it again unless I heard him say it exactly the same way."

"Have you had any problems with anyone lately,

Harper?" Dallas asked. "Aside from the doll that was left for you? Has anything else happened that disturbed you in any way? Maybe something concerning your interactions at the bakery?"

"No...uh, maybe a little," she replied. As she told Dallas about her encounter that day with RJ Morgan, Sam began to fist and unfist his hands.

"If RJ had a problem with my lumber and other supplies, he should have come and talked about it with me," Sam said, unable to hide the anger in his voice. "Dammit, he should have never brought it to Harper."

"You leave RJ to me," Dallas replied with a warning glance at him. "Anything else you can tell me, Harper?" he asked her.

"No, I think I've told you everything." Tears once again filled her eyes.

At that moment the ambulance arrived and Andy Unger and George Ingram, both EMTs, came inside. As Sam watched them tend to Harper's various cuts, his anger once again rose up.

Who had slashed her up like this? Who had hurt her like this? Dammit, he'd like to find the person responsible for wounding her...for attacking her, and beat his ass good right before Dallas arrested him.

Thankfully Andy and George both agreed she needed no further treatment after she indicated her tetanus shot was up to date, and then they left.

"I'm sorry to say, but I'll need your clothes,

Harper," Dallas said. "Can you go change into something else and give me your blouse and slacks for evidence?"

"Of course," she replied. "They're all ruined anyway."

He gestured toward the raincoat she'd already removed so her wounds could be tended to. "I'll have to take your raincoat as well."

"That's okay. It's of no use to me anymore." She got up and left the room and went into what Sam assumed was her bedroom.

"Dallas, what in the hell is going on?" Sam said the minute he heard Harper's bedroom door close.

Dallas raked a hand through his curly dark hair. "I wish I knew who the hell was responsible for this attack."

"She didn't give you much to go on," Sam said.

"She didn't give me anything to go on." Dallas released a deep sigh. "I'm going to scour the area around her front door to see if I can find something… anything that might help me identify this perp. I'll be interviewing more people and checking with the neighbors to see if they saw anyone hanging around here before and during the attack. She told me that the neighbors across the street turned on their porch light when she started to scream. I'm hoping they'll be able to help. I've also got several of my men checking out the neighborhood, looking for anyone who might be lurking around."

"I hope you find something," Sam replied.

"If she hadn't managed to get into the house when she did, I'd be here investigating her murder," Dallas said darkly.

His words caused a chill to race up and down Sam's spine.

"Do you think it's possible it was the Scarecrow Killer?"

"Anything is possible," Dallas replied. "If it was, then he's changed his victim profile. Harper isn't a blonde."

At that moment Harper returned to the room. She was now clad in a long soft-looking blue robe and looked small and vulnerable. She handed Dallas her clothing and he placed it in a brown paper evidence bag. She then sank back down on the sofa next to Sam, who put his arm around her and drew her close to his side.

Thirty minutes later Dallas had left and Sam remained on the sofa holding Harper. "I'm so sorry this happened to you, Harper," he said softly. "I'm so sorry, baby, and I'm so damned angry about it all."

She stirred from his arms and sat back from him. "I'm so scared and I'm so confused. Who would want to hurt me that badly? Who wants to kill me, Sam? What on earth have I done to anger somebody so much?"

Her big blue eyes filled with the mist of tears and her face was still unnaturally pale. He positively ached for her. "Baby, I wish I knew. I'll tell you one thing…until Dallas has the person under arrest, I intend to protect you twenty-four hours a day."

"I appreciate the sentiment, but how do you intend to do that?" She looked at him curiously, hopefully.

"I'm moving in here." He didn't know when he had made that decision, but he felt as if that was the only way to make sure she remained safe. It felt like the right thing to do. "Harper, I'll sleep on the sofa, or I'll sleep on the floor, but I can't just go home and leave you vulnerable here."

She stared at him for several long moments. "My first instinct is to tell you no, that it's absolutely not necessary. But the truth is I'm scared, and having you here, at least for a little while, would definitely make me feel much better."

"Then it's all settled. I'll stay tonight, and tomorrow after work you can go with me to my place so I can pack up a few things." He was grateful to see that some of the color had returned to her face.

"It's going to be okay, Harper." He pulled her back into his arms. She relaxed against him and released a deep, shuddery sigh.

"I don't know what I'd do without you," she said softly. "And I can't believe you're going to disrupt your own life for me."

"Don't you get it, Harper?" He leaned back from her and gazed into her eyes. "I care about you deeply and more than anything I want to be here for you."

She lingered in his arms for several quiet moments and then she sat up and moved away from him. "I want to go take a shower. I need to erase the feel of that man touching me when he was trying to stab me. Right now, I just feel so dirty."

He frowned. "Are you sure you should do that with the bandages that Amos and George put on you?"

She nodded. "I've got the supplies to replace them once I feel clean, and I really need to get clean." She got to her feet. "Make yourself at home. The television remote is there on the coffee table." She gave him a wan smile. "This shouldn't take me too long."

"Don't worry about me." He shot her a reassuring smile. "I'll be right here when you get out of the shower."

The minute she left the room, his smile died on his lips. Staying with her here wasn't a problem for him. There was nothing to tie him to his home, no pets to take care of or plants to water or anyone to answer to.

There was no way he would leave Harper alone with some madman trying to kill her. Once again, a rush of adrenaline fueled by anger ripped through him. Who in the hell was behind the attack? Who hated Harper enough to want her dead? God, he wished he had the answer.

Was it possible it had been the Scarecrow Killer who had attacked her tonight? They had no idea how the murderer got his victims. However, he knew that Sandy hadn't been slashed up all over like that. Her knife wounds were only in her stomach.

When he'd seen the bloody cuts on Harper's arms and shoulder and thought about the terror she must have felt in that moment, he'd seriously wanted to hurt somebody.

Why was this happening to her? She was pleasant and kind to everyone who came into the bakery. He'd never seen or heard about her having a cross word with anyone.

He got up from the sofa and began to pace the living room floor, his stomach tied in tense knots as his brain worked to somehow make sense of what had happened.

Then he remembered the doll and the note. Oh, God, he'd been so stupid. It hadn't been the Scarecrow Killer. She'd been warned before with the doll and note. He was the reason this was happening to her. Why hadn't he seen it before now? It was so apparent. The doll had been her warning against dating him, but she hadn't heeded the warning. This was all about him…about her dating him. His heart plunged to the floor.

If he stopped seeing her would the danger immediately go away? Right now, he couldn't imagine her not being a part of his life, but if he had to distance himself from her in order to keep her safe from harm, he would do it in a minute. Not because he wanted to, but because he cared enough about her to leave her.

He sank back down on the sofa and thought about the tough conversation he needed to have with her when she got out of the shower.

HARPER STOOD IN the shower and once again hot tears mingled with the warm water. The cuts on her arms and shoulders burned beneath the spray, but that wasn't what caused her tears. Even though the wounds hurt, they were all fairly superficial.

She still couldn't believe what had happened to her. Who was the person who had attacked her? What would have happened if she hadn't been able to fight him off? What would have happened if she hadn't managed to get through her front door and lock it behind her? She knew the answer to that last question.

She'd be dead.

There was no question in her mind that he would have managed to stab her to death. That thought terrified her. Despite the heat of the water even more icy chills raced up and down her back. Thank God for Sam. There was no question she'd feel safer with him in her house.

She felt perfectly safe when she was at work at the bakery, whether Sam was outside or not. That was a public place with people coming in and out on a fairly regular basis. She couldn't imagine anyone trying to attack her there.

It was here, in her home, that for the first time since her divorce she was afraid to be alone. It was thoughts of Sam that made her tears finally halt.

She had no idea what it would be like to have him around the house all the time...eating meals with her, spending all evening with her and then sleeping beneath her roof. She knew she'd feel safe but after the last fiery kiss they had shared, she wondered what else she might feel.

By the time she got out of the shower and rebandaged her cuts, it was almost eight o'clock and she was utterly exhausted. The adrenaline that had filled her during the attack and immediately afterward was gone.

Instead of putting on regular clothes, she pulled on her nightshirt and then added her robe on top. She didn't have to worry about her hair; it would do its usual thing and dry curly.

She left the bedroom and found Sam sitting on the edge of the sofa. No smile greeted her and he appeared unusually somber.

"We need to talk," he said and patted the space next to him.

She sank down, her heart once again beating an unnatural rhythm. Maybe he had made the offer to stay here with her in the heat of the moment and now that he'd had a few minutes to think about it, he'd changed his mind.

He reached out and took her hands in his. "Harper, I believe the person who is after you is angry because we're dating. First it was the doll and the note, and then the attack on you. Being around me is obviously dangerous for you. Even though this is the last thing I want to do, maybe it would be best if I distance myself from you."

"No." The word snapped out of her. She drew in a deep breath and squeezed his hands as her mind reeled with his words. "Sam, if you want to distance yourself from me because you don't want to see me anymore, that's one thing. But I absolutely refuse to let some lunatic dictate who I have and who I don't have in my life. I won't lie, I'm frightened, but this just makes me so angry."

"I'll tell you one thing, I definitely don't want to stop seeing you. But it pains me to think that I'm the reason you're in danger," he replied.

"Sam, what if we quit seeing each other and I start dating another man that this creep doesn't like? Will I be terrorized all over again? Will he try to kill me again? Don't you see? I can't give him that much power over me. And the last thing I want to do is stop seeing you. So, it's settled, we're still dating."

"If that's a risk you're willing to take, then I'm all in." He smiled at her, that wonderful smile that lit her up inside and now made her feel safe.

"Besides, we can't know for sure that you're the reason this man came after me," she said.

"After the note and the doll you received, it's an educated guess that I'm your problem," he replied, the somber look once again on his features. "And I don't want us to fool ourselves about that."

"It doesn't matter. As far as I'm concerned, it's settled. I'm not letting anyone push you out of my life. You leave my life when you want to, not when somebody else wants you to. And now, I'm ready for bed. I'm completely exhausted," she said. "Let me show you to my spare bedroom."

They both got up from the sofa and she led him down the hallway and into the second bedroom. Thankfully she felt the bedroom was a nice one, with a queen-size bed covered in a navy spread. There was a long dresser and a chest of drawers, most of which were empty and ready for use.

"You're welcome to stay up as late as you want and the sound of the television won't bother me at all," she said. "The sheets on the bed are clean and there are clean towels in the hall bathroom linen closet."

"Thanks, I'll be just fine," he replied. "After everything that's happened, I hope you get a good night's sleep." He leaned forward and gave her a gentle kiss on her forehead. "And don't worry, I'm on duty here and nobody is going to get past me to get to you, and that's a promise."

"Thanks, Sam, and now I'll just say good-night."
She left his bedroom and went into hers across the
hall.

Taking off her robe, she then turned out the lights
and got into bed. The wind outside had apparently
chased all the clouds from the sky, for a bright beam
of moonlight drifted through her window.

She closed her eyes, but almost immediately her
head filled with visions of her attacker. His eyes had
appeared so dark and so filled with hate. She could
smell his rage toward her, feel his body heat threatening to consume her. In her mind's eye she saw the
knife coming toward her again and again. Her body
tensed in fight-or-flight mode even as she told herself she was safe and sound.

Taking deep breaths in and out, she tried to relax,
but residual fear continued to grip her, tightening her
chest. Now that Sam's truck was parked out front,
surely her attacker wouldn't try to break into the
house. Sam was on duty now and she was perfectly
safe, she reminded herself.

But realistically, how long could Sam stay here
with her? How long might it take Dallas to identify
and arrest the person? Realistically, it could take
weeks…even months. Heck, Dallas might never
catch the person who had attacked her.

A tree branch danced at her window, not an uncommon occurrence, but tonight it shot her straight
up in bed, her heart beating a million miles a minute.

Despite how tired she was, she was never going to get to sleep. She was still too afraid and that fear made her heartbeat race with anxiety. She was afraid to be alone in the dark and in her own bed.

She tried…she really tried, but after another agonizing few minutes had passed with her being unable to relax, she slid out of bed. She had no idea what door she might be opening, but once she'd made up her mind, she refused to reconsider her actions. She was afraid and she knew the only way she could sleep at all tonight was if Sam was by her side in her bed.

The house was quiet and dark, indicating to her that Sam had gone to bed as well. His door was open and she moved to stand in the threshold. "Harper?" He immediately sat up, obviously seeing her in the moonlight.

"Sam…could you…uh… Could you maybe come sleep with me? I… I'm still a little afraid." She was shocked by how badly her voice trembled.

"Of course," he said without any hesitation. He got out of bed. He was clad only in a pair of dark boxers and in the moonlight she couldn't help but admire his half-naked body. His shoulders were so wide and his hips were slim. His broad chest gleamed in the silvery light that danced through the window. All she could think about was how safe she would feel with him next to her.

"I don't mean to be a baby," she said.

"I don't think you're a baby," he replied. "You're a woman who went through a terrifying ordeal."

When he reached her in the hallway, he took her hand with his and allowed her to lead him into her bedroom. Once there she got back into bed and he crawled in on the other side. "Better?" he asked softly.

"Uh…could…could you maybe hold me for a few minutes, maybe just until I fall asleep?" she asked tentatively. It was embarrassing how needy she felt in this moment.

In silent reply he reached out and drew her into his arms and against his body. Feeling his warmth surrounding her, his strength protecting her, she sighed and finally relaxed into him.

"Better now?" he repeated.

"Definitely much better," she replied softly.

She could hear his heartbeat. Strong and steady, it didn't sound like the beat of impending sleep. She also found that his closeness had chased away any desire she had for sleep. Instead, she found herself desiring something else.

Sam.

"Are you sleeping?" she asked softly, even though she knew he wasn't.

"Not yet…why?"

"I can't sleep," she replied.

"Do you want to get up and talk for a little while?" he asked. "Or maybe would you like to go sit on the sofa and watch some television to try to make you sleepy?"

"Not really."

"Harper, what can I do to help you?" he asked.

She hesitated only a moment. "I want you to kiss me, Sam. I… I want you to make love to me." Had she really said that out loud? She felt him tense against her. "I'm sorry, Sam. Forget I said it, forget I said anything," she said hurriedly.

"Harper, why on earth would I want to forget it? I'd love to make love to you, but I don't want to just because you're afraid or you can't sleep. I need to know you really want me as much as I want you."

He wanted her? Just knowing that shot a new, hot desire through her veins. "I want you, Sam. I wanted you the last time we kissed. And oh, I so want you now."

She barely got the words out of her mouth before his lips took hers in a fiery kiss that half stole her breath away. Their tongues danced wildly together as he pulled her closer and closer yet against him.

His hands stroked up and down her back…so warm she could feel his heat through the cotton of her nightshirt. Her entire body warmed and she suddenly wondered if she was having a hot flash.

Oh Lordy, not now, she mentally protested. The very last thing she wanted was for him to see her face and chest turn beet red. The very last thing she wanted to do was break out in a sweat in his arms because of the hormonal mayhem that was occasionally her personal glimpse into hell.

She started to pull back from him and then she realized the warmth inside of her was not a hot flash at all. Rather it was the delicious, Sam-inspired flames of desire.

Now that she recognized what it was, she wanted more. She wanted so much more. She hungered for his touch everywhere on her body. She wanted to be naked with him. With that thought in mind, she completely leaned back from him and drew her nightshirt over her head and tossed it to the side just off the bed.

This was the real moment of truth. Her breasts were not as perky as they'd once been and there was no place to hide her tummy pouch. She knew she was completely visible to him in the moonbeams that crept into the window.

She placed one arm across her breasts and the other one across her stomach. Sam, on the other hand, looked positively gorgeous with his broad, tanned chest and strong upper arms.

"Harper," he said gently. "Please don't try to hide yourself from me." He took the arm that covered her breasts and moved it aside. "You have no reason to hide. You are positively beautiful."

It wasn't his words that made her feel so desirable, rather it was the gleam in his eyes...a hungry glint that made her believe what he said. Suddenly she felt beautiful and desirable and it was a wonderful feeling she hadn't felt in years and years.

He pulled her back into his arms and this time as they kissed, she had the intense pleasure of feeling his naked, warm skin against her own. It felt utterly amazing.

He then shifted her to the side of him and he leaned over her. His mouth slid from her lips to kiss slowly down her jawline and then down onto the length of her throat.

Shivers of pleasure swept over her. She couldn't remember having this wild desire, this crazy hunger for a man ever before in her entire life.

When his tongue flicked across the tip of one of her breasts, a breathless gasp escaped her. Electric currents shot from her breasts to the very center of her being. He sucked and licked, driving her half-mad with pleasure.

"Sam." His name escaped her without her volition.

He raised his head, his eyes glittering like a primal being's. "Do you want me to stop? I'll stop anytime you want, Harper. You're in charge here."

"No…don't stop. Please don't stop," she replied hungrily.

His white teeth flashed as he grinned and then he returned to lavishing her breasts with his tongue. His other hand caressed down the length of her side and then her hip.

Every muscle in her body tensed in sweet anticipation. There were no more thoughts of the attack, or the pain of any of the slash wounds. There was only Sam…sweet, sweet Sam.

His hand reached the edge of her panties. "Sweet Harper," he said, his words mirroring her thoughts. She wished she was wearing hot-pink or sexy black silk underwear. She wished she had on a racy, wispy kind of underpants. Instead, she had on a pair of plain white cotton panties.

It didn't seem to matter as he hung a thumb into the waistband and slowly pulled them down. She arched her hips to allow him to drag them completely off her, then she kicked them to the side.

Her desire for him spiraled even higher. He swirled his fingertips across the sensitive skin of her inner thigh, making her want…need him to touch her even more intimately. She was on fire and when he did finally touch her moist center, she nearly burst into flames.

His fingers moved against her slowly, softly at first and then he picked up the rhythm and pressure as the tension inside her climbed higher and higher.

Then she was there, shuddering and crying out his name as she rode a tidal wave of release that left her utterly boneless. Still, she wanted more…she now wanted him to possess her completely, but as he moved to do just that, she shoved him onto his back.

She now wanted to pleasure him. She wanted to tease and torment him until he could stand it no longer. She wanted to be the best lover he'd ever had… ever would have.

He stared up at her and she leaned over him and kissed him with all her heart, with all her soul. Their tongues once again swirled together in a heated dance. When the kiss finally ended, she slid her hands down and across his chest, then nipped and kissed the warm, firm skin.

His breathing came hard and fast, as did hers as she reached the edge of his black boxers. She began to pull them down, but he stopped her. "You have to stop," he said with a groan. "If you don't stop now, I'll be finished before we get started." He gently pushed her back to his side.

He then kicked off his boxers and moved between her thighs. She welcomed him, grabbing him by his buttocks and urging him forward.

He eased into her and then froze. "Oh, Harper, you feel so good." His voice was a low growl of pleasure.

"Oh, so do you," she moaned. He filled her up completely. Then he began to thrust into her. In and out, slowly…steadily he built a new rising tension inside her. All she could think about was Sam and this moment.

Soon, they moved together faster, more frantically, and their breaths became pants and moans. She moaned his name again and again as the pressure inside her grew in intensity. Then she was there again, exploding into a million pieces as he also found his release.

When it was all over, he leaned down and kissed her. It was a soft, gentle kiss that reached in to caress her very soul. "Are you okay?" he asked.

She smiled up at him. "I'm better than okay. What about you?"

He chuckled. "I am way, way better than okay." He rolled away from her and slid out of the bed. "I'll be right back."

She got up as well. She grabbed her nightgown and panties and then headed for her en suite bathroom. The fear that had driven her to invite Sam into her bedroom was momentarily gone. It had been replaced by the warmth of their lovemaking.

It had been wonderful to feel the strength of a man's arms around her again, to feel his desire for her in every move he'd made. She'd forgotten the utter and complete joy of sharing passion. But she knew the real joyfulness of it had come because it had been Sam. She wanted…needed Sam and nobody else.

Their connection hadn't just felt like a physical one. It had been the connection of heart and soul and she felt closer to Sam than she'd ever felt with anyone before in her entire life.

She quickly pulled her nightgown back over her head and for several long moments she stared at her reflection in the mirror as a sudden, horrible thought lodged in her mind. She had sworn it would never happen. It was definitely something she hadn't wanted to happen, but it had.

She was nothing but a fool, for she had fallen crazy and madly in love with Sam Bravano.

HE PACED BACK and forth in his living room, a rich anger ripping through him. He'd tried his best to kill her tonight. It had been perfect. He'd managed to disable her car and then he had followed her to her front door. Everything had been so perfect, but somehow the bitch had managed to survive his attack.

As he thought of her with the much younger Sam, it completely sickened and disgusted him. And it made him think of his wife, Bettina. After twelve years of marriage that bitch had been going to leave him for a much younger man. In fact, she'd crowed about it, telling him her young lover had more stamina in the sheets than he ever would.

He'd been a good husband to her. He'd spent all the years of his marriage trying to make her happy. He'd worked hard and had been financially generous toward her. He'd made sure she had almost everything she wanted within reason.

He'd known she'd been cheating on him, but he'd figured it was just a fleeting thing and when her affair fell apart, he would forgive her. Until that night, when she'd thrown it all up in his face and had her bags packed and ready to leave.

He hadn't meant to hit her as hard as he had. He really hadn't meant to hit her at all. It had just happened. He'd been so damned angry with her and she'd been so cruel. He'd hit her with an uppercut that had snapped her head backward. Then she had fallen and hit her head on the side of the coffee table. He definitely hadn't meant for her to die, but she had.

Crack. He still remembered the sound her head had made when it hit the wooden surface. For him, it had been the sound of justice. After that everyone in town had thought she'd packed her bags and left him. The truth was, he kept her very close to him now.

Harper had sparked something inside him and he was just waiting and working up his nerve to ask her out. He'd finally decided he was ready for a new relationship with her.

When he heard about her dating the much younger Sam, old memories had shot through his head, bad memories of his wife and her young lover.

He was bitterly disappointed in Harper but more than that she'd stirred an enormous rage inside him that had made him decide she needed to die. She needed to be punished just like Bettina had been punished.

He'd warned her first with the doll and the note. She should have taken that warning and stopped seeing the young man. But she hadn't. And tonight, his rage toward her had been all-consuming, but he'd failed to punish her the way she really needed to be punished.

He finally stopped pacing and sank on his sofa. Oh well, tomorrow was another day. One way or another he'd make Harper pay for her sin. And the payment was death.

Chapter Eight

Sam awoke with the sound of Harper's alarm clock ringing. It was four-thirty in the morning, the world was still dark and he was spooned closely around her body.

"Hmm, I hate to get up," she whispered sleepily.

He hated to leave the bed, too. She was so soft, so warm against him, and thinking about what they had shared the night before fired a new desire for her. She'd been a wonderful lover, so giving and passionate, and he'd not only been stirred by their lovemaking but also their emotional connection.

"Take the day off," he suggested. "Lord knows you've earned it, especially after last night. You could take the day to rest and relax and go back to work when you feel ready."

"Hmm, I could, but I won't. I've got a ten-year-old little girl having a birthday party today and her mother is going to pick up three dozen cupcakes for the event. I can't let them down."

Reluctantly, he rolled away from her and got out of bed. "Okay then, come on, woman. If you insist that you're going to work today, then it's time for you to get up and go bake." He turned on the bedside lamp.

She rolled over and smiled at him. She looked utterly charming with her hair wild and curly and her beautiful blue eyes shining so brightly. "What kind of cookies do you want me to bake for you today?"

"You know I'm partial to your oatmeal raisin ones."

"Then oatmeal raisin it is." She got out of bed and stretched with her arms overhead, exposing not only the tops of her shapely legs, but also a hint of her sexy derriere. Her body excited him. He loved that she wasn't a skinny little thing, but rather she had a little meat on her bones. She had a mature kind of body and he positively loved it.

They parted ways to go shower and dress, him in the hall bathroom and her in her own bathroom. Twenty minutes later they were ready to leave the house.

He drove her to the bakery and came inside with her. It was too early for him to begin working outside so he sat in the folding chair in the kitchen and watched her as she went about her morning routine.

"I think I'll do a batch of brownies for today," she now said. "It's been a minute since I've baked them and they are always a favorite among the customers."

"Brownies always sound good to me," he replied.

So far, the morning conversation had all been business related, but he now decided it was time to talk about more personal things.

"Should we talk about last night?" he asked.

She looked at him in surprise. "Do we need to?"

"I don't know, everything moved pretty quickly and I was wondering if you had any regrets," he replied.

She gazed at him for a long moment and then shook her head. "No regrets here. What about you?" A dainty frown creased the center of her forehead and she seemed to be holding her breath.

He smiled at her. "Definitely no regrets here, but we didn't even talk about birth control. We definitely weren't thinking about that last night."

"I'm on the pill and I haven't been with anyone since I was married." A faint blush danced into her cheeks.

"And I haven't been with anyone in over a year and I'm clean." He offered her another smile. "Thankfully we got all of that out of the way."

"Really?" She looked at him skeptically.

"Really what?" He eyed her curiously.

"You haven't…uh…been with anyone for over a year?" Once again that charming blush filled her cheeks and she averted her gaze from his. "I find that a little hard to believe."

"Well, believe it. Harper, it's the honest-to-God truth. I decided about a year ago that I'd rather be celibate for a while than have empty, meaningless sex with some random woman." He was being perfectly honest with her. He'd had enough meaningless sex in his early to late twenties to last a lifetime. "I smell cookies."

"My cookies!" She whirled around to the oven and withdrew a large baking pan of the golden-brown treats. She placed the pan on a cooling rack and then turned back to him, her hands on her hips. "You are definitely a big distraction in my kitchen, Sam Bravano."

He laughed. "I'm not trying to be. Do you want me to go sit at a table in the other room?"

"Absolutely not," she replied with a laugh of her own.

It felt good. The kitchen was warm and smelled like a touch of heaven with all the things she was baking.

It also felt oddly intimate with just the two of them here while other people were still in their beds and the sun had yet to rise. In the kitchen with Harper was a nice place to be.

He started asking her questions, interested in what all she was mixing up and baking. He watched in admiration as she expertly frosted three dozen cupcakes with bright pink frosting and tiny flowers in white. She then moved on to decorate three different kinds of cakes.

It was obvious she loved what she did and she

moved from one task to the next with a graceful efficiency that he admired. The conversation was easy between them and the time seemed to fly. Suddenly the sun was up and after helping her carry some of the goodies from the kitchen and into the display case, he left her to head outside.

He glanced over to the tattoo shop, which wasn't open yet for the day. When RJ came in, Sam definitely intended to have a little chat with the man. He hadn't forgotten that yesterday RJ had come into the bakery to complain about something he had no right to complain about.

In the meantime, he had work to do. As he got busy, he tried to keep his mind off the fact that somebody had attacked Harper with deadly intent the night before.

If he dwelled on it for too long, he'd be so angry he wouldn't be able to be what he felt she needed right now. What he thought she needed from him now was his calm and steadiness. She needed his light tone and perhaps a little more flirtation to keep her mind off the fear he knew she had to be feeling.

Even though she hadn't spoken of the attack this morning, he'd seen the shadows that occasionally darkened her eyes, shadows that made him want to kill somebody.

He hoped like hell Dallas and his men had found something to help them identify the bastard that was responsible for the attack. He wanted the man who had caused the fear, the pain and the dark shadows in her eyes to be thrown in jail for a very long time.

The bakery officially opened for the day and some of the regulars began to show up. "Hey, Sam," Mark Lindey greeted as he approached the front door.

"Hi, Mark. How you doing?" Sam replied. Mark was in his mid-fifties and owned a small farm on the outskirts of town. He was a divorced man who often stopped in at the bakery for an hour or so in the mornings.

"I'm doing okay," Mark replied. "Eventually I need to talk to you about some work that needs to be done on my front porch. It's rotting and starting to fall apart. It definitely needs to all be replaced."

"Just give me a call whenever you're ready to get the work done," Sam replied.

"It will probably be late fall before I'm ready to get it going," Mark said.

"I'm sure that will work for us. We'll be around whenever."

"Now I'm heading inside to have coffee with my favorite woman, who makes the best cinnamon rolls I've ever eaten in my life."

Sam laughed. "She does make a mean cinnamon roll."

It was just before ten o'clock when Sam saw RJ approaching his shop. He put his hammer down and strode over to the big man. "Hey, RJ," he said as he got closer to the tatted man. "You got a problem with me?"

RJ narrowed his eyes. "I was just wondering how long this crap is going to be out here," he said and gestured toward the supplies stacked to the side of the bakery entrance.

"As long as it takes," Sam replied. The muscle-bound, tattooed bully certainly didn't scare Sam. "My supplies aren't bothering your business and there's no reason to take any complaints you have to Harper. You got a problem with something you bring it to me, but you leave her the hell alone."

"What are you? Her bodyguard?" RJ said sarcastically.

"Actually, right now I am," Sam replied. "She was attacked last night. Somebody tried to kill her...to stab her to death. So, where were you last night?"

"Whoa." RJ took a step backward. "I don't know anything about an attack. I had nothing to do with whatever happened to Harper last night. Don't try to pin anything like that on me."

"I won't, but I'm sure you'll be hearing from Dallas at some point, especially considering your harassment of Harper yesterday just before she was attacked." Sam didn't wait for a reply. Instead, he turned around and headed back to the bakery.

He didn't really believe RJ was the guilty party. RJ might be many things, including a bully, but Sam couldn't see him actually attacking a woman. Despite

RJ's bad boy looks and big attitude, Sam had never heard of the man having any issues with the law.

He got back to work and around one, when the traffic in the bakery was in a lull, he knocked off and went inside. She greeted him with the smile that always lit a warmth deep inside him.

"Hey, cutie," he said as he walked up to the counter.

"Nobody has ever called me cutie before," she said with a laugh.

"Then you've been running around with the wrong crowd," he replied with a grin. "You are definitely a cutie as far as I'm concerned."

She laughed again and covered her cheeks with her hands. "Somehow you always make me blush."

"I love your blushes," he replied and then laughed as her blush deepened.

"So, what can I do for you?"

"Do you really want me to answer that question?" He raked his gaze down the length of her and then leered at her.

"You are a very bad boy," she said. "Let me rephrase my question… what would you like from the display counter today?"

"I'll just take the usual," he said.

The usual was a cup of coffee and three of her oatmeal raisin cookies. "Take a break with me?"

"Of course," she replied.

He took a seat at one of the tables and a moment

later she joined him there with his order. "How are you doing today?" he asked.

"I'm doing fine. I called the garage about my car and somebody is supposed to come out this afternoon to replace the battery."

"That's good, but you won't need to be driving around alone until Dallas gets the person who attacked you last night under arrest."

Her eyes darkened. "I hope that's sooner rather than later."

"Why? Are you tired of my company already?" he said teasingly.

"You know it's not that," she protested.

He reached out and covered her hand with his. "I hope Dallas catches the man sooner rather than later, too." He pulled his hand from hers. "On another note, I had a little chat with RJ earlier. I don't think he'll be bothering you anymore."

"You didn't beat him up, did you?"

He laughed. "Did you want me to beat him up?"

"Maybe just a little," she replied with a naughty grin that absolutely delighted him.

They continued to visit until his cookies were gone and it was time for Sam to get back to work outside. At five thirty, they left the bakery and agreed to order pizza for dinner.

An hour later they sat at her kitchen table sharing a pepperoni pizza and talking about the events of the day. Sam tried to keep the conversation light and breezy, although the afternoon had revealed something that Sam was keeping to himself.

At the time the mechanic had showed up, there were several people inside the bakery and Sam had offered to take care of the car issue with the mechanic for her.

The minute they opened the hood, Sam saw what the problem was...the battery cables had been intentionally disconnected. Sam's blood had run cold at the discovery.

So, it wasn't by accident that Harper had had to walk home from work the night before. The potential murderer had made sure of it. So the attack had definitely been completely premeditated.

He'd immediately called Dallas with the information, but he hadn't told Harper. All he'd said to her was that one of the battery cables was loose and just needed a quick tightening. He considered it a tiny white lie to protect her.

As he now looked at her across the table, her eyes were sparkling as she picked the pepperoni slices off the pizza and then popped them into her mouth.

She'd been through enough without knowing about the car. He not only wanted to protect her physically, but emotionally as well. She'd been so strong through all of this.

She'd been attacked the night before and yet hadn't hesitated in going to work this morning because she needed to bake cupcakes for a little girl's birthday party. Many other women would have taken off work for days or perhaps weeks in order to heal from such a horrible experience, but not Harper.

The plan was after they finished eating, they'd go to his house so he could pack up some things to bring back here. One of the main things he wanted to get was his gun.

They were almost finished with their dinner when she suddenly jumped up from the sofa. "Excuse me," she exclaimed and raced for the hall bathroom.

He frowned. What had just happened? Had she suddenly gotten sick? He didn't feel sick and he had eaten the same pizza she had. After a couple of minutes had passed, he got up and knocked on the bathroom door.

"Harper? Are you okay?" he asked worriedly.

"I'm fine." After another minute or so she opened the door and stepped into the hallway. He could tell that she'd wiped down her face. The edges of her hair were damp and her face was slightly flushed.

"Are you sick?" he asked with concern.

"No, I'm fine," she replied and swept past him.

"You obviously aren't fine," he countered and followed her back into the living room. "Was it the pizza? Did it make you sick?"

She whirled around. "Just leave it alone, Sam. I said I was fine," she snapped and then walked over to grab the pizza box on the coffee table.

There was no question he was surprised by her

sharp tone. He'd never heard that kind of a tone from her before. She froze for a moment and then set the pizza box back down and turned to gaze at him.

"I'm sorry, Sam. I didn't mean to bark at you. I was just…just embarrassed."

He frowned at her as an uneasiness swept through him. "Uh…embarrassed about what?" What was going on with her?

"I was embarrassed to tell you that I…uh, had a hot flash." She averted her gaze from him and it was obvious she was mortified.

He relaxed. He knew all about hot flashes from his mother. Years ago, she would often sit in a kitchen chair and fan herself with a hand towel while cursing at her body.

"Hey, there's absolutely nothing for you to be embarrassed about," he said. He reached out and drew her into his arms. He grinned down at her. "All I care about is that I'm the only man giving you hot flashes."

She smiled up at him in obvious relief. "I can promise you that, and thank you for being understanding."

He gave her a quick kiss on her forehead and then released her. "Now, let's get the leftover pizza taken care of so we can head to my place and I'll pack up some things to bring back here."

"Sounds like a plan," she replied. "And thanks again, Sam."

As they left her house to go to his, he couldn't help but think about how much he cared about her. He definitely wanted to see where the two of them were going with their relationship, but he had to keep her alive in order to do that.

SUNDAY LATE MORNING Harper stood in front of her bathroom mirror, her heart beating a little faster than usual. Sam had told her to dress casually for the day so she was clad in a blue sleeveless blouse and a pair of white capris. Her makeup was light and with a final glance in the mirror, she turned and left the bathroom.

Sam had just finished showering and was still in the second bedroom getting dressed. She went into the kitchen to retrieve the chocolate fudge cake she had baked to take with them and then she sat on the sofa to wait for him.

After they'd finished their pizza and after her hot flash a couple of nights before, they had gone to his house so he could pack up some clothing and personal items to take back to her place.

She had been mortified about the hot flash. She hadn't wanted him to see it happening and so she'd raced for the bathroom to hide. Once she'd admitted to him what had happened, he'd been so sweet about it he'd instantly put her at ease. He was such an amazing guy.

The hot flashes were a part of her life right now

and she was glad she had told him about them. It would have been awkward constantly trying to hide them from him while he was living with her.

Once they had gotten to his place, she'd been impressed not only by the house itself, but by all the work he had already accomplished inside to update things.

The upstairs rooms had all been repainted in a soft, buttery beige and the oak wood floors had been refinished and shone with a glossy beauty.

They'd talked about what would be nice for kitchen flooring and then he had gone upstairs to gather his things while she sat to wait on the sofa in the living room.

For just a few minutes as the two of them had talked about the pros and cons of different flooring, it had felt like they were a married couple discussing it. It had been a crazy fantasy that she couldn't let into her head. They were not and would never be a married couple.

And now she was going to meet his family. Another wave of nerves jangled through her. Would they like her? Sam had told her over and over again that they would all love her, but she couldn't help the doubts that flew through her head.

Would his mother like her or would she have a problem with her handsome, hunky son dating an older woman? What about his brothers? And his sister? What would Harper be walking into? Would it be a hostile crowd?

Sam had slept in her bed since the night of the attack and they had made love another time. It had been just as wonderful as the first time. He had definitely gotten into her heart and yet there was a little part of herself that she held back, knowing that eventually they would part ways.

And they would part ways. There was no way their relationship would last forever. Eventually Sam would tire of her and she needed to remind herself of that fact all the time. She couldn't allow herself to completely buy into the fantasy that they would be together forever. She would never be enough for Sam long-term.

At that moment Sam came into the room. As always, her breath caught in her chest at his bold handsomeness. Clad in a pair of black jeans and a white polo that showcased his strong biceps and broad shoulders, he looked as hot and hunky as ever.

"You look very pretty," he said to her with that special smile he had.

"Thank you. You look nice, too."

"Are you ready to go?" he asked.

"As ready as I can get." She stood and grabbed the cake. It would be around eleven when they got to his mother's house and the meal wasn't planned until after noon. She would have at least an hour or so just to visit with his family.

"Are you nervous?" he asked once they were in his truck and heading down the street.

"I'm absolutely terrified," she admitted.

He laughed and reached out to briefly touch the back of her hand. "Don't be. I've told you before, they're all going to love you, and I hope you love them, too."

"I hope you're right," she replied. They might like her as a person, but would they really like her as an older woman dating Sam?

"You're going to love the meal. I might be partial, but my mom makes the best Italian dishes you'll ever taste." He turned the steering wheel to make a left turn.

"I already got a taste of her cooking when you brought me dinner, and it was absolutely delicious," she replied. With each block that passed the knot of nerves in the pit of her stomach tightened.

"I'll tell you one thing, Mom is going to love that cake. Chocolate cake has always been her favorite kind of dessert."

"I hope she enjoys it," Harper replied.

"Trust me, she will, and it looks absolutely beautiful. Those pink flowers on top really look nice against the chocolate frosting."

"Thanks," she replied. She'd taken special care in the decoration, wanting to make the cake not only delicious but also a treat for the eyes. She was pleased with the way it had turned out.

He finally pulled into the driveway of a large attractive two-story house with forest green shutters and a matching front door. There was a huge wraparound porch with a swing and several outdoor chairs, giving an air of warmth and welcome.

There were several other vehicles parked in the driveway. She assumed they belonged to Sam's siblings and once again anxiety flooded her veins and tightened her chest.

"So, this is your childhood home," she asked when he shut off the engine of his truck.

"This is it."

"It's very nice," she replied.

"Thanks. I had a really good childhood here. This house holds a lot of good memories." He got out of the truck and came around to open her door. He took the cake from her so she could get out and then together they walked up to the front door.

He didn't knock, but instead ushered her into the house. They walked into an entryway with an attractive wooden coatrack bench. On the right was a small formal living room holding a beautiful antique-looking sofa and matching chairs in gold fabric.

Sam led her forward and into a great room where two young men were sprawled on an overstuffed gray sofa. They both stood as Sam introduced them as his brothers, Michael and Tony.

Pleasantries were exchanged and then Sam took her through a large archway and into a huge kitchen.

It was decorated with a Mediterranean flair and a huge wooden table ruled the space in front of four floor-to-ceiling windows. The table was already set with bright yellow and red plates.

Sam's mother, Antoinette, was a short, slightly round dark-haired woman with lively brown eyes and a beautiful smile. Sam had obviously gotten his great smile from his mother. She greeted Harper with a warm hug and then took the cake plate from her. "You shouldn't have done this," she said. "It's gorgeous and it looks delicious."

"Something certainly smells delicious in here," Harper said. "And thank you so much for having me today."

"I needed to meet the woman my son has been raving about," Antoinette replied with another smile. "Now go…out of my kitchen. I'll let you all know when the food is on the table."

"Is there anything I can do to help?" Harper asked.

"Nothing. Go sit, have a glass of wine and relax." Antoinette gave Sam's shoulder a firm shove. "Go."

Sam laughed. "Okay, okay, we're going." He grabbed Harper's hand. "Don't feel bad, Harper. She never lets anyone in her kitchen when she's cooking a big meal."

He led her back to the great room and motioned toward the love seat. "Would you like a glass of wine?" he asked as he went to a small corner bar in the room. "I'm having one," he added as if to put her at ease.

"Okay, then I'll have a small glass," she said. She sank down on the love seat and once again her nerves tightened her chest as she felt Tony and Michael's curious gazes on her.

"I'm surprised you don't want a huge glass of wine if you have to hang around that big lug for any length of time," Tony said and gestured toward Sam. Michael snickered and Sam rolled his eyes.

"Funny man," Sam replied. He carried both glasses of wine across the room. He handed her one and then sank down next to her on the love seat.

"By the way, we were really sorry to hear about the attack on you, Harper. Does Dallas have a suspect in mind?" Michael asked.

"Unfortunately, no," she answered.

"I can tell you this, nobody is ever going to get close enough to hurt her again," Sam said fervently.

"That's our boy," Tony said.

"Seriously, he's staying with you right now?" Michael asked Harper.

"He is. I'm not sure what I'd do without him right now," she replied with a warm glance at Sam.

"How are things with you and Paula?" Sam asked his brother.

Michael smiled. "Things are pretty good with us right now. She would have been here today but she had already planned to spend the day with her mother. We're supposed to get together later this evening."

"I think he needs to break up with her for good," Tony said.

"Nobody asked you for your opinion," Michael retorted.

"Ignore their bickering, Harper," Sam said. "It's a commonplace thing." Sam then looked at Michael. "I'm just glad things are good with you and her right now," Sam replied.

"Yeah, for now," Tony added. "Things could always change between them in the next hour." Tony laughed as Michael glared at him.

"Paula is Michael's girlfriend, but their relationship has been off and on for the last several months," Sam explained to Harper.

"Relationships can be really hard," Harper said with a sympathetic smile at Michael.

"That's for sure," Michael replied. "But we're working on it. I'm really crazy about her."

As the three men began to talk about work and caught up with each other, it was easy to see that the two younger brothers greatly admired Sam, despite their teasing each other back and forth.

More than once Harper found herself laughing as Tony and Michael told stories about a much younger Sam. Sam's brothers were very friendly with her and slowly Harper's nerves began to disappear.

They had all been talking for about a half an hour

when Sam's sister and her husband came in. Lauren was a beautiful woman with long black hair and lively dark eyes. She and her husband, Russ, seemed very nice. Sam made the introductions between them and Harper, and then Russ sat in one of the two armchairs that completed the sitting area, while Lauren headed for the kitchen.

A moment later she came back out with her mother at her side. "Now, what's going on here? I need to get back to my cooking," Antoinette said.

"Ma, I wouldn't have pulled you out of your kitchen if it wasn't important," Lauren replied. "Now, I have a big announcement to make." She paused for a moment, obviously for dramatic effect, and then continued. "Russ and I…we're pregnant."

Antoinette squealed with happiness and threw her arms around her daughter. "Oh, this is what I've been waiting for since you all grew up," she said. "A grandchild for me." She released her daughter and wiped at the tears that had sprung to her eyes.

"Congratulations, Lauren," all her brothers said.

Michael got up and shook Russ's hand. "Good man," he said to his brother-in-law.

"Tell me more," Antoinette said, still wiping happy tears from her eyes. "How far along are you?"

"A little over three months," Lauren replied.

"You kept this secret from me for so long?" Antoinette asked.

"I didn't want to tell anyone until I was this far along," Lauren replied.

"It doesn't matter now. So, am I having a little boy grandbaby or a little girl?" Antoinette asked eagerly.

Lauren laughed. "We don't know yet. We specifically didn't want to know. In the next month or so we'll have a little reveal party."

"You aren't going to shoot off a cannon or get into a hot-air balloon, are you?" Tony asked.

"Yeah, tell us you aren't going to do something wild and crazy just so you can post it on one of your social media accounts," Michael said.

Lauren laughed. "I can promise you none of those things are going to happen. I'm thinking maybe my doctor can let Harper know the sex of the baby and then she can bake either a pink or blue cake covered in chocolate frosting. We wouldn't know the sex until we cut into the cake."

"I can do that," Harper said with a warm smile at Lauren. "In fact, it would be my honor."

"Now I have to get back to my kitchen, but I am so happy," Antoinette said. She practically danced back into the kitchen and Lauren sank down in the chair next to her husband's.

"I hope it's a boy," Michael said to his sister. "I'd love to be the uncle of a little boy I can teach to play football and baseball."

"Hello? What am I in this equation?" Russ said with a laugh.

"We'll let you have the kid until he's out of diapers," Tony said. "And then we'll take over."

"Trust me, Russ is going to be changing a lot of diapers. It's an equal opportunity kind of deal."

Everyone laughed as Russ made a face. It was so nice for Harper to be sharing in this moment with Sam's family. As the men continued to tease both Russ and Lauren, she just sat and enjoyed the laughter that surrounded her.

"I don't know if Sam mentioned it to you or not, but I'm getting ready to open a shop," Lauren leaned over and said to Harper. "It's going to be a dress shop with lots of fun trinkets and jewelry."

Harper nodded. "Yes, Sam told me about your plans. It sounds like it will be a great place to shop."

"I hope all the women in town think so. Any words of advice from one business owner to another?" Lauren asked.

Harper frowned thoughtfully. "Try to work into your budget extra help. It's easy to burn out if you're working the shop eight or ten hours a day, six days a week," Harper said.

"But isn't that what you've been doing at the bakery?" Lauren asked.

"Yes, but I'm finally ready to make a healthy change for myself and hire some part-time help." Harper had been thinking about it for several days and just now realized she was ready to make a change. Did it have something to do with Sam being in her life? Probably.

Sam looked at her in surprise and reached out to grab her hand with his. "I'm thrilled that you're finally going to give yourself a break." She smiled at him warmly.

She then turned back to Lauren. "I would definitely recommend you hire some help now, especially since you're pregnant."

"The good news is I'll be able to bring the baby with me to work every day."

Harper smiled. "That's one of the positive things about being your own boss and making your own rules."

"Come on, my family. The food is on the table," Antoinette's voice rang out from the kitchen.

"Let's go eat," Tony said and jumped up from the sofa.

There were several minutes of controlled chaos as everyone found seats at the table. Steaming dishes filled the center of the tabletop. There was a huge pan of the eggplant parmesan, a stewpot filled with meatballs and a basket of garlic bread.

Even though there was an empty seat at the head of the table, Antoinette hovered over everyone to make sure they all got served.

"Ma, sit down," Sam said. "I'm sure you've been on your feet since early this morning."

"She has been," Michael said. "She was up and

in the kitchen at the crack of dawn. Ma, you know we like it when you sit and eat with us."

"Okay, okay." Antoinette finally sank down in the empty chair. "Now *mangiare*," she said.

"That means eat in Italian," Sam leaned over and said to Harper.

And eat they did. For the next half an hour or so they ate, they talked and they laughed. Harper found herself charmed by the close-knit family. There was not only great food on the table, but there was also an enormous amount of love in the room.

She would love to belong here and to have big dinners with them once a week. She'd never experienced this feeling of close family before, not in her marriage and not when she was growing up as an only child. For her, it was positively magical.

She also felt accepted here. Nobody had said a word that made her feel like she didn't belong. Her nerves had calmed down to nonexistence.

When they were all finished eating, Harper began to help clear the table, but Antoinette shooed her away. "Go, sit and digest and then we'll bring out your beautiful cake."

"Don't even try to argue with her, Harper. She's as stubborn as the day is long," Sam said.

"That is the truth about me," Antoinette agreed with a wide smile. "I am stubborn and I like to do things my own way. Thank you, Harper, for offering to help, but I'd rather you get out of my kitchen."

Sam laughed and took Harper's arm. "Come on, honey. We aren't welcomed in the kitchen."

Sam and Harper had barely sat back down in the love seat when Lauren smiled at her. "Harper, could we have a little chat on the front porch? I'd like to pick your brain some more and I'm sure it would bore the men in the room to death."

"Sure," Harper replied, assuming the young woman wanted to talk more about the ins and outs of running a business. "I'll be right back," she said to Sam and then followed Lauren out the front door.

"At least it's not too hot in the shade to sit for a little while," Lauren said as she sank down in one of the chairs while Harper opted to sit in the double porch swing.

"I didn't want to bore all my brothers and my husband with more store talk," Lauren said.

"I understand completely," Harper said. "And again, congratulations on your pregnancy."

"Thanks. I feel like in the coming months I'm going to have two births…first my store opening and then the baby coming. I'm over the moon about both," Lauren said, her face glowing with her happiness.

For the next fifteen minutes or so, the two women talked about the business of being in business. Harper tried to tell Lauren all the pitfalls to watch out for and Lauren seemed to appreciate any and all advice she could get from Harper.

"You like my brother a lot," Lauren said. It was more of an observation than a question.

"I do," Harper replied. "He's a wonderful, caring and amazing man."

Lauren nodded. "He is, and he seems to like you a lot, too."

"He tells me he does," Harper replied. A touch of warmth filled her cheeks.

Lauren looked off toward the street and then gazed back at Harper once again. "He told us about the attack on you. I'm so sorry that happened to you."

"Thank you. I have to admit it was pretty horrible."

"And I understand he's acting as a sort of bodyguard for you right now."

Harper fought off a sudden shiver as she thought about the man who had tried to kill her. "Yes, he is… thank God. He's staying with me until the man who attacked me is under arrest."

"Does Dallas have any clues about who he is?" Lauren asked.

"Unfortunately, not that I'm aware of, but we're hoping he'll come up with something very soon." Once again Harper fought against a shiver.

"I understand the bodyguard part that he's doing for you, but do you really think it's fair to him for you to tie him up romantically?" Lauren's eyes narrowed slightly. "I mean, let's be real here. You are quite a bit older than him. I'm assuming you can't have children. Your relationship with him would deprive him of having kids and becoming a father in the future."

"He's told me he doesn't want any children," Harper replied, more than a little stunned by Lauren's blunt words to her.

Lauren smiled. "Sam is young. He doesn't know what he wants. He may change his mind about having children six months from now. You seem like a very nice woman, Harper. If you really care about Sam at all and have his best interests at heart, then you should let him go to find somebody more his own age."

She didn't give Harper time to reply and, in any case, Harper didn't know what to say. Lauren got up from her chair. "And now we better get back in there before the boys think we ran away."

Lauren's words resonated deep inside Harper as they all enjoyed the cake she'd baked and then later when they got back to her house.

"That was fun," Sam said once they were settled on her sofa and relaxing. "Did you enjoy it?"

"It was a good time," she replied. "Your brothers were really nice and they're a real hoot and your mother is a doll. Your sister and brother-in-law were very nice, too."

"I could tell they all liked you, too," he said.

Maybe all but one, Harper thought to herself. Sam had no idea what Lauren had said to her on the front porch and Harper didn't intend to share it with him.

Even as they watched a comedy movie on TV, she couldn't get Lauren's words out of her mind. Would she in some way be holding him back from something if she continued to see him?

Was he too young and not in the right headspace to really know what he wanted out of life? He seemed so mature she sometimes forgot about the age difference between them, but now it was all she could think about.

Maybe she needed to distance herself from him a bit. Perhaps she really needed to think about what she was doing with him. Suddenly it didn't feel like just fun and games with Sam anymore. She was in love with him and everything felt far more complicated now.

It was just after eight when she decided to call it a night. She got up from the sofa and turned to look at him. "I'm really exhausted, Sam." She averted her gaze from him. "I'm so tired, I think I'd like to sleep alone tonight." She looked back at him just in time to see the stunned surprise that crossed his features. The look hurt her, but she needed time to think away from him.

He recovered quickly. "Uh…okay. No problem." He smiled at her. "Whatever you need, Harper."

"Then I'll just say good-night," she said.

"I hope you have sweet dreams," he replied.

Minutes later Harper was in bed and staring up at her darkened ceiling. There was no question she was deeply in love with Sam. But was she somehow cheating him from finding what he really wanted, what he really deserved out of life?

Didn't he really deserve a young woman who could give him a family if he wanted? A young woman who wasn't so settled in her ways and wasn't ready for bed at eight o'clock at night? Somebody who didn't suffer from hot flashes?

She released a deep sigh. The trouble with Sam was he was just too young for her. Now all she had to figure out was if she intended to be selfish and keep seeing Sam romantically, or if she loved him enough to let him go.

Chapter Nine

Sam slowly rolled the yellow paint onto the front of the bakery. Harper had picked out the paint last night when the two of them had run to the hardware store. It was a cheerful color that would draw people's attention in a good way to the building.

Even though Sam had always enjoyed the fairly mindless act of painting, today his heart was more than a tiny bit troubled. It had been a little over a week since he and Harper had eaten at his mother's place, a little over a week since she'd first gone to bed alone, and since that time she hadn't invited him back into her bed.

He didn't mind so much not sleeping with her, although he definitely missed her warmth and softness against him, and the scent of her surrounding him while he drifted off to sleep. Then there was the fact that he yearned to make love to her again, but if she wasn't into it right now, then he'd give her the time she needed.

What really bothered him was not only the physical distance between them, but the emotional distance he felt from her. That really bothered him. While she smiled at him and talked to him as usual, he sensed some of their real intimacy had vanished. It was as if she was suddenly holding back from him, and he didn't know why or what had happened.

During the evenings while they'd watched television together, he'd asked her several times if something was wrong between them and she'd insisted everything was fine. But he knew in his heart it wasn't. Things had changed. Something was different and he didn't know why.

The good thing was nothing frightening had happened in the past week. There had been no notes and no strange objects left on her doorstep and things had been quiet and peaceful. But that certainly didn't mean the danger was gone. He remained hyper-vigilant when it came to her protection.

He didn't worry about her when she was at work. There was no way he believed anyone would go into the bakery to try to hurt her, especially given the normal traffic that moved in and out of the establishment. But he did worry about her when they were at her house.

He slept with one eye open and unbeknownst to her, he kept his gun in the top dresser drawer she had allowed him to use for some of his clothing. He not only possessed the gun, but he knew how to use it and would definitely use it to save her life if it came to that.

The sun overhead was hot and made for perfect painting weather. The forecast was for the heat and sunshine to continue through the week. He hoped to get the front of the building painted today except for the trim, and then he'd move to the rest of it starting tomorrow. When he had the whole building painted except for the back, he would then trim it all out. True to her desire, the trim would be a hot pink.

He was hoping to get Harper's take on what she wanted in the backyard after she closed up the bakery today. He knew she hadn't been back there since the day Sandy's body had been found, but he was hoping by now she'd be willing to go out there with him by her side.

He was going to be ready to start work on the back within the next week and so it was time for him to learn what she wanted so he could order supplies.

The bakery had been relatively busy during the morning hours as people came in and left with sweet treats in hand. All her regulars had also shown up. He'd seen Joe and Mark and Ranger inside at various times. At around two there was a lull in business and Sam knocked off to take a break.

The cool, air-conditioned air inside was a welcome relief after his hours in the punishing heat. Harper was behind the counter and offered him a brilliant smile as he walked in. "I can't wait to see how the paint looks," she said.

"I think you're going to be very happy with it," he replied, a bit disappointed that her smile wasn't really meant for him, but rather for the paint.

"You want the usual?" she asked.

"Yes, but instead of the coffee, I'll take a glass of iced tea. It's warm out there today." He pulled out his wallet and handed her the money.

"Go sit and I'll bring it to you," she said after handing him his change.

He took a seat at the table closest to the display case. "You really should be eating a proper lunch each day instead of just eating these cookies," she said as she carried the cookies and drink to him.

"I'd much rather have your cookies than a bologna sandwich," he replied. "Besides, there's all kinds of healthy ingredients in these oatmeal raisin treats, right?"

She laughed and sat across from him. "There's also a lot of sugar."

"Which keeps me moving through the afternoons," he replied. He took a bite and then washed it down with the tea. "It looked like you were fairly busy this morning," he said.

"It was nice and steady, which is the way I like it. The day certainly seems to pass more quickly when I have customers inside. Now, tell me how the painting is going outside."

"It's going. I'm hoping to get the front done by closing time today. Then, I was hoping once you close up you and I could go around back and you can tell me exactly what you want out there. That way I can get some measuring done and let you know the estimate for the work out there."

Her eyes darkened and after a long moment she released a heavy sigh. "Okay. I know it's time…past time really. I have to break the ice sometime and I guess today is as good as any day."

"Harper, I'll be right beside you," he said softly.

She smiled, and this time he knew the gesture was meant solely for him. A flutter of warmth shot straight through to his heart. "There you go again, knowing just what I need," she said.

"I try," he replied lightly. But he obviously wasn't succeeding completely. There was no question she'd withdrawn some from him and he didn't know why. All he really knew was that he was desperate to fix it. He didn't know what she needed from him to bring them back to where they'd been with each other a little over a week ago.

"I'm excited to see the new face of Sweet Tooth," she said.

"It's a sunny, bright new face," he replied.

"I'm so happy." Her eyes sparkled brightly and he loved to see her that way. "I've dreamed of this day ever since I bought the building."

They continued talking about the front of the bakery for about another fifteen minutes or so and then Sam returned to his painting. He'd only been working for a few minutes when Dallas pulled in and parked. "Hey, Dallas," Sam greeted as the lawman got out of his car.

"Hi, Sam," Dallas replied. "The paint is looking really good."

"Thanks, it's definitely a better look than what it was before," Sam replied. He put down his paintbrush. "Are you coming with news for us?"

The smile on Dallas's features instantly fell. "Unfortunately, no. I just was in the area and thought I'd check in and see how Harper is doing. Anything I need to know about?"

"Nothing," Sam said. "Thank God, things have been pretty quiet."

"You still staying with her?"

"I am. I don't want that creep to have another chance to harm her," Sam replied.

"I'll just go in and touch base with her," Dallas replied.

"Do yourself a favor and buy some of her cookies. She makes a mean cookie."

Dallas grinned. "I'll do that." He turned from Sam and headed for the front door.

He came back out a few minutes later with a bag in his hand. "Everything looked good in there," he told Sam. "I wound up with cookies, a slice of cake and a big brownie."

Sam laughed. "Tell me about it. I think I've gained five or ten pounds since I started working for Harper."

"Speaking of work, I've got to get back to the office. I'll see you later, Sam."

"See you, Dallas."

Moments later Dallas was gone and Sam was back to painting. He knew Dallas must be stressing hard. He had a potential serial killer at work in the town and the issue of who had tried to kill Harper. Sam couldn't imagine having that kind of pressure every day.

Dallas had already told them that the doll had yielded no fingerprints, nor had the note that had been left with it. Apparently, the creep had been smart enough to wear gloves. It was the same with the clothing she'd worn on the night of her attack. No fingerprints…nothing to help identify the perp. They had also found nothing around her porch area.

It was just before five when he cleaned up the painting supplies and knocked off for the day. He walked into the shop, where Harper was busy with the last-minute things she had to finish up with before closing. "Can you turn the sign for me and get the lights?" she asked.

"Sure." He turned the sign in the door to indicate the bakery was closed and then he flipped the overhead lights off. "Are you ready to head out back?"

"Let me just lock the front door and then I guess

I'm ready," she replied. She set aside the cloth she'd been using to wipe down the top of the display case and then she joined him by the front door.

He watched as she locked the door and then he grabbed her free hand in his. "It's going to be all right," he said and gently squeezed her hand.

She released a deep sigh. "I know it will be. It's just the first step out there that I'm dreading," she replied. "I can't help but think about Sandy."

"We'll get through this together," he replied and she cast him a tentative smile.

As they walked past the display counter, she dropped her keys on top and then they headed through the kitchen. Her footsteps slowed when they hit the small laundry room. She ground to a halt just in front of the back door.

She looked up at Sam, her blue eyes dark with anxiety, and a frown cut across her forehead. "Sam, please, could you just take a look out there and make sure nothing is out there that doesn't belong out there?"

He looked out the windowpanes in the door and then smiled at her. "All I see is green grass and some pretty purple and pink flowers you must have planted out there at some point or another."

She released an audible sigh of relief. "Okay, then let's go."

He opened the door and together they stepped outside. He felt her visibly relax and he released her hand. "See, it's okay," he said softly. "Now, show me exactly what you have in mind for back here."

For the next hour or so they talked about the renovations she wanted done. She became more and more animated as she explained to him about the covered porch she envisioned. She wanted it big enough to seat at least eight tables beneath it. It was definitely not just a job for Sam, and he would need his brothers' help in constructing the porch.

He did some quick measurements and wrote them down in his pad and then looked around the backyard area. "Maybe we could put some sort of a pretty fountain or water feature in the center of the yard," he suggested. "You know, a visual point that would make it very peaceful to sit out here."

"Oh, I love that idea," she replied and clapped her hands together. "And then we could plant a lot of flowers around it. In fact, I want a lot of plants and flowers in the yard and all around the porch. I want the area to positively explode with color."

"We can definitely do that," he agreed. "We will make it a beautiful and relaxing place for people to sit and eat whatever you offer for sale."

"I have a lot of plans for the menu," she said, her blue eyes sparkling. God, he loved it when she looked that way. For the past week her eyes hadn't sparkled much.

Once he made sure they were both on the same page, and he'd written everything down, they headed out to go home. Home. He'd definitely come to feel like he was home in her house.

Once again, she grew quiet on the way home and then later as they ate the chicken and vegetables she'd fixed in the Crock-Pot that morning.

After eating and cleaning up, they went into the living room to watch some television. She curled up in the corner of the sofa and once again he felt her distance both physically and emotionally.

He wanted to ask her what had happened, why she was distancing herself from him, but he also wanted to give her the time she needed to work out whatever might be bothering her. And maybe he was a little bit afraid of what her answer might be if he pressed her about what had happened to cause this detachment he felt from her.

Maybe she just wasn't that into him anymore but still wanted him to be here for her protection. Maybe if he wasn't playing bodyguard for her, she'd send him on his way. An arrow of pain stabbed into his heart as he considered this possibility, and it was at that moment he suddenly realized he'd fallen deep and hard and madly in love with the baker lady.

It scared him more than a little bit, these feelings he'd caught for Harper. They were bigger and deeper than anything he'd ever felt for a woman before in his life.

He now gazed over to her. Her attention appeared to be solely focused on the crime drama show that was playing. Even though he wasn't that far away from her, the distance between them felt immense.

His heart swelled with a depth of emotion. He loved her, from the curly dark hair on her head to the pretty pink polish on her toenails and everything in between. Her soft and warm body totally turned him on like nobody had done in a very long time. He couldn't imagine being with or loving anyone else. She was his person. But was he really her person?

He enjoyed her sense of humor and the deep conversations they had shared. She was kind and caring and such a good person. She was everything he had been looking for.

He loved the life he envisioned here with her, a quiet life of snuggling together on the sofa, watching movies and eating popcorn…a life of working hard and then planning vacations to be taken together.

He was way past the point where he needed a woman to entertain him. Besides, Harper entertained him plenty. He was far beyond the years of needing to go drinking with his buddies out at the bars.

He was ready for the lifestyle he'd have here, with Harper. As much as he wanted to tell her how he felt, he had a feeling she wasn't ready to hear him…at least not yet. In fact, right now he had no idea what she felt about him or if she even wanted him in her life as a romantic partner. And that thought scared the hell out of him.

HARPER SAT BEHIND the display case and watched outside as Sam and several other men from the lumber yard unloaded all kinds of supplies and wood and stacked it all to the left of her front door. Excitement filled her as the stack of items grew bigger.

She was thrilled that over the past week the building had all been painted yellow with a touch of trim work in bright pink. The front of the bakery now looked a bit whimsical and like one of her decorated cupcakes.

And now, Sam was about to start the work on the back of the building to finish up the rest of her dream for the bakery. Starting in the next couple of days his brothers would be working with him to construct the new covered porch.

She had a feeling he'd intentionally unloaded the lumber in the front of her shop to tick off RJ. She certainly had no problem with that. RJ might hate the new load of lumber outside her building, but there wasn't a damn thing he could do about it.

Sam.

He'd been a quandary in her head and a pain in her heart for a little over two weeks now. She went to bed alone each night wanting him…needing him and yet denying herself the pleasure of having him with her.

She knew he cared about her. He might have even convinced himself that he was in love with her. She'd felt his gaze on her in the evenings, sensed his desire for her both emotionally and physically.

If he wasn't being her personal bodyguard, she would have asked him to leave long before now, but when she thought about the attack on her, when she thought about being in the house all alone, she was still afraid.

However, she was aware that she couldn't keep him with her forever. It was bad enough that he'd put his life on hold for almost an entire month for her. Who knew if or when Dallas might be able to make an arrest and remove the threat that might still be out there? Dallas might never catch the person who had attacked her.

Still, she loved the sense of safety Sam's presence in the house provided her, but she now thought, even with the threat against her still out there and present, that it was time to send him back to his own life. She'd reached the conclusion after yet another night of soul-searching. She loved him enough to let him go.

She intended to tell him tonight after dinner that he needed to go. Even though it was killing her, she loved him enough to free him so that he could find a relationship with a woman his own age. Lauren had been right, it was selfish of her to want to keep him in a relationship where his future dreams might not be met.

Throughout the afternoon Sam carried some of the lumber from the front to the backyard. She hoped that when she had the talk with him this evening, he wouldn't decide he could no longer do the job for her.

Of course, they had a contract that protected her from him just walking off the job. But she would never force him to work here if he wanted out.

They were two civil adults. Surely they could part ways romantically yet still keep up a healthy working relationship, but that all depended on him. And she had no idea how he was going to react when she told him it was time for them to part ways romantically.

Her heart was positively breaking as she thought of the night to come. She was madly and crazy in love with Sam. She'd never meant for it to happen, but it had. It had been supposed to be just fun and games with him, but at some point along the line, things had gotten serious.

She was going to miss him terribly. She would miss the sound of his laughter and their deep conversations. She would feel the absence of his cheerful, larger-than-life presence in her home.

More than anything she would miss his gentle touches and the sweet fire in his forest green eyes when they made love. But his future was important to her. More than anything, she wanted him to be happy and she didn't believe his future happiness was with her.

Thoughts of Sam fell away as one of her customers came in to get the cake Harper had baked for her son's fifth birthday. Neither Allie nor Becky had come in to see her since the night of the community meeting, although both had called her several times.

Unfortunately, the calls had been rather stilted and uncomfortable. It both angered and saddened her that her friends had effectively abandoned her because of who she chose to love. She'd never suspected the judgmental side of them and it hurt her deeply. Well, they'd both be happy after tonight.

Everyone would be happy except for Sam and Harper.

At a few minutes before five o'clock she checked to make sure the back door was locked up and then returned to the front to close up the bakery.

Sam waited for her just outside the front door and he gave her one of his beautiful smiles. "Why don't we order pizza tonight so neither of us has to cook?" he suggested as they headed to his truck. Throughout the course of him living with her, they had taken turns preparing the evening meal.

"That sounds great to me," she replied. "You look exhausted," she added. He looked hot and a fine line of perspiration rode across his forehead.

"I am tired," he admitted. "Carrying some of that lumber from the front to the back today was a bit draining."

"I was wondering if you had it all dropped off out front just to irritate RJ."

He laughed. "I'd like to say I'm a bit evil like that, but the truth of the matter is the lumber truck wouldn't have been able to fit through your gate and the heaviness of the truck would have torn up your yard. Besides, there's still enough left out front to irritate RJ."

She laughed as well, even as a bittersweet pang rushed through her. There would be few moments of shared laughter with him going forward and that broke her heart all over again.

When they got home, he ordered the pizza and then went directly in to shower and she sank down on the sofa to wait for the pizza delivery. It felt good to be off her feet, but a huge ball of anxiety…of dread and sadness began to tighten her chest. She didn't want to do what she intended to do, but she felt like it was the right thing to do for him, and that was what was important.

She decided to wait to have the talk with Sam until after they'd eaten. She jumped up from the sofa and went into the kitchen to get paper plates for the pizza.

She wanted to stay busy doing something…anything. If she sat and thought about the night to come, then she feared she would start crying and never, ever stop.

She reminded herself that she was doing the right thing for Sam and that was all that was important to her. He came back into the living room, smelling like minty soap and the cologne that had begun to smell like home to her. He was dressed in a clean pair of

jeans and a white T-shirt and looked as handsome...
as sexy as she'd ever seen him.

Before she could even greet him, the doorbell
rang. "Ah, that should be our dinner." He answered
the door and then carried the pizza box to the center of the coffee table. "Before I sit, what's the lady's
pleasure to drink? Beer? Soda?"

"I think I'd like a beer," she replied. Maybe it
would provide her a little liquid courage for the conversation that was going to happen.

"There's nothing better than a cold beer with
pizza. I'll be right back." He disappeared into the
kitchen and returned a moment later with two beers
and a couple of napkins in hand.

He sank down next to her on the sofa and placed
the drinks next to the pizza box, which he then
opened. "Mmm, looks good. Hand me your plate
and I'll give you a couple of pieces that have the most
pepperoni on them."

"Ah, a man after my heart," she replied with a
forced lightness.

"I know how you do love you some pepperoni,"
he replied with a grin. He handed her plate back to
her and then served himself.

For the next few minutes, they ate and talked
about the day's events. He explained to her what the
next steps were for the back of the building.

As she listened to him all she could think about
was the fact that tonight was the last time she'd be

sitting next to him eating a meal and listening to his beautiful deep voice. It was the last night for so many things because it was the last night that he would even be in her house.

The ball of anxiety inside her grew bigger and bigger with each minute that passed, as did an immense sadness. Her heart was being ripped in two, not by him, but rather by herself. But as Lauren's words once again played in her head, she reminded herself again that she was doing the right thing for Sam and that was really all that was important.

All too quickly they'd eaten all they wanted of the pizza and the leftovers had been stowed away in the refrigerator. She rejoined him on the sofa and her anxiety was through the roof.

"What do you feel like watching tonight?" he asked as he picked up the remote for the TV. "Are you in the mood for a comedy, or maybe another crime drama?"

"Actually, Sam, we need to have a talk."

He must have heard the seriousness in her tone for he immediately set the remote control down and turned so that he was facing her, a look of deep concern on his features. "What's up?"

A wealth of emotion filled her as she gazed into his beautiful eyes. Oh, this was going to be so hard. "Sam, I've really enjoyed spending time with you. You're a wonderful, caring man."

The frown deepened across his forehead. "Harper, what's going on? What are you doing?"

She drew in a deep breath. "Sam, I'm sorry, but it's time for you to go home. It's been fun, this little fling we've been having, but it's time for each of us to move on." Her words caused her to ache as she spoke them but she wasn't prepared for the look of utter devastation that swept over Sam's features.

"Little fling?" His eyes darkened. "Is that how you see this…us? Harper, this certainly hasn't been a little fling to me." His gaze swept over her face as if searching for answers. "What's really going on here? What about the threat of somebody trying to kill you?"

"You can't play bodyguard for me forever and we both know Dallas isn't going to make an arrest anytime soon. Besides, nothing has happened in the past several weeks. Maybe the creep found somebody else to harass,"

"Or maybe he hasn't done anything else to you because I've been here with you," he countered. "Harper, I don't feel comfortable just leaving you here all alone when I believe the danger is still out there."

His gaze on her was so intense, and not for the first time she felt as if he was trying to probe deep inside her. "I'm sure I'll be just fine."

He slowly shook his head, his gaze still intense.

"I don't feel comfortable leaving you at all. Harper, I… I'm in love with you."

She couldn't help the gasp of surprise that escaped her at his words. She hadn't expected them. When she'd envisioned this difficult conversation, words of love from him hadn't entered her mind.

Now tears of joy and of sheer agony burned at her eyes. Under any other circumstances his profession of love for her would have been exactly what she wanted to hear. Knowing she loved him back but still intended to send him away positively broke her heart.

"Sam, I really think it would be best if you go home now and we start seeing other people." Oh, God, she hoped he would just get up off the sofa and start packing his things. The very last thing she wanted was for this to be a prolonged goodbye.

Chapter Ten

Sam's heart thundered in an uneven rhythm as he
stared at the woman he loved more than life itself.
Harper…her name resounded in his head. He'd somehow felt this coming for the past couple of weeks,
ever since she'd distanced herself from him. But he
had sworn to himself he wasn't going to lose Harper
without a fight, and now was the time to fight.

"Did you hear what I just said to you, Harper?
I'm in love with you. I don't want to date anyone
else. I love you more than any other woman I've ever
loved in my life." He leaned toward her, wanting to
touch her, to pull her into his arms, but he was afraid
to. "Harper, I want to wake up each morning with
you in my arms and I want to fall asleep each night
spooned around you."

She closed her eyes, as if his words were too painful to hear. "What happened to change things?" he
asked softly. "Please tell me. Make me understand.
I thought we were both on the same page, I thought

you cared about me as much as I care about you."
He edged an inch closer to her on the sofa. She was
positively breaking his heart right now.

Her eyes opened, blue misty orbs that gazed at
him in what appeared to be abject misery. "Sam, it
doesn't matter what I feel. What I need you to know
is that we had our time together, I've enjoyed it very
much and now it's over."

Over? It couldn't be over. He didn't want it to be
over. He moved another inch closer to her, so close
he could smell the scent of her, feel her body heat
radiating toward him. "Harper, don't you realize that
you're contradicting yourself? Of course, it does
matter how you feel. And I think if you look deep
in your heart, you'll realize you love me, too." His
heart thundered in his chest with a horrible dread.

"Please, Sam. Don't make this more difficult than
it already is," she said softly.

"Maybe it's difficult because you really don't want
to do what you're doing right now," he replied. He
reached out for her hand, but she jerked hers back,
as if afraid of his touch. "Don't you realize we belong together?" he continued. "Just tell me why you
are breaking things off with me. Harper, make me
understand what's really going on."

Once again, she closed her eyes. This time when
she reopened them there was a hard glint there that
he'd never seen before. "It's over, Sam. That's all you
need to understand and I want you out of my house

tonight." She stood from the sofa. "I'll just be in my bedroom. Please let me know when you're leaving so I can lock up after you."

She was gone from the room before he even had a chance to respond. He heard the sound of her bedroom door shutting, the heartbreaking sound of finality.

For a long moment he couldn't move. His mind refused to believe what had just happened, but his heart hurt more than it had ever pained him in his entire life. Was this really it? No real explanations, no real answers as to what was really going on with her. No glimpse into her mind to give him any clue as to what had prompted this sudden decision.

Did she really not care about him anymore? Did the woman who hadn't had a date in years really want to stop seeing him so she could date other people? None of this made any sense to him at all.

He finally pulled himself up and off the sofa and headed for the second bedroom. As he passed her bedroom, he could hear the sound of her weeping.

The sound of her crying broke his heart even more, but it also deeply confused him. If this was what she really wanted, if she really wanted him out of her life, then why was she crying?

He went on into the second bedroom and sat on the edge of the bed, still stunned by what had happened. What had he missed? He'd tried to be everything she needed him to be. Dammit, what had happened? He finally got up and pulled out the two duffel bags he'd packed to come here. He didn't want to do this. God, he didn't want to pack his things and go home. This was home. Here with Harper was home.

He didn't even think she'd be safe here without him. Somewhere out there was a person who had tried to kill her once. There was no reason to believe he wouldn't try it again, especially without Sam's presence here.

Sam's stomach tightened at the very thought. That, along with his heavy heart, made him pack his things slowly. Maybe he was hoping she'd come back in and stop him. Maybe she'd come in and tell him this was all a big mistake and she was in love with him. But all too soon everything was in the duffel bags and there was nothing more for him to do.

He threw one of the bags over his shoulder and picked up the other one, then he walked down the hallway to her bedroom door. He placed his palm on the door and for several long moments wondered what he could do, what he could say that would change the events of the night. What could he do to make her love him as much as he loved her?

He finally knocked on her door. "Harper, I'm ready to go. Would you at least come out and tell me goodbye?" If she came back out maybe they could have another dialogue about what was happening.

Maybe then she could make him understand why this was happening.

"Goodbye, Sam. I'll see you tomorrow at the bakery." Her voice drifted out from behind the closed door.

A little niggle of hope swept through him. So, she hadn't kicked him out of her life all the way. She hadn't mentioned anything about removing him from the job and her words reassured him that hopefully it wasn't going to happen.

So, he'd have his days to work for her and flirt with her and hopefully get back to the way things had been before they'd all changed.

And why had things changed in the first place? It was a question that haunted him as he left her home and headed out to his pickup.

One thing was for sure. He wasn't about to leave her unprotected. He assumed it was perfectly legal for him to park against the curb in front of her house. If she didn't like his presence there, then she would have to call Dallas and have him tell Sam to move along.

Knowing his plan now, he pulled out of her driveway and backed up and then moved against the curb. He'd stay out here for the night…for every night until the bastard who was after her was caught. If he lowered his seat, nobody would see him if he slept in the truck, and the truck's presence would hopefully keep the bad guy away.

He shut off his truck and powered the seat back, giving him plenty of room to get comfortable. He placed his gun in his lap and tried to relax.

His heart still ached with the events of the night, an ache deeper and more painful than he'd ever felt. Tears burned at his eyes. He was a big strong man, but Harper's rejection made him feel weak and emotional.

He'd truly believed that he and Harper were going to have a forever kind of future together. He loved her with a depth and breadth that he knew he would never find again in his life. He'd planned to be with her through eternity and now it was over.

Harper had been crying in her bedroom when he left, which confused him so much. It was as if she hadn't wanted to stop their relationship but some force greater than her was forcing her to break up with him. What on earth could that force be?

She'd appeared to have gotten over the gossip and naysayers. In fact, it had been just like he'd told her it would be… the gossip about the baker lady and her younger lover had definitely died down.

He didn't believe it was gossip that had driven them apart. So, what was it? He began to think back to exactly when things had changed so drastically between them. It had been after the dinner at his mother's house. That had been the night she'd slept alone and things had begun to change.

He frowned thoughtfully. His brothers and mother

had certainly been welcoming to her and she had seemed to enjoy her time with all of them.

Sure, Lauren had asked her a lot of questions about being a business owner, but Harper hadn't seemed to mind the inquiries. In fact, he knew Harper loved talking business and would want to help his sister out in any way she could.

However, Lauren had taken Harper outside for a private conversation. He frowned. He'd thought the two had merely talked some more about owning a business, but maybe Lauren had said something to Harper that had made her pull away from him.

Was it possible? The more he thought about it, the more he believed this was what might have happened. Dammit, what had Lauren said to her? He knew his sister would never want to hurt him, but sometimes she thought she knew better than he did what was best for him.

He must have fallen asleep for he jerked awake suddenly, his heart thundering a million miles a minute. He grabbed his gun and looked toward her house.

Moonlight drifted down, painting everything in a silvery light. He didn't see anything amiss, but something had awakened him from his sleep. He slid out of his truck quickly and closed the door as softly as possible. He gripped his gun tightly in his hand and every one of his muscles tensed with a fight-or-flight adrenaline.

He checked the front of the house but there was nobody lurking about. He slid around the corner and down the side. He then spun around to the back of the house and again found nobody there. He finally completed his check by coming up the last side.

Nothing. Nobody. He stood by the truck and continued to look around, but there was nothing to give him pause. He finally returned to his truck. As he got back into the seat, from somewhere nearby a dog barked several times. The barks were loud and deep. Maybe that was what had awakened him. He remained awake, looking toward her house for a long time, wanting to make sure she was still safe and sound.

He dozed off and on for the remainder of the night and was finally awakened for good by the sound of Harper's car starting up. He started his truck and when she pulled out of the driveway and headed up the street, he was right behind her.

He followed her to the bakery and watched as she got out of her car and went inside. She didn't acknowledge his presence in any way but he really hadn't expected her to.

He remained parked outside of the bakery until about seven and then he headed to his house. When he walked through the door there was no sense of homecoming, no warm feelings at all. Home remained Harper's house where he had found such joy, such complete soul-deep contentment.

He took a quick shower and pulled on clean jeans and a white T-shirt. Once he was dressed to work for the day, he got back into his pickup and headed to his sister's place. More than anything, he wanted some answers, and he had a feeling Lauren might be the key to the questions that burned through his brain.

Lauren and Russ lived in a nice ranch house just off Main Street. He never knew when Russ would be home or not as his work hours at the firehouse were not regular ones. However, his car was in the driveway when Sam pulled up.

"Well, isn't this an early morning surprise," Lauren said in delight as she opened her door and ushered him in. "Come on into the kitchen. We were just having coffee and discussing the plans for the reveal party."

"Coffee definitely sounds good to me," he replied. One corner of the living room had boxes stacked up. "Inventory for the new store?"

"Yeah, it's not only taken over my living room but also my spare bedroom," she replied with a small laugh. "We're trying to get it all into the back room of the store, but so far we still have a lot to move there."

"Hey, Russ," Sam said as he entered the kitchen and saw his brother-in-law seated at the small round wooden table. He was clad in his fire department uniform so Sam knew he was going into work at some point that morning.

"Sam." Russ half rose, but Sam waved him back down. "What's happening?"

"Not much," Sam replied. "What about you?"

"Your sister is trying to work me to death for this new venture of hers," Russ replied. "And if that's not enough, this reveal party she's planning is going to drive me totally insane."

"Oh, don't be a crybaby," Lauren said with a laugh. "Sit, Sam," she added. "I'll pour you a cup of coffee."

"Thanks, sis." Sam sat in the chair opposite Russ.

A moment later Sam had his coffee and Lauren had joined them at the table. "So, how are things going at the shop?" he asked.

"They're going. We still need to unpack a lot of things and get them situated in the space, but we're working on it. I'm hoping we can open in a month."

"At least six to eight weeks," Russ said.

"Oh, pooh, he's the pessimist in this venture," Lauren said with an affectionate look at her husband. Both Russ and Sam laughed. "I want to get the shop taken care of and opened so I can enjoy my pregnancy without stressing about anything else."

"That sounds like a good plan," Sam replied.

"The only person who is stressing in this situation is me," Russ said wryly. "One minute she's bossing me around about the shop and the next minute she's crying because she can't decide how to decorate the nursery."

"Don't remind me," she said. "How are things with you, Sam? I haven't heard from you since we all had dinner at Mom's together."

"Things are going. I'm still working on the bakery."

"I drove by there yesterday and it looks great," Russ said.

"Yeah, it's coming along," Sam replied and then looked at her sister. "Did you enjoy talking to Harper that day?"

"I did," Lauren replied. "She seems very nice and she had a lot of wisdom to impart to me about being a business owner and I really appreciated it."

"Is business all you talked about when you were outside with her?" Sam asked. He eyed his sister carefully. She looked down to her coffee cup and then gazed up at him once again.

"We talked about you a little bit," she replied.

"Really, and what exactly was the conversation?" Sam fought against a sudden tightening in his chest.

"Oh, you know…just silly girl talk." She released a small burst of what he recognized as nervous laughter.

"Before this conversation goes any further, I need to head out for work." Russ drained his coffee cup and stood. Lauren popped up from the table as well. The two kissed, said their goodbyes and then Russ was gone.

"Now, where were we?" Lauren asked as she returned to her seat.

"You were about to tell me what 'just silly girl talk' entailed between you and Harper," Sam said.

"Oh, you know. I asked her if she liked you and I told her you looked like you were really into her."

"And…"

"And she told me that you'd told her that you didn't want children and I might have reminded her that you were young and might not know exactly what you wanted out of life." Lauren released a sigh and her eyes flashed with a touch of defiance. "Okay, I also told her that if she really cared about you, she'd let you go to find somebody your own age."

Sam sat back hard in his chair, his heart falling to the floor. So that was it. It explained everything. After that conversation everything had changed.

"Dammit, Lauren, why would you say something like that to her?"

"I said it because I love you and I want you to find the right woman for you," she said with a slight lift of her chin. "Sam, I was trying to protect you."

"What gives you the right to interfere in my life?"

"Because I'm your big sister and I care about you," Lauren replied, once again raising her chin defensively.

"If you really cared about me, then all you should want is my happiness," he retorted angrily. "Dammit, Lauren, Harper is my happiness, whether you like it or not. I am deeply in love with her and whatever you said to her really screwed things up between us. And now I need to see if I can fix things with her."

"Don't be angry with me, Sam," she said as tears filled her eyes. "I'm sorry I said anything, but I can't stand it if you're angry with me."

He sighed. "Don't cry. It isn't good for the baby." He scooted his chair back and stood. "I love you, Lauren, but I'm pretty upset and disappointed in you right now. I'm not a little boy that you have to protect anymore. I'm a man and I know what I want. I want Harper, and if I manage to fix things with her, then I hope you never do anything like this again."

"I promise," she said, sniffling with emotion. "I just wanted to protect you, Sam."

"I don't need your protection." He leaned down and kissed her on the forehead. "I'll talk to you later," he said and then strode out of the house and got into his truck. He sat for a moment or two and drew in several deep breaths to steady himself.

Harper had obviously taken Lauren's words to heart. It was the only thing that made any sense. The timing was certainly right. It was after her talk with Lauren that Harper had pulled away from him.

With this new knowledge burning through him, he intended to go and claim his woman. And he believed with all his heart that she was just waiting for him to claim her.

HARPER HAD CRIED herself to sleep the night before. In fact, she'd cried harder about Sam than when her husband had walked out on her after years of marriage. Saying goodbye to Sam had been the most difficult thing she'd ever done in her life.

She'd been stunned that morning to see his truck parked outside of her house and the fact that he'd probably been there all night long broke her heart all over again. Even though she'd cast him aside, he'd apparently still been on duty to keep her safe.

He'd disappeared at some point while she was in the bakery kitchen preparing things for the day. She assumed he'd be back to work sometime this morning…if he intended to finish the job.

At this point she wasn't sure he'd want to continue working for her. It was going to be difficult going from a loving, romantic relationship to a strictly employer/employee association for both of them.

Still, at nine o'clock she saw his truck pull up outside and she couldn't help the way her heart beat an accelerated rhythm in response. As she watched him get out of his vehicle and wrap the tool belt around his waist, she couldn't help the love for him that buoyed up inside of her. Oh, she loved him so much. He was not only deep in her heart, but he was also deep in her very soul.

Even though it pained her greatly, she felt as if she'd done the right thing in breaking up with him. Eventually he'd find a new love, somebody his own age and that woman would make him far happier than he could ever be with her. But the very thought of him with another woman shot an arrow of pain straight through the center of her heart.

To her surprise, instead of going around back where she assumed he intended to begin working today, he beelined for the front door.

"Hey, Joe... Mark... Larry," he said in greeting to the regulars that were seated at tables inside. He then smiled at her and his eyes shone with a love that weakened her knees and caused a flush of heat to roar through her.

She wanted to scream at him to stop looking at her that way, to stop making her feel the way she did. Oh, she desperately wished she didn't love him as much as she did. It would have been so much easier if she didn't love him.

"'Morning, cutie," he said to her.

She stared at him for a long moment. Had he forgotten that she'd broken up with him the night before? Was he trying to torture her on purpose? "'Morning, Sam, what can I get for you?" She tried to keep all emotion out of her voice and off her face.

"I figured I'd start out the day with one of your awesome cinnamon rolls and a cup of coffee," he replied.

She tried not to look at him as she got his order ready and then he paid. She definitely tried to keep her gaze averted from him as he took a seat at one of the tables closest to the display case.

The next ten minutes or so were sheer agony as Sam ate his roll and drank his coffee with his gaze solely fixed on her. She tried to ignore him but she felt the heat of his gaze on her. When he'd finished eating, he tossed his items and then smiled at her, that full, wonderful smile that caused his dimple to dance in his cheek. "I'm heading out back. I'll see you later." And with that he walked out the front door.

Maybe the breakup hadn't affected him as deeply as it had her. He had appeared perfectly happy this morning going back to his normal routine. Perhaps he was secretly glad that she'd let him go and he hadn't had to break up with her. After all, in the weeks that they had spent together she'd been a tremendous amount of work for him.

First there had been finding Sandy in her backyard, and then there had been the disturbing doll and note. Finally, there had been the attack on her. He'd had to do a lot of emotional cleanups for her during the time they'd been together. Maybe he'd already grown tired of her and just hadn't known how to tell her. The thought somehow broke her heart in a different way.

She pasted a smile on her face for the men who were still inside the bakery and then cleaned off the table where Sam had eaten.

There was a fairly steady influx of traffic through-out the morning and then in the afternoon there was the usual lull. She refilled the display case and was unsurprised when Sam came back in.

"Whew, it's hot out there today," he said.

"You want the usual?" she asked.

"Yeah, except no coffee and instead an iced tea." Once again, he took a seat at the table closest to the counter. "Have you had a good morning?" he asked.

"It was pretty good," she replied. She got the order ready and delivered it to the table.

"Thanks. Sit with me for a few minutes?"

She wanted to sit with him. She didn't want to sit with him. She finally sat across from him. As long as they only talked business, she'd be fine. "What have you done in the back this morning?"

"I've been replacing all the rotten boards and once that's all done, we'll be ready to start the building of the new covered porch," he replied.

"I can't wait to have it done. I'm planning a grand reopening when everything is finished. I'll place fly-ers all over town and put a big ad in the paper and it will be a totally awesome event." She was nervously rambling, her gaze going all around the room to keep from looking at him.

"Harper, please look at me," he said softly.

She didn't want to look at him, yet she found her-self gazing up and into his beautiful green eyes even as she steeled herself for whatever he intended to say to her.

"I stopped by and had coffee with Lauren this morning. She told me about the interesting conversation the two of you had on the front porch." His eyes flashed with a bit of what appeared to be irritation. "Harper, my sister meant well, but she had no right to interfere with my relationship with you. I'm a grown man and I know what I want in life and that's you, Harper. I'm deeply in love with you and you're more than enough to make me happy for the rest of my life."

Oh, God, he was positively breaking her heart. Still, she'd made her decision where he was concerned. It was done. It was over. He might be angry at his sister for what she'd said to her, but Lauren had spoken the honest truth. She'd needed to let Sam go so he could find a love closer to his age.

He had so much going for him and eventually he'd thank her for her decision. Eventually he would find a new love that would truly fulfill him in ways she wouldn't be able to.

"Sam, nothing has changed since last night." Each word ripped at her heart as they fell from her lips. "I still feel like it's best if we both go our own ways. I... I'm ready to move on to date somebody my own age."

His eyes filled with pain and once again she cut her gaze away from him. The last thing she wanted to do was hurt Sam. But once again she reminded herself that someday he would thank her for letting him go. One day she would be just a dim memory in his mind.

"Is there anything I can do…anything I can say to change your mind?" His voice was laced with a deep anguish.

Stay strong, a little voice whispered inside her head. Oh, it was so hard to do when all she really wanted was to fall into his arms and profess the depth of her love for him. Doing the right thing positively sucked.

"There's nothing, Sam. However, I do hope we can maintain a good working relationship, but right now that's all I really want and need from you."

He finally nodded. "Got it." His eyes went dark and shuttered against her.

"Now I need to get some work done." She got up from the table and ten minutes later or so he got up and went back outside.

The day felt ridiculously long. Harper's heart hurt even though she kept assuring herself she had done the right thing. She had never expected things with Sam to last forever. But she'd just always assumed he'd be the one to walk away from her. She'd never dreamed she'd be the one to walk away from him.

At quarter after five when she left the shop, Sam was waiting for her by his truck. "I'll follow you home," he said.

"That's really not necessary," she replied.

"It is for me. I'm not going to leave you all on your own no matter what our personal relationship is like. I haven't forgotten that somebody tried to kill you."

Neither had she. "Thank you, Sam." She raced for her car before he could see the tears that filled her eyes. The fact that he still cared about her safety spoke of the love he had for her…a love she intended not to take as her own no matter how much she wanted to claim it forever.

Chapter Eleven

Two more days had passed, two more agonizing days where Harper tried to keep a happy smile on her face during business hours while still crying herself to sleep each night.

The house felt so empty without him. She missed having dinner with him then sitting on the sofa and either watching a show or having a playful argument about one silly thing or another. She missed that banter. She just missed him desperately.

The loneliness she'd felt before Sam had entered her life now seemed more immense than ever. It ate at her as the empty evening hours stretched out before her each night.

Sam continued to play bodyguard for her, which made her sleep better at night. During the days he'd been kind and respectful to her without crossing any boundaries. Still, she felt his love for her every minute that he was around her and as long as he was working for her it would continue to be an exquisite form of torture.

Thankfully today she had a lot of orders going out, so at least through the morning and afternoon she was kept busy with people coming in and out of the business.

It was a gray, overcast day although the forecast didn't call for any rain. Still, the dark clouds reflected Harper's mood. She had a core of sadness inside her that she hoped would eventually ease up and go away but right now it threatened to consume her.

It was during the lull of the afternoon when she was surprised to see Lauren entering the bakery. The woman looked quite pretty in jeans and a pink T-shirt that read Baby On Board with a big arrow pointing to her tummy.

She offered Harper a tentative smile as she approached the display counter. "Hi, Harper."

"Hey, Lauren," Harper replied. "I like your shirt."

"Oh, thanks," Lauren replied.

"So, what can I do for you today?" Why was Sam's sister in here? She'd never been in the bakery before. If Sam had made her come then he'd learn quickly enough that Harper's mind hadn't been changed. Maybe she was here to discuss the gender reveal party.

"My brother has been raving about your cookies so I decided it was past time for me to come in and try them. I'd like a dozen of your oatmeal raisin ones. Then maybe you and I could have a little chat?"

"Okay," Harper agreed, although she couldn't imagine what the two of them had to chat about. Lauren had already been very clear on what she thought about things. "Why don't you have a seat and I'll bring the cookies to you."

Lauren sat at one of the tables. As Harper bagged the cookies to go, she couldn't help but wonder exactly why Lauren was here. What on earth did she have to say to Harper that she hadn't already said? What was done was done, and she couldn't exactly take back what she'd said to Harper that day on the porch.

She brought the bag of cookies to Lauren's table and then sat down opposite the pretty young woman, as the two were the only ones inside at the moment. "What's going on?"

Lauren's features appeared strained and she toyed with the strap on her purse as if nervous. "Harper, I made a big mistake the last time we were together. I should have never gotten involved in your relationship with my brother."

"You just told me how you felt about it all," Harper replied.

"But it wasn't my place to tell you what I thought was best for my brother." She leaned forward. "Harper, I know you broke up with him and if that was because of what I said to you that day, then please reconsider. I've never seen my brother as broken as he's been the last couple of days and it's absolutely killing me to see him that way."

She leaned back in the chair and shook her head. "I had no idea how much he truly loved you. Harper, I had no idea you were the one for him. I should have never, ever interfered. If you can find it in your heart to let him back in, then I know you'd make him a very happy man."

Harper released a weary sigh. "Lauren, I don't intend to change the way things are right now. You were right when you told me it was selfish of me to tie him up romantically. He's a young man and needs to find a nice young woman to date." Saying those words aloud pierced a new arrow into Harper's heart.

Now that she'd made the actual break from Sam, she wasn't going to go backward. The break was destined to happen anyway. Eventually he would want more than she could ever give him.

"I'm so sorry I said anything at all," Lauren said miserably. "It wasn't my place. All I want is for Sam to be happy and now I realize you are…were his true happiness."

"Give yourself a break, Lauren. Your brother is wonderfully handsome and infinitely kind. It won't take him long to find a new girlfriend." Harper was saved from having to say anything else as another customer walked in.

Minutes later Lauren left and Harper breathed a

deep sigh of relief. The rest of the afternoon passed slowly. Only a few people came in and Harper found herself having far too much time to think. And the last thing she wanted to think about was Sam.

Instead, she grabbed some paper and a pen and sat behind the display case and began to draw up a potential flyer she'd use for the reopening she was planning. Of course, she knew the place wouldn't be ready for another month or so but at least the task kept her mind busy for a while.

At three thirty Sam surprised her by coming back inside. "Sam, is something wrong?" she asked. It was unusual for him to come into the bakery at this time in the afternoon.

"No...uh, yes. My mom has a doctor's appointment at four and my brother was going to take her, but he got tied up, so now I need to take her."

"Sam, you make your own hours here, and of course if you need to take your mother to a doctor's appointment, I completely understand," she replied. "Is she okay?"

"She's fine. From what she told me, it's just a normal checkup." He frowned. "But that's not the issue."

It was her turn to frown at him. "So, what's the issue?"

"You. I need you to make me a promise." His gaze was intense and his tone was sober.

"What kind of a promise?" she asked in confusion.

"Promise me that you won't leave here today until I come back to follow you home."

"Oh, Sam, it's only a block and a half away. I'm sure I'll be just fine," she protested.

"Please, Harper. Just humor me." His gaze bore into hers intently. "The doctor's appointment shouldn't take too long. Just promise me you'll wait for me here if I'm a little late getting back."

"Okay, I promise," she replied after a moment of hesitation. After all, it wasn't like she had anything to rush home for, so it was an easy promise to make.

"Thank you," he replied in obvious relief. "I'm taking off now but I should be back by five or a few minutes after."

"Take your time. I promise I'll be here when you get back," she assured him. She sighed as he took off. Why did he have to be such a good man? According to Lauren, she'd apparently broken his heart, yet he still cared enough about her to continue to be her bodyguard. He still continued to want to give her her dream as far as the bakery was concerned.

Most men would have left her to her own devices, but not Sam. Not her sweet, sweet Sam. As always, these kinds of thoughts brought the sting of tears to her eyes. Eventually Sam would get over her and someday maybe she would get over Sam, but not today.

She was fifteen minutes from closing up for the day when Celeste Winthrop walked in. Celeste was a very attractive woman with ash-blond hair and big brown eyes. She was dressed in a pair of long white slacks with an emerald green blouse. She wore big gold earrings and a thick gold necklace. She looked cool and chic and made Harper feel positively dowdy in her black slacks and beige blouse.

Celeste was another person who had never been in the bakery before and Harper steeled herself, knowing the woman wasn't after something sweet to eat but rather something else.

"Good afternoon, Celeste. How can I help you today?" Harper greeted the woman.

"Hmm, I'm not sure. I need to look things over," Celeste replied as she stepped up to the display counter.

"Take your time," Harper replied.

The woman walked up and down the display case, looking at all the things inside. She then stopped and looked back up at Harper. "I didn't see Sam's truck outside. Is there trouble in paradise?" she asked with a sly smile.

"No, he's still on the job here," Harper replied.

"Gossip has it that you and Sam are quite cozy with each other."

Harper sighed. So, the woman wasn't here because she'd suddenly gotten hungry for a brownie or a slice of cake. "I'm not sure what you're talking about."

"You know exactly what I'm talking about," Celeste replied. "You know, there aren't that many good men in this town. Surely you could find somebody your own age to date."

"You're way behind in your gossip, Celeste. Sam and I are no longer seeing each other so he's free for you to chase."

Celeste's nose thinned and her eyes narrowed. "I don't chase men…they chase me," she replied haughtily.

"Good for you," Harper replied, tired of the whole conversation. "Now, what can I get for you?"

Celeste swept her gaze over the items and then looked up at Harper. "I thought I was hungry for a little sweet, but I've changed my mind. Thank you anyway." With that the woman turned around and left the bakery.

The woman hadn't come in for a "little sweet," she had come in to get the latest in gossip straight from the horse's mouth. Now she knew there was a green light with Sam, although Harper had a feeling Celeste would have to wait a very long time for Sam to chase her.

Sam wasn't back by closing time and although she was tempted to go ahead home, she had made a promise to Sam, and she always tried to keep her promises.

She locked the front door and turned off the interior lights and then went back into the kitchen and prepared things for the next morning. Once that was done, she returned to her chair behind the display case and sank down to wait. The bakery was darker than usual because of the gloominess outside that had deepened over the last couple of hours.

Still, she could see well enough that while she waited for Sam, she'd work some more on the paperwork she'd begun earlier.

She pulled out the papers on which she'd drawn a variety of ads to go in the paper and on flyers. She became completely absorbed in the work as she made changes to what she had already done earlier in the day.

She frowned in disgust as she found herself doodling Sam's name over and over again on one of the papers. She was like a love-struck teenager, writing his name repeatedly across the top of an algebra paper.

She'd been sitting there for several minutes when she thought she smelled smoke. Was it coming in from someplace outside? She got up from her chair and sniffed the air. No, it seemed to be coming from the kitchen area.

Had she left something running? Something that had gotten too hot? She couldn't imagine herself doing something like that, but since she'd broken up with Sam her thoughts had been scattered at best.

She hurried back there. The smell of smoke was much more pronounced in the kitchen and she could actually see it drifting in the air. A quick glance at all the equipment she used let her know nothing was on and running.

What in the heck? She now realized the smoke was coming in beneath the door between the kitchen and the laundry room. She coughed, the dark smoke burning her eyes and lodging in the back of her throat.

She pulled open the door between the two rooms. She gasped and stumbled backward. Fire! Tall flames licked at the wood around the back door. Oh, dear God, her building was on fire.

She slammed the door and raced for the front. She needed to get out and the only way out was through the front door, as the burning back door was no longer an option.

She grabbed her purse from beneath the counter and fumbled to get her keys out. With her keys in hand, she ran to the front door. Before she even tried to unlock it, she saw that the stacks of wood and other building supplies had been moved from the side of the door to directly in front of it. They were all now blocking her way out.

When had that happened? Somebody must have moved the items when she'd either been back in the kitchen or absorbed with the paperwork. Who had done this?

She didn't have the time to think about who was responsible as a deep sob of panic escaped her. Despite the items in front of it, she unlocked the door and pushed with all her might. The door didn't budge. She shoved against it again. It wouldn't even open an inch, let alone enough for her to get through.

Another fit of coughing overtook her. Dark smoke was growing more and more intense, filling the room with deadly intent. Her lungs ached and tears coursed down her face, both from fear and the smoke.

Once she was finished with the coughing spasm, she went back to the kitchen. The room was dark with smoke and when she placed her hand on the door leading out to the laundry room, the wood was fiery hot.

Oh, God, a new panic roared through her. It was only a matter of minutes before the fire breached the back door and swept into the kitchen.

She ran back to the front door, pushing against it, shoving at it with all her might. "Help me! Please, somebody help me!" she screamed as she banged on the door until she was completely out of breath.

Trapped. She was trapped in a burning building. Who had done this to her? Another round of coughing punished her and a dizziness caused her head to reel.

Her chest felt tight…so tight and it felt as if she couldn't draw in enough oxygen. She sank down to her knees next to the door. She now couldn't see across the room due to the thick smoke that filled the air. Her head reeled as dozens of thoughts moved through her mind as if in slow motion.

Shouldn't she call somebody? Did she have a phone? She needed to call Sam. Sam. Where was Sam? Wasn't he supposed to be here with her? Where was he? Where had he gone? Confusion muddied her thoughts.

She loved him so much. Would she ever see him again? She was so tired. Why was she so sleepy? Maybe she should take a little nap. Things would be better when she woke up.

Another bout of coughing tortured her. Her lungs burned and she realized someplace in the back of her mind that if she didn't do something soon, she was going to die.

"THANK YOU FOR taking me today," Sam's mother said to him as they pulled up in her driveway.

"You know I don't mind. I'll walk you inside," he said, then parked and turned off the truck engine. He glanced at the clock on the dashboard. There had been a wait in the doctor's office and it was now a quarter after five. He hoped Harper had kept her promise and was still at the bakery waiting for him.

He was definitely eager to get back there before she gave up on him and decided to go on home without him. He still had a horrible fear for her life. He couldn't get out of his mind the night that she'd been slashed up. He would never forgive himself if anything else happened to her.

Even though she didn't want him anymore, he still

wanted to keep her safe from any harm that might come her way. Still, there was nothing worse than unrequited love. He had no idea how long it might take him to recover from Harper. She was and would remain for a very long time a love in his heart and a burn in his very soul.

He'd seen the future with her and he'd loved what he'd visualized for the two of them. Now he had no vision for his future beyond his deep heartbreak.

He walked his mother into the house and she settled into her favorite chair. "I'm glad the doctor gave you a clean bill of health," he said.

"I'm as healthy as a horse," she replied. "Now, where's the remote control?"

It took several minutes for them to find the remote. He kissed her goodbye on her forehead and then he flew out of the house, eager to get back to the bakery.

He knew Lauren had come in to talk to Harper that afternoon, but apparently his sister hadn't been able to change Harper's mind.

Maybe she really didn't love him, but he swore he felt her love flowing from her when the two of them were in the same room. He believed he saw love in her eyes whenever she gazed at him. How could he possibly convince her that they belonged together forever?

The day had turned preternaturally dark, dark enough that he had to turn his headlights on to drive.

As he pulled into the bakery parking lot, he was glad to see Harper's car still parked next to the building. Good, she'd kept her promise and had waited for him.

However, when he stepped out of the car a deep alarm rang through him. Instead of smelling the lingering sweet scent of the bakery, acrid smoke filled the air. The interior of the bakery was dark. He raced up to the door and panic seared through him as he saw the flickering light of flames dancing somewhere in the back of the place.

What the hell? Shock and horror punched into his gut as he saw the building supplies stacked against the front door. He peered inside. It was almost impossible to make anything out through the smoke that filled the place.

Then he saw her… Harper. He could barely see her through the smoke inside. She was curled into an unmoving heap just inside the front door.

"Harper!" He shouted her name and banged on the door as hard as he could, but she didn't move. Frantic, he pulled out his cell phone and called the emergency number. "Fire…there's a fire at the Sweet Tooth Bakery and Harper is unconscious inside," he yelled.

He put the phone back into his pocket and then banged on the door again in an attempt to rouse Harper. Still she didn't respond.

He was afraid to break the door glass, same with the big picture window next to the door. He was terrified he'd cause the fire to explode outward and burn Harper. And if that didn't happen, he was afraid the glass would shatter all over her and cut her to shreds.

Dammit, he wasn't a fireman. He didn't know what to do in this situation. He just needed to get to her. The one thing he could do was remove the items that were stacked in front of the door. Then, if the door was unlocked, he'd risk opening it to pull her outside.

He had to get her out of there as soon as possible. The smoke in the area she was in was thick and deadly and right now she was unresponsive.

Frantically, he began picking up the wood and tossing it aside. As he worked, he shouted for help. His heart thundered in his chest and tears of fear for her blurred his eyes.

To his surprise and relief, RJ ran over from the tattoo shop and began to help him move the supplies from in front of the door. "What the hell?" RJ exclaimed as he worked to help.

"Somebody did this on purpose," Sam said, his blood boiling with both anger and fear. Had RJ done this and was the big man now trying to play hero? He'd deal with RJ later. Right now, no matter what RJ's motives might be, he was helping.

Was it already too late? Had she succumbed to smoke inhalation? Sam knew that smoke could be the real silent killer in a fire.

Oh, God, she couldn't be dead. She just couldn't

be. What would he do without her presence? He'd thought she'd be safe here. He'd believed nobody would try anything while she was inside her bakery. He'd been wrong, so very wrong.

This was all his fault. He should have never left her alone here. He should have never made her promise to stay here to wait for his return. He would never forgive himself if… He couldn't even finish the thought.

Another man Sam didn't even know pitched in to help them move items and before long the doorway was cleared. "If the door is unlocked, I'm going in," Sam said.

"No, man, wait for the firemen to get here," RJ protested. "It's too dangerous."

"She can't wait," Sam cried, even as sirens sounded in the distance. He tried the door. Thankfully it was unlocked. He drew in a deep breath, yanked it all the way open and then stepped inside.

Inside the air was hot and his eyes immediately burned with the smoke. He leaned down next to Harper and scooped her up in his arms. She hung limply and with no response to being moved. A deep sob of despair ripped from him.

RJ opened the door for Sam, and he rushed out into the cooler evening air. Gently he placed Harper on the ground. "Harper… Harper, honey… open your eyes," he said frantically. "Please…please open your eyes."

Suddenly there was chaos all around him. An ambulance pulled up, along with the fire truck and several police cars. Men started spooling out water hoses and carrying them around to the back of the building.

Two EMTs arrived by his side with a gurney. They picked up Harper and then hurried her to the ambulance as a group of onlookers began to gather all around. Before Sam could get his bearings, the ambulance pulled away as Dallas stepped up to Sam's side.

"What happened here, Sam?" Dallas asked tersely.

"Somebody tried to kill Harper." Sam grabbed hold of Dallas's arm. "I don't even know if they succeeded." Sam's eyes blurred with new tears. "God, Dallas, I... I don't even know if she was dead or alive when I pulled her out of there."

"If she's alive they will take good care of her, Sam," Dallas replied. "Right now, I need some information from you."

Sam quickly told him about his mother's doctor's appointment and the promise Harper had made to him to wait until he returned to go home. "Somebody started a fire at the back of the building and then they used my building supplies to block the front door so she couldn't get out. She was trapped in there. It's all my fault. I should have never left her here all alone." His voice cracked with the depth of his emotion.

Sam's fear for Harper's life and his guilt about the

situation nearly cast him to his knees. But he knew Dallas needed as much information as possible to investigate exactly what had happened.

As the lawman continued to question Sam, more people began to gather in the parking lot. All Sam could think about was Harper. How was she doing? Was she going to survive this horrible night? Dear God, had she survived?

Finally, the fire was out. It was Russ who came around to talk to Dallas and Sam about the damage. "The point of ignition was the back door and we believe gasoline was the accelerant. The laundry room is completely burned out, along with the back door area and part of the kitchen. The rest of the interior has probably been badly smoke-damaged but right now it's too hot to go inside to make a full assessment."

"Can I go?" Sam asked Dallas urgently. "I need to get to the hospital to check on Harper."

"Go," Dallas replied. "I'll catch up with you sometime later."

Sam turned and headed to his truck. "Hey, Sam." Joe Rogers approached him. "Is Harper all right?"

"I don't know. I'm heading to the hospital now to find out," Sam replied. He frowned as he gazed at the man who was one of Harper's regulars.

Was that soot across Joe's forehead? How had the man gotten soot on his face? He hadn't been anywhere near the fire. And his hair appeared a slightly lighter color, as if it was dusted with ash. Sure, there had been some ash flying in the air as a result of the fire, but nobody had been here long enough to get soot and ash all over them.

Sam's heart began beating a different kind of a rhythm. Joe? Was it possible? Did he have some sort of an obsession with Harper? An obsession that had turned deadly?

"Excuse me for a minute, Joe," Sam said. He ran back to where Dallas was now talking to RJ. "I think it's Joe... Joe Rogers," he said to Dallas urgently. "He's got soot on his face and, Dallas, he was no-where near the fire. You need to check him out, I think you need to arrest him, Dallas. I believe he set the fire and that's how he got the soot on his forehead. I think he's the one who attacked Harper."

Sam didn't wait but instead turned around, ran past Joe and got into his truck. Joe. That bastard. If what Sam thought was true, then hopefully Dallas would take care of him.

Right now, the only thing on Sam's mind was Harper. It was only in the privacy of his truck that he allowed frightened tears to course down his cheeks.

Harper... Harper, her name ripped through him. She had to be okay. The more he thought about it, the more he was now convinced Joe had been her at-tacker. Had Joe committed murder tonight? The very thought tore through him. Oh, God, he prayed not.

Right now, he didn't care if he and Harper ever got

back together again. She just needed to be alive. She needed to be running her bakery and laughing and smiling with customers. Dammit, she had to be alive.

He drove as fast as possible and finally reached the hospital. He parked and flew out of his truck and then he raced into the emergency waiting room.

Sherry Alyers, a woman he'd dated years before, sat behind the desk. "Sherry, Harper Brennan was just brought in by ambulance. Would you let the doctor know I'm here and need to know her condition as soon as possible?"

"I'll let him know." She got up from her chair and disappeared behind a door right behind the desk.

Sam began to pace the floor, his heart beating so fast he felt short of breath. All he really needed to hear was that she was okay. He just needed to see her for a minute to assure himself she was really going to survive this horrendous night.

"The doctor said he'll be out to speak to you when he can," Sherry said as she returned to her desk.

"Thanks, Sherry."

The minutes ticked by…long minutes that turned into an hour. Sam finally sat. What was taking so long? Was it a good sign that the doctor hadn't come out to talk to him yet? Or was it a very bad sign?

Another hour passed and Dallas arrived. "Any word yet?" he asked.

"No…nothing."

Dallas sank down in the chair next to Sam. "You

were right about Joe. I found two gas cans in his car and he confessed to everything. Seems he couldn't stand seeing Harper dating a younger man."

"That bastard," Sam exclaimed, rich anger taking the place of worry for just a moment.

"Wait, there's more," Dallas said. "He not only confessed to attacking her and setting the fire, but he also copped to killing his wife years ago and burying her in his barn. According to him, his wife was leaving him for a much younger man. The night she was leaving they got into a fight and she fell and hit her head. Harper seeing you apparently triggered him."

"That son of a bitch," Sam said angrily. "So, he's now in jail?"

"Yes, and he'll be charged with enough crimes to keep him locked up for a very long time. I've got men out at his place right now digging up his barn floor." Dallas stood. "Let me go see if I can find out some information for you." He walked up to the desk and Sherry then buzzed him in through the large double doors that said Emergency Room.

Sam tried to digest everything Dallas had just shared about Joe. He'd been...just a regular Joe, who came into the bakery for coffee and a cinnamon roll most mornings. But apparently, he hadn't been just a regular Joe at all. He'd been a man with secrets and a twisted darkness inside him that had caused him to want Harper dead like the wife who had apparently betrayed him.

Dallas finally returned with Dr. Alex Erickson by his side. Sam jumped up from his chair. "How is she?" he immediately asked Alex.

"She's stable," Alex replied. Sam nearly fell to the floor in relief. "Needless to say, she's suffered from smoke inhalation," Alex continued. "I've got her on oxygen and I sedated her. We've run some tests and I don't believe her lungs have been damaged but we'll check again in another day or so."

"Can I see her?" Sam asked.

"Sam, she's sleeping. She won't even know you're there," Alex replied.

"I… I just need to see her for a minute," Sam replied. "Please."

"I don't want her disturbed in any way," Alex said firmly. "She's in room 105."

"Thanks." Sam turned and headed down the hallway that held the patient rooms.

When he reached her room, he stepped just inside the door and his heart squeezed tight. She looked so small in the hospital bed. She had an IV in her arm and an oxygen tube down her throat.

More than anything he wanted to curl up on the bed with her and draw her into his arms. He wanted to keep her from harm, from heartache for the rest of her life.

He remained in the doorway for several minutes, watching the reassuring sight of her chest rise and fall. Thank God she was okay. However, she was going to be devastated when she learned of all the damage in the bakery.

He would rebuild it for her. Whatever it took, if she allowed him, he would work hard for her to get the bakery up and running again.

Finally, he left the doorway, knowing there was nothing more he could do for her tonight. Night had fallen and finally the dark clouds had moved out, revealing a sky full of bright stars.

He remained just sitting in his truck for long moments. It was finally over. He would no longer have to play bodyguard for her anymore. He'd failed miserably at the job anyway.

Still, with Joe in jail she would now be safe to live her life to the fullest without any more fear. Without him. She didn't want him anymore. Now that the danger to her had passed, his heartbreak roared through him harder and more painful than ever.

If she wanted, he'd work to give her a dream bakery, but he'd just be the carpenter who worked for her and nothing more. He had to face the fact, and the fact was that he and Harper weren't going to have a future together.

Chapter Twelve

On the third morning in the hospital, Harper awakened before the sun came up and was grateful that she no longer had the oxygen tube in and the IV was out.

For the past two days she'd been lightly sedated and had drifted in and out of sleep. She'd had no visitors as the doctors had wanted her to rest without interruption.

But she had suffered from nightmares of smoke and fire that had often jerked her from her sleep gasping and panicked. Still, the doctors had been very protective of her rest and recovery time.

The only people she had seen during the past two days were the doctors and nurses who came in to check on her. She'd been told she'd suffered from smoke inhalation, but thankfully no long-term damage had been done.

However, she knew the bakery was probably in

ruins. She hadn't asked anyone about it, hadn't even wanted to think about it until this morning.

She remembered the flames and the smoke, and she remembered that she'd been trapped, but she had no memory of getting out of the bakery and to the hospital.

Sam. Thoughts of him caused tears to immediately fill her eyes. She'd pushed him out of her life... her bakery was in ruins and this morning she felt utterly hopeless and more alone than she'd ever felt.

She dozed off and on until breakfast was delivered. She was grateful for the hot coffee but picked listlessly at the scrambled eggs and hash browns. She really wasn't hungry.

Soon after her breakfast tray was taken away, Dallas walked into her room. "Hey, Harper. How are you feeling this morning?" He sank down in the chair next to her bed.

"I'm okay." Her throat was scratchy and her voice was slightly hoarse, but the doctors had assured her this would eventually pass.

"I need to ask you some questions. Do you feel up to it?" Dallas asked.

She nodded affirmatively. "That would be fine, and then I have some questions for you."

"Basically, I need you to tell me exactly how things went down in the bakery on the day of the fire," Dallas said.

Harper began to tell him what had happened from

the moment she'd smelled smoke. She went through her frantic efforts to shove open the door barricaded with the building supplies until she had apparently fallen unconscious from the smoke. "I don't know how I got out of the bakery. Maybe you could answer that question for me."

"Sam got you out. According to a few witnesses, he worked like a wild animal to move the things from in front of the door and then went in and carried you out."

Her heart squeezed tight. Of course, Sam had saved her...her sweet Sam. Only he wasn't hers anymore. "After you were taken away in the ambulance, Sam noticed something odd about Joe," Dallas continued.

She looked at Dallas in surprise. "Joe... Joe Rogers?"

"Yes. Sam noticed he had some soot on his face and drew it to my attention. Upon further investigation I discovered two empty gas cans in Joe's car. He set the fire, Harper. He was the person who was trying to kill you."

Harper stared at him in stunned surprise. "But wh-why?"

As Dallas told her about Joe, she was utterly shocked by the news. It was so difficult to believe that the man who had been a friendly regular customer had harbored so many secrets and so much hatred toward her.

"According to what Joe told me, he had feelings for you and had just been waiting for the perfect time to ask you out, but then you started seeing Sam and that triggered him and turned his affection into hatred of you."

"It's all just so hard to believe. I would have never guessed that Joe was behind the attacks on me," she replied. "So, tell me what state the bakery is in." She steeled herself for his response. Had it burned down to the ground? Was it nothing more than charred rubble now?

"The back of the building was badly burned, but they got the fire out before it really got too far into the kitchen. However, the whole thing has been smoke-damaged," Dallas said.

She supposed she should be glad that it was no worse than it was, but it definitely sounded fairly dismal. At least she had insurance that should take care of most of it, but it would probably be months and months before she could get it back up and running again.

To her surprise tears began to well up in her eyes once more. She released an embarrassed laugh and reached out for a tissue from the box on her bedside table. "I'm sorry, I seem to be a bit weepy today." She swiped at her eyes with the tissue.

"Don't apologize," Dallas said. "You've been through quite an ordeal, Harper, and you're lucky to be alive right now."

"I'm very lucky," she agreed faintly. But right now, she didn't feel so lucky. Everything felt so overwhelming. She had a burned-out building with heavy smoke damage. She would have to start a cleanup and then a rebuild. And once again she was facing everything alone.

"Do you have any other questions for me?" Dallas asked.

She had a million questions. Was Sam okay? Had he even tried to come and see her? Or had his interest in her...had his love for her already waned?

Of course, she didn't ask any of those questions. In reality she no longer had the right to ask anything about Sam, except one. And that one suddenly thundered in her chest.

"Was Sam hurt while getting me out?"

"No, not at all," Dallas replied.

She released the breath she hadn't realized she'd been holding. Thank God he hadn't been hurt. "I guess that's all the questions I have for you right now," she said.

Once again, she felt the press of hot tears burning her eyes. What on earth was wrong with her? She was a strong woman. She'd faced adversity before. However, everything right now felt bigger than anything she'd ever dealt with before.

"Harper, if you think of any more questions for me, don't hesitate to call me," Dallas said.

"Thank you, Dallas," she replied.

Dallas left and soon after that Dr. Ralph Reeves came into her room. The older man had been Harper's personal doctor whenever she'd needed one in the past. He was a kind, quiet man who treated his patients with kindness and respect.

"How is my patient doing today?" he asked with a warm smile as he sat in the chair Dallas had recently vacated.

"My throat is still a little scratchy, but other than that I'm feeling fine," she replied.

"I think you're well enough to go home today," Dr. Reeves said. "How do you feel about that?"

"I feel good about it," she replied.

"The only way I'll let you go today is if you promise to rest at home for at least a couple of days," Dr. Reeves said. "I know you'll feel like you need to jump into things, especially considering the state of your place of business, however it's important that you give yourself time to finish healing. So, can you promise me that you'll take things slowly and do a lot of nothing for a while?"

"I can promise you that," she agreed. It was actually an easy promise to make. She was exhausted… utterly drained. All she wanted to do now was go home and rest comfortably in her own bed. Anything that needed to be done at the bakery could wait for a couple of days for her to get her energy back.

"Then I'll get your paperwork all ready and you should be set to leave within the hour." Dr. Reeves stood and gave her a kind smile. "Please take good care of yourself, Harper."

"I plan to. Thank you, Dr. Reeves." It was only minutes after the doctor had left her room that she realized she had a problem. Her car wasn't here and she had no idea who to call to take her home.

Millsville was a very small town. There were no taxis on standby or Uber services available to whisk people from place to place. The women she'd once considered her close friends were both at work and in any case, she would be reluctant to call them. She wasn't in the mood to hear any 'I told you sos' from anybody.

She scarcely had time to think as the nurse, Amber James, came into her room. She carried what appeared to be a pair of Harper's jeans and one of her blue blouses. She also had a small paper bag and Harper's purse in hand.

"Somebody brought in some clean clothes for you to put on. We bagged the clothing you came in wearing because of their intense smoke smell. And if you want to take a quick shower before you put on the clean clothes, I'll wait for you."

"Oh, I'd love a quick shower," Harper replied. She could smell the smoke that lingered in her hair and felt it wafting from her body. She couldn't wait to feel clean again.

"Chief Calloway also brought your purse in. He

thought you might need it. We tried to wipe it down to get most of the soot and ashes off it."

"That was very nice of him and I really appreciate you wiping it down," Harper replied. Thank goodness Dallas had realized she'd need her purse when she was discharged and got home. Despite the wipe-down that had been done on it, the purse was still smoke-darkened. Once she got her personal items from it, it would need to be thrown away.

Minutes later she stood beneath a warm spray of water, lathering her hair with the little bottle of shampoo and washing herself with the small bar of soap that had been provided to her. It felt good to finally wash the smoke smell down the drain.

Sam had brought her the clothes. There was no other answer in her mind. He still had a key to her house and he was thoughtful enough to think about providing her something clean to go home in. Once again, her heart squeezed tight as she thought of him and new tears mingled with the shower spray.

Once her shower was finished and as she dressed, her problem returned to her head. How was she going to get home? She needed to figure something out quickly. She finished dressing and sat on the edge of her bed to await her discharge.

While she was contemplating her problem *he* walked in the door. Sam. For a moment her breath caught in her throat. His face appeared drawn and the bright sparkle in his eyes was dimmed, as if he was incredibly tired. But the smile he offered her was one that warmed her despite their current circumstances.

"I heard that you were going home today and I was wondering if you needed a ride," he said.

"H-how did you know?" she asked.

"I have to confess, I've kind of been a pain in everyone's butt here for the last couple of days. I've been hanging out and asking about you. I came earlier to see if I could visit you today, but they told me to wait until the doctor came in to see you. Dr. Reece came to the waiting room and told me that I could see you and that you were being released. So...do you need a ride home?"

"Would you mind?" Even though this felt awkward, she was grateful he'd showed up.

He smiled once again. "Of course, I wouldn't mind."

"I...uh... I'm just waiting for my discharge papers," she explained.

"Then I'll wait with you." He sat in the chair at the foot of the bed. "How are you feeling?"

"Better than the last time you saw me." She didn't want to look at him. She didn't want to let his beautiful eyes, his caring gaze into her heart.

"Does your throat hurt?" he asked curiously. "You're definitely a bit hoarse."

"It hurts a little bit, but not much," she replied. She finally looked at him. "Thank you, Sam. Thank you for saving my life."

The smile on his face fell and his eyes darkened. "God, Harper, when I saw you in the bakery that was filled with so much smoke, and you were on the floor and not moving at all, I... I thought you were gone." His voice cracked a bit and he averted his gaze from her.

"And all I could think about was that it was all my fault. I was the one who made you promise to stay in the bakery. If I hadn't done that, then maybe the fire wouldn't have happened and you wouldn't have been trapped." His voice sounded tortured with guilt.

"Sam, look at me." He slowly raised his gaze back up to her. "You are not responsible for what happened. Joe was. He was the one who set the fire and if it hadn't happened when it did, then it would have happened on another day. You have no reason to feel guilty about anything that happened that night."

He released a deep sigh. "I'm just so sorry about everything."

Amber came back into the room with some paperwork in her hand as she pushed a wheelchair. She handed the papers to Harper, along with a bright smile. "Okay, Harper. You're all set and you're free to leave."

"The bright side of all this is that it's finally over. The bad guy is in jail and I'm still alive," she said.

"Thank God for that," he replied.

"And thank you for all your care, Amber," Harper said as she stood and then sat in the wheelchair. She felt silly sitting in the chair, but knew it was protocol when leaving the hospital.

"It was my pleasure," Amber replied.

"I'll just go pull my truck up," Sam said and then left the room.

Amber pushed her down the hallway and out the emergency room door where Sam had arrived at the curb. "Now, take care of yourself and remember to get plenty of rest," Amber said.

"I will," Harper replied. "Thanks again, Amber."

Sam got out of his truck and helped Harper into the passenger seat. "All ready?" he asked once he was behind the steering wheel.

"Ready," she agreed as she tightened her seat belt. As always, just being around Sam broke her heart all over again. The scent of his cologne smelled like love. His body warmth that wafted toward her made her want to curl up in his arms and never leave.

She drew in a deep breath and released it slowly as he started the truck engine. "Before you take me home, would you please take me to the bakery?" Her heart was already hurting because of Sam. Maybe it was the right time to get all the hurt out of the way today.

Sam looked at her in surprise. "Are you sure you're up to that right now? I thought your discharge instructions were for you to go home and get plenty of rest."

"I don't intend to do anything at the bakery. I... I just need to see it."

EVEN THOUGH HE didn't think it was a good idea, he turned down the street that would take them to the burned-out business. His heart hurt for what she was about to see. He knew she would be devastated by the damage.

He loved her so much and he wished he could protect her from the heartache he knew she would feel. But he couldn't protect her.

He pulled up in front of the bakery. From this vantage point the damage wasn't really visible. "I need to get out," she said. "Do you have time?"

He hesitated a moment and then nodded. "I have all the time you need."

She cast him a grateful smile and then opened the truck door. He quickly got out of the truck and hurried around to meet her.

He frowned as she pulled her set of keys from her purse. He hadn't realized she meant to go inside. Oh, this was going to be so tough on her. He was just glad he would be with her when she got her first glimpse of all the damage. He'd hate for her to face it all alone.

She unlocked the door and pushed it open. Immediately the smell of smoke and wet wood drifted out to greet them. She paused for a long moment and then stepped inside with him at her heels.

The walls inside were dark with smoke damage and the tables and counters were covered with a thin layer of soot. She said nothing as she walked through to the kitchen area where the laundry room was nothing more than charred wood. The back door was completely burned out, leaving a gaping hole in the building.

She stepped out of it and walked to the center of the backyard, her gaze on the back of the bakery. He felt her tears before she began to shed them, silent tears that slowly trekked down her cheeks.

"Harper, we'll clean it…and we'll rebuild it," he said fervently. "We'll make it better than ever." He wanted to do something…to say anything that would stop her from crying, stop her from hurting.

"I knew it was going to be bad, but I still hadn't realized just how bad it was going to be," she said amid her tears.

"I swear, Harper, I'll be right by your side to set this all right." He couldn't help himself. He couldn't just stand there and watch her cry all alone.

He reached out for her and she came willingly into his arms. She buried her face in the front of his T-shirt and began to cry in earnest.

He held her tight, rubbing one hand up and down her back in an effort to soothe her. At the same time, he whispered words of encouragement, of caring and of love into her ear.

She finally stopped crying but remained in his arms. "Oh, Sam, why do you have to be so wonderful?" she asked softly.

He released a small laugh. "I'm not consciously trying to be wonderful. I just... I just love you, Harper."

She completely stilled and then she finally raised her head and gazed up at him. "I love you, too."

His heart lifted at her words even as confusion filled him. "Then why did you send me away from you?"

She stepped out of his arms and stared back at the bakery. "I tried to do the right thing for you." She turned and looked at him and, in her eyes, he saw a combination of confusion and sadness and love.

"What do you mean?" he asked.

"I tried to send you away so you could find a woman your own age, so you could have a family if you wanted one. I sent you away because I'll never really be enough for you."

He stared at her for a long moment. "I hate him," he finally said.

She looked at him in confusion. "Who?"

"Your ex-husband, the man who made you believe you aren't enough. I think he crippled you, Harper. He made you believe you weren't pretty enough or smart enough to hold a man's attention. I wish you could see yourself through my eyes because I think you're a real catch."

She gazed at him for several moments and in those

moments, he found it impossible to read her. "Sam, I'm very set in my ways," she finally said.

He smiled at her. "The good news is that I'm very set in your ways, too." He was rewarded with her small burst of laughter. Encouraged by her response, he continued. "The good thing is you're a woman young at heart and I'm an older man at heart. That makes us absolutely perfect for each other."

"You know occasionally I have...uh...my own personal summers," she said.

"You mean your hot flashes," he replied. "They don't last long and besides, I'm not surprised you're having them because I find you a very hot woman."

He'd been hoping she would laugh again, but instead she frowned. "Sam, I don't want to be the one to keep you from anything you might want in your life."

"Don't you get it? Harper, all I want is to spend my life with you. I never thought marriage would be for me until I met you. Harper, I want to marry you. I want to cook and eat meals with you, I want to watch movies with you and have you in my arms when I go to sleep for the night. I want you, Harper, for the rest of my life."

"I'm so afraid of hurting you," she replied softly. "I do love you, Sam. I love you with all my heart and soul, but I'm so afraid of hurting you."

"Baby, the only way you'll hurt me is if for some crazy reason you keep your love away from me.

Harper, surely the events of the last few days has proven to you that life is far too short not to be happy. You have to trust me. You have to trust in us. If I'm your happiness as you are mine, then choose me. Build a life with me."

Tears began to seep from her eyes once again and his heart crashed to the ground. He had no more he could say to her, no more to give to her to make her see they belonged together.

"No matter what our personal relationship is, if you allow me then I'll rebuild your bakery," he finally said. "I'll give you your dream where it's concerned. That, I can promise you."

"Forget about the bakery," she said. She swiped her tears from her cheeks and offered him a small smile. "Sam, you are one tenacious man. And I want you," she replied, her eyes suddenly shining brilliantly. "I choose you, Sam."

He didn't give her a chance to say anything more. He reached out, drew her into his arms and kissed her with all the love he had in his heart for her.

She returned his kiss, leaning into him as she wrapped her arms around his neck. When the kiss finally ended, he smiled at her. "That's my girl," he said.

She stepped away from him and grabbed his hand. "Come on, Sam. Let's go home."

His heart roared with happiness. Home. Home with Harper. He couldn't wait for his future with her to begin.

Epilogue

Harper sank down in a folding chair and released a deep, tired sigh. All around her people were working to scrub clean the walls inside the bakery.

It had been almost two weeks since the fire. When she and Sam had begun the cleanup work two days ago, Harper had been stunned by the amount of people who had shown up to help. Not only had her regular customers come in to work, but also townspeople she'd never even met came in to assist her.

The work on the outside had also begun. Even though it would take a while for the insurance issue to all get settled, Sam and his brothers had been tearing out the burned wood and replacing it.

Despite the fire and the destruction of her property it had caused, Harper had never been happier in her entire life. Sam had moved back in and every night she fell asleep in his arms.

She was surprised to realize there were far more people who didn't have a problem with their relationship than the few vocal people who did. The nay-sayers no longer bothered her and they had never bothered Sam and that was all that was important.

Sam was not only planning their first trip together, but he was also encouraging her to plan a wedding. He insisted he wouldn't be completely happy until they were married and even though she had never thought she'd get married again, she was positively thrilled by the idea of becoming Sam's wife.

He had brought so much change to her life, wonderful changes that excited her and inspired her. Life really was too short not to reach out for happiness and love when it came your way.

Fifteen minutes later Harper was thanking people and telling them goodbye as closing time arrived. As the place emptied out, Sam came through from the back.

His white T-shirt was filthy and soot streaked his face. He'd never looked as handsome to her. "Hi, cutie," he said to her once the last person had left. He drew her into his arms. "How's my best girl?"

"Good," she replied. "I'll be better if I get a kiss from my best guy."

His eyes twinkled brightly. "I think I can do that." He leaned down and captured her lips with his in a kiss of infinite caring and endless love.

Nobody could predict the future, but Harper knew her future was with the handsome hunk who had unexpectedly walked into her life and had filled it with an abundance of love. Her sweet, sweet Sam had made her life complete.

DALLAS SAT IN his office alone. He leaned back in his chair and rubbed his tired eyes. It was after midnight, he should be home in bed, but lately he'd been reluctant to go to sleep. When he did finally fall asleep, he suffered from horrendous nightmares.

In those bad dreams, despite their mouths being sewn shut, Sandy and Cindy cried and screamed for justice. Despite being tied to poles, they chased him through a dark landscape until he woke up panicked and out of breath.

So far, the killer hadn't made any mistakes. He'd been organized and controlled, both qualities that made him more dangerous and harder to find than the garden-variety messy killer.

As yet, he'd found no motive in Cindy's or Sandy's personal lives that would explain their murders. It appeared the killer had picked his victims randomly, as well as the places he'd left their bodies.

Dallas leaned forward once again and stared down at the thick pile of notes from interviews he and his officers had conducted over the past two months. Nothing. There was absolutely nothing in those papers to give him a clue as to who he was chasing. Right now, he was just chasing his own damned tail.

He knew people were frightened in his town and it killed him that so far, he'd been able to do nothing about it. Right now, Millsville was a playground for a killer who turned young women into human scarecrows. The thing that scared him the most was that it was going to take more murders before the killer finally got sloppy and left a real clue behind.

He couldn't stand the thought of another young woman losing her life. But at the moment he felt like he was just holding his breath until another murder occurred.

* * * * *

COMING SOON!

We really hope you enjoyed reading this book.
If you're looking for more romance, be sure to
head to the shops when new books are
available on

Thursday 2nd February

To see which titles are coming soon, please visit
millsandboon.co.uk/nextmonth

MILLS & BOON

THE HEART OF ROMANCE

A ROMANCE FOR EVERY READER

MODERN
Prepare to be swept off your feet by sophisticated, sexy and seductive heroes, in some of the world's most glamourous and rom locations, where power and passion collide.

HISTORICAL
Escape with historical heroes from time gone by. Whether your pass for wicked Regency Rakes, muscled Vikings or rugged Highlanders, the romance of the past.

MEDICAL
Set your pulse racing with dedicated, delectable doctors in the high-sure world of medicine, where emotions run high and passion, com love are the best medicine.

True Love
Celebrate true love with tender stories of heartfelt romance, from t rush of falling in love to the joy a new baby can bring, and a focus emotional heart of a relationship.

Desire
Indulge in secrets and scandal, intense drama and plenty of sizzling action with powerful and passionate heroes who have it all: wealth, s good looks…everything but the right woman.

HEROES
Experience all the excitement of a gripping thriller, with an intense mance at its heart. Resourceful, true-to-life women and strong, fearl face danger and desire - a killer combination!

To see which titles are coming soon, please visit

millsandboon.co.uk/nextmonth

LET'S TALK
Romance

For exclusive extracts, competitions
and special offers, find us online:

f facebook.com/millsandboon

🐦 @MillsandBoon

📷 @MillsandBoonUK

Get in touch on 01413 063232

JOIN US ON SOCIAL MEDIA!

Stay up to date with our latest releases, author news and gossip, special offers and discounts, and all the behind-the-scenes action from Mills & Boon...

 @millsandboon

 @millsandbooonuk

 facebook.com/millsandboon

 @millsandbooonuk

t might just be true love...

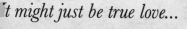

GET YOUR ROMANCE FIX

Get the latest romance news,
exclusive author interviews, story
extracts and much more!